PENGUIN

KING'S P

Simon Sebag Montefiore was born ... London in 1965. At the age
of eighteen he interviewed Prime Minister Margaret Thatcher.
Since then, he has worked as an investment banker and a writer,
interviewing a wide variety of British, American and Soviet
politicians for the national daily newspapers and magazines. He
has debated for Cambridge University against Oxford; worked
on a kibbutz, in the US Senate and down a South African gold
mine; trekked across Burma; driven through Cuba; taken medical
supplies to Soviet dissidents; interviewed Communist guerrillas
and the Philippines Defence Minister during the 1987 coup
attempt; and interviewed the President, the leader of the rebels
and the general of the partisans in the Georgian civil war in the
Caucasus.

Simon Sebag Montefiore lives in Greenwich Village, New York
City, and is writing a second novel and a collection of short
stories.

SIMON SEBAG MONTEFIORE

KING'S PARADE

PENGUIN BOOKS

PENGUIN BOOKS

Published by the Penguin Group
Penguin Books Ltd, 27 Wrights Lane, London W8 5TZ, England
Penguin Books USA Inc., 375 Hudson Street, New York, New York 10014, USA
Penguin Books Australia Ltd, Ringwood, Victoria, Australia
Penguin Books Canada Ltd, 10 Alcorn Avenue, Toronto, Ontario, Canada M4V 3B2
Penguin Books (NZ) Ltd, 182–190 Wairau Road, Auckland 10, New Zealand

Penguin Books Ltd, Registered Offices: Harmondsworth, Middlesex, England

First published by Hamish Hamilton 1991
Published in Penguin Books 1992
1 3 5 7 9 10 8 6 4 2

Printed in England by Clays Ltd, St Ives plc

I

The Cambridge Hunters had never caught anything in a century of Saturday morning hunts except influenza from the damp, flat Fens that stretched from the Wash to Cambridge without so much as a hillock or a valley. The foxes, rabbits and hares of the Fens knew they were safe. On rare occasions, a geriatric rabbit gave the hounds a run for a furlong or two before disappearing down a warren. Over the years, they had become used to the incompetent huntsmen who passed by their hedgerows and warrens every week.

On my first day out with the Hunt, this did not worry me. I have always thought that incompetent sportsmen are the best sort. Like so many British customs, the ritual itself was more significant than its details: everyone was there on their own private hunt. Some chased the hare; some hunted the fox. They each had their own quarry.

The pack had taken a scent. The black and white hounds bounded across the fields like a frothy wave charging up the shore, bearing the boundless energy and enthusiasm of nature. They were yelping and barking with an exhilaration that was infectious to the beaglers.

I wanted to touch them, but they were always ahead of me. Even though I was young then, I felt old beside the hounds. They seemed to have a monopoly on everything that was young and fresh.

The lead beagle was a young male, broad-mouthed, with muscular haunches, and he led the others, leaping with his front paws off the earth, collecting his strength in his broad wiggling back and his sturdy flanks. The others followed, jostling for the position of his lieutenant, keeping their noses close to the leader's tail and to the ground, where the scent was so strong that it was almost a visible scarlet thread across the Fens.

The stodgy gentry of the county and the adventurers and fakes, who are the most unexpected part of Cambridge, joined the undergraduates for this simple rite, which was so different for each person. The glowing vigour of the hunters and their buxom women made them distinct from the adventurers, whose lives in Cambridge were shadowed by hidden pasts. They in turn walked apart from the local squires, whose tasteful air of comfort insulated them from the enthusiasm of the hounds and the bite of the wind.

'I'm no expert, Pike, but I do enjoy my wines,' Mr Party-Jones was telling Sir Pike Pease, the Member of Parliament for Cambridgeshire South West. 'Don't I, my sweet?' he added to his wife in his clipped, loveless voice.

'He loves his wine.' She had a wrinkled, weather-beaten face and grey streaked hair, pulled sharply back. She was dressed in the drab, brown tweediness that passes for good taste in the counties, and she was watching the girls who were following the hunt. Her daughter, Camilla, who was too tall and whose features were rather too sharp, was up there with them. She had done well to get into Cambridge, but now she needed all the help she could get to meet 'someone' for the rest of her life. Mrs Party-Jones had every intention of helping. It was the job of a mother. 'I do hope Camilla's talking to the Nelson boy. He's so nice.'

'I used to chair the wine committee at the House,' said Sir Pike, ignoring her. 'We laid down lovely wines.' He recalled long dinners, savouring ancient wines with his fellow MPs, men with whom it was a pleasure to dine. 'Before 1979. Before the new gang came in.' Twisted images of the new gang rose out of the Fen: Trumply's oiled hair and his telegenic smile; public relations experts; developers like Nelson; and the Woman Herself.

Pease snorted and walked on.

'Still,' said Party-Jones, who was in the City. 'We can't complain. Things are pretty good in the . . .' His wife glanced at him. He stopped, embarrassed to point out the benison of Britain's prosperity in the winter of 1986.

2

'We really must have the Peases over for dinner, dear,' whispered Mrs Party-Jones. 'It's been five months . . .'

'Whatever you say, dear.'

The Reverend Jenkin, vicar of Cambridge's church and steward of the Union Society, his small eyes acutely bright, was almost skipping to keep up with his companion, a fat man with a beard and moustache, who sweated in a three-piece suit and carried an umbrella and briefcase. The little vicar in his black plus-fours, dog-collar and black-rimmed glasses was thinking that he had not been born to this world, but he belonged here: the pulpit and the manor house had ruled Britain from the time of Saint Augustine until the petty bourgeois had temporarily triumphed in the 1960s. If this were Henry VIII's time, I would be Cardinal Wolsey, he thought.

The fat man was peering ahead at the handsome hunters in their navy-blue velvet coats with the brass buttons catching the sun like rows of winking eyes. 'The Nelson boy leads like a lord,' he said in a loud deep voice, watching the young Master of the Hunt.

'The Nelson boy is the son of the developer,' snapped the Reverend Jenkin, who lost all his wit when someone mistook one of the new rich for the aristocracy, whom he was preparing exclusively for his Debrett's peerage of a Heaven.

The huntsmen ran with the beagles, racing them across the fields, climbing over the gates as the hounds leapt joyously, wet-nosed, open-mouthed, long-eared, flying over fences and through the middle of hedges and across little streams. The huntsmen were shouting orders; patting the front hounds; calling laggers into the pack, so that their enthusiasm infected the hounds and their exuberance made the huntsmen happier than they had been all week. Back in Cambridge, there were essays to do – this was our last year. Worse, we were twenty-one years old. There were jobs to get in the real world. Success was a wolf at our heels: success in the City, success in accountancy, success was the fashion.

All the time we asked ourselves: what if we fail the era?

3

This field was the only place left in the world where it did not matter.

Matthew Nelson was Master of the Cambridge Foot Beagles. This was something he had achieved that was beyond the all-embracing tentacles of his father's influence. As he ran ahead, curly-haired and aquiline, with the beagles, Matt imagined that the Mastership was somehow equal to his father's achievements. Though he knew this was not true, here at least he could pretend to himself that it might be.

Each huntsman had his favourite hound, which jumped up on him with unquestioning innocence, stretching its thick, mud-curdled paws towards his face. He would fall to his knees and the hound would lick his face and nibble his ears and smell his hair, while he laughed and laughed as if he was being tickled by a mistress. The exception was a slim, immaculate Indian, whose plus-fours and velvet coat were clearly very new. He was terrified of spattering his new clothes with mud. When the other beagles grew jealous and joined in, the Master blew his horn and off they went again.

It is often thought that British males prefer their dogs to their daughters. They thus bring up the latter to be as like the former as possible.

At the very back of the long column that now straggled across several fields came the camp followers: the girls, far behind the hearty beaglers. Camilla Party-Jones, her fair hair parted on the side, was walking along with her 'dear' childhood friend, Joanna Yarborough.

'You know us Yarboroughs,' Joanna was saying to Camilla. 'Born on skis! Daddy says it's our family motto. Born on skis.'

They talked without cease about many things (skiing, essays on Da Vinci, holidays in the Highlands, Daddy's bank, their brother's army career, the absence of 'eats' at the party in Bankingshire) – about anything, in fact, except men and sex. This painful subject burned day and night in their minds and beneath their grinning faces. They never admitted this

4

to each other – only their mothers understood – but they spoke in a code that each understood very well.

'Matt Nelson is such good style,' said Camilla wistfully, looking after the Master and meaning that he was enormously rich but that was not his attraction.

'He is such a character,' added Jo, which meant that, far from being a character, he drank profusely and vomited with his male fellow-sportsmen. 'Loves his drink, like Daddy. Met him skiing last year.'

'His family do a lot of good work, but he's not really very mature,' concluded Jo. Here was the sad crux: Matt's father was a latter-day Croesus, the most ruthless king of deal-makers, which forced him to sit on charity committees, but his son had not yet noticed the mature attractions of gangly Camilla and stalwart Jo, who were very proud to have won their places in the University. Worse, he seemed attracted to the brainless glamour of secretarial students and social climbers.

The overwhelming majority of the girls out on the Fen came from the secretarial colleges and the Polytechnic, where they were studying subjects as absurd, obscure and inappropriate as anthropology, city planning, typing and divinity. They all wore similar weathered green coats down to their knees, green Wellington boots, thick multicoloured jerseys (bought by their parents during their annual Scottish holidays) and tight jeans.

They laughed and pointed ahead at their boyfriends in the distance, who were hunting and laughing with their fellow-men. Trained from birth that this was the way things should be, the girls found boorish treatment not only attractive but a status symbol. They rose early every Saturday during the university term to hunt the undergraduates.

'They would destroy all this,' came Fergus Fox's earnest Scottish voice, husky with the morning. I knew who 'they' were: Thatcher, the new financiers, the new Right. Fergus Fox was walking beside me, carefully watching the regulars, noting the way they acted and copying their mannerisms. After all, it was our first day out with the Cambridge Foot Beagles.

His protégée (and more) Sally Gilpin was beside him, shining with her conspicuous consumption of make-up: the skin beneath it was clearly visible in the light, as if she had been embalmed. In the open air her thick dark hair, pulled back from her forehead, had the fine sheen of an otter's back.

It was a beautiful day. The Fens were thousands of square miles of green fields and green hedges and streams that ran randomly across the fields. Ahead of us, out of the streams, rose mist, thick white mist in long wisps that curled magically out of the ditches and waterways and nonchalantly rose and twisted into the air.

'And in Cambridge, we can win a small victory over degenerates like Babylon and the right people will notice . . .'

Fox was obsessed with the revolution that had changed Britain after 1979. He wanted to destroy its supporters in the University. It was his dark side.

'I love the idea of hunting,' said Sally Gilpin, imagining her life as lady of the manor and wife of the formidable politician Fergus Fox. 'Thank you for asking me.'

Fergus beamed with pleasure. If only his father, the thin-lipped Highland clergyman, could see him now. This was what Tory gentry had always done. Here he was, taking his place where the rulers of Britain had always lived. How hard he had worked against the Establishment to hunt with the Establishment today. So he walked carefully but triumphantly, as if he was going up to collect a prize but was watching his feet to be sure he did not trip at the crucial moment. This was not part of the new Britain, the heartless Britain at war with itself. This was the real old country as it had always been before the miners' strike and the Falklands, before it had been divided by a brash, new, selfish creed. Here, industry and government, land and society came together as they always had until She came to power. And at last Fergus Fox, President of the Union, Cambridge's most practical politician, was taking his place in the partnership that had always ruled this country.

Fergus began to make an oblique line across the field. The reason became clear when we overtook the vicar and found ourselves climbing over a stile with Sir Pike Pease, the veteran MP who had been sacked by the Prime Minister when he resisted the stand against the unions. He had represented this constituency since his father had died in 1957, and he had never changed his line. Pease was a small, pointed-faced man in his sixties, with black hair greased across his head at an unlikely angle. He stood in a relaxed, hunched-up way in his faded tweeds and plus-fours, with one foot up on the stile. I thought he was like an old hog.

'Oh, hello, old chap,' he said warmly to Fergus. He had known many Union presidents because the University was a vital part of his constituency. He paid Fox special attention because he was an old Conservative, a 'wet' unlike the rest of the sycophants in the party. Of course, Fox is a self-made young man, thought Pease, with his head on a tilt, but there's nothing wrong with that. He's making his way in the world from terrible origins in the Gorbals or somewhere.

'Lovely day,' snorted the hog, as we heard the sounds of the yelping beagles and the horns in the distance.

'Terrible scenes of anarchy in Wapping. It's the miners' strike all over again,' said Fergus. He was eager to win points with Pease – and would have been mortified to know that Pease thought he was from the disgusting slums of the Gorbals instead of the lovely austerity of the Manse. When at last the Woman destroyed Herself, Pease will help me, Fox hoped.

'Ghastly, Fox. Ripping the country in half. Where is the consensus? Where's the great alliance – industry, country and labour? Three hundred years of consensus gone. It's tyranny, I say.' Pease grunted. He shook his head. He remembered the humiliation of reading about his own dismissal in someone else's *Daily Materialist* on the train down to London.

'You know that Trumply's speaking at the Union next week,' Fox told the old man, hoping to provoke more venom. He was not disappointed.

'God dammit! I've got to meet him at the bloody station. I really must be discreet,' said Pease, meaning that he was about to be delightfully indiscreet. 'Sadly, the Blue Rinses think Trumply's a matinée idol and dream about him while

7

they play bingo. This is our government. Yesmen and shady foreign financiers.'

'There'll be a large demonstration about the Bomb, I suppose . . .' I said, keen to be noticed by the old MP.

'You know Joe Rourke, Sir Pike. He's with us on the slate,' said Fergus in his soft accent. The MP smiled warmly, glanced at my new coat and thought, another young man on the make. Not that there's anything wrong with that . . .

We were over the stile. Pease was scurrying affably towards his friends, the Party-Joneses. I was happy. My father and mother thought very highly of Pease and were shocked by his sacking.

'He's a fine man. I know. I've served this country's civil service for twenty-eight years. That's how I know. Pease is a respectable and sensible man.'

'And I have to say it, Frank,' concluded mother. 'I trust him.'

A wave of hopeless disappointment ran through me at the thought of my father: of all the jobs Frank Rourke could have chosen, why had he chosen that one? I thrust it swiftly out of my mind to make way for better thoughts. My parents would be pleased that I was out beagling, which was something they wished they did themselves, and would be deeply impressed that their son knew Sir Pike Pease. My mother would be sure to tell the other wives at the golf club. This was little England at its best, I thought. Dull and slow but as solid as the mud of the Fens. Here was middle England in all its tensions and secret desires, expressed as they had always been. What a perfect system: even the foxes were happy.

Engines were rumbling in the distance. At first I thought it was the beginning of that shot of thunder that filled the Fens when one of the sleek American fighter planes from the Molesworth base rushed across the sky like an arrowhead. The ear-splitting crash through the sound barrier never came. The sound was altogether closer. The whirring engines were so loud and so close that they were suddenly frightening, as if a roaring juggernaut were about to rush out of the mist.

Across the fields, the Master Beagler had stopped and was peering into the gloom. The man with the briefcase and umbrella and the reverend were rushing towards Sir Pike Pease and his coterie to make common cause, eager to discuss the gravity of this interruption. The girls had at last caught up with the rest of us.

Camilla and Jo stood painfully apart. The comely secretaries were giggling nervously, pushing back their hair, rearranging their hairclips and bows, and waiting for their boisterous Beaglers to reveal the mystery. The pack of hounds, breathlessly crying out like excited children, meandered happily across the field, recklessly ignoring the Master's shrill horn calls in their wild pleasure. A rabbit ran a safe hundred yards ahead.

Through the mist, we began to make out a lorry followed by two transit vans, which were bouncing slowly over the pot-holes of a rough farm track that ran along the edge of the field. All three stopped abruptly. We could hear voices and doors slamming. Gradually, we could see a line of figures facing our line. They stood very still out there, like guards in a ghostly parade. The two lines stood peering at one another through the clearing mist for a long time. It was perhaps a few minutes, but the morning was so still that it seemed an eternity. Only the thump of paws broke the strange silence.

One of the figures began to jog across the field towards the beagles. He ran awkwardly in his gym-shoes, slipping in the mud, and dragging behind him a bundle of rags that bounced along the ground. He ran close to the leading beagle. The pack faltered. Several of the cubs bumped into the hound in front of them. Then, as the jogger wove his way back towards the truck and the vans, a delicious new scent electrified them. With a cry of sheer delight, the young leading beagles rushed after this new trail. The rest of the pack followed.

Matthew Nelson suddenly turned around to face us. He made a virile figure, standing there with his Roman profile (similar to his father's, which appeared so often in newspaper cartoons) and his short hair.

9

'It's the anti-blood-sports loonies,' he said. 'The bastards are after the hounds. Trotskyite madmen. I suppose we'd better do something.' The beaglers, scowling rakishly, broke into a slow run towards their pack. The rest of us followed cautiously.

Pike Pease, playing the part of Neville Chamberlain as usual, called out: 'They won't harm the hounds, chaps. Wait for the police. Let's not begin a fracas with these hoodlums.' No one listened to him except Fergus, who nodded ostentatiously, thinking of Pease's cabinet when the Prime Minister finally retired . . .

The antis were not kindly conservationists in round rimless spectacles carrying leaflets. They were more like a medieval army commanded by a cut-throat mercenary captain. Thirty or so of them were piling out of the lorry and the transit vans and advancing across the field in silence. They were dressed in rough anoraks, jeans, soiled denim jackets, gym-shoes and boots. Their hair was in the mohican style so that, except for a central spiky area, their heads were shaved on the back, front and the sides around the ears. Their coats were covered in badges bearing slogans such as 'Kill the Rich'. They were a permanent phalanx of unemployed persons (their fashion sense made sexual discrimination difficult) who travelled the country in vans to appear at violent demonstrations against any grievance God had invented. They were not very interested in chasing dogs. They were waiting for the police to arrive so that they could witness some police brutality.

Standing guard along the field to stop the brave beaglers were a line of skinheads, like jackals with their big jackbooted legs and shoulders and their tiny, pallid, hairless heads. The tallest of the skinheads had a chain tied through a large ring in his left ear. At the other end of the chain there was a live rat, which sat on his shoulder, sniffing the air with a tiny red nose and grimacing with thin yellow teeth. Its naked pink tail hung down over the skinhead's back like a piece of anatomy torn out of a living body. Beside the bearer of the rodent, a tall, big-boned girl with a scarred face, who somehow managed to catch my eye even without a head of hair, moved her jaw slowly from side to side waiting for the action.

The skinheads lived in Cambridge, enjoying their dole cheques and beating up the odd undergraduate. They were here for a day out. They had no political beliefs except that violence was as much fun as hunting.

The captain of this bizarre army of ramblers was Barry Syssons, the head of the Cambridge Left. His band of undergraduate protesters were far too fashionable in their black leather jackets, pixie boots, trousers and polonecks to be streetfighters. If the truth be known, the skinheads made them distinctly nervous, but they admired the 'Kill the Rich' anarchists as real freedom fighters.

The anarchists had crossed Britain from the mining villages of Wales, the slums of Manchester and Bristol and the Gorbals to show their hatred for the new materialistic order and the police, its Gestapo. They had no real organizations. The anarchists were the personification of an attitude: that they were dispossessed and belonged nowhere. They lived off state grants and hated the state all the more for the charity. This was the backlash against the rich, the state and the fascist police.

Lastly, there were three animal rights campaigners, three long-haired hippies still cocooned in the loving sixties. Unfortunately, these three commendable men were so intimidated by their hairless comrades that they hid behind Syssons whispering: 'Are you sure you can control all this?'

Syssons, in his tired Che Guevara beret, carrying a loud-hailer, believed he could control anything. After all, he had led his Cambridge Left on wire-cutting attacks on Molesworth nuclear base; bussed 200 protesters to Manchester to demonstrate against apartheid; and led a hunger strike against American imperialism in Nicaragua. This was nothing for Barry Syssons.

The eight skinheads were no longer standing far apart like cowboys at a shoot-out. They were standing together and they were shouting: 'Y' fuckin' cunts. We'll knock y' fuckin' blood-sportin' fuckin' faces in.' The wind was full of voices, the shrill calls of the hounds, Pease's grunts and the yelled obscenities of the anarchists. The fast approaching beaglers charged at the skinheads manfully and then suddenly lost their nerve.

'Gosh,' said the Master. Matt's voice had gone very faint. All his fellow beaglers stood behind him and stared over his shoulder at the hairless skulls. 'Excuse me,' he said.

'No, cunt.'

The beaglers tried to walk around the skinheads but they just moved to block their way. Meanwhile, the puckish jogger with his bundle of delicious smells was back among the anarchists near the truck. The hounds, encouraging one another, snuffling and sneezing, their noses low on the ground, were bounding towards the trucks.

'Here come the dogs,' said Syssons. 'Get the sprays.'

Joanna saw the spray cans glinting in the sun. 'Matt,' she bellowed grandly at her beagling hero, who was facing the skinheads in the middle of the field. 'They're going to spray the hounds.'

The beaglers tried desperately to get past the skinheads. The skinhead with the pet rat slowly and deliberately pulled his hammer head back and brought it forward so hard on Nelson's forehead that Pike Pease, the vicar and the grown-ups heard it at the other end of the field. The rat, obviously used to this sort of disturbance, clung calmly to the skin-head's shoulder.

'Lord God Almighty, they're cracking heads,' said Pease.

A few of the beaglers had broken through and were running towards their hounds. The girls in their keenness not to miss anything were now too close to watch as spectators. In the panic, they ran towards the hounds like their boyfriends. Joanna saw her moment. The world of beagles and girls was threatened. Nelson was hurt. Now was the moment when her strength could play a real part. She ran to tend to the Master, who lay on the ground bleeding on to the rich green grass. She clearly thought that being a female was like waving a Red Cross flag at an Edwardian cricket match.

Instead, the skinhead who had headbutted Matt ran at her and kicked her in the middle of her face with his Doc Marten boot. Her nose cracked and shattered in a flash of bone fragments, flying teeth and blood that spurted out on to the skinhead's bald pate and then ran down her face over her swelling lips into her Guernsey sweater.

She made no sound at all and continued to kneel over Matt, silently touching her face and following its contours tragically with her fingers as if she had dropped one of her mother's china eggs.

The skinhead rubbed the blood into his scalp. 'Might make the hair grow back,' he called over at the wild skinhead girl. 'It's like fuckin' fertilizer!' The rat smelt the blood and its pink eyes cast longing glances at the red spattering of its master's skull. 'Ain't din-dins, yet,' he said to the rat. He placed it firmly back on his shoulder. 'Get back to your perch, Yuppie.'

The blood had spattered the Indian beagler's new hunting coat, and he was very carefully trying to rub it off. I will allow it to dry, he thought, then it will brush off easily.

'They hit the girl,' shouted the clergyman from a safe distance.

Pease was nonplussed. 'Never mind the gals. What about the hounds?' he said abruptly.

The skinheads and the beaglers were ragging back towards the vans, kicking and fighting on the way, unsure who was chasing and who was running. The hounds were suddenly among the Mohicans by the vans. They jumped up on to the men, who sprayed them maniacally in the face, shouting, 'No more blood sports, down with fascism, kill the rich.'

All over the field, a hundred pointless skirmishes had broken out, among the anarchists who were unsure of their battleplan and the beaglers who were convinced they were defending the very essence of the England they loved.

A police van, followed by a police car, was bumping along the lane the antis had travelled up fifteen minutes earlier. As soon as they were in the field, policemen in their blue uniforms and pointed silver-topped hats began to run across the field, spreading out to corner the antis.

The antis, especially the anarchists, were delighted to see the police. The hunting coats of the beaglers were fascist but they were nowhere near as fascist as a police uniform. Now that was fascist! Before a policeman had even reached an anti, the skins and mohicans were shouting:

'Police brutality! Police brutality!' They picked up rocks and threw them at the police, shouting 'Police brutality' as they did so. Together they began to shout 'Police state' over and over again. Britain is probably the only country in the world where protesters have to invent police cruelty.

It was like a fancy dress battle: the police in their navy-blue coats, big black shoes and silver buttons, unchanged since the days when they hunted Jack the Ripper; the beaglers in their eighteenth-century coats; and the antis in camouflage jackets and anoraks as if they had survived at least one nuclear holocaust already. Among them, the girls in their pearls and colourful jerseys were bemused by the cries of hounds, the shouts of the beaglers and the chanting of the antis. They wondered what on earth these 'yobboes' were going on about.

I stood helplessly with Fergus and Sally Gilpin among the chaos of this English collage. It was our first day out with the Hunt. We did not feel we were quite part of it all, so we tried to keep to the sidelines. Each time we moved to the edge of the fighting, it moved to engulf us again. All around us were breathless men from different worlds clashing in a heaving mass of fists and arms and scratching and mud and boots and shouts. I watched coldly as if it were a newsreel with the sound cut off. The fights formed a tangled forest of clothes and bodies.

The laughing blue eyes were staring straight at me, right through the flying fists and shoving shoulders and kicking boots. My stomach went cold. One of the anarchists standing on the other side of the fighting had noticed us. The eyes were looking at us cynically and wickedly like a socialite might glance at a wallflower at a dance. They had the light, clear, plain honesty that only blue eyes have, but when you were closer, their centre had a hint of yellow, like a cunning animal. The mouth was smiling too, showing the distinctive big teeth at the centre and the pointed little teeth at the edge. The face was lean and regular but full of simian mischief:

the eyes, the adaptable lips and the pirate's teeth. When he threw his head back and laughed aloud, I saw that the anarchist was Babylon.

Jesse Babylon stood with his arms crossed and his legs apart on the other side of the brawl. His bush of fair hair was blowing in the wind and his agile chimpish face grinned at us through the fight. He was dressed in cavalry boots, jodhpurs and a long camouflage battle coat like a commando. He looked as happy as he looked when he was giving one of his rabble-rousing speeches in the Union or setting up some outrageous seductive trap. Chaos was his favourite tonic.

'What the hell is Jesse Babylon doing with the antis?' I asked Fox, expecting him to know the answer.

Fox just shook his head. 'What's it matter?' he snapped, his generous Celtic phrases suddenly contracting into rifle shots. 'Showmanship doesn't win elections. We'll have a surprise for Boy Wonder. And even the PM won't last for ever.'

We were close now and Babylon might have heard. He drew a soft peaked camouflage cap out of his pocket and pulled it over his head in a vain attempt to remain undercover. The cap's sun-flaps covered his neck and ears. For a moment, he played the warrior. Then he laughed and opened his arms over the anarchy in the fields. His performance always amused me. I envied it. It is difficult to admire your enemy but I had to admit that I did. Richard the Lion Heart admired Saladin – and were they not enemies?

I was too young to have real enemies, but in Cambridge you were never too young. At this rate, I thought, the rat race will one day begin in the nursery. Politicians will be assigned constituencies before puberty. Children will be developing property before their voices break. Now, all the old games were played for real prizes. The new meritocracy was above the trappings of old England. It had unleashed the energies that had been dormant since the empire. Babylon was part of the energy

'This is like the Battle of Agincourt,' he shouted, as if he were a film director showing off a set-piece extravaganza with a cast of thousands. Sally Gilpin was no longer so impressed with Fergus's staid charms. Babylon's clownish antics were always enough to expunge Fox from the record. She too was eyeing him for his daring. The battlefield was suddenly my road to Damascus.

Camilla's heart missed a beat when she recognized Jesse Babylon. There he was, among the anarchists, dressed in their gear, walking through the trouble as if he had somehow made it all happen. She was deeply confused. This was Jesse Babylon – how could he be on the other side? Daddy knows his father, she thought, and last week, he was at the party in Bankingshire. Still, how dashing he seemed in his peaked hat and cavalry boots.

The girls from the secretarial college almost forgot the blood that had been spilled. They did not even question what on earth Jesse could be doing with the antis. Politics was like money: it was a complex male mystery that they could not live without. Their mothers begged them to invite Babylon to stay; their fathers mentioned his name in the riddle of finance. They needed no convincing.

'What on earth are you doing up there?' they asked in the same tone of voice they might have said, 'Hello bigboy' if they had been born in another place and another time.

Babylon yearned for the smell of gunpowder. As he watched the Fen turned into a brawl, he was imagining a real revolution in London. The King had been assassinated, the House of Lords massacred to a man, his family house burnt to the ground, the great British class system liquidated.

Babylon would disappear, change his name to Jones, speak in the cockney or Geordie accents he could mimic perfectly, and then the consummate actor would rise like a phoenix-Trotsky to lead the revolution. He was forever taking dangerous risks, playing games, changing places. He was mischievous to the point of recklessness. He had travelled from Cambridge with the antis. He was already leading the anarchists in a singsong of anarchist songs before Barry Syssons realized that the new recruit in the peaked cap with ear-flaps was Jesse Babylon.

'What are you playing at?' asked Fox angrily. He would show this cocky rich kid not to play the fool with serious matters.

'You're too late, Fergus. What a little crew of crawlers,' Babylon said, laughing at Sally and myself. 'Beagling! The Establishment's a moving target. You've joined the old one. The wrong one. It's a meritocracy now. Britain has moved on from beagling. That's why I'm here.'

It was clear that he was not just there for the show. He was there because we were there. When I looked into Babylon's articulate eyes, I realized that he was out on the Fens that morning for me.

The police had herded the antis together. Joanna and Matt Nelson were being bandaged up in the back of a police-car. The policeman who was doing the bandaging asked their names.

'Nelson?' asked the officer again.

'Yes,' Matt said.

'Any relation?'

'He's my father,' answered Matthew, sporting a rakish bandage around his head like a wounded general.

'Those Cambridge grads,' they heard the policeman telling his colleagues. 'We've got Sir John Nelson's boy in 'ere!'

An unexpected sense of satisfaction crept through Matthew as he sat stunned in the back of the panda car. At first he was not able to identify its source. The reason at last occurred to him: something had actually happened to him. When his father asked him for news as he did in his weekly message, typed by his secretary, Matthew could for once answer.

In fact, it might even be worth calling him at work . . . Matthew Nelson, of course, did not know that he would never have been elected Master of the Hunt if his father had not been that panjandrum of the decade, Sir John Nelson.

Joanna could feel her plump face swelling up like an over-ripe plum. She was sure her eyes would be squeezed shut so that she could not see any more; her nose would close so she couldn't breathe. She was pleased that she was there with Matthew Nelson and imagined Camilla watching jealously. If only I was looking better, wished Jo Yarborough.

Mrs Party-Jones, watching through her field binoculars

from the other side of the field, disdained her daughter's lack of activity: One golden opportunity to be noticed by the Nelson boy, she thought. And the girl does nothing.

The antis were still shouting about brutality, police cell murders, tear-gas and electrodes. They were dreaming of the police showing them some sort of cruelty. They had missed the police charges on horseback against the miners earlier in the decade. Now they yearned for a punch or a knock from a truncheon. Death in a police cell would be Valhalla for an anarchist.

At last, their prayers were answered with a terrible act of police callousness. Two policemen had tried to arrest Rat, the skinhead who was named after his pet, which was in turn named Yuppie. He hit one of them and spat at the other. They gave chase.

The crowd, including the girls, Babylon, the already arrested antis and the MP, watched as the bald figure in army boots with a rat on his shoulder was pursued by two big-shoed bobbies in their Victorian police helmets. Never was a chase more lacking in grace: a bald giant and his rat scampering like a jackal with mud sticking to his boots while the awkward officers lumbered after him, dropping their helmets and slipping on the damp soil. At last, one of them tackled Rat like a rugby forward.

Rat continued to run with the officer gripping the top of his legs, but his running became slower and slower. When he finally collapsed on the earth with the policeman on top of him, he was led handcuffed back across the field and through the crowd to the police vans.

'Well played that police officer,' said Pease, as if he was watching his son play in a public school rugby match on Speech Day.

'Oh, hear, hear!' shouted the fat stranger, waving his umbrella, keen to show that he too was familiar with Pease's famous public school.

In the struggle, Yuppie the rodent had lost his grip on his master's shoulder and was hanging in the air, held only by the chain attached to the skinhead's ear. Rat's ear was bleeding from the weight. Yuppie was twisting and squealing in the void like a grotesque hirsute belly dancer. The police were too disgusted to put Yuppie back on his perch, and Rat's hands were tied up. Thus the skinhead's bleeding ears and the dancing Yuppie were examples, at last, of brutality. The anarchists broke into a cacophony of protest, shouting, 'Pig bastard Gestapo.' One of the prisoners even managed to break away but, since his hands were handcuffed, he had no balance and ended up rolling around at the bottom of a muddy ditch crying, 'PIGS.'

The capture of Rat and his pet rodent, Yuppie, would become one of the classic tales of anarchist heroism. During the 1980s the tale was printed, along with black and white photographs of a torn ear on a hairless head and a rat, at least once in each of the 432 separate anarchist newspapers.

'What group are you from?' one of the police asked the muddy anarchist who had been fished out of the ditch.

'Don't think you can find us,' shouted the anarchist.

The skinhead girl with the titian-coloured eyebrows was yelling: 'There ain't no building you can raid . . . no organization you can close . . . no one to catch. We ain't fuckin' sellout pacifist vegetarian hippies . . .' She was pointing at the three peaceful animal rights protesters who were now cowering behind a police van. The officer slipped handcuffs on to her wrists.

'We're the carnivores,' said the first one, calling over at Pease and other huntsmen. 'Now, the People are doin' the huntin'.'

The Chief Constable arrived in a black chauffeured car that crept sleekly along the potholed track like a black serpent. The moment he heard about the riot, the Chief Constable knew very well that the local Member of Parliament would be there. He was a broad, ugly but jovial bear of a man with silver braid wrapped around his barrel chest and his hair greased back fifties-style from his forehead. When he walked past them, the mohicans shouted 'Hitlerpig' in an angry chant.

He patted his boys on the back, smacking them affectionately on the head, softly slapping their cheeks, loudly telling them, 'I'm proud of y', lad. Proud of y'! PC Smart, boyo. Well done, Sergeant Hodgkins. Good work.' And again, 'Proud of y', lads.'

He had reached the MP. He put his arm around Pease. 'Morning, Sir Pike. Most sorry about the disturbances. All my apologies. Our boys were ten minutes late, I gather. We'll be pressing charges, I can tell you, Sir Pike.' He spoke proudly in his gruff Cambridgeshire accent, but with the MP he dropped the virile camaraderie he saved for his men. He knew that the gentry loved genuine regional accents.

'I should think so, Chief Constable,' muttered Pease, who was upset about the hounds. In the Fens, Pease never noticed the pity with which people in London or Cambridge treated the fallen. Here, he himself was free of the sense of humiliation that always followed him elsewhere . . . This was the old country, Pike Pease's country.

Now, the ugly world had soiled even this place. Then he began to calm down. He enjoyed the glow that comes when the natural and ancient alliance of the police, parliament and property stands together. Pease felt much better, like a child between its two parents. He shook the Chief Constable's hand. The copper in turn felt the warmth in the handshake and understood that things had returned to the way they should be. If Pease spoke to the Home Secretary about the Cambridgeshire Constabulary (which was unlikely since the Home Secretary was a die-hard Thatcherite), he would say the best things.

'After the shock, I hope you'll ride home in my car, Sir Pike.' The policeman liked and respected Pease: he was a gentleman and knew how to treat the police.

'I'd like to, Len.' The Chief Constable was relieved to hear that they were on first names again.

'It's good Big Bobby's out here,' said PC Smart, watching the Chief Constable. PC Smart was one of the local policemen, well known to the undergraduates: he usually had the job of guarding politicians when they came to speak at the Union.

'Covering his arse, I'd say,' said the other.

Still, Pete Smart and the local policemen were glad to be on a job with Big Bobby present in person. They knew the beaglers were an anachronism, yet the natural respect they showed towards the police made them both feel comfortable. The young officers knew they were defending the people the police were supposed to defend – the gents. The protesters were the scum of the earth.

'Rent-a-crowd again,' said Smart, who was sweating after chasing Rat across the fields. He took off his hat and brushed back his carrot-coloured hair. He smoothed his neat red moustache.

'Rent-a-Trot,' said a second. 'Why don't you get a job?' he said to one of the 'Kill the Rich' men being led past him.

'Gestapo!' shouted the youth. 'Don't touch me, PIG.'

'Are you a Trotskill . . . Totskin . . . Tortskyist . . .?' asked the officer, struggling with the word.

'Don't touch me, pig scum!'

'Wouldn't want to, mate.'

'I'm an anarcho-syndicalist, if you're so interested, pig,' said the man in the handcuffs, educated by the state in sociology at a polytechnic, enjoying his intellectual superiority over the agents of fascism, who had ended their education at eighteen.

'Humm,' said the officer, amazed at the education of these criminals. 'They all go to college free to learn words like Trotsgill and anarsyndicalists . . .'

'What's the difference between an anarcho-syndicalist, an anti-nuclear anarchist, animal liberation anarchists, Maoists and Trotskyites, Communist anarchists and just anarchists?' asked Smart.

'I think that the anarcho-syndic-whatevers are ones who believe in throwing bottles. The others believe in bricks. Still,' said his colleague in his serious way. 'Why do the Cambridge undergrads hunt when they never catch anything?'

''Cause they're gents. That's what gents do,' said Smart, proud of his worldliness. He knew me from his job at the Union and caught my eye. 'Isn't that so?' he said cheekily, regarding anyone who could walk out with the beagles as 'gents' *per se*. I was delighted to be summed up as a 'gent'. It had not happened before.

The striking female skinhead was led past Babylon, who was surrounded by the girls from the hunt.

'Which side are you fuckin' on?' she said hoarsely.

'Yours,' he said, meaning it, for he disdained the class-conscious hunters. He was a Thatcherite. The real revolution was on the Right.

'Yea, for today. The state's been violent to us. Now we're gonna be violent back. You better fuckin' watch your health tomorrow,' she said, her clear eyes glinting as she pranced past him in her handcuffs. Her face was broad like a big cat's. Even without hair, she had a barbaric charisma. Babylon stepped out from among his tepid admirers and watched her legs and bottom in her tight jeans and motor-bike boots as she was led away. For Babylon, no adventure was out of bounds.

'By the way,' said Jesse Babylon to me, when Fox was walking with Pease and the Chief Constable to the limousine. 'You should come over and talk to us one of these days. It's the start of our last year and look at all the fun you're missing. You're out of time. In the fifties or sixties or especially the seventies, you'd have been on the right side. But now . . .' he opened his hands '. . . we've started afresh. They'll be jealous when they look back. Only in England could you have a conservative Left inspired by snobbery in the guise of morality.' He nodded towards Fox and Pease. 'I'll send Morganthau to see you.'

'Gestapo!' was blurted rhythmically from the back of the police vans. Barry Syssons, clutching the loudhailer he had never used and surrounded by his uptight group of grim radicals, was shaking his head.

'The anarchists have no discipline,' he told his fellow undergraduate radicals, who were all studying economics or English. 'The Die-In next week will go like clockwork without these bunglers. If only they could understand that violence plays into the hands of the Establishment.' He pursed his lips. His cohorts pursed their lips.

Babylon had charmed the police just as he had charmed the

protesters. PC Smart liked Babylon. His speeches at the Union relieved the boredom when Smart was waiting to escort his ward back to London. Admittedly, Smart wondered what on earth Babylon was doing with the antis, but then, he was an eccentric, wasn't he?

Smart was giving him a lift back to Cambridge. Babylon walked through the girls, who were now in the same highly charged state as the rest of us. It had been a battle. It had been Agincourt, Culloden Field, the Somme. The protesters were thugs, hooligans, Trotskyites and dervishes. Babylon asked all the girls to tea at his house at King's Parade.

'We're having a tea party on Tuesday,' he said, enjoying the thought of discussing scones among the flashing blue police lights and the snarling anarchists. 'Bring an éclair.'

'Will Nero be there?' they were asking.

'Oh, yes, he'll be there.' He was climbing into the panda car.

'You're not an anarchist, are you, Mr Babylon?' asked the police officer, who of course called a gentleman either 'Mr', 'Sir' or 'guv' just as his predecessors always had.

'No, I'm a Rabelaisian,' said Babylon. Smart pretended to understand. 'Doesn't all this violence make you feel libidinous?' Babylon asked his friend who was climbing into the driver's seat of the panda car. Any sort of human activity seemed to have that effect on Babylon.

'Dunno what you mean, sir.' The young officer was blushing.

'You know, mate,' laughed Jesse, who had the knack of speaking to strangers on their own ground. 'Violence makes one a bit hot-blooded, doesn't it?'

'Have to admit. It does rather, sir,' said Pete Smart. He put his helmet on the back seat.

'What a fun job it must be.' The door shut and the car reversed up the narrow track.

It had been an English battle of symbols. After all, the hunters did not hunt to kill animals, since the hunt had never killed a harvest mouse. The antis were not really protesting against bloodsports because there was never any blood spilt. Both were in their own way attracted to the Cambridge Foot Beagle Hunt because of what it stood for.

The beaglers were dazed. They did not know what to do with their beloved affectionate beagles. The hounds were dispersed around the Fen, running across the fields, searching for their masters, who had fed them, trained them and caressed them.

They still cried like children, but now they whimpered like blind children who have lost their parents in a crowd. They were black and white spots rushing across distant fields, searching the wind with their dry feverish noses and straining to see through their unseeing eyes.

2

Jesse Babylon sat in the frame of his window and watched the crowd swiftly gather beneath him in King's Parade. Though he watched impassively as the demonstration formed, his frailty was suffused with a feeling of strength and power. If only they all knew, he mused, that I have a way to make them go as quickly as they came. He was pleased that there were so many people, because the more there were, the greater his power would be if they did as he bid.

He rested his head in his hand which he leant on his knee. Music was playing behind him in his room. He was keeping time with his hand on the decorative window-box full of plants. Barry Syssons and his protesters in the street below were watching him nervously. Why wasn't he meeting the minister at the station? Had he overheard the plan on the way to the Hunt? A normal afternoon in King's Parade, with its undergraduates wrapped up in their college scarves and greatcoats, had been transformed in a few moments of Syssons's planning into a rally. Babylon's half-closed eyes observed the scene like a lioness sunning herself on the savannah.

A forest of flags and banners swayed beneath Babylon's bedroom window, rippling like leaves with the wind. Each flag bore the name of a university college or society. Jesse was lazily counting the colleges represented, noting the magical symbol of the Campaign for Nuclear Disarmament on each banner. Just about every college was there, as well as a myriad of local polytechnics, colleges, left-wing clubs, theatre groups and gay rights activists. It was a very different crowd from the anarchists at the Hunt.

They had been the dispossessed. The thousands filling King's Parade that day were the possessed of Cambridge:

only Barry Syssons and his activist friends were there both days. Now, everyone was dressed in variations of Syssons's grim designer protest wardrobe: black boots, trousers and leather jackets. They had short or shaven hair and wore a galaxy of badges which yelled slogans about apartheid, the Bomb, Nicaragua and a pot-pourri of other causes.

When the groups at the Hytlerhouse end of King's Parade began to wave their banners in unison and policemen appeared on the street, Jesse Babylon left his eyrie and went inside. Syssons, grasping his proud loudhailer, was climbing on to the makeshift platform in front of the gateway of King's. King's Chapel stood behind him. From Augustus College all the way to Duvalier, the road was solid with protesters. In the excitement, he forgot to glance up at Babylon's room on King's Parade.

'Don't mention it,' said the Defence Secretary. 'I love the train. It reminds me of when I was up here. There were no girls up here then so we used to await the train from London with bated breath. It used to be called the Fornication Express.'

'Humm. Times change.' Words did not come easily to Pike Pease when his sense of decency was insulted. He managed this rude response, thinking that times may change but commonness is commonness in any era.

Sir Ken Trumply, the Secretary of State for Defence, had come to speak at the Cambridge Union. The minister and his detective were met at the station by an uncomfortable reception committee led by the local MP. Pease's hair was freshly brushed at its peculiar angle and he wore a three-piece grey suit that inevitably contained tweed somewhere in its pattern. Fergus Fox and I stood on either side of him in our blazers with silver buttons and our grey trousers. PC Smart was at attention behind us, with the minister's full-time detective from Scotland Yard. The detective was very supercilious towards the local police force, who were 'bumpkins – and incompetent ones at that' in his opinion. He would not talk to Pete Smart.

'Where the hell's Babylon? Does he have no idea of punc-

26

tuality? He's late for every meeting,' Fox, auburn hair parted perfectly, whispered to me while the minister and the MP were exchanging venomous pleasantries.

Sir Kenneth Trumply stood triumphantly beside the huffy Pease. He could be magnanimous in victory. Trumply had risen over the bodies of Pease and the other old Tories. The battle had to be fought. With Pease in the Cabinet, nothing would have been achieved. Now that battle was over.

Trumply was at his peak. He seemed to personify the era and I felt as if he had been born to his great office and would hold it eternally. His hair was thick and still brown, with a few attractive paintstrokes of grey around the temples. It was greased back and parted so that he looked tidy and fresh like a wartime schoolboy. Success was written all over this handsome figure: the monogram KT was emblazoned on his shirt, the collar of his grey coat was black velvet, and his square-jawed good looks radiated the energy, the confidence and prosperity of the times. The Defence Secretary had managed the 1979 election, carrying the Blue Rinses, the women in the bingo halls, rotary clubs and Women's Institutes who were the essence of Britain's prim stability. How they had loved his youth, charm and enthusiasm. He was the grand statesman of a new sort of Conservatism.

'Welcome to Cambridge. As President of the Union, may I say that we are very proud to have you here,' declared Fergus Fox, his honest Scots accent calming Pease's bitter memories and Trumply's boyish esprit.

The two men stared at each other and then shook hands. A photographer from the local newspaper appeared. Pease's smile was a crooked crack in his weatherbeaten brandy pudding of a face; Trumply's was a dazzling wedding cake of capped, even and snowy television teeth. Pease was remembering Trumply's flirtation during Cabinet meetings with the greatest Blue Rinse of them all, She Herself. You little whore, he thought. Trumply expected the same modesty and generosity that he displayed. Pease must admit, thought Trumply, I have come a long way – and I'm not making such a bad job of it either.

A crowd of undergraduates returning to Cambridge from

long weekends and townspeople who had commuted back to the town from London formed to watch Trumply walk to his car. Fox and I climbed into the car with the great man.

The police rode behind him in a panda car. PC Smart drove. The Scotland Yard detective, who spent his time in aeroplanes and limousines with ministers and presidents, shook his head for no good reason, thinking, these bumpkins wouldn't last a minute in my job where you need a bit of finesse. Pete Smart decided the man was a courtier, not a copper. Neither said a word.

Trumply waved at the crowd, delighted as ever to be liked. As the car headed up King's Parade, Pease sat miserably in the front beside the driver who made things worse by saying in the most affable way: 'Weren't you in the Government once, Sir Pike?'

Jesse Babylon tied a silk dressing-gown cord around each of his large speakers and hung them out of his window. High above the street, he lowered them slowly. They hung from the elaborate cast-iron patterns of the window-box like a pair of black coffins against the familiar red brick of the house in King's Parade. He chose a cassette, placed it in the hi-fi in his room and pressed 'play'. He turned the volume dial up to ten and began to walk downstairs.

Syssons was speaking through his loudhailer in a tone of grim anguish, gripping the edge of his platform so that his knuckles were white.

'Take a look, brothers. The bureaucrat who has sold out this island to American imperialism. Why the fuck are those missiles at Greenham? Why are they in Molesworth? Big Brother, take y' bombs and put them in someone else's land . . .'

Trumply's limousine had slowed down while the police tried to clear the protesters. The police escort pretended that they had known about the protest, but it had been organized by word of mouth inside the university and had been so swiftly assembled with such timing that there had been no chance to stop the minister's car. The Scotland Yard detective and PC Smart stared icily ahead. There had been a slip-up.

Each blamed the other. Police officers tried gently to clear a way through the crowd blocking the road.

Pease was at first amused to see Trumply's procession spoiled. Gradually he began to feel a creeping embarrassment that his constituency was becoming a battlefield. Trumply had come from a Socialist, working-class family. He had none of Pease's contempt for protesters. He simply believed that they were wrong. The dapper Cabinet minister peered out of the window, rather enjoying the fact that his visit had provoked such a reaction.

Syssons, his voice now cracking with emotion, declared: 'Brothers, comrades and sisters, the time has come. Let us show the American cowboy and his sidekick what Cambridge would look like if one of his toy guns went off. At the count of three, let the DIE-IN begin. ONE. TWO. THREE. DIE.'

In one single motion, as if they were tentacles of a leviathan, the thousands of protesters sat straight down on the cobbles of King's Parade and lay as if they had been wiped out in a nuclear holocaust.

Syssons knew that his planning and vision had achieved this extraordinary demonstration of the British people's hatred of American nuclear imperialism. He was proud of himself, but he was even prouder of his brothers and sisters who had come to take part in the Die-In. How sad that the Love-Ins of the sixties had become the Die-Ins of the eighties. Sad but necessary. The Minister would miss his debate. The national press would mention his Die-In (though the press was dominated by the labyrinthine secret influences of the Conservative Party, finance, Sir John Nelson and the Americans). The Prime Minister would see that even Cambridge, the heart of the establishment and the old university of most of the Cabinet, abhorred Her and Her American allies. The head of the Labour Party would congratulate him. As he surveyed the sea of human bodies reaching from one end of King's Parade to the other, Syssons pursed his lips. Maybe some justice was possible in this cruel world of *realpolitik*, capitalism and compromise. Barry Syssons's greatest hour had come.

When the first notes of the *1812* overture blasted out of Babylon's speakers, the crowd instinctively thought they must come from the organ of King's Chapel. Then there was confusion and finally, with a sinking feeling, Syssons looked up at the window. Babylon was not there: only a pair of the largest speakers he had ever seen. The crowd followed his eyes. Syssons tried to continue his speech, but his tinny loudhailer was no match for the overwhelming power of the speakers. His voice was simply lost.

The overture, in a flood of violins, oboes, cellos, drums, double-basses, cymbals, trumpets and cannons, bounced off the walls of King's Chapel, rebounded off the distant tower of the University Library a mile away, echoed against the gargoyles of Augustus and continued to blast out of the speakers. Syssons and his loudhailer made no impression at all.

Jesse Babylon appeared in the doorway of King's Parade on street level, smiling over the seated thousands directly into the eyes of Barry Syssons. He stood there in his yellow cowboy boots, denims and scarlet jersey, with a black great-coat with a baroque collar rising high behind his neck. The tails of the coat were so broad and long that they caught the wind and rose up behind him like a bridal train in a Gothic marriage. When he was sure that everyone of the Die-In had seen him, he began to walk slowly along the edge of the pavement towards the police and the ministerial limousine.

The cannons of Tchaikovsky's *1812* were roaring over the Parade. The music was bellowing out the crashing of gunpowder and the clashing of sabres. The shouts of the protesters were lost, though I could see that they were opening their mouths. Syssons was like a goldfish in a tank – when he tried to speak, just bubbles came out. The police were already beginning to pick up the protesters close to the car and move them out of the way. The cavalry charges of Napoleon's Imperial Guards were being cut to pieces by barrages of Kutuzov's cannonades on the battlefield of Borodino. Every boy or girl there, from Syssons to Babylon, from the minister's chauffeur to PC Smart, felt as if they themselves were there at Borodino in 1812.

The protesters were confused. How long were they supposed to stay dead? The police were arresting people. They couldn't hear Syssons's orders. The Die-In was disintegrating. Starting at the edges and then inwards to the centre, the students jumped up and began to disperse. Dropping their banners and leaflets, they first walked and then ran back to their colleges, while Syssons and his die-hards waited behind to wave their fists as the minister's car slid past.

Sir Kenneth Trumply climbed out of the car and shook hands with Babylon. Babylon climbed into the car beside Trumply. Only Babylon could have invented a ruse of such theatricality that it would both project himself and win him the respect of the great Minister from London. Typically, it was both callous and clever, pulling the rug from under Fox's feet. Fox looked at me with a smile that prayed for and plotted the fall of this dangerous showman. We will find a way, he thought.

Darkness was falling as the car finally drove down King's Parade, past the statues and gargoyles of Augustus, past the Round Church, towards the Union. We drove on in silence, listening to the crumpling sound of the banners under the wheels of the car.

'Consensus preserves but only confrontation can create,' said Babylon. 'That's the lesson of the era. That's what I will say in my speech tonight.'

'Consensus is the English way,' said Pike Pease from the front of the car.

'Only if failure is the English way . . .'

'It's what made us a free country,' I said.

'If she had waited for consensus, we would still be waiting,' said Babylon.

'And maybe we would all be happier,' said Fox.

'I think this is a unique time,' said the slow, careful voice of the Minister. 'This is revolution cemented not with blood but with wealth. And we are lucky to be living through it.'

We had arrived at the Union, an Edwardian red brick building lacking in any sort of charm. The driver of the limousine, who had not spoken since his last painful interjection, seemed determined to finish with one more atrocity of tactlessness.

'Sir Pike,' he said innocently, full of pride to be driving his local Member of Parliament at last and keen to display his knowledge of politics. 'Weren't you once Minister of Defence?'

The car went very quiet.

'Yes,' said Pease very quietly in a hoarse old man's voice. 'Before Ken Trumply.'

'A great speech,' said Babylon's voice from behind me. The debate was over. We were drinking in the President of the Union's office. A crowd was gathered around the minister.

'A great performance,' I said, choosing my words carefully to make my point but conceal my envy.

'You'll hear a hell of a lot more. Just remember my name.'

'I don't think I will ever forget it.'

Babylon's presence made him look bigger than he was, like a genie in an Arabian flask. We circled one another as enemies do, for such hatred is rarely caused by just a difference of ideology.

'Hurrah for the two best speakers in Cambridge.' It was the piping voice of the miniature village vicar. The Reverend Jenkin wore knickerbockers on his little legs like a bantam's drumsticks, and a dog collar. He had the head of a prepubescent schoolboy. 'You spoke awfully well.' And he turned exclusively to Babylon. 'How are your dear parents? I met Sir Edwin and his Lady the other day at the home of my dear friends, the Monaco-Dzerzhinskys, and they sweetly took the trouble to come to say hello.'

The whole crowded room watched Jenkin standing like a referee between the two of us, as if, in this microcosm, the wars of the epoch were being fought in mortal combat. We shook hands, and I caught in Babylon's vivid eyes a glacial contempt that sliced through the warmth of his cheeky grin. Then it was gone.

'By the way, Joe,' said Babylon quietly. 'We would like to talk to you. I mentioned it at the Hunt. Wasn't that an adventure?'

He beamed with a mountebank's delight at the intrigue, but Jenkin interrupted to send Jesse over to the Cabinet minister: 'Oh Jesse, my dear friend Kenneth is dying to talk to you.'

I ground my teeth as the schoolboy haircut and the glasses of the good Reverend drew near.

'What do you make of Babylon?' he rasped, and before I could answer, he added, 'Still, there are Jews and Jews. Kenneth wants to talk to you,' and handed me over to the Minister.

'Well done. I have rarely been attacked with such verve. The Union seems trivial, does it not?' The Minister spoke his Oxford English too precisely, as if he had been taught a new language. 'In the Government there are eighteen of us. Eight are from here and five of them were Presidents. I'm sure you'll be President.'

'Babylon is more likely to . . .'

'Yes, yes, I know who the Babylons are and that is why it is more to you than to a Babylon. It is your launching pad. For my first speech as a Cabinet Minister, all those eight Cambridge people were there you know. I must go. Walk with me to my car.'

Fox shook his hand, thanked him for coming and walked him to the door, through the crowd that lined the walls to see this glamorous politician who had come so far, so fast.

'You'll do well, I did well. I was like you. As a student, I was a Socialist,' he said when we were outside. His hands turned over and over one another and the smile shone too brightly in the midwinter evening. He suddenly seemed so fragile, like a priceless vase that is already cracked and that will shatter, any minute, into a million pieces, leaving only a glossy but worthless memory.

'You changed your views.'

'You're clearly not one of us,' he said. 'After the miners' strike, there's no middle ground.'

'No,' I said. 'I'm not one of you.'

'Ah, but you will be. Everyone will be.'

We had reached the long black car. The driver opened the door. His bodyguard waited for him in the car. We were behind the Union, but some students passed and they whispered, 'Wasn't that Kenneth Trumply?'

'You're at the top,' I said stupidly.

'Whatever happens, remember what I said about Cambridge. Make it yours and it'll make you.' We shook hands and he climbed into the car. The window slid down. The car was moving now. Trumply was sad.

'I have gone further than I ever thought I would,' he said gracelessly as the sleek car slid away. I did not understand his point, but I realized that there was a grave fault somewhere in his strength. He had let me into his secret: the game was up.

The car had gone. When it had disappeared, I turned to find Elliot Morganthau's iron-rimmed glasses and steel-tracked teeth glinting in the street-lights. He lived in the house at King's Parade, with Nero and Babylon.

'There is a spare room.'

'Where?' I said.

'You know where. Do you want the spare room?'

'Where is it?'

'King's Parade. Where else?'

'Why should I want to live there?'

'Well,' he shrugged, 'success is relative. Maybe you're satisfied.'

'When?'

'Now. Tomorrow. It's our last year.'

'Babylon has his room there too.'

'He stays there some nights.'

'I've got rooms for this year . . .'

'Come, come, Joe, you know what I am asking. You know what King's Parade means. Do you want the spare room?'

'Stay where you belong. Always stay with your own sort. They will protect you,' Fox told us with the gravity of a Scottish clergyman's son. He often began our meetings with a sanctimonious home truth aimed at whichever of us was displaying a lack of commitment to the cause. In this case, after Morganthau's offer the night before, I felt that it was aimed at me.

'Anyway, to business. This year, we must destroy them. They're dilettantes anyway. It will not be difficult. I have a plan.'

'When you say destroy, what do you mean?' I asked, sitting on the edge of the bed in his austere room.

'He means wipe them out at the elections,' said Sally sharply, her heavy make-up dividing her face into acutely defined areas of colour like a Chagall window.

'No, that's not Fergus's point at all,' said Simon Saint breathlessly, with the pink virtuosity of a teacher's pet. Simon had the over-soaped face of a buggered-out choirboy, and exuded a rich smell of herbal shampoos and baby powder. 'Fergus means that we should defeat them in debate. Reveal Thatcherism for what it is.'

Fox ran his hand over the parting of his auburn hair and then opened his hands as if to embrace us all. 'You're all right. We will slay them politically and intellectually.'

'In Cambridge?' asked Sally, proud of her efficiency and the neat officiousness of her blue career-girl's suit, with its broad shoulders and knee-length skirt.

'No, Sally,' said Fox, using his Scottish song of a voice like a lullaby. 'If we destroy them in Cambridge, we'll wreck them for life.'

We did not reply. His conviction was so strong that it must be right. 'They're so corrupt, it won't be difficult,' he added, almost apologetically, as if breaking the neck of a blind rabbit.

Fox's eyes wandered around his Spartan room, over the neat piles of paper on the desk and the photograph of his dog-collared, tight-lipped father, but, as always, they settled on Sally. He admired the ways in which she had improved during her two years in Cambridge. The suits were fine, but at once he noticed the ladder in her tights and the uneven make-up on her face. He loved her, but unlike everything else in the world that could be painlessly solved with logic, she always caused him pain. Her make-up and short skirt were slatternly; her torn tights showed a careless attention to detail

35

('God is in the details,' his father always said) and he wished he could trust her. He felt she was always looking for something better, and he knew she was essentially faithless to him.

All this passed through his mind as he sat upright in his desk chair, tidying and retidying the papers on the desk.

'So that's the plan. I am President. Then we have to decide who should stand as my successor at the next election. It is our last year. We must win.'

Saint and I glanced at one another: he is a useless speaker, I thought; a second-rate strategist, thought the cherubic Saint, as he thought of Joe Rourke. Sally stretched and wandered out. Where is she going? Fox longed to know.

Fox and I walked out of Great Court and turned right, down King's Parade, past the house where Nero, Morganthau and Jesse lived. Fox was saying, 'They – and this whole regime – are a grubby bunch of financiers. The rumours about Trumply don't surprise me, and look at Nelson's father. The worst example of power without responsibility. They aren't the Tory Party. We professional people are that. Babylon's the one to fear . . .'

'What about Trumply?' I said.

'The press has found out about the affair with the model. The Blue Rinses made him. Now they will destroy him just as fast.' Then all of a sudden, he stopped.

The elephantine head of Nero and Morganthau's large spectacles were leaning out of their window. Above the sounds of the street, I could just hear Nero's pukka voice bellowing out of his over-ripe face, and Elliot's rich words spurting maniacally from his mouth of glinting steel. We followed their eyes.

Down the wide street bicycled an Armada of fashion: a collage of blonde hair, pedals and buzzing mopeds was heading down King's Parade. These were the girls from the secretarial college, out from their typing courses, the girls from the Hunt. Loose on the town. They were a squadron of social stormtroopers, commanded by their ambitious parents to go up to Oxbridge and barter their pampered bodies for the social investment of a lifetime. Whatever the cost of the secretarial course (which none of them would ever use), the parties, the ball dresses (at £5,000 a gown), their parents were willing to make the sacrifice.

The obese Nero was summoning them up to King's Parade, promising them tea and cakes, but they all knew who he was and who lived in the house and that was enough. This was Babylon's tea party, created out of the chaos of the Hunt. They parked their bicycles and scampered up the stairs. The girls on Vespas jumped off their mopeds. A flood of long hair flowed seamlessly like cream out of their helmets as they pulled them off.

Even Fox was speechless for a moment.

'Appetizing,' he said.

'I will have one of those girls one day,' I said.

'After two years up here, you know very well they're not our sort. They're not in our world. We're not in their league.'

'Then I will change my league.'

My head was full of those secretaries with their skiing legs, their voices like plums and their clear blue English eyes that said, 'Eat me – and I will taste of gold.'

The portrait dominated the room. It showed Andrew Nero lifting a crown on to his own head, dressed as Napoleon in full imperial robes. In the portrait and in reality, Nero's stomach was truly imperial. He sat in a throne of a chair, with his trembling belly fighting to escape from his corduroy trousers like a living creature.

Elliot stood behind the chair with a hand on each corner. A lazy flaxen-haired girl sat cross-legged at Nero's feet. She stuck out her breasts like a war hero thrusts out the medals on his chest. She had taken off her bootkins and stockings and they lay beside her, neatly placed together.

'You don't know Scrubber, do you?' said Nero, who noticed my interest.

'Scrubber is my nickname,' the girl announced in a voice of tight-arsed propriety without looking at me. 'My name is Sophie Croquet-Bowles.'

'You can probably borrow her if you pay me enough,' added Nero.

'Oh, Nero,' laughed Scrubber as if very pleased to be offered.

'She is an avid worshipper of my manhood, the one-eyed trouser snake of King's Parade.'

'It's like a python,' added the girl.

'Well, on to the business in hand,' said Nero, while Scrubber ran her fingers along the patterns on his brogue shoes. 'Let's not embarrass Mr Rourke, who has no doubt been brought up not to speak of such things. Elliot has offered the room. We have asked you here because we want you to join us. You're wasted on Fox with his old Harold Macmillan Toryism and his preacherman's austerity. You're missing out on the whole fun of the decade. Britain has never had a revolution. Why?' They all eyed me.

The girl had looked at me languidly. She had her opinions. 'He is a nothing,' she decided. 'From nowhere.'

Nero had neither Elliot's illusions, nor the girl's simplicity. 'He knows no one. His family aren't anyone. He has neither money, nor genius, nor style. But he has one thing going for him – he will be mine.'

'Elliot,' said Nero when he had thought his thought, 'tell him about the revolution.'

'Britain needs no revolutions,' said Morganthau, 'because we have class without exclusivity. Today, a new upper class is taking over: the Thatcherites. You should be one of them.'

I grinned at their cheek. 'What do I need?'

'You need to be able to read a wine list as well as you read a balance sheet,' answered Elliot.

'There will always be a ruling class,' Nero drawled, 'but it's always changing. Someone has to run the place.'

'And it might as well be us,' said Scrubber, lying back so that her shaggy head rested on Nero's loins.

'So what do you mean by the people who run the place?' I asked.

'Ah,' moaned Nero. He liked that. 'We are the great interests of the land. The Army, the City, the clubs of London, we are the schools, we are the mewses of Kensington and the cottages of Fulham, the manors of Hereford and the old rectories of Suffolk. Joining the ruling class isn't difficult, Joseph, in this great class-ridden democracy. You just have to know how. That's all. It's not so bad – most of the traditions are quite fun. You may like them.'

'No doubt.'

'Cambridge is a laundering process,' he said quickly. 'That is, if you are interested. Change slates. Join us. We are the future. This is the house where the future will be made.'

'And what about Babylon?' I asked.

'Ahhh, Babylon. Babylon wants you,' said Nero. As Elliot showed me out, I noticed that Scrubber was watching me with careless greed, like a window-shopping housewife. The door shut and Elliot smiled indulgently at me so that all the metal in his teeth shone.

'Is Nero really a lord?'

'The art of knowing lords,' he said formally, pleased to have caught me out so soon, 'is to treat them as if they were dustmen. His father came from the North . . .'

'What's wrong with the North?' Everyone talked about it as if it was a Third World country.

'It's a Third World country but Nero lives in the empires of influence that run this country,' said Elliot, conjuring up these hidden edifices with a *Roget's Thesaurus* sauce of words, each one a more outlandish treasure than the last. 'He's not interested in the tips of icebergs. He loves the mysterious powers beneath the surface, where everything is one. There are no loose ends. And in Cambridge, Andrew has a monopoly of the rituals and games of the powers that keep the world turning. It's his hobby.'

'Y' believe all this shit?'

'Implicitly,' said Morganthau, leering down at me, glasses and teeth glimmering in the half light. 'And so will you.'

The stairs curled at a dangerous angle. The banisters were quite rotten. When I tried to turn on an electric light there was a blue flash, so I took them step by step, feeling the wall in the greyness.

The wind blew down the Parade with a vicious iciness that burnt my face like an acid. It stung my skin and made my eyes water. The awnings were shifting restlessly. The sign that advertised 'Intrigues', the tea-shop, swung back and forth wildly on its hinges, which screeched with the wind like a crow. Augustus College was only a few steps down King's Parade, but I found that I was not hurrying. I was enjoying the feeling that this storm was somehow changing me.

I was inventing myself, standing there alone in the Parade beneath King's Chapel. Everything is beginning again now, I thought. There was nothing before this. But my parents were there in front of me, carried on a gust of nostalgia. My father was in his usual grey pinched suit, with his gold club tie held in place with the silver tie-pin in the shape of his initials. How proud he was in his respectability and how satisfied he was in his position.

His clipped voice was telling me about the Civil Service: 'They look after one very well. We have the gold club membership, private medical insurance and ... That's what comes from working for the Civil Service.'

'I can always get a place in a restaurant when I say that Frank works for the Government. They rush to give us a table when I tell them, don't they, Frank?' my mother was saying.

The wind was carrying their voices away. Now it brought the words of schoolboys at my old state school. Their taunts were shrill screeches, as if spoken by the wind and the hinges of the signs in King's Parade.

'Is it true your dad's a tax collector?'

'No, he's a civil servant. He works for the Government. He's a civil servant.'

'He's a tax collector.' They would say it again. 'Aren't you ashamed of 'im? That's not a proper job. Joe Rourke's dad's a tax collector.'

'He works for the Government. He's IN the Government!'

They too were gone. Now the gusts were calm and low like a distant tune played as the wind crossed the tundra and the waves of the North Sea and the Fens. Fergus Fox was lecturing me, as if he were his father giving a Sunday sermon to his dour Scottish congregation.

'Britain today is like a Jacob's ladder. One ladder is going up to Heaven, the other to Hell. More and more are climbing on to the ladder that goes up. They scorn the weaklings who are going down, but one day, the ladder that goes up will no longer be able to hold everyone and it will bend and strain and finally crack. It will throw the ambitious all the way back to earth. They will fall further than they ever hoped to climb.'

Somehow, Fox, Pease and my parents were borne away by the wind that night. Anything was possible to Babylon and Nero. How could anyone wish to stay where they were? The adventure was in making your own destiny. They personified all the golden energy that was changing London and Parliament. I wished to be part of it. The ladder to Heaven was open to me that night. Without a moment's hesitation, I climbed on to it.

And Jesse Babylon, wearing a great white coat that rose up around him like a vampire's cloak, welcomed me aboard, grinning like a demon monkey.

I tried to remember when I had first seen him. It came back with a searing but distant pain, and I made myself forget it almost as soon as I had remembered it. Two years before, almost to the day, I had been at Cambridge for a week.

There was a lining of thick sweat on the walls of the late-night bar deep beneath Cadaffi Street by the time I arrived with Tracy. The college discothèque was underground in a steamy labyrinth of brickwork passages, awash with sweat like a cesspool.

The hideous selection of beer-breathed, pale-faced, thick-ankled women, with their lost enthusiastic eyes and thin hair, were already standing on the dance floor shifting stiffly from foot to foot in time to the music. Some were already exchanging saliva with drunken rowers and boaties, be-muscled rugby players and other local heroes. Through this grotesque scene, I walked proudly with the rounded, strutting Tracy, living every moment of the night before.

Tracy was a waitress in the college dining room, and the

wife of a squaddie airman from Molesworth base. When I asked her up to my room, I offered her tea or coffee, keen to follow the elaborate etiquette of the one-night stand, as I understood it.

'I don't care,' she had yelled, reaching for me. Night after night, I had lain there beside this broad-backed, zeppelin-limbed beast. In this boudoir pantomime, in my journey among her stertorous chambers and spicy canals, I had first learned that lust was the secret unspoken key to the portcullis that divided class from class and enemy from friend. In her uninhibited barrack-room cursing, in her cries and grunts, in the squelching of her juices, I had at last discovered that here was power at its most primitive.

I felt that power as I pushed through the sweating, salivating, salsaing crowd with the bright shining wickedness of Tracy on my arm. She boasted a sexuality so strong that men stared at her as if she had turned herself inside out. The undergraduates eyed her and nudged one another.

'There's the horny waitress from the dining hall. Lucky Joe.'

Suddenly she said, 'There he is,' and disappeared into the crowd, leaving me standing alone. I searched for her feverishly under the laughing faces of the undergraduates until, at last, on the dance floor, I saw her. Then a man's face came down, eyes closed, lips apout with the satisfaction of conquest, and she was gone beneath his plumage of unruly ashen hair.

3

'Aha,' Nero said, lying on his sofa like Humpty Dumpty, his stomach reaching up towards the ceiling. I must have been staring at it, for he boasted, 'This stomach cost thousands. You are one of us, aren't you?'

He poured two glasses of port from a glass decanter and handed me one. 'Total performance. A double act. That is what we need from Jesse and you in the Union, and' (Nero was lecturing) 'for God's sake talk to nargs.'

'What exactly are nargs?'

'The voters, of course – narrow little men without perspective. It is always the smaller men who most hate success – especially in England where exuberant success is a terrible embarrassment,' Nero concluded his social analysis. 'Oh, by the way,' he perked up, 'I've discovered that the Party-Jones family is connected to the banking dynasty, the Turds, through a maternal great-aunt.'

'Really?' I had never heard of any of them.

'You see, Rourke, wherever you see influence, it all connects up. One delicious gilded circle.' And at the thought of this new hidden connection, he shivered with pleasure.

We drank port, Nero on his sofa and I in the big throne of a chair beneath the Napoleonic portrait.

'I shall stand against Saint in the election and wreck that lot. Fox is clever. I secretly quite admire him.' He watched me a moment. 'Why are you joining us?'

'I think you are winning,' I said.

Nero was delighted. He laughed in a loud effeminate way, like an over-indulged Roman.

'Marvellous, you appreciate power. That is the key. Just like me!' His laughter had brought Morganthau to the

43

door, bleary without his glasses, and wearing a night robe.

'Who are the Babylons?'

'They are power, great power,' answered Nero respectfully – this was his religion, after all.

'They own Babylon's Bank in London, Paris and New York. The blue bloods.' Elliot expansively used his hands but was soon on to the more interesting stuff. 'His old man leaves his mother at home in London while he snorkels for gwando-gwando with whatever's on offer.' If Nero's god was Influence, then Elliot vicariously worshipped 'gwando-gwando'.

'Why don't we show him how the other half lives, eh, Elliot? You see we like you,' Nero said, when the laughter had subsided, in his supercilious way. 'I want you to come to my drinkies at the Pitt Club on Friday.' The audience was over.

'One last thing, Joe,' Morganthau said before we got to the door. 'This is a world historical house. After all, Burgess and Maclean and E. M. Forster lived here. Traitors, politicians and writers.'

'Everyone has to make a decision in their lives,' Nero explained. 'Do they want to play the Great Game or do they just want life to pass them by? Do they want to live in King's Parade?'

'Yes.'

'Welcome to the era. Move tomorrow. Time is ticking away,' said Elliot.

'I was born in exquisite luxury and, therefore, I live in exquisite luxury.' He was the Indian I had seen at the Hunt the week before. His accent was more English than Henry Higgins's. This was my first visit to the Pitt Club, Nero's holy of holies but the hated and envied home of élitism for Fox, Leftists like Syssons and the rest of Cambridge.

At the Friday evening debate, Babylon and I had been discussing the riots that were wrecking London. And even in the Pitt a few boys in tweeds were gathered around a television screen that showed blazing buildings, police in riot gear and youths with rasta hairstyles throwing Molotov cocktails.

'If they have not got the means to support themselves they should be sent off home,' said the Indian, turning away from the screen. He was wearing a blue blazer, a striped tie and white silk flannels. Babylon bounded straight into the crowd, just as the Indian had slithered towards me like a cobra across a cold tiled floor, courtier's hand outstretched, and introduced himself as the Maharajah of . . .

'Putney?' I said, thinking he was joking.

'No, my dear chap, Punjab. You surely aren't a member here. I am on the Committee. I'm sure you are a charming person, but I do not think we've passed your membership. Babylon enjoys mixing his different levels of acquaintance, but believe me, he's only playing.' I wondered why he had such strong views on the riots.

'Where do y' live?' I asked him.

'Oh, Geneva, Manhattan, LA, Rome, sometimes London.'

'And India?'

'Well we of course keep a town house in Delhi and the fortress, but society under the Gandhis has atrophied so. And do you know Geneva?'

'No.'

'Manhattan?'

'No.'

'Nor Rome?'

I had to admit that I had never been to any of them.

'But you must have a *pied-à-terre* in London, don't you?' He was looking worried now, and his voice was transforming from politeness to pity, not for me, but for himself for having to speak to me. I did not have a *pied-à-terre* in London.

'Were you at School?' This was a bit much.

'Of course I bloody went to school. Everyone in England goes to school. It is the law.' He looked more pleased with himself than ever.

'I think we misunderstood each other,' he smoothed. '"At School" means "at Eton", where I and many of my friends were educated. Where do you live?'

'Esher,' I said.

'Yes, I noticed your regional accent,' he said with suffocating politeness. 'Do you actually live there?'

'He owns the town.' Babylon had returned to save me. 'You've met the Grand Vizier?' He patted Mr Punjab on the back and added, 'This is my rival and partner at the Union, Joseph Rourke.'

'I see,' said Punjab, awed by Babylon who looked like a deranged hobo. His hair was like a haystack. He was enjoying the contrast between the princely silks and Jermyn Street trousers and his own soiled army flak jacket.

'Come on upstairs.' Babylon dragged me up the wide stairway with old Spy cartoons framed on the walls.

'Frightful old bore,' whispered Babylon. 'But there are worse to come. We did well in the Union, don't you think? Have you heard about Sir Ken Trumply? Had to resign. Apparently, he'll be brought back into the Cabinet in the next year. When the Blue Rinses have forgotten about the poor man. Mrs Trumply was as ugly as sin. Now he'll have to live with her for life. Poor Trumply, he deserved a bonk. He won't be in the wilderness for ever.' Before I could ask about Trumply, we arrived in a big room at the top of the stairs.

Nero was rushing about in his element, all red face and stomach – a word here and a word there, always a bottle of champagne in his hand. At a table at the back, waiters in white coats were opening bottles as fast as they were being drunk. The pops came thick and quick, the music of Cambridge, as more trays of bubbling glasses were carried into the thirsty crowds.

'Waiter, a glass for Mr Rourke,' and Nero steered me into the crowd of blazers, cravats, tweeds and corduroys. 'You are to meet everyone. They are all here.' He threw me at an angular girl. Camilla Party-Jones displayed the incompetence of the daughters of England's rulers. Despite a lifetime devoted solely to social training, she was still incapable of conversing with someone from a background different from hers. Camilla Party-Jones shook my hand as Nero introduced us and began a conversation even more turgid than the Grand Vizier's.

'You're a Beagler. Mummy knows all the Rourkes,' she said. 'Especially the ones who ride around us.'

'Where is that?'

'Wiltshire, but then there are so many of you, Mummy says there's a Denbeigh-Rourke at every public school in the country. Where were you?'

'Camilla darling! You old tart. It has been so-o-o-o long. A whole week and you look *lovely*.' I was saved by another girl, also wearing bright corduroy trousers that went down to the shins, red shoes and a thick sweater. It was Joanna Yarborough, her walrus's face still bruised and stitched from the Hunt.

'You old tart,' gasped Camilla with big-bottomed affection. 'Don't worry, darling. You look like a beaut.'

'Did I hear that you are a Denbeigh-Rourke?' asked the ruddy face of Joanna, and both of them leant forward to catch the next stage in this never-ending game of connections.

'I don't think I'm related to any of your friends,' I heard myself say. My voice was a giveaway. They both looked agonized and confused.

'Oh, really, I see,' they said. They began to scan the room over my shoulder. They were social Hoovers, showing the whites of their eyes, as they tried to find someone more appropriate. There was a silence. Then Camilla said, 'The Rourkes we know have the loveliest house.' This was my consolation prize.

'Who do you know at the Pitt?' Joanna obviously thought I was either a comedian or a gatecrasher. Maybe even a townie – shock horror! When they heard I knew Nero and Nelson and, best of all, that fast-growing legend Babylon, they showed a great deal more interest. 'Is he a grockle?' bellowed Joanna in a stage whisper, studying me.

'Shush, he can hear. He is probably one of Jesse's funny muckers. He was at the Hunt though.'

'Jesse will be President of the Union soon. He is a genius, they say,' said Jo Yarborough.

'Mummy says they are the funniest clan, but Jesse, who I know very well, does not really know how to behave. Not safe in taxis at all but' (and she raised a hand to her lips to signify discretion) 'I know you would not know it and they all look so English and they've been here so long, but Daddy

47

says Jews just don't have morals. Sir Edwin was the same, Mummy says, before he was married. And even worse after.'

Babylon ignored the two gorgons who claimed to know him so well, staggered over and pulled me into the thickest part of the crowd. He nodded at Yarborough.

'That girl will marry a millionaire one day,' he said.

'But she's as ugly as a . . .'

'A dog?'

'Yes.'

'Exactly,' he said. 'She's a Golden Retriever.'

'A Golden Retriever?'

'She hunts a rich husband with the alacrity of a well-trained Labrador,' he said, and began to introduce me to people with dangerous sweeps of his arms. The immaculate Dr Tombs from Augustus could not take his eyes off my guide. 'Jesse is like a pirate. Who do you know here?' he whispered at me before I was dragged straight into Jamie Stagmoor, who was chatting up a blonde girl in a leather miniskirt.

'Emma Condor,' she said, shaking my hand; looking at Babylon, she said, 'Aha, the incorrigible Babylon.' She spoke beautifully, as if the words themselves were meaningless and speaking at all was a tiresome and inexplicable custom. If it had to be done, she may as well make the nicest noise possible. And to me she said, 'So you're Jesse's new mascot.'

'She is gorgeous,' I said to Babylon, when we had moved on.

'Because she's rich.'

'My tutor, Dr Kodell, says the rich are better looking because they eat better.'

'Crap,' said Jesse. 'They just marry better. Here's Darling.'

Darling Darlington, dressed from head to foot in black, with black velvet pixie boots on his feet, stood beside Matthew Nelson, with a dashing bandage and his Julius Caesar profile, towering over a pastel shop-window of secretaries busy looking comely to the jealous fury of the university girls.

'Your father's just done it again,' said Babylon. 'He's just won control of another company today, hasn't he?'

'Yes, thanks, he got control this morning.'

'You must be proud.'

'Very.'

Nelson's father was no longer just a businessman. He had become a modern pin-up, a symbol of the new prosperity. He was a panacea for everyone: teenagers camped outside his gates; blonde gold-diggers with bare midriffs, tanned to coffee in expensive health centres, chased him in night-clubs; boffins at business schools wrote papers on his style of management. From the Prime Minister to the man in the street, he was a latter-day pharaoh, a running soap opera that made us all proud to be British.

Nelson's son in Cambridge was a social cult: it was like being close to Midas. Mothers the length of the counties would say when the tycoon came up in conversation, 'Yes, he is ruthless but my David knows Matthew Nelson and he is an absolute sweetie.'

'Darling, I thought Rupert was coming up for this,' said Babylon.

'Rupert who?' I asked.

'What a Philistine.' Darling scowled.

Babylon was delighted: 'Ru Bonham-Cavendish is an Etonian actor who has played an Etonian in one film. He appears in more parties than plays.'

Darling took this personally: 'Ru's got a helluver lot of talent. As a matter of fact, he's the new Olivier. He's a damn good friend. Anyway, he's rehearsing for a new movie and he's having dinner with the producer. He might not come after all.'

The secretaries buzzed with the name 'Rupert Bonham-Cavendish . . .' 'Yeah, he's a close friend,' Darling told them. 'He might be coming along tonight.'

Scrubber was there too, leaning against Matt Nelson, thinking of tycoons. In her drunkenness, she kissed me wetly on the lips. 'Yummy,' she muttered and then confessed to Matt Nelson in a hearty boom, 'So I'll have Prince Angus, whoever the hell he is. I don't care if he's ugly or stupid, the point is . . .' and here she fell into Nelson's arms, 'he's royal.'

49

Finally we had reached the end of the room; by the fire sat a dark dinky imp of a girl with a compact, tidy body wrapped delicately in purple crushed velvet. She wore no make-up. She sat on a stool with the fire burning behind her, like a movie backdrop, with her legs crossed – a little package of confident and intelligent woman. Elliot was standing above her telling stories.

'The MP,' he was saying, 'took the Margrave on his brief-case in the House of Commons office. And the Margrave said that while it hurt, he thoroughly enjoyed playing his part in a public affair.'

Standing in a semicircle around them seemed to be all the grown-ups in the room. Elliot introduced me to them – Nero's uncle and Nero's stockbroker, who was the father of Camilla Party-Jones. Morganthau introduced me as Babylon's new partner in the Union but the stockbroker cleared his throat and said, 'Don't you think it is a damned good thing that greasy little man, Trumply, got his comeuppance. We can't have the greasy pleb back. Frightfully jumped-up and ghastly on the telly. Remember the terrible way they treated Pike Pease! And the disgusting things . . .'

'I met him at the Union just before he resigned. I thought he was impressive and modest. She wants to bring him back soon.' Everyone turned to look very hard at my out of place twang and, as quickly, they turned away again, as if they had all looked at something forbidden.

'What on earth is this chap doing in the Pitt,' muttered Party-Jones. 'Some Thatcherite on the make, probably.'

'These are the heads that'll hang,' I whispered to Elliot, 'when Brixton comes to Chelsea.'

'It's a damned good thing that the Trumply scandal happened. Got rid of the nobody,' continued Party-Jones, as if I had not spoken.

'Thatcher's got far too many of these sorts of financiers and foreigners in the British Government.'

'You're quite right,' interrupted Elliot. 'They're one reason people voted Tory. Thank God Boadicea has got rid of those stupid old snobs.' Mr Party-Jones turned the livid red of a boiled but living lobster.

'She sacked the decent ones.'

'The old paternalists who had done nothing since 1945? Without firing them, none of this could have happened.'

The girl tactfully changed the subject.

'What do you think of the riots?'

'I feel damned sorry for the police,' I said. I could not stop watching the girl. She was imprinted in my brain like a clear photograph. Her low, cruel voice sounded like a scratched 45 record. Just a whiff of clipped New England hung in the air and I longed to hear her speak again.

'The Bourse' (How sophisticated! I thought) 'is jumping up in leaps and bounds, Nelson is building a new London while Brixton goes up in flames. Maybe we're all getting too rich. Maybe we're ripe for revolution,' she said, her voice crackling like the fire.

Elliot took up the riots: 'The police must learn from the brutish French riot police who use batons and tanks.' He was out of control. 'It is time for a military coup,' he ranted. 'I can't wait to awaken at night to the sound of tanks rolling over the cobbles of King's Parade.'

'No,' said the girl. 'The people will bring back the guillotine, set one up in the Market Square and behead the lot of us. The Army would never launch a coup: they obey the Royal Family.'

'Damned right,' said Party-Jones, tapping Nero's bloated uncle on the shoulder. 'You were a Guardsman too, were you not, Binky?'

The girl smiled and continued. The bores were scared of her. I was. 'The Windsors,' she went on, talking straight into my eyes, 'are Social Democrats, so they'd never order a coup. Anyway, I would be one of the first to be done and I would not mind – my head would look pretty chic on the end of a pike.' It would look chic anywhere, I thought.

I longed for Babylon to return, and my prayer was answered: Party-Jones leapt in the air clutching his groin while, to my amusement, through his legs on all fours crawled Scrubber, followed by Babylon, roaring with laughter, his face red and his eyes staring. As he passed between the pinstriped legs, Scrubber thrust her ample rump into his face so that he collapsed and finally collided with the polished (Guardsman) brown brogues of Camilla's father.

Everyone went quiet as a fast-sobering Babylon looked very slowly from the shoes up the Savile Row suit, over the regimental tie and the striped shirt and finally to the rosy thin face itself.

'What the hell do you think this is?' asked the offended party.

'I am at an orgy. I do not know about you,' snapped Babylon, resting his head on the brogue. Nero saved the day with a glass of champagne. Only the girl kept laughing, curling up on her stool, pulling in her legs and laughing in her husky way, making no effort to conceal her delight. She leant over towards me.

'I'm Katherine Seamark. Call me Kick. Everyone does,' she said. Babylon glanced at her, then followed Scrubber into the crowd.

'Rourke,' said I. I could feel her valuing me like an art dealer.

'You're Jesse's new crush. He picks up people from the strangest places. Well, you've got something. I can feel it. Have you met that bitch?' She nodded her boyish head towards the fawning crowd around Condor. She was a Brahmin python. 'She's a whore.'

'Doesn't look like she needs money . . .'

She bared her teeth contemptuously. 'She does it for fun.'

There was a silence and, made daring by the champagne, I threw myself into her game with the feeling that her spite was something far too amusing to miss.

'And what do you do it for?' I said.

'I do it for the game,' she said finally, but I was never quite sure whether she said 'gain' or 'game'. We were, surely, after them both.

4

Fergus Fox had been thinking about Sally Gilpin. She sat opposite him, holding a cigarette in a holder to her lips as if she were Marlene Dietrich. She was not dressed up for the debate that had just finished. This was the way she always dressed. She blew the smoke out across the room so that it drifted in a cloud towards Fox.

He remembered how he had met her and known at once that he would marry her. He had loved her at first sight. Decisive in all things, he made his decision there and then, in the bar of his college on his fourth day in Cambridge when she walked in with her hair so tidy and her dress so neat. He did not understand that when she walked in that day, she was dreaming of burning her modest off-the-peg dress and cutting her provincial hair and striding into sophisticated Cambridge on high scarlet heels. Who else had she betrayed him with, he wondered? Rourke? And he stared suddenly at me so intensely that I read his thoughts exactly. And that brought him to the question in hand. 'Joe,' he said softly. 'Why were you at Nero's party last night?'

'No particular reason.' Saint and Gilpin watched me with sanctimonious expressions.

'I know for a fact that you were there, I know the time, and I know what was discussed,' Saint announced breathlessly.

'It's no secret. Half Cambridge was there.'

'The other half,' said Fox precisely and cruelly, the Scottish accent sharp now. 'Simon Saint was asked over for tea with Nero the day after you. For the same reason.'

Fox rose from his chair and walked over to me. 'You see, remember what I said about them. They don't even care

53

which of you they ask. You and Saint are exchangeable to
them. What do you have in common? You are both on my
slate and you are both as disposable as a paper cup.'

'Well, I'm joining them.'

'Why?' asked Fox, his voice almost breaking.

'They are the spirit of the time. Your politics are a retreat.
Nero's slate is progress.'

'Remember what Pease said: Britain's democracy has de-
veloped over centuries to provide freedom, meritocracy –
and care for the poor. Thatcher is a short diversion.'

'It is our Indian Summer,' I said.

Sally Gilpin was stretching in her sharp career suit, jacket
and skirt to the knees, with a slit up the back.

'I can't see you tonight,' she said to Fox. 'I'm meeting
someone.'

Fox was already watching Sally again. He imagined her
coming out of 10 Downing Street with him, holding hands.
He saw her shaking hands with party workers in Glasgow
West, his constituency, and was proud how she said the right
thing to everyone. She stalked out of the room, with her
hard lips smoothing her lipstick and her heels hitting the
panelled floor in short staccato cracks. Fergus imagined how
such a girl would have disgusted his father, the presbyterian
preacher, who had taught him to be an ambitious saint.

Scrubber's room was hung with Paisley drapes and filled
with colourful cushions, beanbags, pots of herbs, exotic teas,
hunting prints and photographs of handsome film stars from
glossy magazines. A big brass kettle hung in front of the fire
that burned in the grate. Four muffins were browning on a
barbecue fork. And everywhere around the room, her clothes
were thrown down so nonchalantly that they were part of the
decoration, like the curtains: thick multicoloured jerseys, scarlet miniskirts, pedal-pushers, leather bomber jackets, velvet
trousers, ra-ra skirts, suede boots, jeans with Paisley patches
and white tights with black spots. There were photographs
of her family, the labradors featuring as prominently as the
children.

She sat down right beside me on the beanbag and began to

54

feed me muffins, dripping with jam, oozing butter, and she talked incessantly, with big teeth glistening with lemon curd and the chase. Her girl guide's voice told me stories of hunting expeditions, dressage competitions, standing beside guns at shoots, and of boys met, kissed and held at balls, at house parties and in boxes at West End musicals. I could only listen in repulsed silence as her wide and easy mouth described another adventure on horseback or in bed with the jolly aplomb of a girl used to falling off horses into ditches. These stories were not real things to me, they were simply weapons to exclude me. A conflict rose inside me that tossed me between nausea and lust, but the warmth of her strong rounded flanks burned into me and my worthy outrage was converted by some strange social-sexual formula into another energy.

When I could wait no longer for the breadth of her lips and the fit strength of her riding legs, I pulled her mouth towards me and kissed her in a clinch of lemon curd and lapsang souchong. She would not open her mouth for a second and then it opened wide, with her tongue running its way across my teeth, around my lips and then deep in my mouth in a trail of hot saliva and short fresh breaths. She tore her own shirt off with buttons flying off into the fire, and drew my hands on to her chest like mother earth offering the fruit of her fields.

My hands were shaking. The clips of her bra were the combination of a safelock that I could not find. She laughed and handed me a pair of scissors. I cut the bra off her so that its cups just fell open and buried myself in her breasts, which were large and fertile, as if they had been nurtured for a village show. I moved down her to a ra-ra skirt (fashionable then). She lay back with her breasts upstanding, as if proud at last to be free of the constraints of bras, shirts and modesty, ruddy and fine like a peasant girl in a haystack.

'It's like putting my hand up five not one,' I told her, hands poised.

'Seduce me skirt by skirt then. Take your time.' So I lifted them one by one, revealing more and more of her white tights with their red stripes. At the top, I pulled the top of the tights down in one irresistible movement and worked my hands over her knickers and under them and around and back again so that I could feel the heat, emanating like an invisible smoke.

'When women started wearing tights instead of stockings, they thought they were liberating themselves,' I told her. 'In fact, they were imprisoning themselves in an airless nylon straitjacket.'

Sophie laughed aloud, 'I dunno what the hell you're talking about, so shut up and get into my knickers.' She said it as she would say, 'Saddle up the horses.' Crossed her legs. I tried to prise them open. My hands wandered desperately down her buttocks and under her legs.

'Even Fort Knox isn't impregnable,' she said.

'And this is no Fort Knox,' I added. At last with a great peal of laughter, Tower Bridge opened at high water and I dived between her legs, a pirate opening a chest of treasure. I admired her from between her thighs. Her legs were tawny walls rising up on either side of me; her mons and her belly and her hips were solid and round and curved away until her breasts reared up on the horizon, pointing to the ceiling; and beyond them, just visible between them, a big toothy mouth with open lips, a turned-up nose, blue eyes and thick blonde hair that hung on to wide shoulders. I peeled her open with my fingers like an artichoke and inhaled the smell of a soft breathing coral, with a trail seeping out on to my shaking hands.

'That's perfect,' she was saying. 'Al-l-l-l right-t-t-t. You're a star. Gosh! A little higher. Lower . . . There. There. Now. What a winner. Don't stop now. Go on, we're so close. That's just the ticket.' The repulsive world of the Croquet-Bowleses suddenly tasted sweet. She was the hills of England: here beneath and inside them was the earth and the essence of England herself. And in the taste of her pampered ass, and the swank of her breasts, and the fine blue of her eyes, in this one body, I thought, this riding, hunting, drinking body, herein was the class system of Britain contained in one round-arsed-British-gymkhana-hearty-voiced-jolly-hockey-sticks-blonde-haired-built-to-live body.

I licked up her and down to her anus and spread her legs as far as they could go and kissed her lips so she could taste herself. She was made for the English tongue.

And when I was ready, she held me in her hand and she said, 'You're not my first piece of rough. I've had stable lads. In the stables.'

I wanted to explain that I was far from a piece of rough, but imminent orgasm made me declare a temporary armistice in the class war.

'Well, you're my first piece of toff.'

'And do we taste different?'

'Oh yes,' I said. 'You taste of champagne, and caviar and gold bullion all mixed into one cocktail.'

'The stable lads were really rough. They smelt of saddle leather and horse-sweat. Do the poor taste different? Of course. But Rourke is different. You're on the move. You're not rich and you're no longer truly one of the poor. You taste best of all.' She pronounced 'really rough' as 'rarely raaaf'.

She let go of me and I slid into her, watching her mouth move languorously side to side and her breasts swelling, and I came once and twice as deeply as I could and she whipped my buttocks with her fingers until we fell off the sofa and on to the floor in front of the fire.

We were rolling among the knives and the butter and the pots of lemon curd and the cups of tea. The kettle had boiled dry and it was howling, as the water steamed away, like a man on the rack. Scrubber went down my chest and to my loins and she took me in her mouth and drew me out glistening while she watched me, with her eyes raised like a tawdry angel.

The kettle was boiled dry. The china teapot was shattered. We stood befuddled among the debris as if there had been a massacre at a picnic. We staggered to the bed. I dried her with a towel as her thighs were awash, and we arranged our limbs so we lay together like spoons. Then the door flew open.

I jumped to cover myself. Scrubber lay and waited. There was only one person who would break her door down in the middle of the night. Babylon stood in the doorway, a tousled rakehell silhouetted against the naked lightbulb outside with his hands on his hips, his legs apart and a crooked smile on his face. He walked in without hesitating and sat on the bed, smiling. I thought for a moment, is this the boyfriend?

'Welcome to the Pleasure Dome. We backed the right horse. You're truly one of us,' he said to me gaily. Scrubber was not the least alarmed by all this, but I was not so certain.

Could Babylon have known about this? Did he organize it? It was not right that another man should interrupt us at such a moment. At the time, I thought no one could have set up such a thing, but then I didn't know Babylon, who was a sexual magician, capable of doing both. He probably set it up without Scrubber even realizing. That was Jesse Babylon for you – he was a physical Metternich and a bedroom Kissinger, delighted with his work. His exuberance was infectious and soon we felt almost as if Babylon had been there all the time.

'Joseph, join me for lunch tomorrow at my table in Intrigues in the Market Square. I feel I have met you for the first time. Goodnight,' and he moved elegantly through the fragments of china, wading through the heavy smell of sex as if it was his natural habitat. The door closed behind him.

'Politics,' said Scrubber, 'isn't a science. It's all passion.'

The waitress at Intrigues bore the clear imprint in flour of a man's hand on her black-skirted bottom.

'What a brilliant idea,' said Babylon when he spotted it. 'Do please send the cook my compliments,' he told the waitress, who blushed and waved her new hairstyle in the air. Babylon turned back to me. 'This is enough to make my day.' He regarded the whole of life as a theatrical production. After the night before, I had joined the cast.

Nothing fascinated Babylon as much as secret insights into the lives of others, particularly specimens from different worlds. He would interrogate a dustman or a cleaning lady for two hours, but he might never speak to them again, once he had extracted some terrible secret that had never been told before. The victims of his interrogations remained devoted to him for life: no one had ever shown such an interest in the details of their lives before.

Jesse Babylon caught people like a Victorian explorer who found new forms of life, named them, bottled them in preservative spirits and showed them to friends when they came to dinner.

'If y' don't order now, I'm goin',' said the waitress, who had finished rearranging the strange beehive on her head. 'I'm not standin' 'ere all day.'

'I am sorry,' he told her, looking into her eyes. He told her he adored her new hairstyle and she wriggled with pleasure in her absurd Victorian maid's uniform. 'I love being served by you. It makes my day. Will you always serve me?'

'Of course,' she said, and she broke into a grisly smile. Then: 'I bet you say that to everybody.'

We ordered, and she slunk away into the kitchens where the cook with the floury hand lay in wait. Babylon continued loudly, 'She's had an extraordinary life. The most ordinary are always the most bizarre. She has been subjected to terrible and yet delicious atrocities.'

'Really?'

'She slept with her grandfather at the age of ten and loved it. He was a bearded old man, aged seventy-five. Apparently he was brilliant in bed. He couldn't come so he could bonk eternally. She says she has never found a boyfriend as good. She has one big problem, though – when she comes, she can't help yelling, "Grandpa, grandpa".'

'How on earth do you know that?'

'She tells me everything. Everyone tells me everything.'

Everything about the girl paled into insignificance beside her hairstyle, but she was not ugly. It was clear that Babylon regarded every girl as a challenge and a waitress as a matter of pride. He believed that he could have whomever he wished, and his conviction was so strong that no one ever denied it to him.

'So you're joining us,' he said dreamily, as he stared out of the window at the church outside and the undergraduates rushing by in their scarves and tweed jackets. 'Friendship is like a crown. If every jewel in the crown was the same, life would be extremely boring. So the skill is to create a crown with a variety of jewels – perfect diamonds, worthless rhinestones, pebbles and marble, amethyst and pearl, *papier-mâché* and nuggets of gold. I'm going to put you in my crown.'

'And what will I be?'

'I don't know yet.' His quizzical eyes turned cold and he laughed. I felt honoured to be in Babylon's crown and he knew it: he read people with just a glance and he created characters like a novelist. He was an actor-manager, playing with real men and real women. He beckoned to two boys in the street and they hurried in and shook hands with him. He pointed to the chairs at our table and they sat down and joined us.

'Joe, you know Matthew Nelson and Darling Darlington.'

'Yes, we met at the Pitt,' said Darling, tall and dark-haired, a dramatic giant dressed all in black. 'You're the hack from the Union.'

'Don't cross Darling,' warned Jesse in mocking tones, waving his finger. 'No actor wins a part in Cambridge without Darling. He's a friend of Rupert Bonham-Cavendish, the pre-eminent actor of our generation.'

Baiting Darling was one of Jesse's more mentionable hobbies. 'Either way, Darling is the king of the arts,' he continued. 'And Darling, don't cross my newly won friend here either. He is rich in luck. Rourke possesses luck like others possess houses or cars. He's not the best at anything, nor the worst, but he'll be there at the right moment and he'll say the right thing. Men don't notice him; women are quick to smell luck. Overall, Joe Rourke has an optimism that is self-fulfilling.'

'You need no further introduction,' Darling said quietly.

'Where on earth are you from?' Nelson asked.

'Esher.'

'My father has a development there. A new shopping city. Do you know it?'

'Of course,' I laughed. 'It is the biggest development the place has ever known.'

'Is your father in the City?'

'No,' I said. 'He works in the Civil Service in Reading.'

Babylon watched me carefully. Naturally, he knew dad was an income tax assessor. He could see my parents with their morality and their precise idea of where they fitted into England's complex mosaic. My mother, who was involved with the local Conservative committee, had called again and again for Trumply's sacking after the scandal. Men like Trumply and Nelson had come from below her level in society: so who did they think they were, running the country as if they were born to it? Jesse was laughing at their pride and their snobbery, yet he understood their hatred of Thatcherism: it threatened their position as the moral guardians of the country. Their place was up for grabs. May the best man win. Babylon saw it all clearly but he did not give me away.

'Really? How funny,' Nelson said tonelessly. He wished his father would actually sit down with him one day, on their own, like other fathers did with their sons. Matthew never heard about Nelson's career from his father – only from newspapers, which he scanned every day to know where he was and what he was doing.

'He is creating the new world. He's tearing open London, ripping out its insides and replacing them with a new city he's visualized.' Babylon was excited by his own vision of this new Thatcherite world, but Nelson was embarrassed because he was getting credit for the achievements of a man he barely knew.

Darlington, the lover of beautiful things, had to have his say: 'Look, she's a great dame, but her policies on education misunderstand the essence of British civilization. Education has its own intrinsic value above and beyond any practical use it may have. Macbeth is worth more than mortgages.'

'Money itself does not destroy the arts. It encourages them. All these artists moaning about obsession with wealth. What created the greatest flowering of art? Athens, Venice, Florence, Byzantium? I'll tell you – money. You must be a Thatcherite,' he said to me, 'after all, you're a man of the era.'

'Jesse, you're more into debauchery than Thatcherism,' joked the aesthete.

'They are just different forms of freedom for the individual – sexual and economic. They are entirely consistent. Talking of filth, my true religion, what is the filth at the moment?'

'HRH . . .'

'Prince Angus is in Galtieri College,' Babylon informed me.

'. . . is desperate for a woman. Absolutely desperate,' Darlington emphasized. 'His brothers are always in the papers with this or that model and Angus doesn't even know a girl. He's worried the papers will say he's gay next.'

'How do you know?' I asked.

Darling swept back his hair in a slick confident movement. 'I know because he told me at dinner last night. He's a darling and loves the theatre. I'm very protective of Angus. He doesn't care who the girl is.'

Babylon was flushed with mischief. He ruffled his hair into Viking anarchy and laughed aloud. 'We'll fix something. I know the perfect person. So, I believe, does Joe,' and he laughed more. How he loved trouble – if there was none, he created it, and if there was none to create, he imagined it.

'The other filth is that Emma Condor is here for the whole of the year,' Darlington told us. 'The most beautiful girl in Britain.'

'Ahh, the great Condor. The heiress to all that. That goddess – but she has that boyfriend, von Howitzer, the one who owns the Ruhr . . .' Babylon was thinking aloud. His face brightened, the wheels of his mind were turning. With his happy-go-lucky amorality, the solution cogged up inevitably in his eyes like a big win on a slot machine. The wheels had spun. Had I pulled the lever of the one-armed bandit to cash in my prize, the dial would just have read: 'I shall have her.'

'And – only her closest friends know this – she has one great talent . . .' revealed Darling, who knew everyone from the world where power, money and art met in a whorish trinity.

'Bonking?' suggested the sexual slot-machine.

'She paints like an angel. Great art, fine lines, what an eye for colour and perspective. I act as her art dealer on the side. Ru bought one of her paintings for 1,000 dollars.'

'There it is,' said Babylon. 'You'll meet all these people, Joe. Joe may be Prime Minister – or at least President of the Union. One day. After me.'

'Why are you guys so ambitious? What drives you?' Darling watched Jesse. Nelson was confused by the question. He himself was not ambitious, except to be noticed by his father. Now that was an ambition.

'That's the question of the era. If we don't stand out, we're nothing. We must succeed or we'll be forgotten. If we fall by the wayside . . .' Babylon was interrupted by Darling.

'You sound like those repulsive American bankers, the ones who bought Turd Brothers when my uncle was senior partner. They just threw him out. All Wallenstein Flashberg and Co. think about is success, not people or traditions . . .'

'What is Wallenstein whatever . . .?' I asked.

'It's a crazy American bank that has twenty-five names because it has bought so many other banks. They bought Darling's family firm and sacked his uncle. As a result, Darling is one of those sad Englishmen who hate success because they fear competition.' Babylon grinned wickedly. Darlington waved his hand. 'So that's it,' Babylon finished. 'The eighties disdain the ones who fall by the wayside. There's no romance in that any more.'

The afternoon had passed. It was almost dinner time. Nelson and Darlington were listening to Babylon's latest tale. I was eating crumbs from the table of the court of Jesse Babylon, but I was surprised to find it didn't matter to me: what a table it was. And what crumbs.

'I've always said,' Babylon was repeating, as the whole of Intrigues listened to another anecdote, 'that the more ordinary the people, the more extraordinary the Filth.'

5

'Is this the great war?' I said. 'Is it starting already?'

'Oh, yes,' Babylon told us one day in Nero's room in King's Parade. 'The porter in Hytlerhouse told me that Saint's room has been like a printing press for the last month. Fox has been in there every day. They're not producing a Union news-sheet. They're creating a bloody manifesto.'

'Have you seen a copy?' Morganthau was unelectable to the Committee but was the brains of the slate.

'No.'

'Who's this porter?' asked Nero. 'Can we trust him?'

'Of course,' Babylon asserted. 'He's the one blackmailing the Master of Hytlerhouse after catching him kissing the Margrave just behind the Heydrich Chapel.' As ever, he relished the sordid details.

'Can your blackmailer get us a copy?' Morganthau was excited. This was his sort of politics.

'Naturally,' he said. 'They have to be stopped. We can't have them producing anti-Babylonian propaganda in the guise of Union newsletters, though Fox would try anything.' He looked at his watch and rushed a hand through his sun-streaked hair. 'Wars always begin at the wrong moments. I am late for destiny.' Jesse slammed the door and went out into the snow that was falling so softly and so silently.

'What's destiny?' I asked them. Nero laughed.

'In Jesse's case,' Morganthau ruled, 'destiny is always female.'

Emma Condor had never been kept waiting before. It was a new experience for her. Even though it was cold, she did not mind the wait, because she loved new feelings. Emma had

64

nothing to lose. After all, she still had von Howitzer, her stalwart but stodgy German boyfriend, in London. The dynamic and dangerous Babylon had caught her at a drinks party in London and demanded that she meet him on King's Bridge on one evening the following week.

'You will wear furs and you will wait. Don't worry,' he said, 'I would not dream of touching you, Lady Emma Condor.'

'I am glad we have got that straight, sweetai,' she had answered. She was really thinking, 'You will touch me. I hope you will.'

She wore a fur coat down to her ankles, a wolf hat with a Davy Crockett tail and fur boots. She stared downriver at the stone cannon-balls on Duvalier bridge and the fog that seeped out of the Cam over the hidden winter stone and the grey water. She tried to smell the river, but it was so cold that she could smell nothing except coldness. The college was deserted. Once, a porter with a lantern walked along beside the Chapel, coughing in the cold. She followed the silhouette of the Chapel like the towers of a dream fortress cut with a Stanley knife against the bright night sky. With an artist's eye, the lines of the stone, the perspective of the towers and the twinkling of the lights created a picture for her, as she waited: 'Tomorrow, I will come to the bridge, and I will catch the moment.'

Emma beat her gloved hands together, stamped her feet and considered how warm she was in her clothes and how the air burned her bare face. She had loved dressing up that night, with fur everywhere. She felt an old heat as she pulled the thigh-length boots up her legs, and she wondered about Babylon. He had a glamour but did he want her enough? This nonchalance made him irresistible. He made her, Lady Emma Condor (here, she repeated to herself phrases from gossip articles about her body, her possessions, her paramours and her parties), feel open, gaping open and there for the taking, like a streetwalker.

She watched him come, through the gate and slowly around the empty court as the snow began to fall. He too was in furs and the snow was landing on him, leaving white powder on his hat and coat. He was asking himself, I wonder if she'll turn up? I wonder. Hell, she had better be there. Sure enough, there was a figure at the top of the bridge standing very still, legs apart, one just in front of the other. Ha ha! he thought to himself. Olé!

He did not speak until he was face to face with her and then he stopped, leant forward and kissed her hard on the cheek but close to her lips. She moved her lips nearer his, but he turned away. She was nervous. He drew out of his coat a bottle of champagne and two glasses. She smiled and in the silence he heard the wet crease of her thin lips. He handed her a glass and fired the cork into the Cam. They both watched it fly up and down and away. The sound of the pouring liquid was clear in the night. Babylon was pleased with the scene of the drama and was dying to chat, but he understood the value of silence. They raised the glasses, clinked them in the air, laughed and drank again. Each time the same: the pouring, the toast, the smile and not a word spoken.

'We are not in the real world, sweetai,' she said, her voice the only sound.

'I hope you are right,' he said. He was not acting. That was his only real hope. He strove to make real life unreal, and this came naturally to Cambridge. Her breath was very close now, its sweet warmth heating up his freezing face. He drew away, said, 'A game', and threw the empty champagne bottle into the Cam. 'Come on, play Pooh sticks,' he said, and they ran to the other side to await the bottle.

'But where are the sticks to throw?' she wanted to know.

'The glasses.' They both stared into the river, leaning on the cold stone. The bottle bobbed along, with light catching its outline. 'Fire!' she said and they both threw their glasses. For a second there was silence, then a smashing of glass, a dash of light and lastly, nothing but rings fading in the water. She was still staring down into the river when he brought her face round, cradling her chin in the palms of his hands. He kissed her, on the lips and the throat.

A silent passer-by padding on the soft snow thought they were one, an abominable snowman, loose in Cambridge.

*

There were hundreds of people wandering the world convinced that Babylon was their friend; his only real friends were rivals, whom he believed he would ultimately beat. I counted myself as a friend during the last year, just as I had counted myself his enemy during the first two. To him, friendship was a gamble not a partnership. After a debate, Babylon was lying in a tangle of bandoliers and ruffles with his thigh boots on the arm of the sofa under the photographs of Nero that covered the walls of Nero's room.

'Rourke was brilliant. His Middle England accent is the antidote to an overdose of Babylon. He's learning, watching the maestro.'

Like many who believe their own propaganda, Babylon often used the Caesarean third person.

'Do you think we can trust Joe?' asked Nero.

'Trust no one. Ever,' said Elliot.

'With a real struggle coming, do you think he'll blab to the other side?' Nero said. Scrubber listened, sitting cross-legged on the floor beside the sofa. They trusted her because she was one of them from their world, but they had forgotten that lust can betray generations. She told me every word.

Babylon just said, 'He can never go back to Fox but we ought to watch him. They were his friends for two years. He ate with Fox every night. Rourke's bedder and the porter in Augustus, who are both little friends of mine, say he has not seen any of the Foxites since he broke with them. But let's get the Reverend Jenkin to find out. He's very good at looking into people's souls. It's his job.'

'Do you really think he'll be President?' asked Nero.

'No,' chuckled Jesse. 'No, how could he be?'

That week, the Reverend Jenkin asked me to tea in his little house in Grantchester. I walked there, across the fields with their hard frozen earth, ploughed into a rich curdled brown, speckled with white frost. When I glanced back I could see the friendly towers of Cambridge.

'My grotto to Cambridge, my temple,' he squeaked, as he showed me round the cottage and, pointing to open society magazines on the floor and signed photographs of aristocrats on the wall, guided me through his life of idolatry: 'Gerald was rich, beautiful and clever.' He showed me Gerald's message: 'Splendid evening. Yours ever, Cumberland,' it read, and so on through chinless, pea-brained faces, their pig-English eyes dreading the day an outsider like me would soil their traditions.

'Times have changed since the giants of old,' he told me, and like Nero that first time I had visited King's Parade, the cleric paled. We sat down in the temple and got down to Union business.

'There will be much unpleasantness,' he chirped. 'Are you sound in the phalanx of Nero? I only ask since I, of course, take no sides as Steward of the Union. I only wish the good of the Union and I care very much for you. You are almost the most talented speaker of your day.'

'Thank you. I am sound.'

'Have you seen Fox and Saint lately?' I could not see his expression. He seemed to have spectacle lenses instead of eye-balls.

'No.'

'He is not a gentleman. You are on the side of the gentlemen and that is always preferable. I'm not interested in politics. I don't care about Thatcher but I like Nero's slate because I only know gentlemen.'

'Well, I am not one,' I pointed out.

'You are an exception,' he said, playing with a riding crop. 'Do you horseback ride?'

'Do you mean do I "ride"?'

'Yes,' I said, unaware of the importance of the right phrase.

'One rides, yes, but one hunts more often, usually with my more hospitable parishioners: a season's meets in return for the key to the Kingdom of Heaven, you know. Gentlemen are far more likely to enter, anyway. St Peter is one of us – I'm sure he is an Etonian. And we don't want gyppos in Paradise. Americans don't get in either,' he added sharply.

'Why not?'

'All Jews,' and I got up to go. He led me through an open

door into the study. There, his feet up on the desk, reclined Nero, still listening, eyes closed. He did not look up.

'Sound as a bell,' he said.

Fox produced the newsletter which denounced Thatcherism in an article entitled 'The Butchering of the Consensus' and completely ignored Nero, Babylon and me. The idea was to sabotage our slate's profile with the new undergraduates, who had just come up and would vote for anyone they had seen mentioned in print. It was to be distributed tomorrow.

'Not only that,' Babylon told us. He was sparkling from his triumph with Condor on the bridge, which we had all heard about in graphic detail from the director of that extravaganza. 'That magazine attacks the Government on every page in the most small-minded way. It says that She "hasn't given the grand tradition of the old Tory party a just hearing" and that "the campaign against the unions is a clear demonstration of a heartless attitude to basic British freedoms". I suggest an "Israeli" solution. We are the people who must act. No one else will.'

'Let's just throw them in the river,' I said.

'Voilà,' said Nero. 'Elliot, you hire a van and Rourke, you buy balaclavas; Babylon, find out when it is coming out and where it is stored. Speak to all the porters, cops, bedders, cleaning ladies and printers in East Anglia. We must find it.'

'To the mattresses,' shouted Elliot.

Cambridge was an espionage grey – a *Thirty-Nine Steps* grey – and we stepped through its early light, as alive as eels. Morganthau had hired the van, a shapeless white transit. Nero was too fat and dignified to come, but Elliot was in his element. Until his beloved military coup actually happened, this was the kind of exploit to assuage his thirst for quixotic adventure.

At about three o'clock we drove down to the printers' warehouse down Mill Road way. Babylon had of course traced the printer by speaking to his friend, the blackmailing porter in Hytlerhouse College, who recognized the printers who had brought the proofs to Saint's room.

The difference between King's Parade and Mills Road was the difference between the South and the North, and we drove through its boarded-up streets and little chippies and walls covered in old posters telling us about bands no one had ever heard about.

Outside the printers' we left the van and crept around the back, balaclavas on, instincts on, hearts on. I could hear everything. I could hear more than I wanted – my throbbing chest, cats screeching on back streets, distant windows shutting, traffic.

The magazines lay out in the yard, left there at the end of the midnight print run, anonymous in thick plastic, set in neat piles, waiting for collection. Babylon cut open the top box, wielding his Stanley knife like a professional cat burglar. A picture of Fox and Saint in suits and ties, real politicians, stared out at us.

We packed the van and drove it down Silver Street to the road bridge by Galtieri. Like madmen we threw box after box into the water below, with splashes in the dark. By the time we had finished it was almost dawn, and Elliot returned the van to its garage out of town. Babylon and I watched the boxes rocking in the river, waterlogging, swaying deeper and deeper, until like old dreadnoughts they disappeared, leaving only bubbles on the blue-grey film of the surface. How the Cam must chuckle at our little struggles, I thought as we stared down at the bubbles. Then they were gone too.

There was sweat on our faces as we wandered down deserted King's Parade. We were quiet as we felt the freezing wind evaporate the moisture on our cheeks. The snow was thinner and more slushy than earlier in the week. We sat on the wall beside King's.

'I don't feel the least guilty,' I said.

'Guilty? I feel absolutely exultant. I want to do worse things. I feel brilliant. I could plan a murder, shoot a president or seize a kingdom.'

'Do you ever feel guilty?' I asked this impresario of pleasure.

'No. Morals are only to protect the weak.'

'Are you in love with the Condor?'

'God, no! She is even nastier than I am. We understand each other far too well. We are intimate allies. She is on the payroll.' This was how I first encountered Babylon's 'payroll'.

'I love them all,' he lectured me, 'but it is best to keep them in compartments. That way there is peace. I am quite un-jealous. If they want to have a real boyfriend they come and tell me and I give my blessing. They usually come back after going out with some Army bore for a month.'

'Are we ever going to fall in love?' I said doubtfully.

'If you can buy 'em,' he said, 'how can you love 'em?'

The street was waking up. The milkman was delivering and the post van was working its way down King's Parade from Hytlerhouse to Augustus.

'God, I love filth,' Babylon told the early risers who passed us in the street. 'And how is Scrubber? I haven't seen her for days!'

'She does have one extraordinary ambition: to bonk Prince Angus before she leaves.'

'It's a brilliant idea!'

'It'll never happen, never.' Babylon was gamesome in the morning light, almost laughing.

'Of course it will – we'll organize it. Imagine the trouble, imagine – Scrubber will get her prince. Once.' We both laughed. It was definitely daytime now. The Parade was full of fresh-faced grads on bikes in rowing kit, and scruffy bleary scientists off to breakfast before lectures.

'The poor House of Windsor. Do you even believe in platonic friendship?' I asked him.

'After; but not before.'

Fox woke up suddenly. It was eight o'clock and he had a busy day. There were lectures until lunchtime and then he wanted to check that the *Union News* had reached every single pigeonhole in Cambridge and was on its way to Fleet Street and Tory Head Office. He looked forward to the criminal law lecture of Dr Capone, where mooting was taught. He owed much of his debating skill to the mooting.

And there was something else: Sally was mooting today

and she mooted brilliantly, speaking so concisely in a sharp voice, so efficient, so correct.

Ahh, he lay back in the bed, and congratulated himself. How cleverly he had written and printed the *News* before the beginning of term. While Babylon, with his rich friends, had probably been partying, he was working. The others were just amateurs. The professional would always win.

6

'What of it?' asked Babylon languidly. 'There are many reasons we might have hired a van.'

'So why did you hire it?' Sally Gilpin's scarlet lips parted to reveal tiny sharp teeth, bared for the kill. Fox smiled. This was real teamwork. My female matador, he thought with rare indulgence.

'The evidence seems to point to a clear conclusion. You destroyed the Union magazine, which has cost the Society over £500,' Fergus summed up, with soft-spoken kindness. 'The resignations will tidy things up nicely,' he added reasonably.

Sally smiled at him as she had not smiled for a long time. Now we are working together at last, he dreamed. This is just how it should be.

'If you must know why I hired the van,' Babylon began, 'I recall that night with great tenderness.' I wondered what story we were to hear. 'Sally, on that night, my girlfriend told me that she had no greater desire than to make love in the back of a transit van, with a mattress in the back, parked in the Master of Caddafi's car-park. I simply did not have the heart to refuse her.'

Sally Gilpin's hard lips parted again, but not for the kill this time. She blushed under her foundation and crossed her legs.

'There is no answer to that,' beamed Nero.

'And the cost is still outstanding,' added the President.

'Who organized the printing of this magazine?' asked Jesse.

'Me,' said Fox, suddenly off-balance.

'Who authorized that printing?'

'Me,' said Fox again.

'On whose behalf?'

'As President. On behalf of the Union.' Fox's eyes went from Gilpin to Saint and back, but Babylon gave him no time to escape.

'Since you did it before the beginning of term, the Committee had not authorized it. In other words, Mr President, it was a private venture. It is no business of the Union Committee. Reverend, do you dispute anything?'

Jenkin could not dispute anything, but this was not the way politics should be played.

Fox's lips pursed. Where would he find the money? Not from his father. Could he borrow it from Saint? He suddenly hated Babylon more than he had ever hated anyone, for Babylon had humiliated him in the only way he could be humiliated. Fox found he could barely speak. Nero said nothing. He was content that victory had been stolen from the jaws of defeat. Fox and I were the only ones in the room who could not have afforded to pay, so I felt for him.

I leant over to Jesse: 'We have won the point. Why not let the Union pay the bill? He has no money.'

'Is that my fault? He chose to play the game and I chose to win it.'

'The meeting is over,' said Jenkin. Sally Gilpin crisply gathered her papers together into a sleek black briefcase, but she did not take her eyes off Jesse. Why is it, I wondered to myself, that girls always yearn to repeat the mistakes of all the others?

Fergus Fox had never been to the house in King's Parade, but apparently he wanted to talk to me. At first, I was suspicious and watched his eyes and analysed his words for hidden political codes, but none came.

'It's politics, Joseph, and I lost that round. Your friend was brilliant. If I had the cash, that would be that, but I don't.'

'You can borrow it, Fergus.'

'Jesse could pay it out of the interest on the interest of his weekly income. Why did he push it?'

74

'His games are always real. Babylon has no hobbies, he doesn't play tennis or chess or row. He plays with people.'

'I think Sally admires him.'

'Maybe.' That was the real reason he had come – pure jealousy.

'That's what she really wants; she has such nobility and talent and yet that's all she wants. It's what she's seen on the television and read about in the papers, big houses, and jacuzzis and fancy cars. So far, I have none of that.' This was a different Fergus Fox from the precise President.

'There are plenty of other women in the world,' I told him.

'Are there? I wish I was down in the City now, working already, earning, so I could be ready for her. So I could be comfortable when she needed me.'

'At least, you've made it up here. You're President. What about Saint? He'll run for President, won't he?'

'I wonder if he's up to it,' said Fergus. 'Maybe, I'll have to run again.' He laughed in a broad Scottish roar that I never thought he had possessed. As if he had expelled his demons, the old shrewd Fox returned, with his threatening charm. 'There's so much to do. This is just the start. I've never been handed things. I've always won them. It just takes hard work – and such patience.'

He possessed no doubts because he had to go forward. He could not return to his father and the church. No matter how much he failed, in the end he would succeed.

It was two minutes to eleven and the nominations book closed on the hour. Jenkin and the Union staff were checking their watches. Nero was running for President, but if he wanted to run he needed to hurry. Fox, Saint and Gilpin stood together enjoying the drama, with their collars up, smoking cigarettes they never actually brought to their lips. They just let them burn, filling the room with a sinister mist.

On our side, Babylon was with Condor. Babylon just lolled in the corner, with his legs stretched out across the floor in scarlet velvet boots. Under the careless thatch of hair and the

75

weight of his sleep-heavy eyelids, he observed everyone like a hawk. Condor walked up and down the corridor, with the prowess of a she-leopard behind bars. Elliot was tense. We had organized to put our names down only when Nero arrived, but time was running out. One minute to eleven and not one of our candidates was in the book.

'It is going to be a fun election,' said Fox in the silence.

'One minute.' Jenkin was brisk.

Then Nero lumbered in, as breathless as ever, grasping an open hip-flask and stinking of gin. He rushed at the book, scribbled down his name where it said 'President', and all of us piled in after him, our hands shaking and the ink going all over the book: 'For Vice President and Standing Committee: Babylon, J., Cadaffi College. And for Treasurer: Rourke, J., Augustus College.'

Saint was running against Nero for President and Babylon was standing against Sally, who stared at Condor, keen to find her secret and copy it.

The election was starting. The phoney war was over. Already the Foxites were filing out, Fox, soon to be ex-President, standing straight and paternal, the elder statesman between the bob-haired girl in her career suit and the choir-boy in his blazer. Sally looked back once, searching for Jesse's scarlet boots.

Reverend Jenkin slammed the old book shut, throwing the smoke that hung in the air into waves and whirlpools near the ceiling. The clock struck eleven.

On election day, Morganthau rushed around with lists and schemes, claiming that he had played a major part in the election of President Reagan in 1980. In 1979, he told us, he had won the Cambridge election for Mrs Thatcher by driving around in a van with a loudspeaker, telling the Indians that Thatcher would have an entirely Asian Cabinet, the Irish that she would at once make all racing days into national holidays, and the white area of town that the Tory leader would expel every immigrant in the British Isles.

In our case, he claimed to have won the 'vital' Moonies

vote, which came to three votes in Somoza College and the 'key' gay vote (four fops from Führer Court, Hytlerhouse).

Somehow, Elliot delivered: Nero won the Presidency, despite the rumour that he was a homosexual; Babylon and I both won our positions, though Saint and Gilpin came top of the Committee, which meant they could veto most of our decisions. Still, Morganthau was full of his tales of electoral corruption.

'It wasn't just the Moonie vote. I brought in the gay-lib activists in Hytlerhouse. And I heard an odd story – that Fox burned all our Committee votes even though his people were top of it anyway. So maybe that was his idea of revenge for the magazine and the £500.'

7

Dr Kodell, my history supervisor, beckoned to me the next day as I walked into Octavian Court. He moved extremely slowly, without any movement in his legs at all, as if he was on wheels. Kodell was about to say something when an obese woman wearing a flowery cocktail dress and a bright blue rinse strode up to us and said in a hearty voice, 'Do you fancy a walk to Grantchester, Dr Kodell?'

Kodell ignored the woman and headed back to his rooms.

'What a rude man,' she called after him.

Kodell waited in his doorway. 'That's Lady Belgrano, the Master's wife.' He was so lazy he spoke without moving his mouth, like a ventriloquist. His face was shiny like a *papier-mâché* mask. The only luxury in his appearance was an unexpected and exotic quiff of hair.

'I've never seen her around.'

'Professor Belgrano is the fifth Master of an Oxbridge college she has been married to. And now she's living with Lord Coventry up in Oxford and he'll be the sixth, when poor old Ronnie Belgrano has gone to the science labs in the sky.'

'What happens to her husbands? Does she divorce them?'

'They die – of exhaustion. She is known as the Oxbridge Ferry; she goes from peer to peer.' He peered round the doorway and then turned back to me: 'My colleague, Dr Tombs, is having one of his dinners where he gathers an interesting assortment of characters. The celebrated Professor Cromwell. Max Bright, the PM's public relations man. Old Pericles Gore, the greatest man who never was Prime Minister. The one to watch is Bright. I will see you there.'

At the age of sixteen, the celebrated Professor Cromwell had written his *chef d'oeuvre* in Hebrew, Latin and Aramaic. For most undergraduates, he was more famous for being the last man to have slept with Rupert Brooke. This guru of faded beauty and radiant reactionary genius spotted me the moment I entered Dr Tombs's rooms.

'Frederick, where do you find such beautiful young men?' The Professor bent over and kissed our hands, first mine, then Babylon's.

Kodell introduced us to the dramatic Dr Tombs, whose baldness and fine romantic mouth granted him an ageless mystery. 'Joseph Rourke and Jesse Babylon, the troubadours of the Union, I call them Lucifer and the Pirate,' said Tombs to the Professor.

'Oh, how charming,' said the Professor, tiny, white-haired and moist-eyed. 'I am the Professor,' the old man said in the reedy voice of the old. The top of my hand still shone with the saliva of what I took to be old-world civility. Or senility.

The portraits of skull-capped medieval scholars scowled out from funereal frames at a world that had long ceased to appreciate them. Dinner-jacketed figures stood in the gloom, talking hushed conspiracies. I strained my eyes to see through flickering candlelight a mad red eye here, a white bow tie there, a mouthful of laughing teeth shining with champagne, the silver flash of a cane's handle only to be lost again as the candle's flame illuminated another picture to be imprinted on my mind: a ring on an anonymous hand, a cufflink of blinking diamonds, a line of shirt-studs lighting up a wax-work chest.

The conversation was a blur of exaggerated Oxford English, throwing my eavesdropping ears titbits of politics: 'Ireland is our last colony, the Empire . . .'; donnish venom: 'Oh, what a ghastly bourgeois Sodomite he is . . .'; or art: '. . . if I may say so, you know nothing about him, I studied him for my doctorate . . .' The gravity of it all was tempered by the pure high voice of our host.

When the Professor first spoke to us the room went suddenly quiet, and I could not help noticing that the others were leaning towards us so as not to miss an oracular syllable.

The kissing of hands inspired an audible frisson of wonder, and tearful eyes observed the scene as if it was a revelation.

At last Tombs was back, with elaborately cut glasses of champagne, and after swigging half of it down with relief, we were steered around the room.

In a ritual of whispered greetings, of the rubbing of dinner jackets and the tinkle of glass against glass in the dancing light, I eventually met Mr Clarence, the *Daily Claret*'s editor from London; Pericles Gore, the staring politician with many more years in the wilderness, judging by his sanity; and Max Bright.

Bright stood in the middle of the room, in a loose dinner jacket that made him look like Paddington Bear with a bouffant haircut, and talked like a socialite machine-gun.

'Yea, She knew what to do and She reached the A_1/P_1s anyway because She was a Conservative, but y'know, I helped her reach the Thatcherites, the first-time property-owners, the self-employed, admen and white collar . . .'

'He's rather vulgar, isn't he?' said Tombs in his high voice so that everyone could hear. 'But really, he's very sweet.'

Nero emerged out of the shadows, plumper and pinker than ever: 'The atmosphere, it's all Titus Oates, Philby, Guy Fawkes – what century are we in?' And he was right, it had no century.

A giant introduced himself, leant down, and asked in a low voice, discreet and yet public, 'What do you think of the Professor?'

Again everyone listened and went quiet, except for Bright. Babylon's teeth smiled through the crowd as he desperately fought back laughter.

'He is clearly a genius.'

'Yes, we think so,' answered my inquisitor, without a hint of humanity. Babylon was biting his fist. The spell shattered when the door was thrown open, bringing electric light and with it reality, and a man in a waiter's jacket said, 'Are we ready, Dr Tombs?'

'Thank you, Montmorency, please carry on.'

'Gentlemen,' announced Montmorency (whose name,

when he was not serving at one of Tombs's dinners, was Stavros) clearly and proudly. 'Dinner is served.'

As the candles burned down and the forest of college silver watched over us, we consumed a meal of shameless enormity, divided into ten courses of postured exoticism. Asparagus, ham, trout sorbet, roast goat, venison Rothschild, boeuf Bokassa and glaces Hapsburg were carried by waiters with silver bowls of hot sweet water for our brows and fingers.

I sat opposite the Professor, who mumbled to me about the beauties of Verona, then sang me a ditty about how the Jacobites still ruled England.

Pericles Gore, the old statesman in the wilderness, turned his deathly eyes towards me at last. Loathed by so many for his views on the Empire and immigration, the passionate politician was now, after forty years in the House of Commons, without a seat and alone again with the Dante he had loved as a boy. Once hated as the very protagonist of evil, he was now a mere relic.

'Do you miss the demonstrations against you?' I asked him, knowing that he did.

'They are over now,' he answered, staring over the candles. 'No one bothers any more with the dead. You are talking to a ghost.'

'I met Kenneth Trumply once,' I told him. 'He fell and then he came back.'

'Like me, he enjoyed his circle.'

'Is that politics?' I asked.

'Politics is to provide a public service: Macmillan was a showman, but that fulfilled a public need. You are asking about the individual, though, not the generality.'

'I am asking about you.' I listened to the distinctive voice, with its rolling r's and its nineteenth-century eloquence.

'For the individual,' he said, 'life is a matter of circles. My life has been a circle.' And then he turned away, lest I saw the tears in the light grey of those torchlit eyes.

Outside the snow was thick again as we walked glass in hand between courses, and we went quickly back inside to avoid the cold. Max Bright, his hair made still fluffier by bits of snow, was twiddling with his pink ready-made bow-tie, which had come adrift, and was still talking.

'. . . And that's what we did at the general election. She softened the voice so it didn't scare unemployed men, unmarried men, men with mortgages, eunuchs or inadequate C2s, and Ken Trumply told me that was what won the election . . . Come up to see me in London,' added the swaggering cockatoo, before plunging into another story.

We had changed seats and I was seated with great honour at the right hand of Tombs. Babylon was on his left. There was sweat on Tombs's bald head, and he talked at length about his hatred of ugly people: 'The Aboriginals of Australia have thick lips and flat noses and are the ugliest people on the face of the earth,' he told us in his high voice. He then suddenly jumped up, banged his spoon on the table and declaimed 'The Queen', which we all repeated with glasses raised.

He continued, 'It is time for the conversazione, and I think Clarence will begin the discussion on Shame and the End of English Culture in 1917.'

'Ah' – it was the Professor – 'the arrival in Europe of Brother Eric.' I think he meant Uncle Sam, but no one corrected him. Clarence started after a long and very self-conscious draught of his port. He was the national editor from London.

'I felt shame once. I shot duck out of season.' Babylon, who was by now plainly drunk, burst into giggles in his cuffs. Meanwhile Clarence was holding forth.

'To return to Frederick's point, I believe that the advent of American troops in Europe destroyed the civilization of Europe, the art of Italy, the poetry of German romance, the *joie de vivre* of the Parisians . . . They brought television, a form I despise. Watching television is something one simply doesn't do – like going to a brothel.' Tombs tried to interrupt, but to no avail, so he petulantly banged a silver candelabrum until the editor from London shut up.

'Professor,' he piped, 'do you agree with the Virgilian we have just heard, or is it more Hobbesian?'

The old man peered down the table and said, 'Bananas.'

This threw the table of worshippers into ecstasy. Tombs announced that a more brilliant reference to the influence of America had not been heard in the chronicles of mankind, while Nero thought it was a reference to banana republics in South America. Tombs again took up the buck, asking, 'Is a banana a valid Schopenhauerian symbol?'

'May I have a tangerine then?' said the old man pathetically. He was simply hungry, but this passed unnoticed as Nero vomited profusely into the dessert.

There was a silence, then Tombs exclaimed, 'How aristocratic!'

'If that is a mark of nobility then I am a prince,' said Babylon.

'How aristocratic,' Tombs repeated. 'Over the dessert too.' Thank God the time had come for another walkabout, or so I thought, until Tombs banged the silver and said in the silence, 'Joseph, would an Augustinian Christian agree with the Professor's thought?'

It took about a minute for the fact to penetrate my claret-drowned brain that Joseph was indeed me. I had not an idea in the world as to how an Augustinian Christian was different from any other. Should I get up and leave? Or should I throw up and be an aristocrat? The whole table watched. The old politician's passionate eyes threatened oceans of gore if I could not answer.

The answer struck me.

'Yes.' I said.

Outside the snow had fallen thick and fast, but it seemed to be warmer, or perhaps it was the drink. We spilled out into the night on the snow-covered grass, standing with our black shoes buried and invisible. Babylon threw himself on to his knees in his tails and white tie, rolled a snowball, leapt up and threw it with all his might at the giant shoulder of the character who had asked my opinion of the Professor.

The snowball flew slowly through the air and shattered on his neck, whitening his jacket and head. He spun round, scooped up some snow, and chased Babylon like a polar bear through the Gate of Prosperity.

Suddenly an arctic barrage of snowballs was flying darkly against the anaemic sky. Like a routine out of the *Black and White Minstrel Show*, black-suited and white-tied figures with red, tipsy faces and lost eyes fought a pitched snow battle through the three courts, ambushing from the arches in Octavian Court, legging up drainpipes in Caligula Court and slipping into the snow face first in Tiberius, only to leap up again untired and charge on.

There was sweat and ice on our cheeks and hair as the snowballs hit us, though we were far too drunk and happy to feel them. The Professor and Tombs watched in fascination from a doorway. The old academic was saying, 'Oh, these fresh-faced satyrs playing wild games.'

Nero and I led an attack on the surviving enemy, whose dinner jackets had become snowsuits. We cleared them out past the Porters' Lodge. They did not come back, and Tombs too had disappeared, so we were left to reflect on the empty court as the snow fell and the lanterns swung. We lay in the snow in our dinner jackets. It was 3.30 in the morning but I felt quite awake. All I could hear was my heart beating in the snow.

'Well, what did you think of it all?' asked Nero, lying there like a black snowball.

'Posh.'

'Class is now an open club – and that is the best sort of club. *Nouveau riche* is the best *riche* of all. Money can't get you everything, but I tell you, Rourke, money can get you almost anything. Almost everything. You have no money, so you've got to begin somewhere. These Thatcherite heroes are miles away. They are today's Gods. Bright is the God of image, and Nelson is the god of money and lord of property, and She, She is the God of Power and Britannia. But where was Nelson five years ago? No one had ever heard of him. He came from nowhere to everything in a couple of years. That is the eighties. This is the definition of a British revolution: when a new class of people send their children to public schools. They don't need guns or guillotines, they just need the right vowels. Then they don't need to storm the Bastille, because they can talk their way in. You might become

President of the Union, but that's nothing without money. Money is like wine – you can probably survive without it, but you can't live.'

We got up and looked at each other, red faces and red eyes shining in the brightness of the snow.

'God bless money,' I said aloud.

'Money bless God,' said Nero.

8

'I believe in heroes. Even now, I worship Alexander the Great or Napoleon. Nowadays, most schoolboys have barely heard of them.' Jesse was holding forth loudly in Intrigues. The hairstyle on two legs who was the waitress brought Jesse another free cream-cake.

'I'm risking my job,' she said, winking.

'How very silly of you. I'm full up anyway,' grunted Babylon. 'Is that another new hairstyle? You look like a piña colada.'

'What's that?' she said, leaning over him so that her fragile hairstyle rocked dangerously.

'It's a cocktail.'

'Maybe that's what I am,' the piña colada flirted, and returned to the kitchens. Babylon was pleased for a moment and then carried on . . .

'That's because today's schoolboys dream of tycoons. They are the modern marshals. They don't need gunpowder and cavalry. They conquer empires by telephone. The children just have to read the papers to hear all about it. It's all the papers write about.'

'A few articles on millionaire life-styles can't overshadow the heroics of old . . .' interrupted Elliot, who regarded himself as a bit of a Cicero.

Babylon's voice rose, as if he was at the Union: 'Everyone can see the works of the new heroes. They are the malls and houses and developments and building sites rising up in every city across England. We can all hear the roaring of the drills and the lorries in our beds at night. The people of Britain can hear the heavy footsteps of the modern marshals as they sleep. What a time to be alive!'

Babylon fell exhausted into his chair, thinking of these pinstriped phalanxes. He waited a moment, watching me, while he thought about Nero's speech to me. Nero had naturally reported it to him. 'And what are you going to do?'

Babylon, the great inquisitor, shifted his eyes towards me without moving at all. He was smiling like an executioner, for that was the essential question for all of us. How easy it was to talk of Thatcherism, but where would we find our success? What if we didn't? God forbid. I stared out of the window. The skinheads who lived in the town were sitting on a bench by the church, eating hamburgers. Their girl was watching us through the window.

'I know what you should do.' Babylon suddenly sat up. 'Go and see Max Bright. He'll see you after Tombs's dinner and I'm sure he'd give you a holiday job over Christmas. Public relations – that's the future. This is the age of the package. The PR man is the priest of today. Bright is Her High Priest. He doesn't run the country but he tells us how it's run.'

Babylon was glowing with the pleasure of the fixer, for if I failed in London with Bright, Babylon at least had played his role. And if I succeeded, he would have one more finger in the pie. He would have his man in Max Bright's office. If I really succeeded – aha, there was the problem.

He reached for the bowl of whipped cream on the table, and glazing it with his finger, he flicked a cloud of cream into his smiling mouth. His friendship was like a razor – you could lick the surface, but never the blade.

Charm was Max Bright's world. His bouffant hair bounced as he spoke and he never stopped.

The office on the top floor of High-Ginentonic and Bright's greenhouse-style headquarters in Beaconsfield Square, London W1, was a garishly bright pink. Bright sat at a glass desk, with an oversized screen playing rock music videos soundlessly beside him. The phone rang continually. He answered each call without the slightest interruption of his flow.

He was just saying to me, 'Yea, you understand, like I do, that PR, reaching people in their homes, from dukes to

87

dailies, one-parent families, workers, bankers, that's it, that's my creed, and when the PM, when She asks me who should be in the Cabinet . . .' when the phone rang. Without hesitating, a hand heavy with a generous rhinestone picked up a pink phone in a fluid motion.

'Ah, Ken. Great to hear you . . .' Here he put his hand over the receiver and said to me 'Sir Kenneth Trumply', then he removed his hand and on he went: 'And when Our Dear Lady asks who should be the next Secretary of State for Foreign Affairs, I tell her, I say, how about Ken, he's done his time in the desert, he's better now than he ever was. We need a presenter, and the housewife in Birmingham loves Ken's voice and his hairstyle, all right, Ken, so we're getting there. She's missing you, Ken, and so am I . . .'

Bright put the phone down and continued to me, 'Ken is most popular with Bs and Cs; primitive housewives still see Ken as a gent while young males admire his flawed past. Who wants the perfect man in the Government? No, men in all sorts of jobs living in all sorts of areas want a bit of colour . . .'

The phone was ringing again. The rhinestone swept down for the blue phone . . .

Bright's husky voice was just one of his arsenal of seductions. The other weapons varied, from the bouncing adolescent hair (he was about forty, even then), the jolly check suit, with baggy turn-ups, a winning smile, a permanent tan, the neutral accent, and a cockney wink. This latter was by no means the genuine article.

Bright flourished as the man who came from nowhere. The press was convinced that he was born in a Melbourne slum, mothered by a runaway beauty queen and fathered by an itinerant labourer. In the sixties, he would have claimed to be an East Ender and called himself Winking Willy, but by the time he arrived on the scene it was old hat being a cockney. So he chose Australia. In fact he was the son of a town councillor from Brighton.

Suddenly the flow stopped, and he leant back in the deep black leather-bound chair with its metallic arms. 'You must know a lot of business people through Cambridge,' he said slowly.

'Not really,' I confessed. He said nothing. The silence was as refreshing as a cool breeze in a heatwave. 'Oh, except Sir John Nelson. I know him through Matt. His son is one of my best friends,' I exaggerated.

'That's what I hoped you'd say,' gushed Bright in an irresistible burst of huskiness. 'Come and work this holidays then. We'll see how we fit.' The green phone was ringing.

'The businessman needs public relations as much as a politician, Joseph.' On the first day, Bright called me into his giddy-coloured office, where he lay in a white suit on a pink sofa. He did not move, though he was already talking into a magnolia plastic phone and I could hear his voice from the moment I arrived in his secretary's office. At last, he turned the phone off and continued talking to me without drawing breath.

'There's only one client I lack in this country. I have the Government, the Ministry of Finance, the Conservatives, the Labour Party and every businessman you care to mention except one. The biggest of all.'

'Who's that?'

'Think,' he said. 'One giant. One man who more than any other has come to be part of every man and woman's vision of the eighties. A financier whose development of London will be as definitive as Napoleon the Third's creation of Paris. Apart from Margaret, I mean the Prime Minister, he's the one they will remember. Not his name, but his buildings. Her ideas and his bricks. That's the way I'd campaign, her ideas and his stones.'

He lay there staring up at the scarlet ceiling. 'And then, there's you. Why are you here? It's no coincidence.'

'Nelson. Sir John Nelson.'

'That is it, kiddo. Nelson, the last big fish. The biggest fish in the ocean deep.'

'So what can I do for you, Mr Bright?'

'Call me Max and get me an appointment tomorrow. The

89

two of us. Him and the new revolution. New England and Nelson. They're the same account. One account.'

'Of course, I have to have him,' thought Sir John Nelson. 'He is the PM's man. So I'll hire him. He came to me. I did not have to go to him. To chase him. And here he is chasing me, brought to me by a friend of my son's. But do I have to listen to all this?'

Sir John Nelson sat crooked on the sofa. He had been equally uncomfortable in the vast-backed damask embroidered chair that was placed behind his desk. It had been the chair of some Pope, and Nelson sat hunched up in it as if he knew it had been made for someone else. So he moved us to the sofa in the corner with an awkward gesture from a nervous hand, but he was no more comfortable there. Meanwhile, of course, Max's sales pitch was whirling round us like a gravel-throated hurricane.

'Yeah, Sir John, your buildings aren't just bricks and mortar, they're a new way of life not just for yuppies in the docklands but for thruppies, suppies, guppies, A, B2s, even C10s, B52s, F15s. Your houses aren't merely residences, though God, they're that too, and I'd be happy to live in one, they're a new London, a new Birmingham, you're actually creating communities around your malls and your centres. It's art – and I wanna show the people that. She thinks so too. She thinks your constructions are her words in stone. And, that's a story, what a campaign, what a story to tell . . .'

Nelson knew that his projects were profitable, but if this fancy-haired smoothie was able to convince everyone that they were a sort of art, even a manifesto, so much the better. Nelson stopped listening. He was a man of economy, anxious about time-wasting and repelled by weakness. Resting, or even hesitating, was a weakness, and he had to go on without rest or friends or indulgences. Houses and racehorses and sponsorships were different. They were not personal. They were simply another form of promotion. At last he interrupted Bright and he turned to me.

'It is good you're a friend of Matthew,' he said, carefully

uttering the name of his son as if he rarely said it. He thought back to his own life. I was not likeable as a boy, thought Nelson. I was friendless as a young man. I was anxious for a friend but despised friendship. What trust, what nakedness it requires, he thought. How do others find it so easy to parade naked before their friends? How good that Matthew should have such friends. Nelson felt ambiguous about his son – the boy was so easy-going and sociable, so unlike his father, who was both jealous and contemptuous at the same time. The boy was a fool, a weak fool like his mother, but Sir John Nelson was confident that he at least was strong and clever enough for all his family. So why not be happy that Matthew had friends? And he smiled at me tortuously.

'Mr Bright, let us get on and sign the contracts. Thank you for the presentation (if that is the right word for that gibberish, he thought). What are the rates?'

'Oh, I leave that to my accounts man,' said Max languidly, with a bounce of his hair.

'I do not. I deal with the top man, myself. That is why I am here now. There is no shortage of PR men these days, Mr Bright.' This was delivered in a single bored tone as if ticking off a schoolboy.

'It'll be 600 grand for this year, plus the cost of . . .'

'Joking aside, I will not pay a penny more than £100,000, all-in.'

'Sir John, 500 grand.' Bright was miserably out of his depth.

Nelson pressed a button on the telephone beside the sofa.

'Veronica, please get me the head of Saddam Brothers.' Saddam was the ultimate advertising rival to Bright. Everyone used one or the other. 'I've heard they're cheaper,' Nelson commented simply. He was not sitting crooked any more. The figures had enervated him so that his dry thin head looked precise and tight like it did in his pictures. He was a grand eagle of a man now, and when Bright's blonde locks bounced as he said, 'OK, one hundred,' Sir John nodded, cancelled the order to his secretary, and then for some reason returned to me. I sat forward in my chair, fresh in my new suit, staring wide-eyed at this modern master. 'When this boy is with you, let him sit in on the meetings.'

'We don't usually involve interns.'

'Well, involve this one on my account,' said Nelson, while I thanked him profusely. He looked very pleased for the first time because he was helping a friend of his son Matthew and therefore helping his son. Nelson did not really understand that friendship required a personal relationship. He regarded 'friend of Matthew' as a title rather like 'accountant of Nelson plc' or 'Commissioner of Parks'.

Max was grinning across his whole face, with his hair bouncing and the checks on his suit winking and the gold buckles on his Italian shoes shining. The fees don't matter, he was thinking, because we'll get it all back on expenses.

'Many thanks, Sir John. Or Johnny? Or John? Or is it Jack? Now we're partners, what would you like to be called?'

'Sir John.'

The meeting that was to change history was already four hours long. The delicious sandalwood and seashore smell of Scrubber's loins had started on the tip of my tongue as soon as the meeting began. It travelled with a gradual warmth up into the perverse knocking shops and massage parlours of my brain and then down my body into my boxer shorts. There the smell exploded into a masterpiece that destroyed the line of my suit and my concentration on the meeting.

I was trapped by my own imagination, since I could not even rise and leave the room without bending double to hide something that had clearly not been provoked by the administration figures for Nelson plc's headquarters in Park Lane. So there I sat with one hand nonchalantly gripping Scrubber's delight under the table and the other pretending to take notes on a pad of paper. The smell of pine and the sound of moist caresses was soon all I could hear and all I could think of. It was on my hands, and my pad of notes. It exuded from Max Bright's briefcase and the accountant's calculator like a fleshy pink mist. Even the Perrier bottle in the middle of the table and Nelson's model of his new skyline for London, which was placed proudly in front of him, even the interim results of Nelson Construction read aloud in Long Island Lockjaw American by a tanned investment banker with an Italian suit and round tortoiseshell glasses, all smelt of Scrubber's cunt.

'Universal Imperial. I want to make a bid by June,' said Nelson in the middle of the banker's sentence. Everyone went silent. Max's hair stood on end. The sheer enormity of his statement removed the bulge in my trousers and any vestiges of Scrubber's anatomy. Nothing smelled better than the smell of money.

Nelson had said very little. He had welcomed everyone to the meeting, and then the banker from Wallenstein, the bank with more names than Edward the Seventh, had spoken for an hour, followed by the pale accountant from Bludlez, Slumba and Ded, who kept fiddling with his single lock of brown hair in order to cover as much yellowy pate as possible.

The management consultant was from the firm that offered its clients such discretion that it had no name. Its writing paper was headed: '. . .and Co.' and it was like a highly paid masonic cell, with offices in every capital of the world which were so secret that each was unaware of the existence of the others. The management consultant's rendition of administrative cutbacks for head office had driven me from vague daydreams to my odyssey through a throbbing bonanza of rampant Rabelaisian perversion.

The lawyer from the great partnership of Invoice and Invoice was an effete, wet-palmed and girlish-voiced rocket scientist (a brilliant technical creator of incomprehensible structures). He had said nothing, though his four cast-iron brief-cases overflowed with papers. Within minutes of sitting down, he had spilt coffee all over his tie.

'Any comments?' continued Nelson. Everyone sprang into a bureaucratic war-dance.

'I shall commission a 1,000-page report by 400 of our analysts worked on by thirty-two secret teams who will not even know the name of the company they are to write the report about,' said the management consultant.

'Wallenstein's top can-do m & a team, with thirty professionals, 345 analytical models, 234 secretaries and 401 analysts, will work day and night. They will live in the office. They will not sleep or even know a weekend has passed. Eating or bodily functions will not interrupt them. As a team, they will enjoy their work. Wallenstein is a place where good guys can come first,' said the banker.

Nelson did not wait for Bright, the accountant or the lawyer to speak. 'I want your comments now.' Panic passed across five overpaid faces. Nelson's face expressed nothing.

'I could not recommend such a step. Your balance sheet has an excess of debt, your cashflows . . .' the accountant dried up under Nelson's unseeing stare. The preppie banker made an attempt to scotch the idea.

'We, as professionals, could not support your bid for a company that is the unassailable blue chip conglomerate of the British establishment. We advise restraint, Sir John, and believe that Nelson plc, a company not ten years old, should attain managerial maturity before attempting to buy Britain's oldest and largest company.'

'Is that the advice of Wallenstein or of you personally, McGill Peabody?'

'I, well, I . . . Alrighteee. It is possible, if your share price was supported so we utilized every unit of value in your own shares,' said Peabody, who suddenly visualized the fees that he, McGill Peabody, would earn. Universal was worth $25 billion and the fees would be at least $100 million, probably more since any bid by an upstart like Nelson, however rich, would be fought tooth and nail by the financial establishment. I could buy a house in Eaton Square and an English country estate in Bankingshire, thought the banker. And then, he imagined the praise of Mr Wallenstein showering down on him like golden rain.

'Alrighteee,' he said again.

'Which would be illegal,' the castrato rocket scientist added, at the same time as trying to scrub his tie with an indiarubber to remove the coffee.

'Your friends around the City would not support such a bid for nothing, but we at . . .and Co. would be able to organize such a structure, though, of course, it would need to be secret and it would cost you $100 million, on top of the fees to lawyers, bankers and public relations.' The voice of the nameless consultant was without accent or tone. As a young analyst, he had spent so long working on computer spreadsheets at . . .and Co. that he had actually forgotten how to speak. After ten years, . . .and Co., realizing his worth, sent him on a course to learn how to speak again.

'It's illegal. You could be prosecuted under the 1901, 1981, 1982, 1983, 1987 and 1726 Financial Acts. I cannot allow this talk, I cannot support it . . .' the lawyer's unbroken voice soared, like Nelson's share price.

'Whose lawyer are you?' said Nelson.

'We act for Nelson plc. $200 million of shareholders' money spent on one bid. We act for the shareholders, not you personally,' the lawyer cried bravely, though already he knew himself to be helplessly excited by the structures he would have to design to make such a bid possible. Imagine the holding companies, and nominee companies, and shell companies, he was thinking. Brass plates on anonymous doors in Monrovia, Liechtenstein, Monte Carlo, Grand Cayman, Borneo, the Falklands and Ulan Bator flashed before his eyes.

'Clearly, I should hire another lawyer. Invoice and Invoice tell me I cannot expand my business. Perhaps we need some American lawyers. Wallenstein will help run the figures, and . . .and Co. will run through the synergies. I want to see a legal structure by Monday from my helpful lawyers and I want Bright here to come up with a PR programme so the papers are on our side. Our share price must be supported. Who will approach our friends?'

Everyone shook their heads. The lawyer put his head in his hands. His sleeve sank into the mayonnaise on the sandwich plate beside him. The man from Bludlez tried to hide behind his one lock of hair. Peabody said he could not do such a thing. Wallenstein would not wish even to know such a thing was going on. It would have to be done personally. Only . . .and Co. understood what had to be done.

'It must be done by someone who does not exist, Sir John, then the whole plan can be denied by you yourself and all of our organizations.'

'Thank you,' said Nelson. 'Please stay behind, Max and um . . .' A bony hand pointed at me.

'Joseph Rourke,' I said.

'Yes,' said Nelson, who did not move as all the advisers nervously packed papers into cases. The fit tennis-playing banking Adonis and the body-building consultant were gone in a flash of tanned muscle, fine-suited torso and patent leather shoes. The other two waddled out, the fleshless frame of the rocket scientist straining under his four armour-plated cases that banged the door-posts, and the accountant repeatedly trying different positions for his one lock of hair before facing the cruel Mayfair streets.

'You will approach them,' said Nelson when the lock of hair had at last disappeared behind the closed door.

'I certainly cannot and will not,' answered Bright without a hint of the usual huskiness.

'No, not you,' answered Nelson. 'Joseph Rourke will do it. He is perfect, are you not, Joseph? You're not even here. You're in Cambridge. No one would ever guess that a student with a holiday job could be involved in the planning of this enterprise. No student has ever had such an opportunity, but I always help my children's, um, their friends. You see, these big law and banking firms are weak bureaucracies without any entrepreneurial flair. It is therefore appropriate that we turn to the individual. Joseph Rourke.' He rose quickly and left the room.

9

The gaze of Britain had settled on this Square Mile of gold.
All the hopes of old England had shifted, moving away from
the disused docks of London and Liverpool and the empty cot-
ton mills of Lancashire, and the flooded mines of Wales and
Yorkshire. Now the grannies with their savings and the schoolboys with their ambitions culled from newspaper stories on
Italian shoes and mock-Tudor mansions were buying shares,
those tickets to Rolls-Roycedom. And they were turning to
the City, a factory that made nothing but money.

It was lunchtime: the rushing bankers formed a giant pattern of pinstripes merging and parting, like the opening of a
living vertical blind. Like a 1980s Dick Whittington, I came
to London on Nelson's mission. He was rebuilding London.
It was his City.

Godfrey La Goncourt's offices off Threadneedle Street had
the air of an antique shop with an ancient black door and
a bow window tinted the mellow golden brown of good
furniture.

An old butler showed me in through a hall that was a
museum of the Goncourts, a history of the Europe of rail-
ways, Napoleon III and Bismarck. There were prints of
Goncourt châteaux and Goncourt carriages, and family trees
of the Goncourts of Germany, Austria and England. There
were vases donated by monarchs of long-lost kingdoms with
picturesque Ruritanian names. History had made their
money beautiful.

This Goncourt had given a new shine to a tired old name,
building a new fortune very different from the genteel millions
of his crusty ancestors. In brilliant escapades, Goncourt was

97

creating a financial services empire of his own. To the City he was a miracle, where old money met the gaudier dazzle of the new.

I waited nervously in a long conference room, far away from the treasures outside: there was a long ugly glass table with ten tubular metal chairs around it. Modern panelling decorated the walls, shining with new gloss and still smelling of fresh varnish. A print, *Edward VII leads Baron La Goncourt's Arc de Triomphe winner 1901, 'Big Money'*, hung over the table, yet I was very much in 1987 now.

A distracted vibration fired into the room, shaking my hand like one of Don Quixote's windmills and then throwing himself into a pile of untidy arms and legs in the chair to my left. Goncourt was very different from the svelte creature of hair grease, silk and aftershave I had imagined.

'Hello Joe, what can I do for you?' he asked in a patrician mumble. His priceless suit made him look even more dishevelled.

'I am from Nelson,' I said.

'Ah, the great Nelson.' Goncourt was one of those merchant princes who truly admire the self-made.

'He will bid for Universal Imperial this summer. His share price needs support. Will you support it?'

'Will it be profitable?'

'A profit is guaranteed. There is nothing to lose.'

'Guaranteed profit is an unusual concept. It must be illegal.'

'It's not illegal, but either way, I don't exist. It is untraceable. Our conversation never happened.'

I waited breathlessly for the reaction, but he did not seem to have heard. His eyes were staring up at his ancestor's winning racehorse. I stared nervously down the table, at the inevitable Perrier bottles and the little pads of paper inscribed 'G La G'.

Goncourt was dreaming: 'What did they have, my ancestors, that I don't? How could they dine with kings, and win races with 'Big Money' as well as making it? Here I am, neck and neck with spivs like Nelson and Brooklyn cab drivers like Wallenstein. Where, where is THE DEAL?

The big one. The one that will push me above the wolf pack. Where is that Deal?'

'Why are you involved?' he said abruptly.

'I am a friend of Sir John's. I am working for Max Bright, who is doing the public relations.'

At last his eyes left the painting and looked at me closely, as if I were a new racehorse. Where is this boy going? he wondered restlessly. Are we passing one another on his way up or down? Up, he decided, but he lacks clarity. He's young . . . Where's the Deal? I am getting on. There is so much to do.

His eyes were grey, so light that I wondered how he could see through them. They were almost opaque. His hair had thinned and receded, and he had a donnish, petulant face in which the bones around the eyes were the dominant feature, together with an aquiline nose.

'Our friend has a strange way of doing things, but then that is why he is what he is. Naturally, you won't have my answer now, but let me say that Nelson wants Universal Imperial too much. No one in business should become so emotional about a mere balance sheet. Who else are you seeing?'

'Wallenstein and Walter Hinton.' They were names as big as his own. In his desperation for the big deal, he was suddenly tortured by the possibility that a Hinton or a Wallenstein could make a riskless profit that he could not. And suppose Nelson won, what if Goncourt was not involved in the conquest of the century? He smiled again, and so great was the luxury of even a grin that I positively melted with gratefulness to him. He may not have agreed to buy the shares, but he had smiled.

London was under surgery. Two years ago, it had been the decaying capital of a lost empire; now its cancers were being torn out and this new London, with its myriad developments, its wider avenues and its new shopping villages, stood alone as the capital of cosmopolitanism. Sitting in my black taxi, as I travelled from the City to Park Lane, I could see the ancient city enjoying a second childhood.

At four o'clock I was at the Park Lane offices of the conglomerate publisher Hinton Incorporated, of New York and London. It was only a few miles across the City but a million miles from the Victorian memorabilia that masked Goncourt's desperate hunger.

The girl at the desk inside the angular offices looked like an air stewardess in a TV commercial, or a *Playboy* centre-fold: a mouthful of perfect teeth, big tombstones with a gap in the middle that seemed to say in broad Nebraskan, 'Come on boy, just room to squeeze you in.' She handed me a security badge as if it was a war medal. I went up in the lift and watched myself in a gilded mirror. I made faces and struck corporate poses, making my shoulders enormous, pushing my hair back, smiling all teeth like the receptionist. I emerged at another reception desk, in a suite so lavishly and intensely decorated that I felt quite suffocated. The place was buried in scarlet carpet and the walls were of gilded stucco, like a cake out of control. I walked out of the lift dreaming I was in the palace of a Third Empire debauchee who had combined a love of gold and thick carpets with the American obsession for glass buildings. Hyde Park stretched out like a giant's picnic below us.

I identified myself to the second receptionist, and did a double-take – the girl was identical to the one downstairs. Could the gap-toothed all-American nymph have raced me up the stairs?

'Are you by any chance a relation of the girl downstairs?' I said.

'No,' came that same Midwest 'taulk', 'but we both work for Mr Hinton.' And her hooded eyes peered towards a mighty pair of golden doors at the far end of the coridor.

'Where are you from?'

'Oklahoma.'

'And the girl downstairs?'

'Nebraska, but we both work for Mr Hin–'

'Where were you recruited?'

'In Washington Deee Seeee.'

'Is it a fun city?'

'Aw, just awesome.'

'Why?'

'Senators,' she gasped, as if the very word itself was enough to ruin her knickers.

'Which are your favourites?'

'The Kennedys are so-o-o cute. Jack Jr told me all Republicans are scumbags . . .'

'But Mr Hinton is a Republican . . .'

The phone rang and she sat up very straight and flirted with the receiver. 'Yes, Ambassador Hinton, no sir, yes sir,' and to my shock she handed the phone to me.

'Walt Hinton here. You're a fine boy. There's nothing so fine as a Cambridge education. I believe in it. You're going to have to wait, so sit down and have a read . . .' and the line went dead.

'I suppose he is very busy,' I suggested to the secretary.

'Aw yeaa, he is on the line to the President all the ti-i-me.'

In my mind all I could hear was Hinton's thickly macho voice booming down the line at me. The girl brought me some magazines and coffee, prancing around in her airways suit with her long legs, her big breasts steering her along like rudders. Every magazine was crowned with a cover picture of Walt Hinton – with the President, with an ex-President, with the Shah, with the King of England.

'Ambassador Hinton likes his visitors to have a taste of him,' said that voice from somewhere behind me, but I could smell her clean soapy American body. I wondered if Hinton had had a taste of her. Most likely, I thought, and why not? She is more fun than dividends.

All of a sudden those great doors opened wide as if kicked by a grizzly, and sure enough, out came the bearish figure of the man himself. In an old English pinstripe, he strode at me with such energy I was afraid he might not be able to stop and would run me over. A great red hand came down and greeted me, while another encircled my shoulders and marched me into his Olympian office.

The room was filled with bronzes of bemuscled Greek athletes. He saw me looking, and as he parked me at one end of a sofa he said, 'They are Athenian, and you know why I got 'em?'

'No, Ambassador.'

'The Athenian empire and the American empire are damned similar – great democracies, maritime powers, the greatest traders in the world, and the greatest art in the world too.'

'I never thought of that, but it's a very clever idea.'

'You think so and you are from Cambridge, so write and tell your professors that I said it.'

'The reason I am here, and . . .'

'You're a fine boy, and I want to help you, but . . .'

'And I want to say what an honour it is to . . .'

'You are damned right it is, but you see I started from zero. I didn't go to university. We did some bad things and some good things but we won. I started blind, but now things have come together.'

This was an understatement on both counts, for his father had been imprisoned for gangsterism when he was a boy and things came together to such an extent that he was one of the three richest men in America. 'I am an old man but I have my kids and my grandchildren and I collect art. You know, I have known two of your monarchs and I have served three Presidents as well as running all this – and I adore your young Prince James. I tell you, Joseph, he is going to make one hell of a king.'

'I come from Nelson.'

'Don't tell me – he's going to buy Universal Imperial.'

'Yes . . .'

'And he wants me to pay for it?'

'No, he will pay you to help him.'

'You got a great job, kid. A boy your age should not be involved in such dirty work. When I was your age, I was playing golf and tennis all day at our place in New Hampshire.'

This too was not quite gospel. At my age Hinton had been his father's employee, in charge of fixing the races at racecourses across America by bribery, drugs or worse; in the true American tradition, however, he had converted himself into such a bastion of taste and old money that he had become something of a joke.

'People helped me when I was young and ambitious. I might even help you and Sir John. He built these here offices. They're mighty dandy. He's changed the face of this city. There's only one man of that influence in each generation, a Hearst, a Hinton, a Nelson. Good luck, fine boy, don't fly too close to the sun. Remember Icarus.'

The wheel spun round. It slowed. It stopped. The arrow pointed to the word SELL. 'What do y' think, sell or keep buying?' said Lew Wallenstein. He did not wait for my answer. He just lifted up one of the battery of scarlet phones on his mahogany desk and said, 'Sell.'

We sat in a glass box in the middle of a dealing room crisscrossed by rampart upon rampart of telescreens, and telephones. All around were colourful men in button-down shirts and rolled-up shirt-sleeves, and sharp girls in business suits with short hair, lying across the screens, gripping three telephones a hand, yelling numbers. But they all kept an eye on Wallenstein in his strategically transparent office. And, like hungry hawks, they watched the famous spear he held in his hand all day and his turning wheel.

It lay in the middle of his desk, a wide dial like a clock with an arrow that he spun and spun all the time. Around the outside of the face in different colours lay the words that the dealers cared so much about. The words 'SELL, BUY, FIRE, HIRE, YES, NO' were distributed at random round the circle. His hands were like the man – hairy, dark and squat. Wrestler's hands. Wallenstein was the bull of the bull market.

As the arrow came to 'SELL' I could see that the traders were already poised, straining, their hands hovering over yet more telephones. He pressed a panel on his desk, leant towards the microphone built into his inkwell, and said, 'Sell.' When he gave the order, we watched as the whole floor flew into a feverish confusion of movement.

He swung his chair back to face me, a crude powerman's smile on his mouth, his model spear, about a foot long, pointing directly at my face.

'So you're the kid from Cambridge, right?' He was a pug, as broad as he was tall, with shaven thick black hair that grew low on his forehead. The office had no luxuries. Everything was glass. A framed poster on the wall read: 'BUSINESS IS WAR.' Behind Wallenstein stood a white-haired butler, wearing an incongruous black jacket and holding a gold tray, but the tycoon acted as if this man was not even there. His hand was back on his toy, spinning. He could not stop.

'What do you think of this?'

'Chancy.'

'Chance is everything to me, y' know. You, do you have researchers up in Cambridge go by the name of economists?' His voice was broad cab-driver's Brooklyn.

'Yes, a lot of my friends read it.'

'Fine, but my economist is this,' he said, and he spun once more, 'and it is just as right as your puck-assed Cambridge economists. At Wallenstein there are 7,000 traders in London, New York and Tokyo and they're the best. They don't need a fuckin' economist, though we have to have a few for appearances. They read all fuckin' day, they look like goddam geeks, they can't ski, they're too ugly for the dames, they get paid 200 grand a year and they know fuckin nuthin' about the markets. It's all chance – it is chance that you are here now. Why do you think I saw you?'

'Because I was at Cambridge.' That generous prize-fighter's smile flashed again.

'You gotta be jokin'. I only saw y' 'cause Peabody, one of my guys on the Nelson account, told me someone might be callin'. What do you think of Cambridge?'

'A snob's fairy-tale.'

'And what do you think of the English class system?'

'A sewer of shit.'

I hoped I was saying the right things. Wallenstein, with his famous little spear in his hand, was the terror of every boardroom from Milan to Manhattan, a beast of the markets, a green mailer, a merchant bandit, not banker. He hated the English, the poor, and all Gentiles. So I was trying to answer accordingly.

Wallenstein spun round in his chair. 'Get's two *cap-puccinos*, Groom,' he snapped at the dignified waiter, who left the glass box. 'What are the poor?' he said, leaning towards me over the dial. It was the question of the eighties.

'They are the people who have not made their own luck.'

'Good boy,' he said, 'now we talk business; fire away.'

'You know that Nelson's going to bid . . .'

'Of course I fuckin' know, we're workin' on the deal . . .'

'He wants you to help support his share price. And he'll pay you to do it. It's the biggest deal this country has ever known, and without your help it's not going to happen. He really needs you, Mr Wallenstein.'

'Not even the guy who wipes my ass calls me Mr Wallenstein. Call me Lew.'

'You can make the deal or you can break it, Lew.'

'I like that, kid. Tell me, what do y' make of my dealing floor? It's the biggest in Europe.' He pointed the spear at me.

The dealing floor was as big as a football ground. Blinding white lights burned down to give Wallenstein's employees extra energy that they might otherwise miss. They were living in an unreal world, without the light of the sun and without fresh air. They only saw the grey of dawn and the dim of dusk, when the purple half-light of neon replaced the rhythm of the markets with the beat of the night-clubs.

'It's like a ballroom,' I declared, and it was. It was a twenty-first-century ballroom in a Busby Berkeley dance extravaganza.

'So the Cambridge preppie thinks my dealing room, which goddam turns over more than Haiti, Jamaica and West Africa put together, is a ballroom.' He put on his fake Raffles accent, jovial sarcasm itself. While in Cambridge I was the tax collector's son; to this Brooklyn street kid I was the classic Cambridge man.

'Look at it.' He peered through the window, waving his spear towards the dealing floor. 'It's booming. Up and up and up! Everyone's buying – teenagers, grandmothers, everyone! This is meritocracy for you. With all this fuckin' cash around, who needs a goddam class system? See that little broad over there?'

He pointed his spear through the glass at a miniskirted, blonde-haired, pneumatic sales assistant, who smiled proudly back at him and tossed her head back as she remembered the jacuzzi in his plush flat in Eaton Square and the drinks cabinet in his Roller . . .

'That's Penny. Great kid. Great fuck. Do you score easy, kid?' and he nodded towards the chic women talking into the phones.

'Let me tell you this,' and I dramatically took my eyes away from the dealing dancers at their financial ball and clamped them to his eyes like black pennies, 'I could have any of those women I want.'

'I like you, kid. Ask me a question.'

'What do you spend your money on?'

The indulgent smile was wiped off his face. 'I am above all that shit. I don't need that. I am not one of your English gents making a shitty million and buying a little mansion in the Home Counties. I stopped counting years ago. I could have retired at twenty-three and I'm forty-seven now. Numbers ain't nothing to me . . .'

His voice was pure Brooklyn. His fury had all the scorn of the man who has left his home town far, far behind. It brought colour to his cheeks. The traders could see he was angry and waited. They knew the boss.

'You don't seem to realize, boy, I am one of the richest men in the world.'

The butler was back with two steaming *cappuccinos*. 'Well, thank you, Groom. Y' know, the skill of life is to use people for what they're good at. For example, Groom will agree when I say that the British have the best name for class in the world, and as every retailer will tell you, you need class. That is why Brits make the best butlers in the world.'

'Thank you, sir,' said Groom.

'But they're shit bankers. So when I bought the antique firm of Turd Brothers, stockbrokers since 1779, for 100 million fuckin' dollars . . .'

'You fired the lot . . .'

'Yea, we found that most of Turd Brothers had died in their seats without telling anyone, so we just carried 'em out. But we kept Groom, the most expensive butler in the world . . .'

'Sir, really!' Groom relished his boss's praise, though it was a long way from the panelled splendour of Mr Turd's private partners' room.

'It's true, Groom. You see, we paid 100 million dollars for Groom because he is all that is left of the mighty lion of the city, Turd Brothers. I paid 100 million for you, Groom.'

'Most honoured, sir.' Groom was a pillar of stability in an asylum of avarice. His long nose had been moulded to sniff the bouquets of the fine wines favoured by the partners of Turd Brothers, instead of bringing frothy *cappuccinos* to insolent traders, but he was the highest-paid butler in the world.

'Kid,' said Wallenstein at last, 'do you really think that my firm will both do the corporate finance work for a bid and trade in the shares on the quiet? I am afraid the answer has got to be . . .' and he spun the wheel, with his eyes glinting at me. I was dead before I was even alive.

The arrow whizzed around. The dealers were less busy now and the boss winked at them, sharing the joke. They watched his wheel. It slowed down, passed 'FIRE' and 'SELL'. It stopped dead at 'NO'. He looked up at me.

'Sorry, kid, I guess it is just bad luck, but it says "No" if my eyes don't deceive me.' There was no luck in the wheel. He literally made his own. He stopped the arrow when it suited him. The dealers were laughing. He was laughing. I had nothing to lose.

'Like you said, we all make our own luck,' I said to him. He just watched me as I leant over and pushed the arrow round the dial to 'YES'. 'Your eyes did deceive you. The Wallenstein wheel says "Yes".'

The smirking traders went quiet on the floor. Their eyes turned cold. No one had ever spoiled the boss's game, except for Peregrine Snorter-Grouse, the last partner of Turd Brothers. He had been fired on the spot and then arrested for trespassing on the premises. Wallenstein shot me a look like an ice axe. His face warmed. He showed his white teeth again.

He remembered the end of that gook from Turd Brothers with enormous satisfaction. He loved the way he had cried out, 'It's not cricket, it's just not cricket. You'll destroy Turd Brothers, the cream of the City . . .' as he was led handcuffed out of the building.

Lew knew its effect: it created fear. And fear made money. It was fear in the darting eyes of the traders that he could feel now. There were two sorts. One was the fear of losing your job. And then there was pure fear – to a man, the employees were terrified of Wallenstein. They were scared of his voice and his physical force and his energy. This, thought Wallenstein, is the best fear of all.

'You are quite right, Joe,' he said simply, and he pushed the dial round to where it read 'BUY'. 'I'll support Nelson's shares. The deal's too good to be true. If he's willing to go that far, he can't lose. You got it. Luck, my ass. There ain't no such thing.'

10

'You're all so ambitious,' Darlington said to me in his sauce of fashionable accents, the voice of the Chelsea brasserie. 'While I spend my Christmas hols in an apartment in Manhattan, dealing in a pair of brilliant young British artists by day, dancing all goddam night, you spend yours working with Bright down in London. That's ambition for you.' He was ambitious himself, but somehow in that time of bankers and property developers, the theatrical world claimed to be a land of learning and innocence. It was the beginning of a new term at Cambridge. We were at dinner at Darlington's house off Mill Road, where he had assembled a crowd as varied as his dialects.

Syssons, the leader of the left in Cambridge, glared at me with disgust in his eyes. He had glared ever since Nero, Jesse and I had defeated his motion to rename the Union the 'Mandela Society'. Prince Angus stared down the table. Drippy Macduff-Swittle, balding and lisping editor of the *Univ*, the Cambridge newspaper, sat with his Arab leggings on the table and his Palestinian *keffiyeh* over his shoulders.

'Takes all sorts, Barry,' he laughed, with saliva flying.

'You are right,' I said, 'and we are ambitious. No more ambitious than you are in the art world.'

'But for what? For personal gain?' Darlington's life had been such a flood of trust money that he simply could not imagine how anyone else could actually need a thing. He had everything, and believed he had been born a cross between Mick Jagger, Matisse and the Duke of Devonshire, in whichever order.

'When I was at Eton, I was wild out of my head. Played in a band, of course. Bass. Vocals, sometimes, when Charlie

Kensington – y'know Charlie, he owns Kensington – was too stoned to play.'

'Did you record anything?' I helped myself to the bean-sprouts, peppers and Szechuan beef on the table.

'Sorry it ain't soochi. Look, recording, *ça n'est rien*. My uncle is in the business, so getting a contract was no hassle.'

'What does he do?' I had learnt from Babylon how to interview: the art of making people feel important.

'Oh, Joe, he spends most of his time trying to keep out of the gossip columns.'

'Why?' I dreamed of seeing my name in a gossip column.

'He has enough strife without the tabloids. He's a record producer. Manages the Baby Eaters. People say they're wild. There is a lot of shit flying around. Like they actually eat babies.'

'Is it true?' The Baby Eaters had entered the charts at No. 37 and then disappeared into oblivion, but everyone had to humour Darlington that they were the new Beatles.

'Get out of my trousers,' he laughed. 'They are a bunch of great guys. Real musicians; much underestimated. Piles – he is on lead guitar – dropped out of the Royal School of Music. They are always treed out of their heads, and they believe in black magic. Ever heard of Aleister Crowley?'

'Is he the famous footballer?' asked the Prince.

'Well, he was some guy. 'Struth, he had powers. Piles gave me the story. Just freaky. Unreal. Still, sometimes when they are just planet fucking, strange things happen . . .'

'Good for selling records . . .'

'Yeah, but the uncle does not need the strife. It is a dirty biz. I'm into the art world myself . . .'

'Art dealing?'

'Yeah. I keep on the ball. I've just bought the new Hockney book. A gift at forty-five quid. I already had it, but the reproduction is so much better in the new editions. Some of the shit they turn out as art books these days really gets in my trousers . . .'

On the other side of me sat Prince Angus's bodyguard, a typical policeman, proud of his strange job as the constant companion to his ward. The Prince was chatting away to Babylon at the other end of the table.

'Do you carry a gun?' I asked the copper.

'Couldn't tell you that, sir.'

'You must meet some interesting people.'

'Oh yes, sir, I've bin to some dos.'

'What about girls? You must get your pick of them.'

'No, sir, His Royal Highness behaves in the most exemplary fashion, and I'm a happily married man. Not much holiday though.'

'It must be the most prestigious job in the force.'

'I have, um, heard it said,' he admitted modestly. While the policeman was not the most dramatic of companions, he was better company than the Prince. I looked down the table to see Babylon working his most dastardly spells on the Prince, who listened in shocked rapture as my friend explained that 'life is an adventure'. Emma Condor sat on the other side, smiling beautiful lies of agreement to Babylon's Satanic plans.

The place was more like an art gallery than a student's house. Darlington provided a home for the actors and arties crowd, disgusted by the barefaced ambition of the hacks. But Darlington had his own little ambitions too, so Prince Angus was often, incongruously, a guest.

Opposite me at the table sat an obese girl with spiked pink hair, a T-shirt covered in safety pins and badges, and a miniskirt that should have been banned by law. Her hippopotamine legs needed felling. Her badges announced slogans like 'All men are fags' and 'Israel is fascist', and one had a picture of the British Isles with the slogan 'US Airbase 1' beside it.

'Your mate, Kick, actually approves of having American missiles just outside Cambridge at Molesworth,' said the girl, seeing me reading her badge.

'She would. She's American.'

'Does American citizenship give her a right to destroy the world?'

'Sweetai,' came that inevitable drawl from the cheekbones and blondeness of Emma, 'Kick is ghastly. Only the other day she said she fancied Darling because he had a castle with real slits in it.' The radical punk and the titled heiress had become strange allies.

'She's really got her eye on Ru Bonham-Cavendish, but most chicks have,' added Darling, mentioning his friend, the next Henry Irving. 'I'll get him up here for a roar soon. Ru loves to party and to act: that's his life.'

But Barry, that white-faced shaven-headed conscience wearing a beret on the crown of his head, intervened with more ideological dogma. He was the sort who would tell you not to smile because there were children starving in Ethiopia – Barry Syssons was known as the 'Grim Reaper'.

'It is her blatant Americanism that most offends Karen and me. Why should our island be a launching pad for American imperialism when that iniquitous force is supporting contras, the racists in Africa and the fascists in Palestine?' Karen and Barry represented the New Left. The intelligent socialists of old were extinct. In Britain, a socialist country with a King, a class system and a welfare state, there was nothing left for them to achieve. Even trade-union leaders now sat in the House of Lords. Instead the New Left had fallen upon a list of causes unrelated to socialism and to one another. Across the country, earnest young middle-class radicals had chosen a 'Set-Menu', with dishes as varied as Gay Rights, Palestine, Anti-Blood Sports, Nicaragua, Disarmament and, for the main course, South Africa.

'Because we believe that American missiles are better than Soviet tyranny. You may not have heard, but one of the few things that unite Britain and the US is a fondness for a system you have evidently taken for granted, called Democracy.' It was Babylon, shooting from the hip.

The Prince was faintly disturbed. 'How can the Israelis be fascists?' he said to the Grim Reaper, the head of Cambridge Left.

There was a silence as Syssons fiddled with his beret. The fool! Barry was upset. Did the Prince not feel the anger of the youth of the world against this fascist power? What irony – that the victims of the Holocaust should become the new Nazis. And could he not see that it was all connected to Gay Rights and local democracy and the Sandinistas? Did he not know that the Sandinistas had overthrown a cruel American tyrant (here, he winced with anger at the mention of another fascist power) and were teaching kids to read? Barry, with Karen fuming beside him, was so angry about so many issues that he was near combustion. He ran through the 'Menu' in his mind. The Grim Reaper had accepted each idea as a gospel to save a suffering world.

'I dunno much about all this crass strife,' said a cool Darling, oblivious to the passions flying around him. 'All I know is that the Russian Rev sure made some fantastic art. Take poetry, Mayakovsky, or even movies . . .'

'And that brings us to the new Russia,' said Karen with a sudden glow. 'Now the Soviets hold the moral high ground' (this being a favourite television phrase) 'with Gorbachev.' She uttered the name like a saint.

'Gorbachev,' Barry told us, 'is a true liberal, believing in democracy, like we do. Gorbachev is far more the leader of the free world than Reagan or Thatcher.'

Drippy Macduff-Swittle ended the subject: 'I don't see why you are all worrying about missiles and whether Jews are fascists or not. There is a plague coming that will wipe out everyone. A new Black Death.' He spat as he lisped.

'Rubbish!' we all said. 'What plague?'

'It's just been found. It only kills queers so far. It started in Haiti from the blacks screwing pigs and it's in New York and San Francisco.'

'Oh, sweetais, we have all heard of the gay plague . . .' Emma said clearly.

'But its OK providing you are not a poove,' added Babylon.

'Keep your prejudices about the rights of minorities out of this,' yelled Karen, crossing her tree-trunk legs.

'We have got to agree,' came Darling's voice to my left. 'It can't just be a gay disease. A lot of the world's greatest artists are gay. Look at Wilde, or Warhol.'

'What is the disease called?' asked the Prince.

'It's called blades or aids or jades or something like that.'

'That's it,' said the Condor enthusiastically. 'It's called AIDS.'

'And we're all going to die of it, are we?' Babylon's voice

was sarcastic. He hated Drippy. This plague was his enemy's story.

'Well, I won't,' he answered, 'because I am a good Catholic boy and I behave myself, but immoral types like Babylon will be the first to go.'

'Oh yeah,' Babylon came back, 'you're only moral because you can't find anyone to be immoral with you. You're a hypocrite.'

'Go off to the zoo and fornicate with the animals.'

'So some gays die in America and you say it is going to come to England and kill the rest of us.'

'Some of the doctors say it will, and there's no medical reason it should stick to the homos, is there?'

'Syphilis wiped out everyone at the turn of the century. Killed de Maupassant, even Churchill's father,' I said. 'This could be the new syphilis.'

Babylon closed the subject: 'I'll tell you all – no one seems to know about this except Drippy. Even the Government doesn't. It doesn't mean anything. We're not going to die. Just because some gays die in America, we won't die. They'll find a cure.'

I walked home with Drippy and Syssons. Babylon disappeared to Emma's bed. We came through the dirty streets of Mill Road and skirted around Midsummer Common. It was a misty night and we wanted to get home alive. As we walked past the green we spotted two tramps dancing with one another in the fog. We watched for a second. One bearded man lunged at the other and smashed him in the face with a bottle. The other head-butted the first. We hurried on.

The other two were going to 'paste up' at *Univ* to print the next day's edition.

'Maybe you should come and look in,' said Syssons. 'There might be something that interests you and your friends.'

'Tell me,' lisped Drippy. 'Is your Babylon determined to be President of the Union?'

'Yes, and he will be, probably.'

'I doubt it. Why are the Hebrews so ambitious? They are all bankers and hacks. I like him personally, but he is just riddled with Jew blood.'

Syssons, the champion of oppressed minorities, did not come to my friend's rescue, for the modern Left were free with scary words like 'fascist' but selective in the minorities they chose to defend.

'They are agents of America; in Palestine they are actually massacring the Palestinian people,' said Syssons. He remembered the TV documentaries he had seen about the Palestinians. The ideas of the New Left were created by the latest documentary they had seen. Syssons adored those programmes narrated in a harsh urgent voice, about wounded and angry people in far away oppressed lands. When he saw the riots in Ireland, he knew the British army were 'fascist'. When the TV showed him the Sandanistas setting up schools in Nicaragua, he travelled all night by bus to demonstrate in Leeds against American imperialism. And South Africa, television's child, was the Grim Reaper's favourite source of fury.

Apart from the causes on TV, he believed the world was a free, caring place. But TV could change his opinions in seconds. It created new places and new angers. That harsh, urgent voice was his music, his Bible. No other places existed – only South Africa, Palestine, Northern Ireland, Central America. He was the conscience of Middle Britain, the *maitre d'* of the Set-Menu of the New Left, created by TV and believed in by the Good.

'Whatever your *nouveau riche* Oriental friend thinks, there is no way he or any of you lot will be anything . . . And the Arabs?' Drippy sighed. 'Such a beautiful people.'

We had arrived at the *Univ* offices. It was two in the morning. The newspaper was nearly finished. In the dingy underground rooms, drained trendy undergrads in denims, overalls and black crouched over old-fashioned typewriters and leant over large layout stands putting the newspaper together. It was the first issue of Easter term. The first Union Committee meeting of term had passed uneventfully. We had been back a week.

'Well, well, well.' A familiar Scots accent broke my train of thought. 'If it is not the wee fall guy. I warned him,' said the voice, 'but he said he liked Nero better. I warned him, did I not, Rourke?'

The journalists stopped typing and watched me. I turned around. Syssons, Drippy and Fergus. The blazer-wearing Fox shook my hand as he always did.

'I would like to see the article if it is so terrible.'

'Condemned men are allowed their final requests.' The Scots accent purred in a comforting way. It was reassuring even as it condemned you.

Those three were a strange alliance, as they stood there humiliating me. Bitter, lefty Syssons in his beret, the revolutionary from the People's Republic of Cambridge; Drippy, the Anglo-Catholic with a will to power; and of course Fergus Fox, ex-Union President, Scots opportunist, now Chairman of the Cambridge Conservatives, driven by old scores.

'Run and show this to Nero,' said Fox. He handed me a draft front page of the next day's *Univ*. There were photographs of Nero at an old garden party and of Babylon and me in black tie at debates. The headline read 'FASCISTS RUN UNION', and the sub-title 'ELITE CONNECTION WITH APARTHEID'. The story chronicled the defeat of the Cambridge Left's motion to rename the Union after Nelson Mandela. This defeat was apparently the result of a Pretoria-based conspiracy jointly financed by the Establishment and the South African secret police.

'It's rubbish,' I said. 'You can't publish that.'

'It is published,' said Drippy.

'And you are all fascists,' said Syssons.

'It's just a frame,' I protested. 'Why the pictures of us in black tie? That is what one wears for debates. That's what *you* wear, Fergus, when you're a speaker.'

'Really? But there's no picture of me in the paper, is there? Who is to know we all wear black tie at the Union? After all, a tiny minority of Cambridge, yet alone the country as a whole, come to the Union.' Fox opened his arms and smiled sympathetically. 'You see, you're sunk.'

'It's a frame.'

'It's news,' said Drippy.

'And either way,' said Fergus, 'it's a winner.'

*

I ran back along King's Parade and yelled up at Nero's window.

Upstairs Babylon was drunkenly telling Morganthau about his discussions with Prince Angus.

'So I just said, "If you want to learn a thing or two about the opposite sex, Sir, me and Emma can help. We know just the girl." He seemed delighted . . .'

Dizzy from the wine and the fresh air, I sat down in Nero's throne. They went quiet.

'They've got their own back. They've got their revenge for their magazine. We're at war.' I threw open the paper.

'And I had such a good evening.' Babylon was nonplussed.

'It is to the mattresses now, to the mattresses.' Elliot's voice cracked with excitement: he really was the Mafiosi now.

'You should never have gone to that South African party at the embassy. They are fascists. Why the hell did you go . . .?' I exploded at Nero.

'It is not a mighty moral question,' said Elliot. 'It's *realpolitik*.'

Babylon calmed us: 'Nero has the same weakness as I – if Lucifer was the host, we would still go to the party.'

Nero's face was straining. He looked at the paper again and again. Just when it was all so near, with his Presidency just started: 'It's our Pearl Harbor, it's the end, I've been President for two days and this has wrecked us. It's the end.'

I I

Dr Tombs came out of his rooms in Octavian Court. He turned left. Dr Kodell turned right out of his door. They met in the middle, facing the Gate of Honour. The Gate of Prosperity was noble behind them. They stood shoulder to shoulder: Tombs in a grey cloak and a wide-brimmed hat at an angle, Kodell in a faded blue velvet jacket and grey trousers.

'Seen *Univ* this morning?' Kodell's mouth barely moved.

'Yes.'

'Our boys are finished, are they?'

'Yes.'

'Shame.'

'Master on usual form?'

'Lord Belgrano is plantlife.'

'Quite.'

'Ave.'

'Ave.' They parted and went back to their rooms. I was buried.

'Resign,' said Fox.

'Yes, resign,' echoed Saint.

'For the sake of the Union Society,' said Fox. His voice was so entrancing I almost obeyed him on the spot.

'For the university, for the name of Cambridge,' added Saint. We stood in the secluded Stroessner Gardens. It was spring, but our breath was still visible. We were wrapped up, under scarves and greatcoats, facing one another on the clipped lawn within the circle of roses. It was an exciting end to my short political life. Fox, Saint and Syssons, in his beret, faced Babylon and myself, with Nero, sad and fat, watching cleverly with his piggish eyes. Fox shivered like a cat that is being caressed.

'We are not going to give up. We've got more nerve than that.' Nero had not slept. He was stumbling breathlessly like a wounded warhorse at a medieval battle.

'So you'll resign tomorrow, instead of today. To save face.' Syssons's metallic voice was harsh after Fox's.

Babylon stepped forward, with all the energy Nero lacked. His fair hair was wild and his eyes cool and grey-blue like a wolf's.

'Get it into your disgusting little heads,' he said into their faces, 'we are not running scared. We are not going to resign.'

'There is no face for you to save,' said Syssons. 'You are fascists, you have collaborated with the South Africans. Nero has visited the Embassy for a party. I have the proof. You are a public-school conspiracy. We know it all. Resign.'

The Robespierre of the rose garden was shouting, his mechanical voice ringing over the lawn. Fox was embarrassed: the fool believes his own propaganda, thought the Scotsman, who believed only in what was possible.

'You'll resign at the Committee Meeting. We'll vote you out,' said Fox, and the three trooped up the steps past the great statue of Sir Alfredo Stroessner, the founder of the college in 1840, who had discovered the electrode. Drippy was waiting for them at the top. His little head was outlined for a moment against the horizon. We were left standing, wordless, in the cold garden.

The *Daily Claret* man from London sat on the edge of Babylon's bed, in the sprawling untidy room in Cadaffi. Mr Crockett wore a large parka (with fake fur around the hood and an orange lining) and thick schoolboy spectacles, and there was a notebook on his knee. He had a likeable, plump face. Babylon had friends in Fleet Street. They wanted to know what was happening up at the Varsity so Crockett had come to Cambridge.

I had met Mr Crockett's train, the evening train from London, and escorted him by cab to Babylon's room. The cabbie was intrigued by our visitor, and peered at him in his mirror.

'So you're up 'ere, all the way from London, to see about the debating society? Must be more important fings goin' on in the world. F' example, 'ave you heard what the Cambridge Council 'as done to us cabbies . . .?'

By the time we had reached Great Gate the cabbie had not drawn breath: 'I always thought Mr Foot was a git, but this Mr Kinnock is diabolical. It's his Mrs that I blame it on. She wears the trousers. I don't understand what makes people socialists. Unhappy childhood, I suppose. Still, I make a good living for the wife and kids . . .' The man from London paid the taxi.

Babylon, playing the languid aesthete for Fleet Street's very impressed Youth expert, lay back in silk pyjamas and smoked a cigarette in an ivory holder. Emma Condor was making tea. The journalist began.

'Is there any truth in the allegations in the *Univ*?'

Babylon exhaled: 'They are the most brazen collection of lies since Stalin's Great Trial.'

The journalist scribbled. Very quotable. 'And are you an élitist secret society intent on making Cambridge once again the preserve of the landed classes?'

'Joe's father is a tax assessor in Esher. So much for the landed classes.'

'But are you all public-school boys?'

'Joe went to a comprehensive. I was at public school.'

'How do you feel about the allegations?' Mr Crockett asked me very earnestly.

'They are an insult. They are an insult to my belief in consent, the ideals that have made us a free country.' He wrote down every word. My accent, fainter than it used to be, was the proof of the pudding for Mr Crockett of the *Daily Claret*. 'They are an insult,' I added, for no good reason.

'What are you going to do?'

'I shall pursue these liars and cheats until they have taken back their rubbish. I will not sleep until the truth is out. I shall fight this Trotskyite . . .'

'Trotskyite what?'

'Conspiracy: Barry Syssons, the head of the Cambridge

Left, is leader of the militant anarchists of the loony Left. He leads a clandestine 'Kill the Rich' cell in East Anglia, which recently raised an army of thugs and skinheads to attack the local Hunt.'

Mr Crockett was overwhelmed by Babylon's master-stroke. His editor, Mr Clarence, Dr Tombs's friend, would love the story. He might promote Mr Crockett to Deputy, Associate, Under News Editor, or even mention his name when he dined with the proprietor, the remote Mr Sidney Operahouse, that capricious global demi-god. He had to wipe his brow with his sleeve and take a deep breath before asking very slowly, 'Are you saying you are the victim of a Militant infiltration of Cambridge life and that your Union opponents are the unwitting puppets of this anarchist plot?'

'Yes,' said Babylon. Mr Crockett took a photograph of Babylon in bed before he left and rushed back to London to file his copy, whispering and almost singing, 'Mr Clarence will be pleased with me, Mr Clarence will be pleased . . .'

'Fifteen love,' said Babylon.

Condor brought us more tea.

There was silence in the hot Union Committee room. Saint cleared his throat. Morganthau and Fox, veterans of old campaigns, had joined us young Turks: Saint, Babylon and I sat around the scratched table. Sally Gilpin was crossing and recrossing her legs in her executive battledress. She was stimulated by the audacity of Fox's plan. Perhaps he is appropriate, after all, she thought. The Reverend Jenkin sat at one end of the table.

'Mr President, are we ready?' Nero nodded. 'Then go ahead, Fergus.'

'It is a tragedy when a society as respected as the Union and as respected a President as Andrew Nero reach a point when they are no longer compatible. I believe that the sooner company is parted the better. May I ask the Steward's opinion?' Saint's cheeks flushed with fresh excitement.

'I think that the article in *Univ* has disturbed the smooth running of the society, that is all.'

'Is it not true that,' Saint started to read from notes, 'the political associations of Lord Nero have compromised him . . .'

'You mean social associations,' countered Elliot. 'He was in the embassy for a drink, not a rally.'

'If I may continue without facile interjections, I also believe the use by Mr Babylon of the national press has further reduced the reputation . . . The *Daily Claret* is owned by the Operahouse interests which . . .'

'You have written a very mediocre speech for him,' Elliot said to Fox in a stage whisper.

'He writes his own as it happens.'

'Quiet,' said Jenkin.

'I therefore ask for a vote of no confidence in Nero. Now,' said Saint. The show of hands was against us. Fox formally asked for the resignation of the three of us. Jenkin sat tight-lipped.

'I am afraid the game is over,' said Fergus. 'I am waiting.'

Nero had the eyes of the hunted. I winked at Babylon.

'You can wait if you like,' said Sally. 'The debate will be worse for you. You will be humiliated. Cambridge is burning. They hate you. And we are so patient. We are in no great hurry.'

In spite of himself, Fergus wanted to kiss the girl for knowing what Right was. At once, he checked his own enthusiasm. So this was the end of the great Establishment party. They had worked hard. After all, they were smart as well as privileged, but they would not survive the debate.

'You will be waiting until kingdom come,' Babylon said firmly. 'The Committee has no authority to overturn the choice of the electorate. Mr President, do you have any other business?'

12

The Chamber, with every seat, bench and floor filled, waited for the Christians to be thrown to the lions. The wall of faces stared at us as if we were no longer really alive. We were condemned men beyond pity, like cattle at the gates of the abbatoir. The lynching mob was quiet, but some people pointed us out to each other as if we were already headless.

Fox was standing at the back with a posse of Hytlerhouse's rugby players. He was pleased with the turn-out, but things had to be done with discipline. Everyone had to play their part like clockwork.

Syssons sat among the throng on the other side. All the people offended by our rise had mysteriously crawled out of the woodwork. Tracy had come to see her humiliations avenged. The Augustus bar crowd had come to see me brought down to size. Drippy was standing up near the door. Dr Kodell slipped quietly in. The Reverend Jenkin came and sat beside us. Mysteriously, the Pitt Club had appeared too: a helpless Party-Jones; reptilian Mr Punjab in a tweed suit; Yarborough, who thought this was a beagling meeting; Nelson, Darling, Kick, Scrubber and the Condor. Everyone loves a hanging.

There was silence as the President asked for any questions.

'We are going to be lynched,' I whispered.

'We will go down fighting to the last man,' said Jesse.

'Like the three hundred at Thermopylae.'

No one had said anything. Saint turned and nodded ostentatiously at Fox. He smiled back and tapped a boy in front of him. The boy got up and threaded through the crowd, stepping over the people sitting in the gangway. The crowd murmured. The show! Roll up, roll up. The drums were beating.

The unknown enemy reached the dispatch box and produced a large card with a speech written on it. Fox smiled at me across the sea of staring faces.

'My name is Norman Crunchwell. Pinochet College.' The weaselish voice stammered at first and then began to rise with a sanctimonious confidence. 'We have all followed the sad scandal at the Union Society. I myself was proud to help in that article. What followed was a public outcry in the national press against the guilty ones. The outcry was louder in Cambridge itself.'

The crowd was restless. The horror story was starting.

I heard Fox's voice leading shouts of 'Guilty' and 'Boo' that ricocheted round the hall, from the Scot's lullaby accent to Syssons and on to where Drippy spat them back across the Chamber.

'The truth is that three members of the Committee are part of the racist and élitist conspiracy that is against the very principles that all students believe to be the most basic. Ladies and gentlemen, there are fascists on the Committee you yourself elected.'

At once the group around Syssons chanted, 'Fascist scum, scum, scum, fascists.' Then clear as a bell came the awkward tongue of Drippy: 'Name them. Name the fascists.' The crowd took up the cry. It seemed all thousand of them were shouting, 'Names.'

Crunchwell rose to the situation. 'I shall accuse them by name,' he said, and the crowd roared its approval. 'Andrew Nero . . .' Nero, high in the President's chair, turned quite white. 'Jesse Babylon and Joseph Rourke. The fascists,' he shrieked, his words high and feverish. 'Fascists.'

The hall was alight. The sheep had become wolves. Every thin-lipped mouth from every hate-mottled face on every bench and every seat was chanting, 'Resign', and, 'Fascists', in time with the drums I was sure I could hear.

How can there be so much hatred, I asked myself, borrowed from others? How can they cry themselves hoarse for a cause that does not exist? And Syssons, the Grim Reaper, with his mob of Robespierres, righteously adding us to their Set-Menu. The sound of all that loathing drove the energy out of me. I just sat there looking into those strained red and white eyes, paralysed by the scale of the injustice. I was strapped into an electric chair, taking the shocks, open-eyed, interested in a detached way by my own demolition. Did the shocks hurt? What did they do to my body afterwards?

Nero buried his face in his hands. His ears were red. His shoulders were throbbing. This was far from his gilded connections and corridors of power.

Crunchwell was standing in front of the crowd, pretending to conduct a magical orchestra that played symphonies that went 'Resign, resign, out, fascist scum, out . . .' Then he walked out. He was supposed to be the ordinary student, the angry man on the Clapham omnibus. Now he was off home to write an essay, or to have a coffee and a fag. Sally, her lips fellatio scarlet, was a pouting sexual hyena. Saint bristled with pride, a weak man given a moment's strength by the crowd. He had planned all this down to the smallest detail. It was his moment.

Babylon's face was a sculptured mask of defiance. The actor had taken the clay of the laughing monkey face and with harsh strokes and chisel blows given it lines of strength. His frivolity was gone. He leapt up to his feet and strode to the dispatch box. He stood in front of it and he waited.

The shouts of the animals detached him from the spite and the stamping feet. The noise rose, and with it his isolated strength. They chanted, 'Sit down, fascist, resign.' He waited frailly before them, thin as a rake but as sharp.

He turned and winked at me. Soon you could once again hear the individuals, the Glaswegian, the lisp, Syssons. Babylon spoke quietly so that everyone leaned forward to hear him. I wished I had dared.

'I stand before you alone,' he said. 'I look at your faces tonight so that I can mark them down as faces I shall never greet but with pity and shame for you. You are like any lynch mob. You have shown yourselves to be the basest, and the most cowardly flock of sheep. You have yelped –' (here again the ringleaders tried to restart the catcalls but they were overridden) 'yelped at the three of us, a farrago of utter lies. You have hidden your faces in numbers, you have acted as cowards and weaklings have always acted. Quite apart from your methods, none of us has ever been near a fascist. You insult the victims of fascism, for you yourselves are using the weapons of fascism. You burned our letters, sold bitter lies to the newspapers for your own selfish ambition. But this is the age of confrontation: we are never going to give up. We are not afraid to fight. Bring back Torquemada, bring back McCarthy, for you are their successors. Resign? Never in a million years!'

When he sat down, they clapped.

13

Babylon took us home in glory. The glistening limousine rolled over the cobbles of King's Parade and stopped outside the house.

The chauffeur, a bull of a man, stood proudly beside the car cleaning the silverwork, while he haughtily scowled with motor snobbery at any ordinary car that went past, saving his special disdain for Cambridge's bicycles, which he regarded as cars without engines.

Babylon sat in front and the rest of us – Nero, Morganthau, Scrubber, Emma and Kick – rode in the back, languishing on the thick clean leather seats. Jesse produced doughnuts and white wine. As the car squeezed through the narrow streets of Cambridge and out through the flat featureless fens into the fresh rolling countryside of Bankingshire, we put our feet out of the window, shook the wine bottles and cheered as we passed the old men in cloth caps who sit eternally outside pubs in English villages. As we drew closer, I began to feel excited and cock-eyed from the wine. I could not wait to arrive. The chauffeur watched us through his mirror. He could not take his eyes off Scrubber's fleshy legs, which hugged the leather seats – and she could not take her hands off me.

'What did you think of Cambridge, Royce?' Jesse asked the driver.

'A bit of a one-horse town, Mr Jesse,' said Royce, who had not noticed the Chapel or the Great Court, but only a large number of cars without engines.

Babylon smiled as he watched us in the back. He had an overwhelming confidence that it was his day. How could we fail to be impressed by the house he was going to show us?

Everyone he took home remained devoted to him for life. He was as relaxed as we were excited, and as he anticipated our admiration, he lay back in his seat beside his father's chauffeur and thought how lovely life was.

A sign on the gate-posts announced 'Goldtrough Hall'. Elliot licked his lips as we passed it. If only I had an old rectory in Suffolk, he thought. An avenue of old oaks guarded the road like a vigil of gnarled veterans and ended with a vast Regency house, long, with a great central façade and a doorway that was pillared like a Greek temple. Unsteady on our feet, we stared at the house, then we turned towards a park of rolling luxuriant greenness as if even the grass of Bankingshire was rich. When I am married I am going to live in Bankingshire, decided Scrubber, whose parents lived in Accountantshire. There was a lake at the end of the park, with a little temple on its far bank.

'Mummy wants to build another folly,' Babylon told us, 'but she's not often here. Daddy loathes her.'

We left Royce standing beside the car with his eyes raised towards the house. As far as he was concerned, the Babylons had always lived here, in permanent prosperity. When Eve sank her teeth into her apple in Eden, the Babylons were already ruling Goldtrough. Royce's world was inconceivable without them.

'What do you think of the house?' asked Jesse.

'It's like a bloody museum,' I said.

There were passages lined with priceless pictures, cellars of rare wines and rooms of gilded furniture that all seemed to have belonged to Marie Antoinette. I was simply struck dumb by it all: how could I catch these people up? I kept asking myself, How can Jesse be so ambitious when he has all this? What more can he want? Where can he want to go from here?

The girls' eyes spoke of marriages and dynasties, parties and pearls, as we walked down endless corridors full of treasure. Except Emma — she prowled around, hands on her hips, legs akimbo, in her short skirt. Though Scrubber claimed to study history of art, she was not familiar with Reynolds or Velasquez: she did notice we were impressed, so she gathered the pictures were worth something. And Jesse's daddy was a baronet too.

But it was Kick's slick walk, and the calculus in her murderess's eyes, that I liked the most. Every picture was valued in dollars, pounds and francs too. It did not daunt her. She knew she was made for the Best. She enjoyed it in conspiracy with me, like cat burglars casing a joint.

The portraits become more and more modern, until at last we came to Sir Edwin standing at the end of the corridor as if he were himself one of the pictures.

'Which one of you is Joseph Rourke?' asked Sir Edwin. He was tall and thin, and his slow purring voice cast the spell of an Indian snake charmer. He brushed his grey hair back high on his forehead and his eyes were blue, yet his face had the oriental elegance of the man who would be on top of the pile wherever he had been born. 'You have all deserved a rest, but I gather you have come down to Goldtrough to plan your revenge. It will not be the first plot Goldtrough has known. Shall we eat, Montgomery?' he asked a portly butler with wide hips, spherical head and body, and baggy striped trousers.

'It has been ready for ten minutes, Sir Edwin.'

'Grub's up.' He led the way in. Disastrously, Elliot trod on Montgomery's foot as we went into the dining-room.

'I'm frightfully sorry,' Morganthau said, hoping no one would notice. He wanted to be invited again.

'It was a pleasure, sir,' answered the dignified butler with a bow.

Kick and Condor sat on either side of Babylon's father. He turned from one to the other, enjoying their hatred and judging them. He preferred the passion of Kick's Boston spite to Emma's cold languor. Sir Edwin had known many women like these in his time, but he was still attracted to Kick. 'I could move her into Goldtrough, quietly, so as not to shock anybody,' he calculated, 'and she would entertain for me and defend my interests, and look after me. Like her mother did.' Sir Edwin loved to make such calculations but could not admit to himself that he was lonely.

At our end of the table, we persecuted Scrubber about her love life.

'The Prince knows exactly who you are,' Jesse informed her. 'Next term is the term for you. It's your last chance.'

'You haven't told him,' she said, delighted that he had.

'Oh yes, I have.'

'You didn't.'

'I told him your desires, your height, how you taste, the number of fillings in your teeth, your vital statistics . . .'

'I hope you did not tell him everything . . .' she giggled coyly.

'You mean about me?'

'That too.'

'I told the Prince every detail.'

'What did he say?' She was tipsy.

'Well, he was extremely shocked; in fact, he did not speak for two days afterwards . . .'

'Oh-h-h, no-o-o, but not about . . .'

'What – Nero, Joe, what else?'

Scrubber pouted and winked and blushed.

'Oh, I can't tell you,' she said.

'Go on,' we all said.

'I can't.'

'Give us a clue.' We were fascinated.

'OK,' she said. 'Law and order.'

We were stumped by that. Scrubber sat there sipping her white and red wines alternately, chuckling, showing us her cleavage and her wine-stained teeth.

'I've got it, I know.' It all went back to Tracey, who still worked in Augustus's dining-room. (The table at our end went 'O-o-o-o-o-h'). At the beginning of term, when we were talking ('Oh-h-h yea-ah'), she confessed that one evening while on her way back from a party down the Mill Road, she had bumped into PC Smart.

'I don't believe it!' said Nero.

'Gives a new meaning to the Beat.' Morganthau was on to another story for immortality. 'That man's devotion to duty confounds me.'

'So,' we all said, 'is that it? The secret? The policeman? PC Smart?'

Scrubber went every shade of red before she admitted it, not out of shame but out of pride.

'That is what I call Community Policing,' said Elliot.

She laughed with her mouth wide open. It was all good clean fun, like hunting, winning the Pony Club races . . . or screwing a policeman.

'He was such a sweet little chap. I hadn't the heart to send him away,' she said.

The candles had burned low, the girls had retired, and we moved up to sit next to Sir Edwin. The port decanter clinked peacefully as we passed it round the table. Cigar smoke and old alcohol made us happy and bleary-eyed, far away from the exhausting witch hunts of the Union. But Cambridge is like a tattoo: you can hide it but it is always there.

Sir Edwin had that priceless ability to make you feel that you were the only person in the world that he wanted to speak to.

'When you have found a way, Jesse, to destroy your enemies in the Union, what then?'

'I will stage the debate to end all debates. I will speak against Oxford. It will by my swansong. It will make us all. And I will end as President.'

'Have you heard about AIDS up there?'

'Just about,' I said.

'Not really,' said Nero. 'We're not gay and we're not addicts of anything, so we're safe.'

'Not so. In America everyone is dying of it – children, girls, all sorts of people. Virgins will be back in fashion.'

'We don't even know any virgins, Dad.'

'I quite like them,' said Sir Edwin with a thin smile. 'Now,' he turned to me, 'tell me about your friend John Nelson. Max Bright has told me all about you.'

'Nelson,' I pronounced drunkenly, 'will soon be the undisputed dominant businessman in this country.'

'I very much admire you, but may I give you some advice on the City?' His tone changed. His eyes had narrowed. He placed his hands together like a priest. They were deeply tanned and fine, yet strong. There was a gold ring on the little finger.

'In the City, we do not like too much show. Publicity makes the City jealous; people ask questions. There are times,' he said casually, 'one has to cut people down to size, for the City's sake, you understand. After all, everyone has things they would rather forget.'

'Not everyone can have skeletons in the cupboard,' I said.

He laughed a laugh like the sound of pouring sherry into a glass. 'You're quite right, Joseph.' He was talking only to me. 'But you see, the Establishment has no skeletons. It just has History. It is people outside the club who have skeletons.'

'But what's the City to Nelson? He's beyond the City.'

'No one is beyond the City. The City is not an island. It is a mirror of this country today. In the Docklands, Nelson has torn London open to create a new city. Who do you think has paid for all that grandeur? The City. What the City gives, the City can take.'

'How many men build a city of their own?'

'There's the rub,' he said. 'There is no greater vanity in the world.'

'Wallenstein, Bright, Nelson, they cannot fall. They are the gods aren't they?'

'After Big Bang, they have become national heroes, but they are making too much money – they put their salaries in the papers and they are going too fast for the English, the nation of shopkeepers.'

The room was silent, and Sir Edwin grinned so that handsome lines creased his face. 'Far be it from me to say there is going to be any scandal about anyone.'

The sofas were made for extravagant giants. The gold leaf on the lamps and the pillars had been designed to provoke revolutions. Kick and I sat far apart on chairs at opposite ends of the room, playing delicious games with one another. She combined instinctive sensuality with icy expediency. I wondered which would win in the end.

Jesse's father had gone to bed, with a glance at Kick from the top of the stairs. The others were lost in the palace. Laughter flared up from one wing and then there was silence. Somewhere, a piano began to tinkle. Someone was singing Sinatra.

She lay down on the sofa. She watched her skirt ride up, judging the angles like a scientist. Then she looked at me. 'I am probably the only girl you know who is equal to men. I talk like a man. I can talk about anything.'

'You can talk anyone into bed?'

'Don't need to. Just wait.' And she waited. Her long legs in their lace stockings ended with the black band of her suspenders.

'What are you after?'

'This minute?' she said as if it was obvious.

'Afterwards.'

'I want to be kept on edge. I want variety, money, I want to play the grand game. I want a man who's a firewalker.'

'You want to marry a house like this?'

'Boring to run. Great to live in.'

We were like dwarfs in the drawing-room. She looked the part of Sir Edwin's young mistress as she lay there. She pulled back her shoulders. The dress was turquoise and ended tightly on one shoulder, leaving the other bare. The angle from shoulder to flank was a sharp one. I stared at her arms, her shoulder-blades, the long muscled neck, the firm shoulders. All I could hear was that mid-Atlantic voice that was husky like it had taken a few Bourbons too many.

'Nothing is left to chance in your life. You never make a casual move, do you?'

'Casual? I don't even goddam know the word. I am too valuable to be casual. I'm a survivor. Always on my own. Daddy's some banker in Boston or Connecticut or Maine or God knows where. And he knows everyone. Except his daughter. And Mummy lives her own life, so I have to look after Number One.'

She had colour in her cheeks now. Above the stockings there was a hint of white thigh. She had the logistics just right. They were slim athlete's legs, strong and confident, and she knew their power.

'You are ruled by luck and instinct.'

'Except when passion and policy meet . . .' I said. 'Casual sex will end soon anyway. AIDS.'

'Casual sex is an art; it is a modern right like freedom of

speech.' She laughed like a pioneer swilling gold gravel in his pan.

I walked over and stood there looking at her. Everything fitted together so well, like a proud machine.

'So?'

'So.' She made me speak in volleys.

I sat on the sofa. She did not sit up, but an arm of flawless white flesh reached up to feel my face and twirl my hair. I so wanted to touch that skin above the stockings, but she kept fires specially stoked to burn boys who strayed too far.

'I am not going to get burned.'

'Brave boys get burned.'

'They're ashes now.'

She did not look up to see me go but she was smiling, the cobra. She was thinking: What fun, what a bloody game!

Emma's languid words were drifting down the corridors.

'Mummy just goes on and on at me. If only they had got me a brother. You've got to marry the right sort, she says, no Americans, no Catholics, no Jews, no one from Account-antshire or Stockbrokershire or from the North or South London or . . . Hello, Joe.'

They were in the billiards room, which was large and dark with a tangle of antlers around the walls. The two of them were lying on the billiard table, drunk. Babylon had his eyes shut, his flies were undone and his shirt was open. His hair was tousled.

'Come and join us,' he said. 'Where've y' bin?'

'With Kick.' I got on the table and lay down flat with my eyes closed. Condor was between us. The big light above the table was out, and lights shone faintly around the walls, behind big antlers. The green baize felt soft and affluent against my cheeks.

'Get burned?' asked Babylon. Had he been listening? I looked at him and lay down again.

'God, no,' I said, though it had been close.

'Keep still,' said Emma. 'I'm asleep.'

'Could you marry someone from Esher?' asked Jesse.

'Dunno,' she said. 'Mummy never mentioned it.'

134

'There you have it, Rourke.'

'I'm never going to marry, never. I hate children. If I could buy them when they're fifteen, I'd marry,' I said with my eyes closed. Emma's smell was chic and dirty, all hair-spray, French perfume and old wine. It was a good picture: two boys and a girl dead on a pool table.

'I don't want to marry. I just love kissing boys,' she announced.

'And besides, what's the point in having babies anyway? They'll all either be raped, burned in riots, become drug addicts, die of AIDS or be nuked in the final holocaust.'

'Joe, that's miserable,' said Emma with feeling.'I'll train my children to be muggers, instead of stockbrokers. Money destroys everything. Like those coke-snorting American bankers in those boring New York novels about decay and greed in the land of the free. American novelists forgot adjectives long ago and replaced them with brand names.'

'In those books, money is a sort of corrosive.'

'What is it then?' Emma slurred her words.

'It reflects whatever you are.' Babylon was wide awake. 'If you're mean, it is a big number in a bank account. If you're power, it is an entrée. If you're into art, it is a Matisse. If you're nothing, like the ones in those bland books, it'll make you nothing. It is a medium, a panacea. It's not just a fact.'

The light was a blue glow growing brighter on the horizon. Streaked with the red of fresh blood, the rays were pointing out into a grey sky.

'This is called the Walk of Alcibiades,' Babylon said in a fresh morning voice. There, at the end of the hedged pas-sageway, stood a white Grecian in a cloak. The stone gleamed in the light.

'He is one of my greatest heroes.' My voice was hoarse.

'Of course, he is like you. You know what you want. You will have it. No loyalty will stand in your way. Yet you will enjoy your deceits and strangely, you will be admired for your betrayals.'

The mansion jutted up above us into the dim light.

'It looks like a sinking ship,' I said quietly.

'We are the only two survivors.'

'And Alcibiades,' I protested.

'You lived through your heroes up at home, didn't you? They were your real life.'

'I did.' It was not exactly true, for I had no heroes until Babylon. They died when I came to Cambridge.

'At Cambridge you don't need to dream. It is what you make it.'

'But you already have the house, and the land, and England.'

'The land has no spiritual value. That's an English fallacy.'

'If you don't want it, I'll have it.'

'My only pride in the world is as a Jew. It is the only thing in the world I believe. There is nothing more hallowed. It is History itself.'

I wanted to tease him, but he stood so seriously beside the statue, his profile up against the sky and the house far behind him. I felt he was a bit mad.

'It's easier for you to keep your religion. You can afford it,' I said to the two statues.

'Wealth is a religion all of its own. Jews are not in any class. Just Jews.'

'Do you mean a culture, a race, Israel?'

'All those things. It is a way of life. Judaism is about feeling. That is the Jew's role in history. To feel.'

'That's a rationalization.'

'No,' he said. 'Sometimes I feel I am living for six million who are not.'

'Your father was probably sitting in Boodles for most of the Holocaust.'

He did not hear me. 'Imagine the talent and the variety and the cosmopolitanism of those communities in Galicia or Budapest, the Ukraine or Paris. All dust, as if they had never lived. When I laugh, I'm laughing for all of them.'

Did he believe this? His grey figure turned and disappeared into the house.

Babylon was the classic British Jew, assimilated into the gentry, but under light hair and the Saxon eyes flowed the

136

hot, restless blood of another race. Britain had granted the Babylons the peace to build their fortune. In return they had surrendered their culture for the philistinism of the shires. Two thousand years of wisdom and learning, art and war and tragedy were at last to be destroyed by peace. They would disappear in the mist that silently covered Goldtrough as the sun rose. Freedom was the deadliest exterminator of all.

Sir Edwin stood watching me from the southern wing of Goldtrough, dressed in plus fours and a hacking jacket.

'There's to be a bid,' he said. 'And you are involved, you, an undergraduate.' He put on his leather gloves, long finger by finger.

'How do you know?'

'Max Bright.'

'You should buy shares in Nelson,' I said, taking the plunge as Nelson's ambassador. My heart was beating and my face was hot, despite the dew that sprinkled cool droplets on to my forehead.

'No one your age has ever had the chance to play such a game,' he said, as if he had not listened. 'I am going out riding.'

He swished the crop through the air, as if to clear it.

'The others are up, having breakfast. Your friend Elliot is very excited – he has worked out the strategy to vanquish your Scottish enemy. Apparently, he cheated in the Union election and you're going to get his allies to confess all.'

'How on earth am I supposed to do that?'

He laughed out loud: 'I don't understand the details, but it involves you, a girl and a tape recorder. Sounds almost as entertaining as working for Max Bright.'

'Good riding,' I said.

14

Babylon kicked his leg high into the air, spun round, squatted on the floor with his hands flat on the ground and then leapt into the air. Condor turned the music up again and then joined him, moving round the table like a long-legged, sleek-haired, slit-eyed cat. He wrapped a hand around his crotch and, keeping both feet on the ground, he propelled himself forward in time to the beat of the music with his other hand lassooing the air. Emma danced behind him, copying his moves and pushing her hips into his bottom.

He suddenly turned towards Jo Yarborough's dining-room table, where the rest of us sat formally eating our chicken Kiev while Babylon danced round her flat up in Cambridge's Newnham village. He waved his finger and said clearly: 'Go – Joe. You have a job to do. She is waiting.'

'I'm not sure I want to do this. I don't think it'll work,' I said. The others tried to listen above the music. Jo Yarborough watched his every move, in silent worship and joy at having Jesse Babylon and his 'exclusive circle' at her dinner party. Party-Jones yearned for him just to look at her. She imagined him asking her to a ball in London . . . and then she saw Condor's svelte confidence and she good-naturedly accepted that she could only dream. Jesse turned the music off.

'It'll succeed because it is so daring that no one would ever dream of doing it,' Jesse said. 'Elliot, is the tape ready?'

'Oh-h, yes,' answered Elliot, iron teeth a-glisten, 'the tape waits Joe's Irish love melody and her frigid orgasmatron.'

'What are you planning, Jesse?' asked a confused Yarborough.

'Something naughty, if it is Babylon,' commented Party-Jones.

'This will achieve the triumph. Then I shall organize the great debate against Oxford to celebrate.'

'Can we all come to it?' asked Yarborough.

'I've got so-o-o many friends at Oxford,' added Party-Jones.

'You see, tonight's plan will make all of us. Not just Joe and me and Elliot, but all of us. In ten years' time, we will be running this country. It's a meritocracy this England, and we will work and fight the hardest and we will be the best. Tonight will be the night it all started.'

No one argued with him. We were all sure that whatever Babylon decreed would happen. He was unstoppable. He laughed at me.

'Get on with it. You might even enjoy it. Dirty work is always the best.'

Condor turned the dial on Yarborough's hi-fi and Babylon was dancing again. The others envied his grace.

'You're trying to get me drunk,' said Sally Gilpin in her thin-lipped clipped voice with the ritzy innocence of the small-town slattern.

'Quite right,' I said. She had always cast *oeillades* at Babylon during Committee meetings, but equally I had caught her watching me with her cold mannish eyes. On the day we returned from our weekend at Goldtrough, I had passed her in the street, slicing through the tourists with her jaw forward and her power shoulders. She accepted my invitation to supper in my room with alacrity.

'To what do I owe the honour?'

'I've been plucking up the courage,' I claimed.

'For two years?'

She had dressed up to the nines, in a razor-shouldered jacket with a sharp short skirt and pumps the same scarlet as her lipstick, for the honour of drinking my plonk wine and tinned soup, but she did not seem disappointed. She was intensely feminist, but far too clever to burden her career with either scruples or feminism. The less nonsense the better might have been her motto, so the direct approach was doubt-less the best. Talk about it, and doing it is not so far off.

139

'How old were you when you lost your virginity?'

'None of your business, is it?'

'No.'

'Seventeen.'

'How many boys have you slept with up here?'

'Rourke!' I filled up her glass again. 'Two.'

'Do I know them?'

'Both of them.'

'Let me guess.'

'Go on then.'

'Fergus Fox.'

'He's been in love with me for ages.' She felt suddenly confident of her attractions.

'And how was he?'

'What do you mean by that?' she asked archly. I said nothing, but Sally relished her single-minded supremacy over weak silly man-kind. 'He was very serious and very earnest,' she said at last and then laughed too loudly. I could see the thickness of her make-up on her face as it stretched to laugh. The delicious irony of her hubris excited me.

'And the other?'

'You know him very well.'

'Not Jesse?'

'Of course.' She was proud of her scalps. That is how I fitted into her strategy, for first she had screwed us in politics and now she would screw us in the sack. No wonder Babylon had not volunteered for this part of the plan.

We were sitting beside each other on the floor. I poured some more wine, put my arm round her and wondered what Jesse would have done. She saved me the worry. She put down her wine glass, arranged her hair and fired me a dry kiss on the lips. She got down to it with the thoroughness of a warehouse storeman checking his stock.

I found myself detached from her in our intimacy and I watched her thin mouth, stretching this way, convulsing upwards and sideways and all ways. There was sweat on her made-up face, and always that flagrant pencil line of a mouth opening and twisting as if she was in agony. She was tight and dry and she held me in vice-like grips until she came in

140

controlled gasps like a man. There seemed to be no mess. It was careful, clean and quick. Afterwards she lit a cigarette.

'I've given up smoking. But post-coital, it's OK.'

'Oh, no better finale.' We lay naked on my bed in King's Parade. We were in the intimate afterwards when there are no secrets, but we were only intimate in the way that boxers are when they are alone in the ring.

'I suppose the Union thing gave you a bit of a shock,' she said, holding her cigarette.

'You won – you finished my political ambitions.'

'Going to give it up?'

'Suppose so. You lot are pros. We can't compete.'

'Quite right. Fergus never makes a slip.' Her sharp pretty face, which I had kissed with such distant lust, almost concealed its pride of conquest, but the thrust of her predatory jaw hid nothing.

'Yeah, but he needn't have mucked around at the election.'

'What do you mean?'

'He needn't have destroyed the ballot papers. I know all about it.'

'Well, he overdoes things. Still, it was a laugh.'

'Who was with you?'

'Saint, Fergus and me. When Jenkin wasn't looking we just burned about twenty-five ballot papers.'

'Jenkin suspected something.'

'That's the whole joke. No one can prove it, unless we tell them.'

'Yeah,' I said, 'that is the joke.'

'What?' She suddenly sounded worried. I hoped the tape was running.

The doe-eyed Syrian boy, with his head slanted back and his lips parted slightly to reveal dazzling white teeth, stared at the camera. Naked but for a loincloth, his thin muscular frame was berry-brown and his legs were long and smooth.

'Was he good, Drippy?' asked Jesse, pointing at the photograph, which was next to one of a Scottish castle on a hilltop.

'The Macduff-Swittles used to own the whole of Earlshire but we're down to the last four farms now,' explained Drippy, standing proudly in his Turkish pantaloons in his room in Cadaffi College. 'And that's my friend Abdul. I don't know if he was good, Jeshie, but wasn't he noble?'

Syssons, with a Palestinian *keffiyeh* wrapped round his neck, was lying on a beanbag in the corner while Francis, a red-haired boy with a very pale face, who was the King of the Catholic Mafia, sat upright in a chair by Drippy's desk.

'Well, Wourke,' said Drippy, lisp and all, 'what have you got for me?'

'Play this tape,' I said and I handed it to him. He put it in the cassette player.

'I hope it's nothing to do with Darling's Baby Eaters,' said Barry in a rare joke.

'Just listen,' said Babylon.

The tape came on and played my conversation with Sally Gilpin from the night before. Babylon turned off the tape. The room was silent.

'So the tables are turned,' said Drippy.

'They were fools, but it goes to show what compromisers, what scum all you Tories are. No principle in any of you.' Syssons got up and walked to the window. He threw it open and stared out at the spires and rooftops of Cadaffi, feeling sick and disgusted with the *realpolitik* that had made Fox his ally.

None of them understood that there were real questions of right and wrong out there. He wrapped the *keffiyeh* tighter round his neck and remembered the day he had seen a TV documentary about Israel's attack on Lebanon: Israeli soldiers with murderous American M-16s shooting at Palestinian freedom fighters with their Kalashnikovs, the guns of freedom. He had walked into his mother's kitchen and spotted that her tablecloth was in fact a *keffiyeh*. He had peeled it off the table and wrapped it round his neck. He still wore it.

'These tapes are already in the hands of Fleet Street,' said Jesse victoriously.

'And the Steward of the Union, the Reverend Jenkin,' I added.

'It's quite a story. There's a touch of irony. "Fox destroyed by malice." You are clever boys. I'll publish it tomorrow. Can I interview you both?' Drippy was flushed. It was quite a scoop. 'You crafty little Hebrew,' he said to Jesse.

'It is quite extraordinary the corruption that goes on,' said Francis vaguely. 'Look at the Vatican.'

'I hear that you are a male Mata Hari,' said Dr Kodell without opening his mouth, but with unusual relish. I wondered if perhaps Professor Belgrano had died, or Kodell had finished his *chef d'oeuvre*.

'I do not know what you mean, Dr Kodell.'

'Dr Tombs and I were most worried. So was the Professor. Even old Belgrano was upset. We thought you were victims of an unjust, but competent Inquisition. I witnessed the scene in the Chamber.'

'It was horrible.'

'I thought Nero and yourself were rather passive. Babylon was most impressive.'

'He saved the day. And now he is organizing his debating carnival against Oxford to crown it all.'

'He is a real Babylon.' He had the snobbery of the historian for his period. To Kodell, the great families of nineteenth-century finance and industry were the true aristocracy. 'I think the whole taping concept was brilliant. Burgess and Maclean would never have thought of it, but Philby would have done it even better.'

'How do you know that?'

'Kim used to spend long nights drinking together with the Professor, but no matter how much he drank, Philby never gave away a thing in twenty-five years. The Professor knew Philby terribly well.'

'How well?'

'Terribly well.' He did not change his expression.

'Is your book on the industrial revolution finished yet, Dr Kodell?' He was writing a new book about how the lower

143

classes 'aped' their social superiors at the time of the creation of modern Britain. This explained his love of the 1980s.

'Almost.' He waited a moment for effect and then said modestly, 'I have stumbled on the foundations of the sexual liberation of women.'

I gasped and he half-smiled, proudly. 'Quite by chance, I have realized that the mechanical rhythm of the factories brought many working-class women to their first orgasms, which their insensitive gin-drinking husbands had been unable to give them.'

'It is a discovery that will change the way the whole of twentieth-century social history is written,' I said dutifully.

'Two hundred years before the sixties, working-class women were having orgasms from the movement of the machinery in those primitive assembly lines. I imagine that, but for the roar of the machinery, those factories would have been filled with the gasps of orgasmic women.'

'What a discovery!' I said. 'It could alter feminism.'

He nodded gravely, confident that it would win him the Chair he so obviously deserved.

'The only reason I approve of feminism is that it's greatly improved the standard of modern pornography,' he said. 'What did you do with the tapes?' he asked, returning to earth from the orgasmic cries that had turned the industrial revolution into the source of his most vivid sexual fantasy.

'We made copies – we sent ten down to London, two to Tory Head Office and the rest to people who had covered the trial, and we gave it to Macduff-Swittle. Fergus Fox will never even be an MP,' I said triumphantly. 'He is politically destroyed now and for ever.'

'Deadly,' said Dr Kodell approvingly.

15

'Sir John, we at Augustus could imagine no finer honour in our thousand-year history than to have our new science labs named the Nelson Laboratories,' said Professor Belgrano.

'Hmmm,' said Nelson.

'At Saint Cadaffi's, the new Mandela Women's Centre is in desperate need of funds. How delighted . . .'

'Great idea,' bounced in Max.

'And at Hytlerhouse, the Quisling Building is in desperate need of repair, as your son will bear witness, as a typical Hytlerhousian . . .'

The wealthy may have no friends but they are never alone. Sir John Nelson was in Cambridge to visit his beloved son and heir, Matthew. Max Bright had advised him that in order to avoid revolution, the rich traditionally gave some money away. Naturally, Nelson did not take kindly to giving anything away until Max suggested using the money to build a grand edifice that would for ever bear the great name of Nelson. What better place to build this eternal monument than Cambridge, where the son and heir was studying?

At once, Bright's awesome publicity machine rolled into action. The papers were awash with tales of how the man who was rebuilding London was about to donate a million, or 100 million, or 50 million (the exact number varied – the *Daily Claret* said a million while the *Daily Materialist* estimated 20 million; the *Blue Tit*, which lied when it did not guess, decided on 150 million) 'to give to the people of Britain a new educational institution as part of Cambridge University, where Sir John's son Matthew, aged twenty-one, is reading geography. Sir John is to visit Cambridge to discuss the details of his donation with the authorities during the last weeks of the Lent Term. Sir John, who owns houses in London, Paris and Mustique, is estimated to be worth . . .' (to quote the *Daily Materialist*).

The meeting with the dons of Cambridge ended without so much as a complete word from Nelson, who was singularly unimpressed with their grovelling. He had not listened to much of the discussion, leaving Max to manage the details. His bid would require giving enough money away without wasting more on these overfed and under-worked professional beggars, concluded the tycoon.

'They've never worked a day in their lives,' he grumbled to Max.

He set off down King's Parade, followed by Max and PC Smart with his bodyguards – and a gaggle of press men. Matthew and I walked at the back of the procession. The locals and the undergraduates on the streets stood watching as the Roman head they all knew so well passed by them.

'That's John Nelson come to give a new college,' they whispered. 'God, that guy's rich. What a life-style, but he looks pretty ordinary, doesn't he?'

Barry Syssons led a small Cambridge Left commando, who stood beside a banner which announced in scrawled brush marks: 'NELSON FASCIST DESTROYER OF WORKERS' RIGHTS.'

Finally Nelson arrived at Matthew's rooms at Hytlerhouse and sat down awkwardly on the edge of his son's bed. Max threw himself into a chair and crossed his legs, revealing his pink fluorescent socks. He could see that Cambridge had a certain grandeur, though he thought it needed more colour – like his office.

'That was a gr-r-r-eat performance, John boy,' he said to Nelson, who shivered at his bonhomie. 'The PM will notice and She will love it – self-help, self-improvement, do-it-y'self values. Yes, I mentioned it to her myself this morning when we had our daily tête-à-tête' (pronounced tederted) 'that the middle-of-the-road Bs and B2s, teachers, Greens, social workers and ex-Liberals with two kids and one car will be impressed.'

'Good.' Nelson was hunched up on the bed, but his eyes

saw only the balance sheets of Universal Imperial rising up before him in a pillar of golden numbers. At last the dons were gone, and Matthew, Babylon and myself stood at the door watching the chirpy adman and the morose mogul. 'So we decided to make a visit to call on you, Matthew.'

'Thank you, Dad,' said Matthew, delighted to be noticed after being ignored since his father's helicopter had hovered low over the towers of Cambridge and then landed in the Great Court of Caddafi College.

'Y' next move has gotta be the Scottish castle. Sure, it's an old chestnut, but it always works . . .'

'Max, I have enough houses,' said Nelson.

'It's not to live in,' explained the tireless Max. 'Scottish castles are great British institutions, loved by old age pensioners or first-time house buyers as much as by garage mechanics and dukes, but really they are loved by the City. They don't yet trust you, right?'

Nelson nodded, suddenly Nelson the deal maker – lithe and sharp.

'They trust people with castles in Scotland. If you buy a real historical gem which has fallen into ruin and then renovate it out of love for ye olde England, I'll place the story in the *Daily Materialist* with a shot of you in tweeds and the City will love you. They will say, "We may not know who his grandfather is but he appreciates history and class so we will lend him money and buy his shares."'

'Good. Do you have one in mind?' asked the man of few words but many pennies.

'Bonnie Prince Charlie's castle is on the market for twenty grand. It'll cost twenty grand to renovate enough rooms for a feature in the *Materialist*. So for forty grand, the Monopolies Commission will let you take over anything within reason and opposition to your peerage in the year-end honours will disappear.'

'Thank you, Max.' The cockatoo grinned at his own ingenuity. Nelson turned towards me. 'Will we see you this holidays, um . . . er . . .?'

'Joseph,' said Max with tact for which I was grateful.

147

Matthew was pleased that his father could not remember my name.

'Yes, of course. Joseph,' added Nelson.

'I'll be working with Max.'

'There is a lot of work to do. Work never hurt anyone and look what it brings.' He paused. 'It is time to go, Max. Goodbye, Jesse. Goodbye, Matthew. Work hard, Matthew.'

'Goodbye, Dad.'

'We are winning the world,' announced Babylon to Darling and Morganthau from his table in Intrigues. 'Tonight will top it all. What a partnership, Joe.'

'Is your speech done?'

'Who needs a speech? I've never written a speech in my life and I'm not going to start today.'

'Have you seen the papers,' asked Morganthau, with cream stuck to the metal grids on his teeth, 'about Nelson and how he visited his son and his young protégé, one Joseph Rourke? Your friend Max obviously likes you. I'll read this one. It's from some glossy magazine for the successful, self-assured and attractive 1980s woman: "Joe Rourke is twenty-one years old with handsome, satanic looks, curly auburn hair, and he is breaking hearts up at a Cambridge filled with a new generation of young Thatcherite heroes. He is the protégé of Max Bright, the PR man to everyone from Sir John Nelson to the Prime Minister Herself. 'Success need not hurt people,' he says in his deep voice with its now faint accent. Last week, Joe walked with Nelson and Max Bright down Cambridge's romantic King's Parade, populated with creatures out of Brideshead, where the men are thin, wealthy and elegant and the women are pale, with painted lips, wearing torn Yves Saint Laurent. Rourke is one of the Jesse Babylon set . . ."'

'Poor you, Joe. Shit, man, once the press are after you, you're dead,' said Darling. 'Look at my uncle – the gossip columnists won't leave him alone. Those *paparazzi* make Angus's life hell – and as for Ru Bonham-Carter, he can hardly talk to a chick without the *paparazzi* getting pictures of him. The bastards.'

'I don't mind a bit of the press,' I said.

This upset Darling: 'Where you come from, you might think it's clever getting in the gossip columns, but you'll learn that people of class know that all publicity is bad. Look what Ru goes through as punishment for his talent.'

Darling rose and disappeared into the street for the sake of his poor rich famous friends. 'Excuse me, I've gotta talk to my stockbroker. The market's goin' through the goddamn roof.'

'So tonight of all nights, tonight is our night,' said Jesse almost quietly. Like any good actor, he knew when to take his bow, so he walked out into the street, where he bumped into Matt Nelson and then Syssons.

Jo Yarborough emerged out of the market-place, carrying a handful of shopping-bags, and made a beeline for him. Drippy, Kick and Emma were around him suddenly and he was the centre of them, walking through them with his legs kicking forward and his monkey face grinning like a wicked clown.

Elliot and I watched through the window of Intrigues, sipping our *cappuccinos* with the waitress standing beside our table.

'What am I compared to you and him?' said Elliot's rich voice. He sat there in his tweed jacket, his corduroy trousers and his brown brogue shoes. 'You are already with Bright and Babylon, the next President of the Union, the star, look at him but what am I? I am nothing. I don't belong here – I am American in London and English in America, and everywhere, I am a Jew, an ugly Yid. Look how at ease Jesse is with his body. If only I had some money and an old house in Bankingshire.'

'But you're an American Jew.'

'I am far more at home in the salons of Vienna and the cafés of Paris than the ghettos of Poland.'

Babylon paraded through the streets outside, kissing the cheeks of girls who admired him with luminous eyes and patting boys on the back who wished they possessed his grace and his abandon – as I did. Our coffees were cold before he disappeared from our view.

The debate was Babylon's debate and the Chamber, which was filled to the point of bursting, awaited Babylon's entrance like Westminster Abbey before the Coronation of a beloved young king.

On one side of the Chamber were the familiar faces of Cambridge and on the other the strangers from Oxford, dressed in a carnival of silly hats and striped blazers, full of the boorish competitiveness that rages between two such similar institutions. I stood at the door, listening to the ebb and flow of the sound of the crowd, then Drippy slipped in beside me.

'Jesse must be pleased with this,' I said.

'Oxford hate Babylon. They are dwunk and they are going to destwoy him. You wait,' he lisped with an unattractive grin.

'Why are they so drunk?'

'Because Fergus, Barry and I spent £500 on drinks for the two busloads coming from Oxford.'

'Poor Jesse.'

'His race is used to suffering.'

The doors were thrown open. Everyone went silent for a moment. The Oxford army blew their whistles, threw rolls of tissue paper in the air and fired water pistols, but it was a false alarm: three bedraggled *paparazzi* from London crept in and crouched near the door, heavy with constellations of cameras and lights. They were followed by the well-connected, heavily oiled gossip columnist of the *Daily Materialist*, dressed in a suavely cut double-breasted suit: in his tasselled new loafers he stepped over the spectators sitting on the floor to reach his reserved seat at the front.

Barry Syssons and his band of black-clad Grim Reapers, with their 'Kill the Rich' badges, sat at the front. They made no effort to hide their repulsion for the beautifully suited social columnist of Britain's most conservative tabloid as he stepped over them, trying not to scratch or soil his peerless shoes on their donkey jackets and badges.

Worse, the perpetually tanned secretaries from the typing school arrived in their pastels and coloured pullovers and sat on the floor beside Syssons. A wave of healthy lust swept the Chamber as the excited girls blushed a vivid British red. The persons of the Cambridge Left protested at the girls' multicoloured membership of the upper middle class by turning away. The well-fed and tanned nymphets for their part wondered who on earth these grim ruffians could be and decided that they must be townies, since no undergraduate could possibly look so peculiar. They soon turned their attention to the Roaring Ruperts from glamorous Oxford: they all knew someone from Oxford. Their mothers had told them it was a must.

Among the Cambridge benches, while Party-Jones and Yarborough worried about the attractiveness of the secretaries, Kick's ultrarays scanned the scene, appreciating these subtleties and searching, always searching for the winner of all winners.

Babylon appeared in the doorway, with the half doors swinging behind him. Scarlet satin boots reached his thighs like Rupert of Hentzau, and from his belted waist to his backcombed whirlwind of hair, jewels and leather tingled and crooned as he strode slowly over Syssons's disgusted puritans and the fascinated secretaries, who were crammed together like sardines in the walkway. Oxford watched this exotic highwayman with his eyeshadow and his flying cuffs as if he was not English, not man, not woman but some devilish showman in an oriental circus.

He waited at the dispatch box, glancing languidly from side to side, catching eyes, and at last the mumble that had greeted his entrance died away into a victorious silence. Even Oxford, with £500 worth of whisky in their veins, were confused by this show of confidence. A crazy girl from Lady Grantham College ran up to him and kissed him on the lips. Never one to miss an opportunity, even in front of a thousand people, his hand was at once behind her neck and they were kissing like lovers. Suddenly she broke off and rushed back, wet-mouthed, to her seat.

Babylon the actor-manager enjoyed his triumph for too long. His smile laughed at everyone in the way a so-called artist might laugh when he has sold a pile of bricks to the National Gallery for a million pounds. By the time he at last sat down, Oxford was firing its water pistols and yelling slogans.

While President Nero shouted 'Order', Babylon was up on his feet, revelling in the trouble he himself had fermented, to lead Cambridge's defence, while the first speakers struggled pathetically to be heard. Babylon picked a quartet of giants, including Darling, who stood an athletic six foot two, and he stood in front of them with a mad dash in his eyes, answering every outrage with something fouler. He was a windmill of obscenities and flying jewellery, laughing, waving at friends, pointing out troublemakers. He led his giants up through the gangway to seize one troublemaker, who they lifted up and threw physically out of the Chamber. Jesse always claimed that when he was excited his blood turned to red wine, and he now returned to the Chamber like a drug-crazed buccaneer.

When it was his turn to speak, everything had gone too far to stop. As Oxford became drunker, the Cambridge contingent became more sober, until they were just waxworks watching a mad show. Babylon was not the first, nor the last, leader to believe that the man who created the volcano can control it. He had dared his own success to destroy itself and he had succeeded.

'Ladies and Gentlemen . . .' he began, but he got no further. A crew of gin-crazed boaties leapt at him across the Chamber. Babylon's men ran to stop them, but they had already reached Jesse, who was not exactly a streetfighter. Matt Nelson and I jumped up to join them. One of the boaties tried to head-butt Darling, who valued his face more than any Hockney. Darling threw him a right hook that bloodied his mouth and sent him flying back on to the shocked gossip columnist, who had once written a whole column on the woman who had poured wine over Kenneth Trumply. Now this really was a story, though his suit had been speckled with beer and blood.

The biggest of the boaties headed for me. I stopped him in his tracks with a swing shot to the point of his chin that almost broke my knuckles. Matt and Jesse were struggling with the boatie whom Jesse had earlier thrown out. Darling twisted him into a half-nelson and then propelled him like a ball down a bowling alley into one of the benches.

Babylon stood shaken and breathless, with his hands on his hips and sweat on his face. He raised his hand and to everyone's surprise he won a silence. He waved a bejewelled hand in the Oxford direction as if to say, 'You see, they are in the palm of my hand,' but they were not. The photographers snapped away, their clicking the only sound. He never started his speech. Already, party foam and water rained down on him.

'Why are you a poof?'

'Are you really Cambridge's best speaker?'

'Why are you wearing jewellery?'

'Could you do everyone a favour and sit down?'

The questions were shouted out one after another until they were an unanswerable barrage, and he stood up there like an undergraduate Gordon of Khartoum, waiting patiently for the Mahdi's spear to end it all.

'Gentlemen of Oxford, go fuck yourselves,' he said very clearly, and then we walked to the door, while Cambridge watched his back sadly. Oxford swarmed like maddened hornets. It was almost three years since I had first seen the master speak, and now the swinging saloon doors shut behind his curly fair hair, covered in the party foam, and he was gone.

Babylon was standing in the Union bar smiling weakly like Laurel in the Laurel and Hardy films. There was make-up running down his face. Embarrassed friends who had shaken his hand after so many triumphs passed without daring to catch his blue bloodshot eyes. Strangely, they greeted me with a friendliness they had once saved for him. Girls whom I had only met with Babylon kissed me on the lips as if I had won the Battle of Britain. The passive spectators were as guilty of cowardice as they were of the crime itself. They had betrayed him with their passivity, and all could feel his blood still hot on the daggers hidden wet in their cloaks.

At first, I admired the way he took it all, and then I realized he was enjoying this his finest scene: Babylon as Sydney Carton going to his death with head held high.

'This is my lying in state,' he said.

Fergus Fox was the last to pass us. Fox paused for a moment in front of Babylon, as one might stand before an old tombstone to read its long-forgotten name. He said nothing, for he himself was one of the dead and Babylon was proud to have been his slayer. Fox shook my hand. He smiled at me with great indulgence, nodding his head.

'Well, well,' came the sing-song Celtic drawl. 'That changes everything. Now Joe Rourke will be President of the Union in our last term. How about that?' And he disappeared into the crowd, leaving the bagpipe tune of his words hanging in the air.

Babylon did not come home to King's Parade that night. Long after midnight, the door opened for a second, casting a pencil-thin line of light across my face for just long enough to wake me.

The door clicked shut but there was no sound. Suddenly I was very wide awake. I could hear the turning spokes of a bicycle as it was wheeled along the cobblestones under my window. I listened to the drip of water falling from a pipe near the roof and the single note it made as it hit the pavement below. Then I heard the breathing and the softest rustle of clothes until there was sweat on my forehead and I was afraid.

Her wide wet lips descended on my mouth with the taste of brazen lust and good claret. She pulled back the curtain and a bright half light revealed the grey outline of Scrubber sitting on the edge of the bed, smiling broadly and proudly as she watched me. We looked at each other for what seemed a long time. Then she threw one leg over me and in one movement her dress was pulled up high over her hips and her loins were above my face, stinking deliciously with the wealth of a woman's body, filling the room with her irresistible pungent odour. She wore no underwear. I reached around her buttocks and pulled her down to my face. The insides of her thighs glistened in the moonlight, slippery with her own excitement.

She rose and fell like an ocean-going liner, with a squall at sea, all hands on deck and no captain on the bridge. The funnels were pumping smoke into the wind and the engineers were working like a chain gang in the stinking bowels of the ship, their bodies covered in sweat, shovelling coal into the giant ship's furnaces to fuel her as she sliced through turbulent seas.

When she kissed me, my whole face tasted of her and she licked my lips, my chin, my cheeks so as not to miss her own glissando. After it all, when she was so open that my whole hand was inside her cauldron and she was pouring liquor out of her sopping chambers, leaving a trail to celebrate her coming to me, Fox's words came to me again. 'That changes everything.'

Then Scrubber said, 'Everything will be different now. You'll have to run for President.'

She worked her way down my body. I could see her eyes were shut. Could I betray him? The best, the only, the most entertaining friend I had ever known – could I turn on him now when he was humiliated? I could win, for who could beat me? I cannot. I will not do it. Suddenly, Scrubber's eyes were open and bright and staring up at me: I knew there and then that I could stand against him, I would stand and I would win. I could do anything I chose to do. And I would.

'Why did you come?'

'Because I wanted you,' she said, her face very close to mine and an all-enveloping smell around her of both of us, the smell of harbours, salt and sweat.

'If Babylon had triumphed at the debate, you would have gone to his room tonight, wouldn't you?' I knew the answer already, but I did not mind. I was glad she had come to mine.

'Sherry?'

'Thank you, Dr Kodell.' The offer was unprecedented. I was either to be expelled or given a scholarship. Kodell fetched the drink with his brothel creepers never leaving the carpet, as if he had wheels on them. He would live for ever, I decided, for he ate well in college, drank little, rarely left his chair and walked without his feet ever leaving the ground.

'I was sorry to hear about the Babylon débâcle. It has been said it was a case of hubris.'

'It has been said, but not by me.'

'I am watching you . . .'

'Thank you, Dr Kodell.'

'. . . expecting great things. You see, you are being tested.'

'We are friends, you know.'

'Cambridge is for friends . . .'

'That's just it.'

'. . . but it is also the key to the Kingdom.'

'Cambridge is famous for its friendships. Here friends mean something.'

'Success brings more friends than anything.'

'But not Jesse . . .'

'He would probably respect you if you stood.'

'And hate me.'

'It is your time. You are the man of the moment. The Day personified. Do not fail!' he said, with his eyelids heavy. 'You have two days to decide.'

'How do you see this in the context of the rise of the Babylon family?' He sadly lifted one tired eyebrow, as if he was seeing families rise and fall before his weary eyes.

'Elites come and go.'

'I shan't stand.' The sleepy eyes wheeled around to face me like gun-turrets.

'Where does history start for you?' he asked.

'1917.'

'It is your October.'

Nero cornered me in my room. He sat on my desk and placed his hands with their short pink fingers on the table as if to make his point clearer.

'You must not run. It is not the thing.'

'I just don't know. Is he going to run?'

'Not if you do.'

'But he might not win . . .'

'Winning. Winning. He was born to sit in that chair.'

'That is a damned good reason for him not to.' Not one of

156

my allies supported me, but the outsider could not be surprised at that.

'I don't mean born as in class. I just mean that he was made to sit in that chair.'

'You did mean it like that.'

A cruel swinish turn came to his eyes. 'Don't take out the chip on your shoulder on Jesse Babylon.'

'If he was made to be President, he wouldn't have fucked up his speech.'

'But Joe, imagine him up there in the President's chair. You can see him, can't you?' He was right, for I would never sit as easy in that chair as Jesse Babylon would.

Even the Reverend Jenkin wanted to dissuade me. He put his arm through mine while I was on my way to Augustus, so that I could not escape.

'Let's walk around my church,' he ordered, like a castrated sergeant-major. He did not beat around the bush. He took off his broad-rimmed black hat, straightened his glasses, pushed back his hair, adjusted his black plus-fours and began: 'I shan't mention Judas, since he has become something of a cliché. In fact, Jesse thinks he was a Jewish freedom fighter and approves of him. Anyway, let me tell you that all this Thatcherite nonsense of the last few years doesn't change the fact that some people are prepared to rule and lead by birth and blood and education. Jesse Babylon is one such person.'

'I thought you didn't like Jews.'

'The fact that most Jews are ghastly has no bearing here. He comes from a princely family, not from some sort of tailor's shop in Poland. Don't worry, I am not born to rule myself. I have many friends from great families, it is true, though I hate to talk about it, but since you force me, I am happy to tell you that Princess Distilla is a close, darling friend. In fact, she is by far the sexiest of the royal family. Anyway, I was saying that these days people have somehow forgotten their place. I know mine and all I say is that you should know yours.'

He replaced his black broad-rimmed hat, raised it to me,

and waddled off into the church. The skinheads who lay on the bench by the church drinking beer watched him go quizzically. If God is like that man, thought the girl, then he is not our God.

There is an archway in the middle of the wide white building at right angles with King's Chapel. Babylon and I faced one another in this archway, whence we could see the happy-go-lucky thoroughfare of King's Parade and, in the opposite direction, the river. It was dusk the day after the debate, though it seemed later. There was no better place and no finer time to discuss whose name would be in the nominations book the next day. Though I had dreaded the scene, Babylon was smiling in the grey light, for he had always loved drama and he had chosen this stage for this act.

'PROFESSOR DINOSAURUS DIED THIS YEAR 1732 – A LEADER AND TEACHER WHOSE WISDOM AND GENIUS WILL NOT ONLY BE REMEMBERED BY THE MANY WHO KNEW HIM BUT WILL ALSO BE KNOWN FOR EVER BY ALL GENERATIONS TO COME.' Jesse read out the inscription that lay on the floor of the arch. We looked at one another and said together, 'Ozymandias.' Babylon recited the poem perfectly, as if he had planned every moment.

'My name is Ozymandias, king of kings. Look on my works, ye Mighty, and despair . . . Nothing beside remains. Round the decay of that colossal wreck, boundless and bare, the lone and level sands stretch far away.'

'So things pass. Nothing is permanent.'

'You have luck, Joe. We all know that you have the most self-fulfilling luck. Where did you learn to be so lucky? When you meet someone, you are so polite, you say the perfect thing and they like you. People notice you but not too much. You are good-looking without special features. When you speak, everyone agrees you're good. And now this. You have all the luck in the world.' I realized that in Babylon's eyes this was a roll-call of mediocrity, but how could I argue? He spoke better, and when he spoke, even in ordinary conversation, he spoke creatively and differently and brilliantly. Babylon had an exuberance that invited the world into his magical castle, but he never even let down the drawbridge. 'Anyway, you had better run . . . run with your luck. You never know when it might end.'

He turned and walked back towards the Cam. It was almost dark as I watched him go. He stood staring into the river for a moment and then he went over the bridge and out of sight.

16

Cambridge that summer was a circus where the master of ceremonies had lost control. The audience was no longer sure what was play and what was real. Even we actors on the stage could not be sure where the game ended and where serious things began.

When the trapeze artist lost his balance, tripped and hurtled to the ground, the red-nosed clowns laughed and played the fool beside the shattered body. When the fire-eater caught fire and was burning to death in front of the audience, mothers pointed it out to their children, saying, 'Look at that. Isn't it clever?' The children roared with delight, until all that was left of the fire-eater was a smoking pile of ashes and tangled cloth. It had to be all right. After all, this was Cambridge, and Cambridge was a circus.

Matthew Nelson's garden party was the first act of our last summer in Cambridge. Hytlerhouse's luxuriant Lebens-raum Gardens were filled with boxes of glasses and Pimms bottles, bought in bulk at low prices from Nelson's global drinks subsidiary. In the middle of the empty green gardens, Matt, Darling and Francis were mixing the drinks with lemonade. Matt poured a bottle of sherry into the bowl too.

'We'll get everyone stoned,' he said simply, and the way he said 'stoned' sounded American. Matthew possessed the easy social graces often found in the children of shy and awkward parents. His hair had grown long, he had a faint tan and he looked more like Julius Caesar than ever. He wore a collarless shirt with a baseball jacket on top of it.

'Are you sure it is right to pickle the drink? Isn't it rather playing a trick on our friends?' Francis spoke very slowly, like a religious affairs correspondent on the radio. His face was pale. The afternoon sun made it paler. He wore a cream cricket jersey and a neck scarf. I didn't know him well. He was Catholic and troubled – that was all I knew.

'Have a drink,' said Darling, handing me one. There were all sorts of fruit in it. The garden was still quite empty. 'No one is here yet, but I can tell you – everyone, ya everyone, will be here soon enough. Ru Bonham-Cavendish is coming, if they let him out of the rehearsals for his new movie. He's playing a young aristocrat from the thirties. Some actor.'

'Has he played any other part?'

'Look, he's got a wide range. He played an Old Etonian at Oxford in the forties in his first movie, so this part is completely different.'

'Is your Dad coming?' I asked Matt.

'Him and Max, I think. If they have time. I'm not quite sure, but I hope so.'

'I hear your old man's just bought a little Hockney for a couple of smackers,' Darling began again . . .

I swigged down my drink. He filled it up again. I swilled it coolly and sweetly in my throat. I wandered off and bumped straight into the Reverend Jenkin, who put his arm through mine.

'Aha!' He was drunk already. 'Aha, Mr President of the Union. Hurrah for the great team that has sent the stinking, yelping proles back to their holes. I was dining the other day with the Vice-Chancellor. Sweet little man. Doesn't know how to behave, of course. I was telling him how after Nero we thought it would be Jesse, but we didn't mind you. I called it the Apostolic Succession and he rather liked that.'

The garden was slowly filling up. The guests formed a collage, with the rich grass speckled with white blazers and pink faces.

'You know, friendships get lost in May Week . . .' said Jenkin, without elaborating. 'I am going to introduce you to the Margrave.'

'The Margrave of what?'

'Never you mind.' He led me up to the Margrave and introduced us.

'Joseph Rourke, I am delighted to make your acquaintance

at last,' declaimed the Margrave, like a bad Shakespearian actor. He must have weighed about seventeen stone. His girth was held in a three-piece pinstriped suit. His feet were so large that his shoes were specially made for him. I recognized him at once: he had been at the Hunt, with his trademark briefcase and umbrella.

He saw me looking him up and down. 'My suits are made for me in London Town. I relish each measuring.'

'Do you live in Cambridge?'

'Yes, I teach. I have followed your career in the Union with great mirth and that of your friend Mr Babylon.'

'You follow politics?'

'Margaret – the tabloids insist on calling her Maggie – is a close friend; so I dabble. I must say these occasions take me back to my schooldays at Eton . . .'

Jenkin, who was still with us, winked obviously and asked, 'What, Margrave, was your favourite sport at Eton?'

'When we were at Eton we used to do favours to one another that you in the younger generation, I believe, call blow jobs.'

Babylon arrived with both Emma and Kick in tow. He was on top of the world, and seemed to have forgotten the Union in the pleasures of the flesh. He threw down his Pimmses quicker than they could be filled up. Elliot and Jesse dragged me away from the Margrave and into the gardens.

'Have you been talking to the Margrave?'

'He was telling me about his schooldays,' I told them. They had asked the question as one. They were both laughing and slapping their thighs.

'Has he told you about the favours?' bubbled Elliot.

'Yes.'

'And what about the sailors in America?' said Jesse.

'Or has he shown you the inside of his briefcase? All it has in it is a bottle of vodka and a gay porn mag called *Nazi Boys and Tendercocks*.'

'What does he do for a living?'

'Nothing. He just walks up and down King's Parade looking for rough trade.' Elliot was in his element: the Margrave could have been a product of his imagination. Except it was all part of the circus.

The party was booming. Scrubber had appeared and was filling our glasses out of a jug. In the process she managed to pour most of it all over us, but we didn't care. We were feeling tops.

The garden was no longer a tranquil backwater. It was alive. There was no music, but couples were dancing to their own: some red-haired girl had stolen the Reverend's hat and the Margrave was drinking neat vodka out of a bottle that, sure enough, was stored in his briefcase.

'I am a don,' he told me as he opened the case. He did not notice the *Nazi Boys and Tendercocks* being stolen by the warm wind and carried away across the gardens, revealing pictures of moustachioed young men in leather boots. The usual rugby bores were singing songs that went 'Roll her over in the clover . . .' Nelson was filling up the glasses.

The Condor was on tour through the chaos, kissing a boy here, greeting a girl there, laughing with one group, earnestly nodding her head at another. But everywhere eyes followed her. She was not a natural. She was trained to be the ultimate social Hoover. All the same, she was a hell of a pleasure to watch. She had a talent for walking. Her pyjamas were the sort karate men wear. When the wind blew, she was a sail on a sailing boat. As she passed she let her hair blow in my face. It was fine hair. I wanted to open my mouth and bite it. But she just giggled, touched my face for a second and went on her way.

Darling and Prince Angus were standing with a leather-jacketed, tanned young man. Long thin blond hair hung rather deliberately over his perfect face from an immaculate centre parting. This was the great actor – Rupert. Darling rushed up to me.

'I'm real worried about the *paparazzi*. Ru wants a quiet day and so do I. Shit, is that a photographer?' Sure enough, there was an unmistakable photographer standing by the garden gate. 'I'd better hide. Last thing I want is my shot in any of those rags.' The photographer paid no attention to Darling.

In the distance, we heard the whirr of a helicopter landing. Throughout the garden, a shiver of self-congratulation was almost visible, for Sir John Nelson was coming to the party.

'Have you heard, he's bought Bonnie Prince Charlie's castle?' boomed Yarborough.

'He's a real lover of history,' said Camilla, who had read the *Daily Materialist*.

'How d'you know?'

'Some friends of Daddy's know Nelson very well,' she lied, keen to show that she did not desperately scour the *Materialist* every day for news of the rich and overbred.

'Bought Nelson shares at 270. Now they're 880. Marvellous,' Nero was telling Francis. 'The markets are raging. Thanks to Nelson, much of it. What can he take over next – Universal Imperial? Too big even for him. Never seen a market like it. More Pimms, please . . .'

Nelson arrived at the garden gate in his sober pinstriped suit, with the grinning Bright beside him in a baggy white suit and a red bowtie. The photographer started clicking, after a wink from Max. Bright surveyed the garden, social-Hoovered the crowd and headed for Prince Angus, who was shepherded by the irrepressible Max to Nelson's side. The photographer took shots of 'Philanthropist and tycoon Sir John Nelson chatting to his old friend H.R.H. Prince Angus at his son's garden party . . .'

Poor Ru, the famous actor, and Darling stood awaiting some attention. ('Ru specially asked to be incognito today, so I had a word with the *Materialist*,' Darling told me later.) Nelson walked tensely through the garden, which parted for him like the Red Sea. All eyes followed him. After he had talked to Matthew for all of a minute, and said to me, 'Big meeting in a couple of weeks', the helicopter whirred into the sky and this god was once again carried away to Olympus.

Soon it was dusk and the party had broken up into lesser parties, hidden on the lawns and in the bushes. Strangely, the noise of all those people was still there, the singing, the clink of glasses, hollow bottles, laughing girls' voices, but the people had become invisible. The Margrave had walked off with his feet pointed outwards, briefcase in one hand and a youth in the other. Emma and Babylon had disappeared.

From one bush we heard Scrubber's distinctive sounds, and sure enough, out she came with Roosevelt Douga, the

Nigerian from Caddafi, who was famous for writing his essays in his Rolls-Royce. His wealth stemmed from a £100 million Red Cross grant, made to help the starving after the Biafran War.

'It's all true what they say about black boys,' Scrubber told the gardens. 'Wow, it's true.' Roosevelt smiled, and his white teeth shone in the light.

Nero and I walked on. A young blonde girl, unmistakably from the secretarial college, emerged from the gardens.

'I know you,' she said to me, ignoring Nero. 'You're President of the Union and I'm a friend of Jesse's.' There was barely a girl in England who did not seem to be a friend of Jesse's.

'I know you. You're Camilla,' I said, guessing her name.

'They're all Camilla to me,' muttered Nero under his breath.

'No,' she said. 'Mandy de Troy. I'm a cousin of Jesse's mother, you see . . .' Nero gasped, for she was a Bankingshire de Troy, descended from Queen Victoria's foreign minister . . .

'Ah,' said that worshipper of Connections as he left us, 'the gilded complexity of it all.'

'I'm very drunk,' she said.

'So much the better. Let's go for a walkabout.'

The air was warm, the girl was lovely, and I did not have a bloody care in the world. She unzipped my trousers. 'Yum, yum,' she said, with such inappropriate tweeness that I wanted to laugh at her. I stroked her hair, stared up at the trees and a darkening sky and smelt the freshly cut grass.

'You're a virtuoso,' I told her.

'What's that?'

'You're at the secretarial.'

'Do you ever have girlfriends who aren't?' she asked.

'You mean do I kiss girls without secretarial diplomas from Cambridge? You must experience all classes of woman to be a man.'

'Not Sharons. Yuck. How could you? They're unspeakable.'

'They're not unspeakable.' I said. 'They simply speak

differently.' She had not noticed my accent, since it was inconceivable to her that any friend of Jesse's could speak anything but King's English.

She came up again laughing and happy, playfully wiping her mouth, as if her lips were smeared with jam.

'I enjoyed my party,' said Francis, 'but I was so distracted.'

'What by?'

'Everything, you know, but Matthew kept expecting his father to come.' That was how we got on to John Nelson again.

'He's getting a peerage, you know.'

'That man is so brazen!'

'His new City in the docklands is historical. The unveiling of a new Rockefeller, a modern Pharaoh.'

'Yes,' said Francis frigidly. 'Mind you, I invested all my money in the market and a lot in Nelson shares. It can only go up, though I am no expert.'

'Don't y' worry about it,' said the waitress, whose hair now resembled Cruella de Ville's bob. 'I've put five hundred quid into the Stock Exchange myself. It's the best fing, innit?'

'I hate money.' Francis ignored her. 'I shall be a Cardinal or an MP.'

'Be both.'

'Mummy will make sure I am one or the other. You're in business already. It's very tawdry, isn't it?'

'Only when you have it already. What does your father do?'

'He makes lentil soup.'

'That's all?'

'That's all.'

'Are you religious?'

'My parents are converts to Catholicism. All converts are religious.'

'Do you go to church a lot?'

'I go to Mass every morning.' He pronounced it 'marse'. It was posher than plain 'mass'. I wondered what he had to confess. He was an exemplary moral person, except for his

166

wanton snobbery. We stared out of the window again. Kick went past in boots and a skirt that showed her knees. Francis put his teacup harshly on the table. Everyone looked up. The waitress asked if anything was wrong. As usual she had the flour hand mark on her skirt.

'The cook must be a pervert,' I said as I showed him. He looked handsome, but his reddish hair hung in his eyes.

'Women are such tarts.'

'So are men,' I said.

'They just play with people.'

'What do you think of Kick?' I asked him. He turned his eyes away. He was wishing she would come back past us. Me too. I wanted to see her knees again.

'Everything,' he said. 'I think everything about her.'

'Buy Nelson Leisure, dalling,' said Dominique d'Elite, the Eurocrat who worked in London for Wallenstein. She was reading the *Materialist*'s famous gossip column. Oh God, she was thinking, the von Howitzers are in it again.

'And buy 20,000 Nelson Leisures,' Jesse added into the phone before he put it down. 'Marvellous girl,' and he kissed the perfectly groomed beauty who lay beside him on the bed, her body just hidden enough by the pink pages of the *Financial News*. She was too disinterested to be English.

'When did Nelson buy that?' I said.

'God knows.' Babylon was beginning to look at his girl as if he wanted me to leave.

'Yesterday,' said the girl.

'With Dominique, you make money by making love.'

'He owns 29.9 per cent,' said the brunette, without looking up from the society gossip column.

'How the hell do you know so much?' I asked her.

'I work for Wallenstein. I am Jesse's *banqueur*,' she pouted, It sounded like 'bonker'.

'What a life,' I said. Babylon's room was a bewildering rubbish dump of share certificates, boxer shorts and female underwear. I was not sure which interested me more.

The summer was spinning. The great British public danced to the music of stock exchanges that would rise for ever. The newspapers every day chronicled the latest success of Sir John Nelson's ambition as if it was a national victory. Every newspaper wrote of nothing but 'exclusivity'.

Britain's sober people were dreaming of 'exclusive' suburbs, cars, houses, designer labels. 1987 was the year when anyone could get rich anyhow, but especially on the people's stock market. According to the newspapers, just about everything was now 'exclusive'. That summer was the season of universal exclusivity. Yet in the Middle East, Khomeini's young Muslim fanatics would die in suicidal attacks for their God. We in 1987's 'exclusive' England could not understand it, for our only God was living. We knew no other.

The girl under the *Financial News* had finished her gossip column and decided it was time to get back to London. She stepped out of bed with a fluid efficiency that somehow allowed me to see things I knew I should not. She dressed in clothes with legendarily exclusive labels that were both luxurious and practical – a *mélange* of wealth and austerity.

'Were you at Cambridge?' I asked.

'Two years ago, then the Sorbonne.' She handed Jesse a dressing-gown and he stepped into it obediently. She found a shirt and took command of his dressing. He meekly put on whatever she suggested.

'And you recommend that we go into the City?'

'Oh, yes,' she said. 'It goes up and up. It hasn't stopped for five years. It is the engine that is driving this country, it is the motor that is propelling America. Oxbridge is the incubator of the City.'

We followed her to her BMW, parked outside Great Gate. She revved the engine. 'The Bull Market has changed the mind of a generation. It has turned a nation into Tories. We have all become optimists. It must go up.' I could not place her accent. It was the tongue of the Eurotrash: Swiss, German or French, tastelessly blended with Manhattan.

Babylon kissed his prophetess goodbye. She swung her curtain of sleek hair to the side of her face.

'*À bientôt,* Dominique,' he said.

'*Bel-ami*,' she said in the superior cosmopolitian way she might have said 'little boy'. 'I'll tell you when to sell.'

As Dominique drove off, with her light hair flying behind her like a wedding train, I suddenly noticed that the skin-heads who sat around all day in the churchyard were walking down King's Parade, with the mohican girl at their head. They watched the car until it was out of sight and then they watched us.

17

'Well?' Nelson spoke only after the silence had become un-
bearable. Even with the air-conditioning on, the conference
room was too hot. All those extra-terrestrial ambitions and
all those tense egos were crammed round this one long table.
There were about fifty people in the room. Behind each of
the leading players sat at least ten assistants. It had a mirror
effect: behind McGill Peabody sat ten other clean-cut, tanned
young bankers; behind the pallid wet-palmed solicitor sat a
veritable tribe of identical rocket scientists.

'Who the hell are all those people?' asked Nelson.

'The Team,' said Peabody religiously. 'The Jocks.'

'Hmmm,' said Nelson, wondering why using American
football slang had become the key to success in Wall Street.

'Why doesn't Wallenstein begin?'

'Alrightee,' sang McGill, the fit, fresh young banker, in
his happy country-club American.

'Is everything in place?'

'Applecart Auchincloss have raised twenty billion in a mez-
zanine financing of equity, loans, notes, NIFFs, MUFFs
and bonds.'

'Are they watertight?' Nelson's words were taut but quiet,
so we all leaned forward each time he spoke.

'We must move by June. Now we're watertight, but
nothing is watertight for ever,' said the voice of Bermuda
shorts, tennis shoes and knickerbockers. 'Alrightee, let's run
with the ball!'

'Thank you for that.' Nelson loathed this type of American
physical keenness. This man is a buffoon, he decided, a real
HYP – Harvard, Yale, Princeton – but unfortunately it was
too late to have Lew Wallenstein take him off the bid.

Bankers behave as if they are right little supermen, thought Sir John, but Wallenstein Inc. had simply asked another bank to raise the money. Hardly a difficult task, since he was borrowing the money at an outrageous rate of 15 per cent. 'What about the Special Fund?'

The nameless management consultant, so young and so together, this mega-bid machine, began: '. . . and Co. have run up a series of programmes for strategies, disposals, long-term resources allocations, and our special Efficiency Unit, as well as your very own Nelson hyper-Extraordinary Team, have been working twenty-five hours a day . . .'

'What about the Special Fund?'

'If you could just pass the ball to me for a mo', my guys at Wallenstein M & A have been putting in not twenty-six hours a day, but a good twenty-six and a half hours a day on this job. They can take the pace and play the game.'

This jolly Yankee backslapping didn't impress Nelson one bit. He banged the table and waited.

The flaccid lawyer and the accountant with his one strand of hair jealously watched the banker and the consultant, who were tanned and cosmopolitan. In their dreams, the lawyers and accountants also worked out in chic gyms, greased their hair back and played tennis every day. As for Nelson, he was outside their experience. He might have been from another planet.

'The Special Fund is being assembled, though not by . . . and Co., but we can say that all the mechanisms are in place. Nominee companies are being set up . . .' The lawyer was as breathless as a thirsty dog at all those brass plates.

The consultant went on . . . 'And everything is ready.'

'As you know, the details are being handled elsewhere by another committee,' said Nelson. 'You are part of the group that is to assist me in the greatest bid this century in this country. We are nearing the launch. At the moment, it is set for June. What about about the Universal's share register?'

'Funds hold 30 per cent, management only 10 per cent and the rest is small shareholders.'

'Any other comments?'

'Alrightee! As the titular leader of the team, I will hold this ball until we are over the touch line. I would like to tell

171

you all – you are all damned fine professionals and I'm proud to have you all on board. I have always played to win, Sir John. I am a pokka playa through and through. The Team is a Winner. Thanks, team.'

'A polo player?' asked Nelson abruptly. 'What the hell has that got to do with it?'

'Pokka, the card game, Sir John.'

'Ah, poker. What of it? I'll play you if you're so good. I played poker with Sydney Operahouse last week and won a million pounds.'

Poker was Nelson's only indulgence. Everyone congratulated him.

The banker explained himself: 'I don't actually play, Sir John, but when I say I am a pokka player, I mean I am a professional and a player, unencumbered by rigid structures and morality.'

'When this is over, I'll have your shirt off your back and win back some of your fees. Meeting is over. Thank you all. I hope you are all poker players. Max and ... um ... er ... please stay behind.'

As usual, the accountant's strand of hair had to be arranged. Each of his team arranged their hair before leaving. The four cases of each of the ten lawyers had to be fitted through the door before we could be alone.

'Gr-r-r-eat meeting,' said Max, who found keeping quiet a terrible strain.

'These bankers and people. Bureaucrats. Civil servants.' Nelson shook his head.

'Yeah, exactly, professionals in ivory towers. I was talking to Her today. She says Confrontation is the only way to win freedom from the institutions, hidden interests, the oligarchies, unions, clubs. The Tory party is full of 'em. She's gr-r-r-eat. I lovva. Talk to Her every day.'

'Good. We are ready to go. Any PR angles?'

'Glenfiddle. Your castle in Scotland. The renovation has created br-r-r-illiant vibes. I was talking to Party-Jones, senior partner of Party and Jones, the leading stockbroker. He is the ultimate stick-in-the-mud and he says to me, "That Nelson, I thought he was a shark, but he really does care

172

about Britain, the traditions. He really wants to learn, look at that castle he bought . . .'' You see, Sir John.'

'Now what?'

'Just before the bid comes, we need another story. Now many of the locals in Scotland are afraid you're gonna fire some of the old retainers on the estate and treat it like a business.'

'Well, I am,' said Nelson.

'No, you're not. Absolu-u-u-tley not! On the day of the bid, I suggest you give every man in Glenfiddle village a free brace of pheasants.'

'Where on earth do I get pheasants?'

'We'll buy 'em from Fortnum's.'

'Max, Fortnum's are the most expensive shop in the country. I have a friend from the old days. Owns a chain of butchers. You can buy them from my man.'

'Gr-r-r-eat, Sir John. Now Joe Rourke is here,' he dropped the name for Nelson.

'How is Cambridge? Down for the day? Good. Now you must hit Operahouse, Goncourt, Hinton and Wallenstein. That'll cover us. They are my friends, you see. Now Wallenstein's a man unlike the clown he sends to our meetings. If you have technical questions, speak to . . .and Co. Good. That's it.'

The mohican girl and her skinheads were walking straight towards me down the wide hot street. The streets of Cambridge seemed wider in the summer. Undergraduates with bottles of wine, sportsmen on their way down to the river and secretaries in short skirts on bicycles filled the streets. The stones appeared to be a lighter colour, and I walked down King's Parade past my house towards Grantchester, where Kick was having her picnic. Nelson's monotonous voice echoed in my ears. The bid really was coming. Twenty billion pounds' worth of bid for the very citadel of British business.

The girl and the skinheads scared me. I found myself sweating. I hoped they would not notice me but they had seen me already. The girl had a scar on her face close to her mouth but lower. She prowled too close to me, so I could smell her, and the men followed, glaring out of hairless skulls like beasts. They walked right down the middle of the street. I could hear the leather in their boots creak so close that sweaty hot day in King's Parade. Which is the truer power, I asked myself, their sort of force or Nelson's?

Babylon turned to me and said in a soft dreamy voice, 'They were young, beautiful and rich. Cambridge was their playground and the world was their oyster. That hot summer, they poured the wine as if the cellars would never run dry and the markets rose as high as the summer sun . . .'

'They thought it would never end. But then the war came.' I finished Babylon's favourite cliché. Prince Angus clapped.

'How funny. How very funny.'

The party was out near Byron's pool on the meadows beside the Cam. The sun was so bright that the river looked like a stream of mercury on this grassy bed of rich thick green. Francis was rubbing cream on to Kick's back. Nero lay in a pair of baggy khaki shorts, like a Victorian explorer, with his bare stomach a fleshy mountain reaching for the sky.

'This time when the war comes, it won't just end the idyll. It'll be Armageddon,' said Francis gloomily.

'There won't even be time for an Armageddon party,' said Nero, who was considering that after the Bomb, all his connections with Influence would be meaningless.

'I've enjoyed every minute,' announced Babylon. 'I couldn't have laughed more or kissed more. I am ready to fuck my maker.'

'Tell me,' came the old BBC voice of Prince Angus, 'when are you going to introduce me to this girl? I could perhaps take her as my partner to the May Ball.'

'Whenever you like, Sir,' said Jesse, whose tales of sexual adventure had at last found favour. 'Perfect for the ball.'

Out in the meadow, the party was a social Bacchanale. Scrubber was being chased by a band of rugger players, who in turn were being followed by a breathless Margrave, who was sweating through his three-piece white suit. The boys caught up with Scrubber and began tearing off her clothes, to her obvious delight. She grabbed the Margrave's umbrella and used the handle to poke playfully at the crotches of her drunk attackers.

Babylon, Angus and his bodyguard looked out at this scene. Babylon wished Scrubber would behave. After all, here was the King's son who wanted to meet her and all she could do was roll in the hay with a crew of repulsively drunk sportsmen. Around the periphery, girls like Yarborough were socially Hoovering for partners for the great May Ball. If only the Prince, if only he were to notice them . . .

'Is she here, this charming girl?' asked the Prince.

'Can't see her, Sir,' lied Jesse, while the rest of us listened as we sunbathed.

'You said she would be here. Have another look around. Is she discreet?'

'Very.'

'By the way, who is that girl?'

'Which one, Sir?' said Jesse innocently.

'The naughty one over there.'

Babylon was miserable. After all his plotting, all the foundations so carefully laid, she had to wreck it like this.

'That girl – who is that girl?'

'Ah, there she is, Sir. Well spotted, Sir. That is Sophie.'

'I could hardly miss her,' said the Prince. Scrubber's legs were covered in mud and one of the rugby players had his hand down her blouse. 'She doesn't look very discreet to me.'

'I can't believe it's her,' said Jesse pathetically. 'It's so uncharacteristic.'

'You must of course be joking, Jesse.'

'Only half joking, Sir.'

'I see,' said Prince Angus.

We lay there in the sun. Mandy the virtuoso lay behind me and I used her soft long thighs as a pillow. Her skin was smooth and cool. I longed to take her into the meadows. Yarborough was talking very loudly with Party-Jones.

'Matt Nelson has bought a GTI turbo with extra lights and a souped-up engine, but I prefer Andrew's BMW. It is blue and has a sun-roof.'

'Cargirls,' Babylon whispered, 'are the lowest form of simpleton – machine snobs.'

'You're such a pervert,' Francis said to Jesse, once Angus and his bodyguard had left. 'All you think of is these disgusting plots.' He sat by the river with Kick Seamark beside him.

'Why not be a pervert. More fun than being a monk.'

'It'll kill you, before the Bomb.'

'AIDS? Crap,' bellowed Nero.

'It's creeping up on us without us even knowing. All we can think of is the markets. It'll be a punishment for us having no hearts.' He looked at Kick sitting there with her short haircut, a designer rag covering her breasts and her feet dangling in the water. She was a picture.

'Don't worry, Francis, I'll die with SAFE SEX engraved on my heart.'

Francis did not hear Jesse, for Kick was beside him. He had never been happier in his life. He was smiling like a child, while Kick's eyes were slits in the sun staring out at the river.

18

'The date is set. The date of the launch of the bid,' said the accentless and anonymous consultant.

'This is a happening I'm going to tell my kids about one day,' said Peabody.

We stood outside by the river in Southwark on land owned by Nelson. It was undeveloped and the old warehouses, built in red brick, stood empty, overshadowing the narrow Victorian streets. They had consciously built their warehouses and old breweries for posterity: these were cogs in the wheels of a world empire. The gateposts were as high as the buildings and the names of the companies were still proudly announced in tall steel letters.

'The date is June 15th,' said Nelson, who stood as always alone by the waterfront, watching the tugs bounce by and the scummy water breaking on the banks of the Thames.

'*Parfait!* Gr-r-r-eat stuff,' exclaimed Max beside me.

'No leaks,' Peabody and the consultant said pointedly to Max. Even Nelson turned towards Max.

'No leaks, Max,' he repeated. PR men were notorious for their leaks.

It was the day of the Ball. Jesse and Darling punted the Prince upriver. I punted Kick up behind them, listening in hysterics to their conversation as it wafted to us over the flat water and the reeds.

'So are you going to take Sophie to the Ball?' asked Jesse.

'Yes, she did look fun,' said the Prince, 'but what would the papers say? I believe her nickname is Scrubber.'

'How would they know she was called Scrubber?' said Jesse.

177

'Yeah, she's a sweet gal,' joined in Darling, who loved everyone, except gossip columnists.

'But I have to be very careful, you know,' the Prince said innocently.

'That is what we are here for, sir,' volunteered Darling, taking off his Rayban sunglasses for effect.

'We are all patriots, Sir,' added Jesse. The bodyguard perched uncomfortably at the other end of the boat was very surprised by Jesse's declaration of medieval fealty.

'Oh, thank you, thank you both.' Angus was visibly moved. The two royalists smiled.

'So you see, Jesse, this Scrubber or Sophie, I'll have to meet her some other time.'

'You can meet her at the Ball, Sir.'

'What a lovely idea, Jesse, but better not take her. I shall take Kick Seamark. There are so many people trying to take advantage of me.'

'I know just the type, Sir.'

Kick, who was listening like I was, smiled dazzlingly and spontaneously to herself. It is appropriate, she thought, because he is a prince and I am the best. She was attractive not only because of her arrogance and her body, but also because she prided herself on an ability to discuss history or literature: though she thought that Tolstoy had written *The Hobbit*, Trotsky had authored *War and Peace*, and Tolkien had masterminded the Russian Revolution, at least she knew the names.

Behind us on the still river that day was the punt weighed down with the solid load of Party-Jones, Yarborough, Matt Nelson, Punjab and Francis.

'After the way he's behaved, who is Jesse going to take to the ball?' came Party-Jones's willowy voice, above the swish of the boat through the water and the splashes as Nelson plunged the punt pole into the river.

'He can't take all of them, that's for sure,' bellowed Yarborough.

'Do you think he'll take Emma Condor?'

'She is so pretty of course, but he treats her badly.'

'To tell you the truth, I wouldn't take it.' This was far

from the truth. Both girls would have taken anything from Babylon. There was silence.

'You old tart,' bellowed Yarborough. 'You've always fancied Jesse and you haven't even got a tongue sarney from him.'

'Nor have you, you old tart.' For some reason, 'old tart' was a term of great affection in Yarborough's set.

'What if he takes Sophie Croquet-Bowles?' asked Party-Jones, her weak voice drifting to us over the reeds. She didn't say 'Scrubber' because she wished everyone to know that she was a friend of the Croquet-Bowleses from Account-antshire and did not merely know her from Cambridge.

'What a gruesome twosome! So he's not going to take you?'

'Oh, I don't think I am in the running really but you might be.' 'Really' was pronounced 'rarely'.

'Really. Who says? Where did you hear that? Who told you?' Yarborough's features took on a rosy hue and her eyes turned to the sky. If only this were true. For weeks the two girls had thought of nothing but the May Ball, for it was the test of their careers so far (as opposed to their studies, which they would never actually use) and they were going through purgatory in anticipation. By this point they had given up hope of Babylon asking them. Now they would be happy to go with anyone.

Their greatest crosses to bear were Scrubber (Party-Jones: 'Does no one realize that she is wild?' – this was a euphemism in polite society for insatiable harlot); the secretaries (Yarborough: 'Everyone knows they are the stupidest girls. All they can do is spend money on clothes'); and worst of all the glamorous Seamark (Party-Jones: 'She's an American gold-digger') and Condor (Yarborough: I can't see why everyone thinks she's so attractive – she's far too thin').

'I'm not at all sure who to take,' said the immaculate Indian in his three-piece white suit, holding his swagger-stick like a fan.

'Nor me really.' Nelson was punting. Both desperate girls stiffened. This could be it. Were they about to be asked? Yarborough knew that if either of them were to be asked, it had to be her, not the flaccid Party-Jones; the latter was convinced that she was a good deal more ladylike than Yarborough.

'I might ask . . . um . . .' Party-Jones was about to expire with excitement . . . 'um . . . Mandy de Troy,' said Matt.

'She is a very attractive and pretty girl. At the secretarial college, I believe,' said Punjab. The girls were dying to say something, to achieve justice, to show these boys that they were wrong to consider such a thing. Party-Jones managed to hold in her indignation about the secretaries but Yarborough could not.

'But they're all so stupid!' she shouted.

The outburst surprised the boys. It gave everything away. The two girls blushed visibly, wearing their desperation naked on their cheeks.

'My father met your father at a dinner in the City,' Yarborough added to Nelson, hoping to make things better.

'Good,' said Nelson, proud and pained at his father's renown.

'There is some talk of a peerage,' suggested the Indian.

'Yes, there is.'

The girls eyed Matt's Roman profile. A peerage! Matt's father was to receive a peerage! They were friends of Matt. They marked themselves down for life as friends of Matt Nelson with a capital F.

Nelson observed their pig eyes and red faces carefully. 'Are you going to the Ball?' he asked Francis, who was lying in the boat staring at our punt up ahead hoping to catch a glimpse of Kick.

'No. Kick won't come with me. She is going with Angus. I don't know what to do. I've been to marse all morning but it's no good.'

'So where are you going to go tonight?' asked Yarborough in amazement.

'Nowhere.'

Yarborough was unimpressed by Francis for two reasons: first, she was irritated that Francis had decided not to go to the Ball at all when she was desperate to be taken by someone, and second, neither she nor Party-Jones could believe that anyone could actually want to miss a ball for any reason.

A crowd of shirtless boys and girls with torn dresses were dancing around a vast cauldron of bubbling vodka. The Margrave was holding forth to Nero.

'My first day at Eton, I was unceremoniously buggered by a duke with a broomstick and I never looked back. The boys up here who do my garden are always offering themselves to me for small sums of money . . .'

Babylon and Condor were dancing on a floating platform. He was shirtless and shining with sweat or oil, while she wore only a bikini, like a girl in a James Bond film. She was long and sleek and shiny. I stared at her body – the ultimate girl, a diamond. So far, I was only good enough for rhinestones. Babylon yelled at me, 'If I lose the beat, I'll die,' and he danced all the rhythms, wiry and frail, kicking his legs high in the air.

On the way back with Kick, we saw a figure standing alone on the first bridge. It was Francis, who had walked back from the party hours earlier. He followed us along the banks, watching Kick glide by looking so good.

Kick waved and blew empty kisses. 'Darling,' she shouted. 'Ahoy darling.'

He nodded but he did not move, so we went on.

'You shouldn't lead him up the garden path,' I told her.

'Oh, Joe, but he's so sweet. He's mad.'

'For a madman, he's got good taste.'

'He would do anything for me, that idiot, anything. I'm sick of his religious rubbish. His "marse" every day. If he wanted me so much, why all this "marse"?'

'He's not going to the ball.'

'Of course he'll go in the end. Everyone does.'

Kick opened a bottle of champagne, firing the cork into the banks of the Cam, filled her glass and lay back again. She crossed her legs. She had great legs. They were pale honey now and pampered. I followed them up. She kept them tightly crossed.

'I never wear knickers. Love the ventilation.'

I looked desperately back up her dress while she laughed like a sophisticated smuggler. She leaned forward, put her hands round my waist and pulled me on to her. The punt-pole went in with a splash and the glass splashed into the water off the side of the punt. I fell between her legs. I could smell the wet wood of the boat and her sweat and her skin. I turned over so I was staring up at her face, and we kissed.

I ran my hand down her leg and back up until I was near the top. My fingers could feel the heat. Her hand grabbed mine like a vice.

'No way, you naughty boy,' she said playfully. I blushed. We headed back to Cambridge. I was furious, more with myself than with her. That heat of hers kept coming back to me. It was not just a game.

'I wanted you.'

'Well, I'm bloody honoured,' I said. 'I'll put that on my curriculum vitae.'

'I just loved it. You might have noticed.' We were back in Cambridge. Tonight was the May Ball. I was taking Scrubber. Babylon was taking Condor, and even Party-Jones and Yarborough would be there on the night.

There was a rumpus down by the lock. The currents were strange there. The water swirled into little whirlpools. Someone had probably dropped a punt-pole. There were students and police standing by the side of the water shouting at us. I waved at them. Maybe this was security for the May Ball. They were pointing at us, pointing at the water. Kick sat up and just looked into the river, so hard that her eyes opened a little but no sound came.

I saw the hair. It was like an anemone, the way it swished to and fro with the river. Every strand seemed to be dancing to the river's tune. The face was porcelain white, a beautiful mask. He lay just beneath the water. The water was his element. It became him. He was too lovely to be frightening, but Francis was so very sad in the water. They were shouting from the river bank. There were men in diving suits, with oxygen cylinders, all calling over to us. Francis did not hear a thing. He would not be going to the ball.

19

'Where's Francis? Anything wrong? Mind if I sit down?' Drippy arrived late for dinner before the ball. He was arrogantly wearing his Swittle tartan kilt, knowing that the English regard Scotland as the home of the old nobility. He had been in London for an interview with the editor of the *Daily Snore* and had just arrived back in time for the ball.

No. Nothing was very wrong. Babylon had been telling us about his adventures during a *coup d'état* in Bolivia when Drippy appeared at the door. Prince Angus, who was already drunk, kept saying, 'I can see what the girls see in him. He's quite a raconteur.'

Kick, who could drink any man under the table, was haunted by the cool porcelain face lying just beneath the water. Every time she lifted her glass to her lips, she saw the face floating in the wine. Now we were all staring at Drippy over the shells of eaten snails and oysters which made rough pyramids along the table.

'You all looked as if I was a ghost.'

'Pull up a chair,' said Jesse, who suddenly felt for his enemy.

'So what is wrong with you all?'

'Well,' someone said. 'Well . . .'

Drippy was not listening. 'Tell me,' he said, throwing down a glass of wine, 'did Fran come in the end?'

'No,' I said firmly.

'Well, he might have done. It's not such a stupid question.'

He glanced directly at Kick and winked like a conspirator. 'What's he doing tonight then?'

Kick recoiled physically and stared into her wine. The Prince looked pained.

'He's not doing anything.' Something in the way I said it made him turn to me slowly, still smiling stupidly, but with a cold fear in his belly.

'Is something wrong?'

'Yes,' I said.

'There has been an accident,' said the Prince.

'Well, what?' Drippy's voice was strangled.

'He has been hurt.' I could not say it.

'Is he OK?' The saliva on Drippy's lips was a ragged foam.

No one could say it. Everyone had stopped eating. At last Babylon said it, almost brutally.

'He is dead. He drowned this afternoon.'

Kick winced, but she was going to the ball. She was not going to be weak about anything. Not even this.

Drippy's face disintegrated before us. As he fought the tears, he twisted his mouth as if undergoing a human decompression experiment. He got up and ran out, the kilt silly now, staggering to the door, blinded by tears.

For a moment we thought, Let's throw in the towel, let's miss the ball, but it only lasted a second. We began to talk again slowly. Babylon told his stories with such energy, with his hands beating the air to illustrate his point, and his eyes sparkling, that we all listened. His exuberance invigorated us, as if he were saying, 'Let us dance at the ball for our friends who are not there to dance with us.'

Every stud in the Maharajah of the Punjab's shirt was polished and perfectly in place. He wore a winged collar, starched so sharply that I thought it might cut his throat. The shirt was as stiff as a board with the line of studs that glittered in the street lights – they were ivory encircled with gold. Altogether he looked as if his tails had been poured on to him, not buttoned.

A triumphant Camilla Party-Jones was on his arm, with a gash of a grin on her face and bony crooked shoulders thrusting abruptly out of a tangle of frills. She tottered over to me on her high heels, like an electricity pylon after a storm.

'What do you think of my dress?' she asked.

Before I could think of a polite lie, she told me, 'It's the best. Mummy and I bought it specially.'

'I thought as much.'

We were in the street outside Cadaffi and from every side the visions of the night descended: girls were running down from Bokassa College in gymshoes and slipping on high heels as they went into the ball. Excited herds of rosy-faced rock-shouldered gymkhana-riding belly-laughing County girls emerged from taxis, while the cabbies leaned out of their windows and whistled through their teeth, saying 'Bootiful!' Flocks of giggling blonde Verbier-skiing sunburnt Chelsea Chicas leapt out of small cars so tightly stacked with well-lined flesh, ball dresses and made-up faces that it was difficult to tell where each pair of legs belonged; while grand jetsetters and their svelte women, like fine racehorses with delicate muscles rippling across silky backs and ankles, arrived very gravely in limousines from London with men to open the doors, and enough diamonds to sink the *Titanic* all over again.

The air was leaping, as if every one of us was about to go on stage in a Broadway chorus line.

'Gosh, Joseph, look.' Camilla pulled my arm and pointed an imperious hand through the crowd of penguins and frills.

They marched through the couples, smacking their Doc Marten boots on to the tarmac, swigging beer from cans and chucking them over their shoulders. Tall in their boots, strong in their leather, they wore military green jackets, zipped up tight around the waist so that their shoulders seemed unnaturally broad and threatening. Inhuman and frightening, with bitter eyes burning out of bald skulls, the skinheads patrolled the wonderland of a May Ball evening.

They were ogling the rich bitches in lust and disgust in equal portions, scaring the boys and gaming for trouble. The crowds parted for them, and cars slowed to let them pass as if they were dangerous animals in a safari park. They sat down on the other side of the road, spitting and laughing and shouting 'PIG' at a solitary constable on duty in the street while the undergrads hurried inside.

'I hope they're not going to the ball,' said Party-Jones.

'I shouldn't think they are.'

'Only the best for this ball. Very few people get tickets.'

'What are they drinking in here?' I asked.

'Darling is on the Committee. He told me Bollinger '63, and Moët in a fountain. Only the best. The best of everything.'

She was getting on my nerves, but we were nearer the front of the queue. The skins made me uneasy. The girl was with them, I had noticed, the one with 'Property of Skins' written on the back of her jacket. She had a new haircut, peroxided and long on top, short at the sides. She was watching us all. She was always watching.

'What kind of wedding are you going to have?' I asked Camilla. If she said 'The best' again, I would throw her to the skinheads.

She giggled, hugged her shoulders with her own hands, and her eyes gazed at the dashing men from London.

'A big one,' she said.

'And what kind of house?'

'A big one,' she said again. We were at the front of the queue. I was looking for Scrubber. Drippy, sporran swinging, reclaimed Joanna Yarborough from the crowd.

'And what kind of husband do you want?' We were in. We went under the archway, but I waited to hear Camilla's answer.

'The best.'

'Try Harrods,' I suggested.

We sauntered through the marquees and the halls and the arches. The ball bore us away from the term at Cambridge and out of this world. It was June 15th, the last night of Cambridge. Round tables, each bedecked with bottles of champagne in ice buckets and sideboards laden with pineapples and oranges, mangoes and apples, mixed sophistication with the plenty of a harvest festival. A band was playing in front of the great dance-floor of shiny wood that stretched the length of the tent, but it was not quite empty. Jesse was on it, dancing with Emma, close to the band.

As the saxophonist played, Jesse's tailed figure bobbed as

he kept time, while the band played faster, stamping their feet and clapping their hands. Couples stopped and watched him dance. He was one of the sights. Then they would walk on into the next marquee, where a disco played with the thud of electronic drums and the flash of lights, firing on to the dance floor like a cannonade. In the middle of the room, a champagne fountain rose out of a pool and already there were people round it, holding out their hands, dipping in their glasses, rubbing the champagne into their hair, as if Moët would make cripples walk and blind men see.

'It's so exciting,' said Scrubber. 'It's like a dream.'

The death in the river was as remote as a death in a detective series on television. Here, no one would ever sleep, or die, or even need to dream. It was all there, under the Big Top. Even the couples were a picture – under the lights, at the tables, all night in never-never-land. Kick had brightened up too; she smiled at me across the table as if the scene on the Cam had been just another circus act, part of the ball, like the band or the fountain.

Prince Angus was awkwardly enthroned at a table at the back of the big tent. 'Royalty must be discreet,' his body-guard had told me. Soon there were *paparazzi* snapping away and Kick, happy that she had now been recorded for posterity where she belonged, was bored. Angus was as perky as a wretched schoolboy, but rather than be seen to be legless he stayed sitting down, worrying about how to keep Miss Seamark happy.

'There's Angus,' said Scrubber, looking comely in her ball dress as she paraded around the royal table, eyeing up the princely talent. I introduced the shy Prince. He was soon wilting beneath the gamma rays of her tropical lust: this big blowsy thing wanted him, how marvellous. This sexual battering-ram was heaven-sent for Seamark. She gave up her seat and kept everyone's glasses filled to the brim. Her evening had been saved. I sat myself down at the table and wondered who the hell I was supposed to dance with for the rest of the ball.

Francis was the topic of the night – the trapeze artist who

187

fell from the wire. At the bars, in the loos, at table, the name was on everyone's lips. Francis would have been mortified to hear the number of friends he had acquired. Everyone claimed to know him. He was a 'darling love' to every girl who had never met him; he had drunk a pint with every boy at the ball in pubs he had never been to. Hundreds of people who had either seen the frogmen or heard the howl of the police siren, or known the guy who had a pigeonhole next to Francis's, had become involved in a real-life drama, and it made their evening.

'I can't believe it happened. We saw it. Everything,' said Kick. She did not want to say his name. It was a spectacle, not a man, in the Cam.

'But why did he do it?' asked Camilla Party-Jones.

'I suppose it was the pressure of exams.'

'I don't think that mother of his helped,' yelled Yarborough.

The suggestions flooded in from every side – the eager imbecility of Camilla, or the grave confidence of inscrutable Matt Nelson, or Jo Yarborough, shaking all over with the excitement of it all.

'His father was an alcoholic.'

'Gambling debts.'

'Interbreeding.'

'Bankruptcy?'

'Too much money.'

'Aren't you rather jumping to conclusions?' said the Prince sensibly.

'A love affair. Bonking Roman Candlesticks!' yelled the buffalovine Yarborough, breathless and overheating with the idea of this élite cadaver who she had known so-o-o well! We all turned to Kick and then at once pretended we had not. She did not mind, because her part in the tragedy had already been altered in her own account.

'He couldn't love. It was Catholicism. Who has ever heard of a happy Catholic?'

'Drippy is Catholic and he is alive,' joked Scrubber, already ensconced on the princely knee.

'Well, it's a great shame, but I think we'll all get over it very soon,' concluded Party-Jones, who for some reason was convinced that she had suffered a lot more than Francis.

Scrubber dragged Angus on to the dance floor. He tried to escape with all his strength, but her powerful arms held him like a clamp. For a moment, when a slow dance came on, the struggle was so intense that I feared the bodyguard, uncomfortable in his black tie, might intervene. Of course, the determined girl won. The Prince relaxed as each song played into the next, and he began to like it. Three songs later, the Prince would not have been separated from the mother-earth warmth of Scrubber for all the crowns in Europe.

'Anyway, I shall miss Francis, I mean I shall really miss him. I can't really believe he's gone,' said Kick.

'Why will you miss him?'

'All those free dinners,' she said drunkenly.

'What?' I said.

'Yes, I'll miss him,' she said beautifully, tears in her eyes, but I could have sworn she said it. There were crowds on the dance floor now. Scrubber and Angus were lost in the méleé. It was about one o'clock in the morning. We went to dance.

Babylon danced up with Emma in tow. He did not look at me. He just put his arm round Kick and led her into the centre of the dance floor. Through the crowd, you could just spot that head leaping up towards the lights – the hands, the shoulders, the legs kicked up like Nijinsky. He loved life itself. It was a pleasure to watch.

'If he'd been born in the slums, sweetai, he'd have been a rock star.' Emma was beside me. It was the kind of thing he would have said about himself. And he was probably right.

We sat down for a time, just watching the people. There was Punjab, dancing in small rigid steps and then taking Party-Jones glasses of champagne from the bar with the courtesy of an elderly and well-cuckolded husband.

Mandy de Troy, the virtuoso, walked round on Matt Nelson's arm, grinning, with her big teeth glowing in the rich purple of the neon lights. I am on the arm of Midas, she was thinking, what treasure there is at the end of this arm. And was not Sir John, the father of the man she would make love to, coming in a helicopter out of the sky that very night?

'Do you realize,' said Elliot, who was in Nero's party with Dr Tombs and the Professor, 'that we are witnessing the end of an era? The last great bow of promiscuity. Stare, enjoy it. Sample its delights, redolent of the juices of youth, before it is gone for ever.'

Couples were ostentatiously marching out into the gardens to take their pleasure in the full glare of Elliot's envy. He had a thin-haired girl with him, imported from London, who sat poker-faced and dull-eyed.

'Are you enjoying yourself?' I asked her.

'I'm hating it,' she said. 'It's all cliques. Luckily I have brought an excellent book to read.' She got out a Jane Austen novel from her cleavage and began reading it.

Tombs was observing her with disgust. 'I've always said that a woman with thin hair is like a man with small genitalia,' he said in a high-pitched stage whisper. The girl stared at her Jane Austen even harder and wished the world would swallow her up.

Nero suddenly called over to me: 'The news is breathtaking. The bid. I've just heard. You've known for ages, of course. He's bid today for the flagship company of the Establishment.'

A slick-haired character from the City, who looked as if he worked for Wallenstein, leaned back and said, 'Nelson is one hundred per cent shrewd operator.' Neal von Smith's braces were covered in dollar signs and he had a knowledgeable, grave manner of imparting information as if it were very secret indeed. He always finished each revelation with a few nods of the head and a sharp intake of breath through clenched teeth. His accent was half-American and he could read a French menu better than a Frenchman (though in fact he was from Wimbledon, which he believed to be extremely parochial). He had a deep tan and a supertanker of oil in his hair.

'That's Nelson's kid?' He nodded towards Matt, who

passed us on the way to the gardens to receive one of the virtuoso's most symphonic favours.

'Nelson may well come tonight,' I said.

'I know that. I'm on the deal. Wallenstein.' He flipped an embossed card out of the top pocket of his tux and picked up a cordless phone from the table. 'Give me a call if you wanna job.' He dialled a number: 'Von Smith here. Falco, give us a price. New York close? All right. Tokyo? What's manganese doing? Then sell it for fuck's sake.'

Dr Tombs watched the banker as if he were a fascinating new species.

'Are you going into the City?' he asked in his clear voice. Both Nero and Elliot had jobs in the City.

'I suppose the City is what this generation does,' commented a surprisingly lucid Professor, who sat there like an ageing child with tears running down his cheeks. Tombs popped an éclair into the Professor's mouth. 'In my generation, everyone went to the war. Now they go to the City. Either way, they never come back. I haven't sent all my young men to the City. Burgess and Maclean went to the Foreign Office. They loved it there – and everyone loved them.'

'Is Dr Kodell here tonight?' Tombs was asking. 'He is one of those brilliant young men who never quite fulfil their potential. You see, he is not quite a man. He knows not what he is. He gives me a strange feeling here.' And he placed his hand on his belly where the white waistcoat ended and the striped tail trousers began.

The banker put the phone down again. He noticed that Tombs was neither a tennis player nor a skier and was therefore not quite a man either.

'Nelson's price in Tokyo is 7065. Yen. He needs his own shares to increase in value. Let's hope he's got loads of friends.'

'He has –'

'– and even more enemies,' added Nero.

'How's the markets?' I said.

'Footsie's up 70 points on Nelson's announcement this afternoon. Dow was up 50 at the close. The Swissies and the Zipperheads, y'know the Japs, piled into the property sector.

The market is reaching for the sky.' And to make his point he gestured up towards the top of the tent, the Big Top.

The roar of the helicopter's propellers was suddenly over the marquee so that the canvas undulated and trees outside were blown sideways. Everyone rushed outside to see him arrive, looking up at the chopper hovering like a mythical bird. The chopper touched down on the grass and its propellers slowed until they were clearly visible and the noise died down. A side door opened and that familiar thin profile in black tie was walking towards us, followed by his ever-growing entourage of well-groomed and well-heeled assistants with great names and minute brains.

'What a night. We'll never forget it. The night of the Bid and the night of the Ball,' I said. Suddenly, I understood the vast release of energy that had poured through Britain in the eighties. All the efforts of all those millions of people were at that moment captured in the thin austere figure of this paramount hero. 'What a great time to be alive. This is a great ball, isn't it?'

'That chopper is a beautiful machine,' the banker said poetically, as we followed the entourage into the marquee. 'With this bid, my bonus could pay for this little party ten times over.'

Babylon threw back the flap of a side entrance to the marquee and walked up to Emma and me as we made for the gardens. He stood face to face with me and stared at the arm that was on the Condor's waist. My hand dropped away.

'What are you?' he said. 'What is in you? Do you have no code? No heart at all?' All our careers passed before us as we faced one another on this last night – and my Presidency reared up bitterly between us, when we should have remembered the laughter and adventure of the three years.

'No.' I was scared of him for a fleeting moment.

'You're scum, you have taken everything, but you're nothing. For all you've taken, you've gained nothing.'

And he walked out, out of the tent, out of my life and out on to the street. He had not spoken to Emma. He had not even looked at her. As he went, he saw it all in the red-hot clarity of his anger. He no longer wanted any part of it.

*

She kissed me as we danced. From the night Jesse first kissed her on the bridge, I had dreamed of this. I always visualized her in her furs. I had put her out of my mind, and that May Ball night I had not dared to hope. She was my friend's untouchable girl, but then in his strange way he had given her to me just as he had thrown the Presidency into my lap. He had trained me for both. Her lips were traitor's lips and I loved the taste of them. I had resolved to take over Jesse Babylon, to copy him better than he could himself, and now I had succeeded.

I held the back of her neck and kissed her in the middle of the dance floor, with smoke rising from the floor and lasers slashing through the darkness.

Babylon climbed out through the gate. The bouncers watched him, swigging stolen champagne and smoking pot they had bought at Liverpool Street station. It was 3.30 and they felt they had done their job. The boy was out in the street; he loosened his white tie, leaned back against the doorposts and breathed out. He was glad to be out of the ball, with its smoke and its silly girls. He told himself he did not mind about Emma, but really he minded very much.

He ran his hand through his hair, and asked himself why, why he had done it to himself, why he carried on madly when he knew it would end as it had ended. And it had ended. He tried to hate the desperate little people with their materialistic obsessions, but he could not really do it, because millions of people had enjoyed the materialism of the era. None more than he.

So he just cried until he could taste his own salty tears. He enjoyed crying. A man should be proud he can cry, he told himself. He walked along a bit, back towards the centre of town, but he wept so freely that he sat on a wall opposite the pub, the Baron of Beef, and listened to the evening as it became the morning.

Music rose from the distant marquees like the sounds of a circus. Jesse recognized his favourite songs, which reminded him of happier times. Then he heard the crunch of a beer can in the street and he listened as the creak of leather got closer until it was right in front of him. He opened his eyes and saw them.

I led Emma out through the open door of the marquee into the garden lit up with lights, and I held her hand as we danced outside and then walked on until the music became more and more distant. We could hear other noises, laughter in the street. Her kiss was the key to the kingdom. The portcullis had opened, and I collected it all, the castle, the lot. She playfully ran away and I chased her until I could kiss her again. She had a light tongue, and lips that tasted of champagne, coconut suntan oil and Parisian scents. In her lips, I tasted everything I wanted.

Five men's heads surrounded him. They were bloodless, homeless faces, with lips that had never allowed themselves sensuality and eyes that hated him before they knew him. There was no hair on their heads, and he could hear the creak of their boots and the thud of his own heart. They stood like jackals in their green wide-shouldered battle-jackets and tight jeans tucked into stormtrooper boots that went up to their knees. He could feel the coolness of their jackets and those loveless eyes. They smelt of cheap after-shave, leather and beer.

Babylon's neck was wet with sweat and he wished the wet tears on his cheeks would dry. He feared his own weakness. There was the girl there, too, somewhere among them. She smelt different, and he could see her hair and the wetness of her eyes shining in the street lights. His breathing came quicker. He stood up. He was too scared to pray.

Burning torches on stakes lit up the Cam. There were boats, punted by boys without their tails on, their shirts and waistcoats made whiter still by the play of the fires. One punting girl had taken off her dress altogether, and she stood on the punt platform like something out of a Victorian brothel, all petticoats and suspenders in the smouldering torchlight.

'Where's Excalibur?' Emma said. The river was on fire

with the flames of the torches reflected vividly in its smooth waters.

I just saw Francis's unseeing eyes in the water and turned away.

'Whatcha lookin' at?' the biggest skinhead asked him.

'Nothing actually,' said Babylon.

'Do y' 'ear that tongue in 'is head?' the skinhead asked his friends. 'We've bagged a right one 'ere.' He turned back to Jesse. 'I asked yer what you was lookin' at,' he said, bringing his face and his breath very close.

'I said nothing. I'm going home.'

'You bin lookin' at moi girl, 'aven't y'?'

'Not at all,' said Jesse.

'Why not? Do y' think she's ugly?'

'No, not at all.'

'Are y' insulting 'er?'

'No.'

'If y' insultin' 'er, yer insulting me and if y' insultin' me yer insultin' all of us.' They all laughed.

'I don't think she's ugly,' he said desperately.

'So you 'ave bin lookin' at moi girl, 'ave y'?'

They moved in closer.

'Are y' tough,' asked one of them, 'you toffee-nosed little shit?'

Babylon did not say a thing.

'Well y' better be, 'cause we're going to beat the shit out of y'.'

The Prince took his tail coat off. He was back in his rooms in college. He said goodnight to the detective who slept next door. As soon as the door shut, Scrubber leapt on him. She undid his waistcoat and began to push the braces off his shoulders. Then she flicked off his tie. He was paralysed as she went about him. Of course, trained to be careful of fortune-hunters, he was aware she was all too keen, too fresh. How could any decent girl be so forward? How could any woman brought up properly know so much? It was a mystery to him, yet she spoke in the same accent as him. She had been to a very nice school. His mother, the Queen, was a Governor.

'Are you sure we should?'

'Should what?'

'Be here, together.'

'Absolutely sure,' she said in her heartiest voice, a voice that evoked horses and shooting lodges and things he knew about.

'I don't think my position really allows me this sort of, um, well . . .'

'Rubbish! It's nothing to do with your duties. Look at Edward the Seventh.' He frowned – the number of times he had been warned about the disgusting example set by Dirty Uncle Bertie.

'And besides,' she told him as she reached for his trouser buttons, 'I am a citizen of this kingdom and I am a darn sight better cause than opening some boring old super-market.'

He struggled. He had tried morality and affairs of state to dissuade her. He was delighted he had failed but still apprehensive.

'I don't really know much about this sort of thing,' he said carefully.

'Don't worry, Angus,' she said as she lowered herself on to him, 'I do it all the time.'

Jesse tried to break out of the circle, but a skinhead head-butted him in the face. Blood cascaded from his head until it was in his eyes and he could hardly see a thing. He could only wait for the next blow that came down on him from unknown hands belonging to unknown faces that hated him and enjoyed beating him within an inch of his life, until there seemed to be pain everywhere and he was wet every-where, in his trousers, his socks, his head and his arms. He could hear them chuckling all round him as he staggered from the blows.

Every time he fell in one direction they would smash him towards the other, until the punches were dulled by the agony and his face seemed to be hanging from his head. He wanted to be sick, but he could not find anywhere to be sick out of, so he just coughed and hoped it would end. He could hear the girl's voice yelling, 'Stop it, he don't mean no harm. Leave him, he's OK, one's no good for a fight.' They told her to get out of it and kept hitting. He was spluttering. His face was wet. He was suffocating but beyond crying. He did not just hope it would end; he wished it was the end.

The band was playing like hell. We danced again until I was hot. So I undid my bow tie and threw off my tails. I pushed back my hair. I felt the invincibility of success as I posed and strutted to that music. I felt so powerful. The Condor had opened her dress. As she danced she held it and fanned herself with it, showing her long legs and her suspenders. I watched her legs and the muscles working in them so smoothly, and the spring of her hair. I could see her dancing by the Cam in her bikini. It was only yesterday; it was a world ago. I recalled every inch of her as if it was a photograph.

I led her out quickly into the gardens. It was lighter now, and the torches were only just necessary. I pulled her by the hand and she knew why and hurried after me. As soon as we were out of sight of the Big Top, I threw down the zip of her dress and she smiled at my impatience, and stepped out of it. I pulled her down, running my hands over her rearing breasts and the kiln of her loins. I licked her from head to foot as she lay on her dress, stretched out on the grass surrounded by rhododendrons.

A hand like a charmed snake found my buttons, studs, zips. As if by magic she undid them so softly I barely noticed they were gone until I felt the cool air on my thighs. The touch of her lips alighted like butterflies here and there for a second before taking to their wings again.

She pulled me on to her as the light grew brighter. As music from the marquee played tunes I would always remember, I shared her with the morning.

When he fell to the pavement, he could still hear the music in the distance, songs he would never forget in his nightmares. The punches had turned to kicks that rained on his head and on his stomach and in his groin. The coolness of the paving stones soon turned to the heat of the wetness that spread under him like water. Still he could hear the girl shouting at them, and he heard them slap her and swear at her. He did not feel the slash of the knife but he heard its metallic click as it fell to the stone beside him. He just hoped he was not dead as he lay in that maelstrom of boots and fists. He hoped not, because he had always enjoyed life. He knew that now and he had always known it.

The air smelt of newly mown grass. I wondered at her body and the richness of its smells and its capacity for enjoyment. There were so many different textures, from the hardness of her ankles to the softness of her hands and the virgin-smooth of her thighs. I penetrated her with my hands from back and from front. She was on the horns of a dilemma: whichever way she moved, there was pleasure.

The streets were empty now and quiet, as if an army had just evacuated an occupied town. As we walked back to King's Parade, the helicopter's engines began to whirl and it seemed to rise out of the Big Top itself, banking in a wide arc around Cambridge and carrying this emperor back to the balance sheets of his empire.

We raised our eyes to follow him across the sky and I knew the bid would succeed. The chopper carried History among its passengers and I was bound up with History.

'Oh dear,' she said. 'Oh, God.' There was a little crowd around a figure on the pavement. Beside a boy dressed in tails was the punk girl, on her knees in the gutter, the striking girl who watched us so closely. She had a bucket of water and was bathing the head so that her lap was thick with blood. Her arms were bare where she had ripped her clothes to stop the bleeding, and she did not look up. There was a policeman there, calling for help on his radio. It was PC Smart.

''ello, Joe,' he said. 'Terrible business. Poor bugger. Those skins got him. Terrible mess 'e's in.'

'Who is it?' asked Emma.

'He's from the ball,' said PC Smart. 'Take a look, sir.'

'Not anyone we know, is it?' said Emma sleepily.

'I wouldn't look if I were you, young lady,' said the policeman, who felt faint himself.

'Who is it?' I asked. There was something about the head, despite the blackening blood.

'He's a good friend of yours, Mr Rourke. I could of sworn it.'

'It's Jesse,' I said.

I bent down, shaking my head. I wanted to help.

'I'm tending him,' said the girl.

The real story had not been at the ball at all but in the gutter outside. I edged nearer the caked head.

'Don't come near me, Rourke,' he said painfully. 'Don't come goddam near me.'

20

'Sir Methuselah Botham-Jagger,' Sir John Nelson said into the speaker-telephone on his desk to the Chairman of Universal Imperial. 'This is Nelson calling. As you know, last night, Nelson plc launched a bid for Universal Imperial.'

He did not wait for Sir Methuselah to answer. The room was tense, hot and overcrowded: Max, Peabody the banker, the well-bred assistants, the suave but anonymous consultant, Norris Ded the accountant, with his lock of hair sweat-stuck to his head, the rocket scientist lawyer Mr Invoice were all there, attended by hundreds of assistants.

Colleagues, tax experts, debt experts, equity experts, troubleshooters, lunch-orderers, coffee-makers, proof-readers, briefcase-bearers, country desk officers, number-crunchers, marketeers and black-liners kept joining the meeting. It was becoming like a medieval court, with each baron increasing his feudal retinue. Soon there will be jugglers too, I thought. We all stared at this one man at his vast desk, sitting in his new high-backed chair in his Docklands office with only a glass wall between him and the greatest city in the world.

'I own 6.7 per cent and it is only ten in the morning. I sincerely hope that together we can bring together the old and the new to create a company of which London can be proud.'

London stretched out before us from the window of Nelson's new office. The powerful grey flow of the Thames whirled and bucked in small waves, seahorses of foam and currents that crossed the surface like a muscle tensing beneath a giant's skin. Beyond the river the variety of London created a skyline of concrete and brick and glass, skyscrapers, green parks, markets and cathedrals, old townhouses, Victorian stations and shopping arcades. Above it all, the cranes and hulks of building sites marked the places where Nelson was holding surgery.

'To tell you the truth, Sir John,' the chairman of Universal Imperial answered on the squawk-box in a languid silver-tongued voice, 'your offer is anything but welcome. It is inadequate for shareholders. What is more, there is no man less suitable to even contemplate Universal Imperial, yet alone have the effrontery to sit on its Board, than you.'

'I regard that as a compliment, Sir Methuselah. Your shareholders deserve a management which is willing to share with them the vast hidden values locked up in your balance sheet for the use of a small number of hereditary directors, such as yourself, whose only claim to their positions is birth. Your declining ivory tower is against the whole spirit of the dynamic new England.'

'Fantastic. My phrases, of course. All in my press release. Love it,' Max whispered in a loud outburst of huskiness that probably reached Botham-Jagger, if not the whole Board of Universal Imperial.

Nelson spoke calmly and strongly. He was at his best now, for he was living the bid and his awkwardness was reserved only for human relations and other trivialities. When it came to business, he had the grace of an athlete.

'I should inform you that I have appointed Babylon's to act for us in London,' the patrician voice announced out of the squawk-box.

'We have Wallenstein.' McGill Peabody thrust his chest out with pride, his tan turned a shade darker and the exhilaration that he felt when he scored a hole in one at the Kennebunkport golf course rushed through his even body, trim with surfing and tennis.

'We will also appoint Watch Yorbachs to serve us in America.'

'Nelson has appointed Bagalboy Piranha Fish in New York and Sellyermutha in Tokyo.'

'We have five banks on the job, Sir John.'

'We have . . .'

Peabody mouthed, 'Six'.

'. . . six,' said Nelson.

'Now we'll have to appoint another three banks,' whispered Peabody.

'I hope you will behave like a gentleman during your bid, Sir John. Even in war there are rules and manners, as I have been taught since school. Good morning.'

'This battle will not be won on the playing fields of Eton. Goodbye, Sir Methuselah.' Nelson swung his chair round so that the back faced us. Through the glass wall, there was London.

'Gr-r-r-eat performance,' said Max. 'She is on your side. She told me just now. You spoke like a pro.'

'Grand slam, Sir John,' announced the knickerbocker glory from Wallenstein.

She has come to kill me. That is clear. Babylon watched the girl from the hospital bed. He was swathed in bandages. His body ached and stitches criss-crossed his body like a railway map. The whole attack was as distant as a scene from a film, yet she was part of the scene and here she sat beside his bed, watching him like a zoologist, as she had always watched him.

Babylon tried to understand why she had waited with him for the ambulance and why she had visited him every day since the beating up. Did she feel guilty? Had she come to finish him off?

As he watched her, he realized he had watched her over the years as much as she had watched him, because she had a coarse sex appeal like the acrid stench of burning manganese. He liked her body and her cheeks and the cut of her gib as she walked like a rakish sailor. The upturned nose and the big generous teeth gave her face an openness, and the scar that reached from the corner of her mouth to the point of her chin made her a pirate on Captain Morgan's frigate in Jesse's feverish imagination.

Her proven dangerousness made her attractive as much as it scared him. With her faded denims, torn at the thighs, and her stormtrooper boots and her reddish hair cut short at the sides, she would put her feet up on the side of the bed and watch him curiously.

'What is your name?' he said at last.

'Jewels,' she said in a voice of street gravel and Hackney housing estates.

'Why? Your eyes?' Her eyes were green and cruel. She had learned to watch because she had been on her own for a long time.

'No, 'cause I don't need no jools. I don't need nuthin'. I'm an alleycat,' she laughed loudly with her mouth wide open.

Babylon smiled. 'What do you do?'

'Nuthin'. Why work when y' get paid not to work?'

'You must work some time, you know,' said Jesse, thinking of his friends with their diaries full of interviews for jobs in the City.

'Look, Jesse-boy, in the olden days, the people worked and the toffs played.'

'That is approximately correct.' The over-educated are always confused by the simple logic of the under-educated.

'Well, naw, the rich work to stai rich and the people don't work at all. They got the dole. That's democracy, innit?'

'I suppose you're right,' admitted Jesse, who could not see any fault in her analysis.

Jewels had always found Jesse fascinating. She and her skinheads had picked him out, for his exuberant *joie de vivre* was an obnoxious challenge to their world and they hated him with a hate they loved. They had first seen him at the Hunt a year before. They knew he was both a traitor to them and an enigma. They longed to injure him and they waited for their chance. Jewels hated him but she wanted him to want her, because he was a glamour boy in his baggy white trousers and his red striped blazer, always singing, always dancing. To Jewels, he was Clark Gable in her grey lost little world. If she could not be near him, then she wanted to ruin him. It was the only way to get near him. How else does a skinhead become acquainted with the heir to an empire?

'So if y're such a fuckin' hard worka, what's your sort of work?'

'I am an undergraduate, I work . . . I might go into the City or the media or advertising . . .'

'What's that – white colla worka, blue colla, what izit'-grad?'

'White collar,' he laughed. He liked her. She was new. She was fresh.

'Y're a fuckin' winged colla worka, if the truth be told,' she shouted and laughed in an explosion of teeth, freckles and red hair.

She is a charming beast, thought Jesse. It would be fun to kiss that mouth and lie between her legs. So rough! What an experiment! And he smiled for the first time since the Great Ball.

'Let me get out my diary. My days are full of strife and grief. Meetings every moment. Life is busy,' Darling was telling me as we wandered through the West End.

It was Saturday in new London. Chelsea and Kensington were no longer the private reserves of the Yarboroughs or the Botham-Jaggers. Of course they still lived there, but this was the time when everyone could shop there and everyone could eat there.

The cafés were filled to the brim with girls in designer clothes, with coffee-coloured bellies won on the beaches of Marbella and purchased on the sunbeds of suburban health clubs. Their boys wore white trousers, blazers, sunglasses and Italian shoes, bought in cheap high-street shops that made these hardworking estate agents, clerks, management trainees and salesmen feel like playboys. They drank *cappuccinos* after Martinis in restaurants which were called 'brasseries' with cosmopolitan names. Vivid disco music blasted out of open-topped cars.

Bankers from Wallenstein or Babylon's, who had foolishly bought their blazers from the most expensive tailors in Jermyn Street (if in doubt, an investment banker will always pay twice as much as necessary), were discussing which airline business class was more comfortable. Wealthy Italian girls doing arts courses in London, plainly dressed in boots and denims, were telling one another how crude Turin was, though their fathers had made their money there. English Chelsea Chicas in their graceless baggy clothes in bright colours were claiming to each other that they were completely Scottish, which was for some reason far more élite than being English.

Darling and his arty friends felt that they were superior to these intruders from suburbia. Yet how were they to identify the suburbanites? They drove the same cars and wore the same clothes and ate in the same 'brasseries'. They were all as happy as one another, because it was an intoxicating time to be alive.

'I'm pretty busy too. Let's see. I've got meetings with Max on Tuesday, Thursday.' I took my Filofax out as we walked. It was an enormous black directory costing a large sum of money. Not everyone possessed the real McCoy, but this was the era of the schedule when the very ownership of a diary was a status symbol.

The hype of entrepreneurialism, beamed daily on TV by Max and his rivals, had created a national mania for 'meetings' and time-planning and being busy. The thought of Nelson would make young people reach for their diaries to organize more meetings to develop more strategies and create more networks. In their diaries, all the people in cafés in the West End would technically be at 'meetings'. Spare time was an embarrassment, for work, work, work and the consumption of its earnings had become the religion of the nation.

'Max Bright will love John and Jon. The moment I show him one, he'll pay whatever it takes. When it comes to art, he is a man of discernment,' Darling was saying. He wanted me to organize a meeting with Max so that he could sell him the most fashionable new art. I was more interested in watching the streets, enjoying their colour and enthusiasm. 'London is full of money. There has never bin anything like it.'

'Not just big money, Darling, it's full of small money but it is being spent and enjoyed. It is better than the dark days when there was no money to spend because no one had the spirit to make any.'

'Money only exists to enjoy. Those property boys and those banking boys are making big bucks. The markets are going into the stratosphere and Nelson – what a guy. He's got style. He's buying a John and Jon.'

We had arrived at Darling's cottage in Chelsea, where his rooms had black and white floors, chrome chairs and nothing on the walls. It was dinner time in the summer.

The Prince was supposed to be a regular, but he was still worrying about the latest revelation in the tabloid newspaper the *Blue Tit* about Scrubber. Matt Nelson, quiet and almost invisible, was there, playing with a car tyre which Darling claimed was high art.

'It's a John and Jon.'

'Who the hell is John and Jon?' asked Matt, who sat cross-legged with his torn jeans tucked into his multi-coloured rugger socks. The wok steamed at his feet. Darling passed around plates laden with Szechuan chicken, rice, lobster with ginger and cashew nuts.

'Matt,' Darling told him self-righteously, 'they are just about the most famous living English artists. Forget Bacon or Hockney. These guys were there first. Did you see the *Mop and Bucket* in the Babylons' drawing-room, or the *Toilet Brush* at the Party-Joneses's house? They are all by J and J. Kick's mother buys in New York. She was lucky to pick up a John and Jon for 60 grand.'

'John is a darling. He is such an . . . an artist. That is all you can say. So is Jon. He has such an eye. Mama loves her *Washingmachine*. She says it was a bargain,' said Kick. She was watching me, despite Emma's presence, for she suddenly had a strange inkling of the world I was moving in.

'Your old man's looking at one, Matt. *Emptybath*. Lovely piece. Jon told me at the Botham-Jaggers' that it was John's idea. It is certainly more John than Jon to leave the plug in and a tidemark around the bath. A perfect touch.'

'Don't mention the Botham-Jaggers to me,' laughed Matt Nelson.

'And are you buying one, Darling?' asked Kick, with a prawn held precisely between poised chopsticks.

'You bet, I'm negotiating at the moment with the Trust to buy the *Car Tyre*.'

*

'We will win. I have always won. This is the biggest battle. Nelson shares must be supported. Please talk to our friends. They must be sustained at the 890 pence level. That is all, Joe.'

Sir John Nelson's secretary had told me to meet him on the quayside of the vast Docklands development. Already a town had arisen out of the empty crumbling warehouses and ugly doomladen chimneys that had somehow made the horizon beautiful in their lonely and obsolete grandeur. There were concrete foundations and skeletons of brick buildings. The night sky, glowing with the lights of London, shone through the scaffolding like the skeleton of a dead man. Cranes, hundreds of feet tall, shaped like crucifixes and emblazoned with Nelson's name, turned silently on their axles high above us. Squat trucks revved their engines and bulldozers roared. Behind us, great lights lit up building sites like film sets, where workers earning double salaries worked all night, with their drills roaring and their cement mixers churning, to create a new city on old London.

The ground was open, like a deep wound, crisscrossed with wide muddy girders and walls. Men in their yellow Nelson hard hats worked like a race of ants under the lights. It looked like an operation on the body of a giant. In Nelson's surgery, we were staring into the pulsing body of a living creature.

'Is this illegal?' I asked him. Nelson stared at me.

'No. It is not illegal but it not legal either. The laws are new. Badly drafted by bureaucrats. Unclear. If it was illegal, I would never suggest it. Is that all?' he asked the nameless consultant, the leader of the Extraordinary Team from the secret nameless American firm that was working sleeplessly to make the bid work.

'That is all. It must be done now.'

'It will be done now. Are you going back in, Sir John?'

'No,' he said, standing in the shadows away from the glare of site lights and the rumbling machinery. 'Take the car back, you two. I shall stay out here on my quay. I want to walk through Nelson City. Check the deadlines. Builders always take short cuts. They have to be watched.'

*

Scrubber had become a superstar. Darling had her at the opening of his gallery in St James's, and it was not long before a thinner, blonder and, sadly, more demure Sophie Croquet-Bowles was going out with that dashing young actor Ru Bonham-Cavendish, while running her own interior design business. Interior design is the art of spending vast quantities of other people's money at the best stores. Scrubber was very good at it, and her clients loved to use the 'ex-royal girlfriend'.

One day Scrubber was the unwashed high whoress of slut Sloanery. The next, she was Prince Angus's new girlfriend. Or was it his fiancée? Or was it the next Queen? The news-papermen (Sydney Operahouse owned the *Blue Tit*), fat, pasty-faced brawlers, in anoraks with straps bearing an arsenal of lenses and films, camped permanently outside Scrubber's flat in the Fulham Road.

'If I can get a picture of the little tart, with her big knock-ers, I'll be made. If the editor likes it, it'll be syndicated. I'll get five grand, ten grand. I'll buy a car,' thought the camera-men. They tried to climb up to her room, but Scrubber pushed away the ladder; they pushed down the window of her car, but she wound it up again on their fingers and valuable lenses. If she was at a party, they awaited her arrival and departure and the next morning her photograph would appear on the front page of every paper in Europe.

'I can't bear it,' she would say. 'I have no privacy. They never leave us alone. Just because I am who I am, it doesn't mean I have no rights!' Camilla Party-Jones and Jo Yar-borough showed her a respect they had reserved for Matthew Nelson, but it was not long before Scrubber had left them far behind.

Housewives the length of Europe read their newspapers, dreamed of buying the dress Scrubber was wearing that day, and said, 'Poor girl, the pressure she must be under.' And lorry-drivers and workmen in motorway cafés in Liverpool or Lyons clicked their tongues at Scrubber's minidresses and the bulge of her breasts lurking beneath her silks and laces and said to their mates, 'Trust that Prince Angus! What a corker. Lucky 'im! He must be a randy devil. And I bet she goes.'

The truth was that Scrubber loved it all. For the rest of her life she was the 'royal girl', the 'ex-royal girlfriend', a job for a lifetime built on ten minutes of incompetent royal passion. She had become a Lillie Langtry and a Nell Gwynne rolled into one for the eighties.

Darling, Nero and Kick, despite their attempts to defend the royal personage against such a wicked trick, were soon delighted to be included in 'Scrubber's Royal Set'.

'Those *paparazzi* bastards,' declared Darlington. 'They're putting her through hell.'

Scrubber's mother told the newspapers that the possible marriage 'would be a very good match for the Croquet-Bowles family', which no one doubted. No one consulted the Prince about the story at all. Relieved to be rid of the *paparazzi* at last, he was nonetheless confused. He called his bodyguard into his flat in the back of Buckingham Palace, as he looked at yet another front-page photograph of Scrubber.

'Inspector,' he said.

'Yes, Sir.'

'After what occurred between this girl and me,' came the old-world voice. 'Does it mean we are automatically engaged?'

'Oh, no, Sir,' explained the bodyguard. 'You can't always believe what you read in the tabloids, Sir. They often get it wrong, you know.'

'It has a ghostly beauty, does it not?' Goncourt's eyes never left *Vacuumcleaner* by John and Jon. The priceless piece of art stood on the floor beneath the Leonardo da Vinci cartoon in the drawing-room of his Little Venice house. 'I bought the da Vinci and my wife bought this. It is not exactly my cup of tea, but she absolutely loves it.'

Only someone who has never done a day's housework could ever believe that a vacuum cleaner is a work of art. It is of course a John and Jon,' I said in a voice of tired sophistication, to make clear that there was a J and J in every house I visited.

'It is time to buy Nelson shares, is it?'

'Yes, we must keep it at 890 so that the share offer keeps its value.'

'His original offer still holds good. Nelson will subsidize me if the shares lose money?'

'Yes, of course the deal holds good.'

'Then I buy,' he said simply, looking at *Vacuumcleaner* again.

'The pheasants worked a treat,' Max was telling Sir John. 'The *Daily Materialist* covered it and had a centre spread of the grateful villagers. The City was touched. Yeah, touched. Your shares are up 5 pence on today's close .895. Spoke to Ken Trumply today. Gr-r-r-eat mate of mine. And the PM. She says he is doing a brilliant job at Finance and, I've gotta say it, he . . .'

'What is your point?' said Nelson.

'There'll be no referral to the Monopolies Commission, unless Ken has no control over his civil servants. Just in case, though, we need to build up your history a bit, say you come from a mercantile family, nothing big, but put you in a British context, show that you have been rich for a long time, generations, not this rich, of course, but genteel, always comfortably off. The Brits don't like people to MAKE money; they like to think the rich have always been rich.'

'Do what you think, Max, but do not over-do it. Just do what is necessary.'

Scrubber's diary was a large golden volume as thick as the Bible. When it came to her Bible, she was a fundamentalist. She was running her finger down the pages, saying, 'Can't do Monday, Tuesday, Wednesday. Ah, Thursday, 7th July. Can do. How swee-e-e-et of you. Put me on the Committee, and Ru, if you like. It is an important cause to both of us.'

People all over the nightclub were opening and closing their voluminous diaries, drawing them out of suit pockets and handbags as if they were pistols, after coming off the dance floor or going into the restaurant.

Scrubber was sitting with her parents, Ru Bonham-Cavendish (the latest boyfriend of the ex-royal girlfriend), now playing an Etonian in the fifth film in a row, Darling,

Kick, Matt Nelson and an array of very sleek and very brown friends. They were talking about charity – or rather a very chic social committee which claimed it was meeting to raise funds for charity. Nero and his banking friend from Wallenstein, Neal von Smith, were talking business.

Throughout the drawing-rooms of the club, watched over by its middle-aged and dignified waiters, the pin-striped insurance brokers were slapping each others' backs, twanging one another's braces and showing off to girls who dreamed only of expensive cars and smart restaurants; bankers drinking champagne entertained impressed European clients and silent Japanese; others caressed attractive secretaries still in their working suits, who, dazzled with the glamour of this power lifestyle, were itching to add their bodies to their bosses' many possessions. PR men, advertisers, financial printers, corporate entertainers in white tuxedos were waving portable telephones as if to say, 'Look at us, we are part of the era,' while impresarios and art dealers, who are always fashionable, drank cocktails with pretentious names such as 'Bellini' or 'Mozart'.

The old playboys from times when it was chic to do nothing at all wandered through the crowd like strangers, feeling left out among all this energy and exuberance.

'Nelson's share price is up at 895. The money we're making out there is phenomenal,' von Smith was telling Nero and anyone else who cared to listen. 'I think our horse is gonna win.'

A beautifully dressed sun-lamp-kissed admirer with acquisitive eyes watched him and murmured to me, 'He earns 200,000 a year so he can get away with it.'

'What happens to you if he doesn't?' asked Nero, winking at me.

'He will win if Neal's behind him.' Even the girl knew about the bid, having read about the Scottish castle and the free pheasants in the *Daily Materialist*'s gossip column.

'That would be a CLM,' Neal said grimly in his half-American accent.

'What is that?'

'Career limiting move. He will win. McGill is sure of it.'

'How clever,' said the girl. 'CLM. Come on, Neal, let's dance.'

Mrs Croquet-Bowles, who was reputed to be intelligent, had been wildly impressed by her daughter's social ascension to Mount Olympus, and now she was determined to make a good impression on Matt Nelson. She was an emaciated woman with thin brown hair, a hawkish nose and all the sensuality and grace of the brittle invitation cards which she lived for and loved.

'Your Daddy's having such an exciting time, keeping everyone on their toes. We are so pleased to have you with us tonight, aren't we, darling?'

Mr (he had no known first name) Croquet-Bowles, a thin, bald and graceless man who had risen to be one of the four deputy chairmen of Party and Jones, the stockbrokers, grunted.

'Absolutely, darling.' He was always faintly embarrassed by his wife's social acuteness, but he was also intelligent enough to know that he would never have reached his present position without it.

'We think that, frankly, your father is absolutely brilliant. He is rebuilding London, like Haussmann did with Paris. My husband and I love Paris.' She wielded the name of Haussmann as an example of her celebrated intelligence.

'Mummy, do you know Joe Rourke? He works for Max Bright, particularly on the Nelson account,' said Scrubber, who was swiftly learning the social skills of her mother. Sex and food had become duties mainly necessary to keep men happy which interfered with social planning and dressing. I realized that Scrubber would never again fuck with the abandoned lust that she had at Cambridge. Now she was a Golden Retriever like the rest.

'We have heard so much about you. Don't you come from . . .'

'Esher.'

'Oh, Mummy!' said Scrubber, embarrassed but unashamed.

'. . . yes, that's right. What an interesting life you must have led,' said Scrubber's mama (mar-mar), meaning exactly the opposite. Matt Nelson had escaped into the crowd.

212

She went on: 'I was so interested to learn in the *Materialist* yesterday that John Nelson comes from a very distinguished family in the Midlands, who owned the local factory up there. My husband always said that he came from nowhere, which of course we all think is marvellous' – this was lip service to Thatcherite meritocracy – 'but the Nelsons always had enormous style and you can only inherit that. Look at the way he bought that historic castle and did it up and behaved so well to the villagers.'

Mr Croquet-Bowles announced, 'It does make a difference. Botham-Jagger is a bit of a stick in the mud, but I can tell you that many of the other Universal Imperial directors are coming round to Nelson. They say he is not so bad, has behaved relatively well. Party-Jones says he might win after all.'

'There you are,' said Mrs Croquet-Bowles.

21

Winter had come. Sir Edwin Babylon took me out to lunch
at his club. As soon as Babylon appeared at the door, the
waiters were like characters in a film that has suddenly
been speeded up: off they went, laying out the club silver,
shining the table, bringing the best wine, waitering like mad.

The rooms of the place were high and square. Great portraits hung on the walls of severe servants of the Empire,
whose very name recalled romantic victories over helpless
natives in far-away corners of the globe. There were men
sitting in deep armchairs reading newspapers, but as we
passed they lowered them just an inch and nodded their grey
heads.

Finally we sat down at our table. The head waiter bowed
as we did so and said in a joyful grand voice, 'Sir Edwin', as
if the name itself was wine to him. Babylon waited till he had
gone to fetch the wine list and then the pussycat turned to
me. His eyes were a light grey with green in the middle of
them, and his hair was pushed back in a band of grey, as if it
was made of good iron. When he spoke, it was like the
pouring of syrup.

'It is funny that we find ourselves on separate sides.
Nelson might win. After all, he's paying a lot and his image
has greatly improved, thanks to you and Max perhaps. What
is more, he claims to be an outsider, yet he is supported by
the PM, and Ken Trumply at Finance, who see Universal
Imperial as a den of Butskellism or 'wetness', as you young
might prefer to call it. Not that I am under any illusions
about the man. He is a genius who will do anything to win.
Look at the way his shares have performed.'

He looked at the tables around us and, delighted to catch

his eye, the red-faced and smooth-cheeked men of prosperity smiled back sleekly.

'He is too flashy. The British like ugly men who are neither poor nor rich. Nelson is not ugly enough and certainly not poor enough. By the way, I have a new chap working for me as a sort of personal assistant. He is very clever. Scottish. Fergus Fox. He was at Cambridge with you.'

'I know him well. We were competitors at the Union,' I told him lightly, though the news of the arrival of Fox in Sir Edwin's office made my blood run cold. 'How is Jesse?'

'Much better. He's about to move to the Docklands with his new girlfriend, who is a strange choice to say the least. It is a shame you see so little of each other now.' I agreed with him, for that was the greatest shame of all.

'Thank you for the lunch, Sir Edwin.'

'Let us not let Sir John Nelson come between us.' The mention of his name sent a shiver of recognition through the tables around ours and it reverberated from table to table as a dozen well-fed jaws began to discuss Nelson's bid. 'You know you are walking a dangerous tightrope,' he continued, 'and you should enjoy it. I am enjoying watching you from afar.'

'Good.'

'This floor is a family. It's a great fuckin' bed and we're all in it together. These guys are mine. Give me 10,000 bachelors with crippling mortgages. That is what Wallenstein needs.'

Wallenstein stood in the middle of the trading floor with his famous spear in one hand and the other hand on his hip. He was not talking to anyone in particular, but he knew everyone was listening to his gems of wisdom.

Penny winked at him as he passed her desk.

'How are y', kid?' he said. The whole trading floor leant over in their direction to hear the conversation.

'Tired. You know,' she said.

'I know. ' He gave her a macho grin. 'Sleep faster.'

Groom stood elegantly behind him with a single *cappuccino*

on a silver salver, emblazoned with the fine crest of Turd Brothers.

Neal von Smith met me at the mirror doors, where he ostentatiously checked his hair before greeting me.

'We're winning,' he said simply. 'Are y' busy?' This was the banker's perpetual greeting and it represented a challenge – are you as busy as I? I grunted that I was. 'Here at Wallenstein, you can be a director in five years at the age of twenty-eight. I would envisage a year as a graduate analyst, two years as an associate and, er, a salary of approximately 100 big ones. Then business school raising the learning curve to achieve a leverage in salary of, er, let's say, 150 big greenbacks. A swell firm,' he concluded, as we reached Wallenstein and the unblinking Groom.

'Thanks, Smithy,' yelled Lew, so that all the traders on their phones looked at von Smith over their screens and thought: That is Smith of corporate finance. The boss knows his name.

'Chino for Joe,' bellowed Lew at Groom, who walked impassively to fetch it.

Wallenstein put his arm around me and, twirling the spear dangerously (some employees longed to be wounded in order to be noticed by the great man and deliberately walked especially close to risk being hit), said, 'What can I do for you?'

'It is time to buy, as we discussed. He is near winning, but he needs the push on the share price. Ramp it. If it wavers, the whole bid wavers.'

'Gotcha. Naw problem. How is Peabody performing?'

'All right.'

'He runs around like a dame, worryin' about his body. Let me tell y', an investment banker never runs. He's not a banker, he's a fuckin' bimbo.' Wallenstein strode off down a bank of screens, yelling at an unfortunate trader, 'You bin in the toilet for twenny minutes and the market's moved a couple of points and y' missed it. In future, shit in y'own time, kiddo . . .'

'One *cappuccino*, Mr Rourke,' said Groom, with the faintest hint of a smile.

*

216

'Why did you do this to me?' Babylon asked her point blank.

'Y' needed it,' she said brutally. Then more truthfully, 'I wanted to be near you.'

He had been moved from the hospital in Cambridge and now he sat stiffly in a chair, in a silk dressing-gown and slippers engraved in gold with his crest, like a battered Noël Coward. The Thames flowed beneath the window of the old Victorian hospital, built by a philanthropist manufacturer.

Babylon had wasted his character on the tittering cargirls, social Hoovers and country oafs of his old life, but this was a flaw in his personality. Jesse had wasted his creativity on worthless dinner parties where his *bons mots* were worshipped for a moment then forgotten and unappreciated. Somehow, Jewels had gleaned this from watching him.

'The art of life is to give y' talents to those who'll love y' for 'em,' she said. 'They was dust in the wind, y' mates. They'd laugh, but they'd forget y'. Where are they now?' She sat and watched his lean face and she was sure that she was the one who would love him and appreciate him as the other worthless ones could not.

'I never belonged with them,' he told her. 'I will always swim the Jewish way: against the tide.'

Jewels needed the comfort that he alone could offer in the world she had known. She wanted his energy behind her, but the money and its trappings meant nothing to someone who had never known normal English middle-class life. Jewels did not give a damn for his wealth and his ancestry, but she appreciated that he could be the first family she had ever had. So, for all her unspoilt charm, she, like all of us, had her axe to grind.

She came from Tower Hamlets housing estates. Her father was the block's caretaker, a craggy-faced Victorian moralist, with greased-back hair and a cigarette always on his lip. He hated Jewels as much as he hated the blacks who lived in the flats. 'Standards are falling,' he would say. 'No one knows how to be'ave any more. It's these immigrants, that is what it is. And my daughter's no better, I'm sorry to say.'

She left home and stayed with the boys she met at the clubs where she and her friends danced and smoked. They were punks when she first met them, 'new romantics' when she first slept with them, and skinheads when she became one of them in the mid-eighties.

When he was stronger, Jewels, wrapped against the cold in a duffel coat, took Jesse to her squat beyond the East End down near the docks, in a row of disused houses that marked the border of Nelson City. He stood stiffly at the doorway and they looked out at the new imperial London, lit up with searchlights that made tunnels of light into the sky. There was glass in the windows now, and plants in the atriums of the shopping arcades, but a strange unnatural emptiness lingered in the new streets as if time had not yet begun in Nelson City.

Jesse missed Goldtrough and the grandeur of his old world, but then he realized that this was a real adventure. Now he was out on his own with this strange thug of a girl in a squat God-knows-where. Even he, the raconteur and viveur, could not have invented this strange *affaire* with the girl who had almost killed him. Babylon broke into a smile, for now he was truly alive. He had changed his life and that is one of the best things a man can do.

'Is it finished?' Jewels said.

'Yes. Nelson's son was up at Cambridge with me. My father told me that Nelson was about to win the bid he launched . . .'

'What the fuck do I care?' she said, laughing again, her longer hair blowing Titian red in the dusty wind that blew down the stark avenues of new London. 'Come in, it's getting dark and it's cold.'

She turned on the naked light bulb that lit the room with the yellow texture of Edwardian gaslight, and she lit an electric ring that glowed orange in the half-light.

For the first time in his life, Jesse was not sure what to do. Jewels went to the corner of the room and turned on a tinpot record player. Jesse braced himself for a deafening onslaught of punk, but a ridiculous crackly French love song began to play, with schoolchildren singing '*Enchantant la-la-la*'. The two of them burst out laughing to hide how the song somehow moved them.

'Y're gonna dance with me,' she said roughly and she went and stood close to him. He put his arms round her and danced formally to the music. '*Enchantant,*' he thought.

Their difference of accents and worlds robbed him of his decadence and she of her roughness. The jaded pair suddenly felt young and unsure. He smelt of soap and aftershave and she smelt of cigarettes and leather, and they danced nervous circles around each other as the record played over and over again. She seemed to him freer than anyone he had ever known, and he felt he had never known anyone before. She was the first. She was like music itself, for she could be played anywhere and she would sound just as fine.

He kissed her very slowly and she kissed him back. They kissed for a long time, and then they fell together on the old mattress and peeled their clothes off. They smelt each other's skins, savouring the moment. He appreciated her strength and her energy.

Jesse remembered how he had always revelled in his own nakedness, flaunting his body like a militiaman's truncheon as he approached the bed. Now he felt strangely weak. Jewels, who had taken rough men, sailors, dockers, wanderers, skinheads and streetfighters, and treated them to sweat- and blood-drowned fucks that were like street brawls, was now attracted by his elegance and fragility. She was surprised to find that she treasured him, she who had valued nothing before.

It was dark, and the darkness took out the incidentals so that they felt they were truly alone in London.

Suddenly, the walls exploded in flashes of light. They were firing fireworks and rockets over Nelson City.

'We have control, Sir Methuselah. We have at this moment 54 per cent of the acceptances. I control Universal Imperial.' Nelson stood silhouetted against the afternoon light of the August sky, high over the river. The autumn sun caught the new glass in the windows of Nelson City beneath and around Nelson's office. The Thames shone a melancholy gold.

In the office, McGill Peabody was slapping backs, shaking his head and saying over and over again, 'We ran with the ball, we played the game and we won. This team's a winner. Sir John is a true sportsman.'

Max, on a portable phone, was in his element, with his voice husky, his hair on end, spreading the news to his network in a relentless parade of famous names: 'Yeah, Prime Minister, we got it. Thank you. Ken, we've got a majority. Gr-r-r-eat! Yeah, the chopper's gotta land on Nelson's heliport and take us on to the offices of UI. Call Esmond Powerlord at the *Materialist* and tell him the news ... Yeah, yeah, is that Mr Operahouse? Hi, Sydney. We won. The front page of the *Blue Tit*? Gr-r-r-eat ... Bye. It's top news. Hunky dory. Start drafting the press release ...'

Nelson was listening to Botham-Jagger at the other end of the line. He put down the telephone. Everyone congratulated him. He smiled distantly, standing straight and elegant before the window, with his aquiline profile. He is an emperor now, I thought, and I am here to see him enthroned. How Kodell would relish this moment, for this is History!

'We have won because of hard work and good advice, unfettered by bureaucracy and institutionalism,' said our Caesar.

The chopper soared high over Nelson City as the sun began to go down on London. Its towers and halls and arcades stood unreal and unlived in beneath us, like a toy city. We flew along the river, over barges filled with coal and majestic bridges lined with commuting cars. The people massed in the streets, rushing to the underground stations, walking home and already fanning out into the City to eat and dance and spend their money.

We landed on the roof of the charmless Universal Imperial building, standing square and thick like a stone pug.

'Let's blow 'em away. Let's let 'em know who won, who played best,' shouted the excited McGill Peabody above the spinning rotors of the chopper. Nelson, suddenly silent and rocklike in the satisfaction of his triumph, turned to him with scorn.

'We are all to act with the greatest courtesy,' he said tonelessly. 'Their building will be sold. Their staff rationalized.

Their brands will be consolidated into international names for quality. Their directors will be pensioned off. Their loss-making subsidiaries will be closed down or sold off. Universal Imperial will be a first-class British company again.'

We were shown down to the boardroom with Nelson walking first, followed by Peabody (who was oblivious to his recent humiliation and kept saying, 'This team's a winner'), Max, speaking ceaselessly into his cordless telephone, and myself.

The high and broad oak doors were opened by doormen in UI uniforms. The directors sat at the long table with the white-haired Sir Methuselah in the chair at the far end. They stood up as one man, taking their cue from Botham-Jagger.

'Please be seated,' said Nelson. Only the Chairman remained standing. He was a fine figure of a man in his seventies, his suit immaculate, his hair virgin white, his face the healthy outdoor rare-roast-beef red of the man who has led a vigorous life of war, business and sport.

'On behalf of the Board, welcome to Universal Imperial, Sir John.'

'Universal Imperial is Britain at its finest. I shall make changes to ensure that the company remains the best, without, I hope, altering its unique traditions. I would like to ask all those present to remain on the Board for the present and to ask Sir Methuselah to serve as my Vice-Chairman.'

A beam of pleasure crossed the old man's face for a moment, for he valued face above all else. He had dreaded a humiliation from this jumped-up rogue he so hated. Now he would be able to leave with decorum and dignity. In a quivering voice, he accepted.

'Tonight, Nelson City will be opened. I invite you all with your advisers and wives to join us there tonight.' Nelson turned automatically and walked out of the room and back to the chopper. The rotors were still turning. Botham-Jagger's mandarin's face was set in an expression of relief and an overwhelming sadness.

'I have bought the largest company in Europe, the realization of a dream I had when I was a boy. I have worked since I was twenty to achieve what I have achieved tonight. The running of Universal will be very different now. I will turn the company into a modern corporation, with incentives and share schemes for staff. No job will be secure without a clear role. There will be no more jobs for life. Merit will replace the old school tie.'

The crowd beneath the podium on the steps of the Nelson Arcade stood in silence, revelling in the knowledge that this speech would go into legend, but trying to understand the dour messages they were hearing. The business world would never be the same again. The thin economical voice echoed off the concrete façades of new wine bars and brasseries, office blocks and pubs, flats and houses and off the older buildings across the river.

'That said,' Nelson continued, 'the whole Board is fired now.' He stopped and smiled over the heads of the crowd, who were trying to gauge this man of decadent ambition and personal austerity.

'That was a joke,' he added. 'I hope you like the view – as far as you can see, I own it. Thank you.' The bemused applause crackled from building to building like volleys of machine-gun fire.

The fireworks began to explode overhead, throwing strange dashes of light into the crowd and on to the river. A rocket's blazing flight revealed Botham-Jagger and Sir Edwin Babylon, two discreet well-groomed lionheads lost in the crowds. Sir Edwin spotted me.

'Well done, this is the moment of triumph. He can do no wrong now. He is so high and mighty that I wonder if any man could rise further.'

The old Chairman smiled wryly. 'One is never too young to be on the winning side,' he said.

Fox was suddenly beside me, shaking my hand and watching me closely as if he was searching for my secret alchemy.

'Well, well, well,' came that long-lost Scots tune, as elegant and precise as it had always been. 'We face one another again. Chuff chuff goes the Nelson train.'

'It's over now.'

'No, it's only beginning.'

'Nelson won.'

'You wrecked my political career with your friend Jesse.'

'It was a long time ago.'

'It was yesterday. My father read in the newspapers that I was a cheat. It broke his heart.' His voice was softer than ever. He said it again. 'You broke his heart.'

The softness hung in the air for a moment. A firework landed in the Thames.

'I'll avenge it,' he said.

'Vengeance always diminishes the avenger, Fergus. You should know that by now.'

'Then I shall make you debase the thing you love. This is a victory for the Right of the party, but even you know that this is a creed for balance sheets, not humans. While She is winning, I'll follow her to the end of the world, but when She begins to stop winning, we 'wets' will make her pay for everything. She will be blamed for Nelson and more. She will end her days hated and despised and bitter. She will travel full circle.'

'We have grown up under her. She may have a multitude of faults, She may be terrible, but we will never know better again.'

Nelson had gone. The fireworks were over, but for the pressmen, the PR men and the great British public, the party had just begun. The bankers from Wallenstein had dropped their jackets and were down to their braces and their pink shirts, telling tales of the bid, full of heroic acts of arrogance and conquest. Von Smith and Peabody were talking about the fees and the vast bonuses they were to receive at year-end.

Wallenstein himself was lecturing Penny the sales assistant, whose legs alone were longer than the rest of him: 'The commission . . . structure in the markets . . . have changed since I started thirty years ago. They were $\frac{3}{4}$ per cent then. Now they're $1\frac{7}{8}$!'

'Oh, yeaaah, baby,' said the bimbo, who clearly did not appreciate the importance of the history of commissions in the global markets. The management consultants had loosened their ties but remained together as a solid and

223

exhausted phalanx of nameless gloom. The public relations men and women were gathered around a triumphant Max, who was struggling to cram so many important names into every sentence that they were no longer sentences at all: 'Thatcher, Operahouse, Trumply . . .' Meanwhile the accountants and lawyers, who had barely seen the light of day for months, wandered dazed through the crowds, staring like aliens at the bright lights and the female species.

Lastly, the citizens of London danced and sang and delighted in this new pleasure dome, where they could buy their white suits, and blazers, and culottes and dresses with French and Italian labels. They were shareholders and property owners, though their mortgages were too large and they knew nothing of shares, but this market had given them happiness and independence and self-esteem.

The cafés and brasseries were serving *cappuccinos* and rosé and Cointreau and Martinis and croissants as if this were Paris. A discothèque in the Nelson Hotel blared out synthesizer music, and long-legged, long-haired girls with short skirts danced in groups in the streets.

Only the local East Enders stared at the flash lights and the excited Londoners who had made them foreigners in their own streets.

I stood down by the river on the quay behind the Nelson hotel, away from the crowds and the music and lights. Once clippers from Jamaica, Shanghai or Cape Town had delivered tons of silk, molasses and grain to this very spot. Nelson had re-created that old spirit in the manner of today. The new construction was still going on. There were roads to smooth, tar to lay, windows to clean. In the unnatural glare of their searchlights, builders in tin hats and overalls worked to the last minute.

Here I could hear the boats and platforms banging against the quaystones and the clink of their chains as they rose and fell with the grey water. The city and the sky glowed with the prosperity of the age. Cars hooted on distant bridges. A boat blew its horn downriver. The disco music reached me like the memories of a circus.

Two figures were dancing down by the water in the shadow of the wrecked houses that marked the edge of the development. The boy with a haystack of hair was kicking and strutting in a way that made my eyes strain and my stomach tighten. Babylon was dancing by the water. They danced out of sight.

Kick was beside me, a dark perfect imp in her boots and her short skirt that showed the knees that had driven Francis crazy.

'You won. I knew you would. You are up there with them,' she said huskily. With the simplicity of those who honestly believe that their friends are the most successful people in the world, she believed that I had won the great bid.

'Britain will always remember tonight and these years. What a time to be alive. What a time to be young, when everything is golden. The fun of it, of eating out, of dressing well, of buying a flat. This is the time when everyone looks at Nelson and says, I could do that. There is nothing in my way. There have been rich men before, but who has created a new city like this? Who will ever leave such a monument? Nelson is a man who has taken his place in the stars.'

'It's like the Third Empire, but with direction and morality. What will it mean to the future?'

'History will say: look at what Nelson did. Everything is possible.'

Like a fine apple with a worm in it, there was something rotten in Kick. I wanted to bite the apple before it was gone for ever.

'When I have a lover,' she said, 'no one looks after him like I do. His interests are mine. He loves going to bed with me, because I make him love it. Forget these parochials, these Emmas, your bimbos. I can talk them out of court, I can beat them as a conversationalist, as a woman and as a whore.'

I waited until she had finished. Summer was long gone and it was suddenly very cold. The water swilled in waves and foam, breaking on the quay.

We stood close on the bank, her hot breath firing up like a

miniature geyser in the winter air. It was dark and the river rolled and washed up the bank and banged the moored boats against one another, so that their rowlocks spun and their timbers creaked. The clouds were rushing, now an impenetrable black, now wispy and transparent. Her neck was thrown back, shining white in the dark. I kissed her throat and moved to her lips. She could not refuse me this time.

I pushed my hand up her skirt from behind and she parted her legs. I reached up and over her tights; she wore no knickers and she was a copious, curdled stream stinking of men's dreams, worth the wait, worth waiting for ever.

This was the night of the possible. The builders were whistling and cheering behind us, as scent-drenched, rive-gauche-jacketed, Lady Haute Couture, shoulder-padded, Bond-Streeted, twenty-carat Kick stood there with her legs open and shining.

'Let them watch,' she said open-mouthed, bare-teethed. 'This will make their day. It will make their life. They will never see the like of this again.'

There was wealth everywhere and we were celebrating a market that would never fall, an exclusivity that was universal, we felt we were fucking for democracy. Her little hot, steaming river ran down her legs and into her tights and through my fingers and thence into the cold and dull grey-watered Thames.

We fumbled in the cold, with buttons and zips and coats and boxer shorts until we were skin to flesh. I was hard as if I would never be any other way again. If at first we were cold, we could have melted all the snow in the Arctic by the end. As we wrestled, our breath visible and still tasting of the wine from the great party, our saliva grew cold on each other's cheeks.

We travelled far and so far and so, so often that there was no time to be cold. We just made love all the harder, until we were sore and she had felt the last of the heat shot deep inside her and the heat we had made had gone.

'What do you think of me now?' Her words were as husky as I had ever heard them. We did ourselves up and looked at

226

one another. The builders, standing together like workers in the brochure for a new Soviet dam project, were resentful now and watched us in hateful silence.

'I love you,' I said untruthfully, though how I admired her body and her lust and her pursuit of pleasure.

'Don't lie to me, Rourke.'

I told her again but she had believed me the first time.

There was suddenly a cold wind racing along the Thames and along Nelson's new streets, carrying the paper that the revellers had left high into the air.

'You always loved me. There will be a storm tomorrow. Look at the seagulls.'

'I've always loved you,' I kept saying because I enjoyed lying. And because it was a cold night.

22

The storm awoke me. For a moment, I thought the world was ending. Emma was holding me beside her. The scaffolding in the building development opposite my flat collapsed with the agonizing sound of tearing and twisting iron. The girders crashed into the pavement, shattering the paving stones and bouncing like deadly matchsticks along the street. The wind shrieked like the voice of a tortured man, rising in terrifying crescendos, dropping only to rise again.

By the time morning came, London had been ravaged. The trees of the squares, planted hundreds of years ago, had been felled in one night. They had crushed sports cars and railings beneath them. Cars had been upturned and trains derailed. The building sites that covered so much of London had become like battlefields of felled cranes, destroyed scaffolding, smashed glass. In Covent Garden, in Chelsea and of course in Nelson City, the shattered remains of the tables and chairs of the new brasseries, restaurants and cafés peppered the streets, like the morning after an earthquake.

Bright called me from the office.

'As if the storm isn't enough, there's something wrong with the market. Get down to Wallenstein's now. Nelson and I will be down later.' In 1987, there was only one 'market', the sharemarket, where even grannies and schoolboys were buying shares.

Wallenstein stood like a man of granite in the middle of an empire that was disintegrating before our very eyes.

'Joe, the market opened late. The storm fucked up the systems. Fuck knows why – it opened in freefall. We're down 100 points already. New York's 'bout t' open. If New

York goes down, the whole show is over. Everything we built.'

'New York's open,' shouted Penny from the rampart of telephones and screens in front of us. Lew and I watched the green numbers as they flashed on the screen: Dow Jones 2589.

'Why don't you just sell everything?' I said.

'We're in Catch-22,' said Wallenstein. 'Our holdings are so goddam big, we'd cause a Crash just by selling them. So we're selling slowly everywhere. But slowly. Confidence is the key.'

The floor had gone silent. Everyone watched the figure. Suddenly, the numbers began to drop: 2250 ... 2240 ... 2230 ...

The floor gasped in the silence so that you could feel the air contract as they inhaled. They watched Wallenstein now and they looked back at the screen: he was the king of the market. Like blind puppies, each one believed that somehow he would have a trick up his sleeve to save the day. Wallenstein kept his eyes on the numbers: 2225 ... 2210. He moved his head to watch the floor.

'OK,' he said, quietly. 'Let's get out before the whole fucking ship goes down.'

In a fluid slow-motion mass, the floor exploded into a crazed tangle of telephone wires and screens with men and women straining to get their orders through. Everyone was shouting, a thousand voices yelling 2190 ... 2150, the numbers that told the story. The salesmen and traders were waving phones, their eyes desperately watching the screens as they said, then shouted, finally cried, 'Sell. Sell. Sell.'

Wallenstein watched them impassively, unsmiling and observant. Groom was beside him, grey-haired and nonchalant, the eternal *cappuccino* on the Turd Brothers salver.

'Ever seen a Crash, Groom?'

'1929, sir, and 1973.'

'So this is no surprise?'

'It is said, sir, that what goes up must come down. Another *cappuccino*?'

The situation was desperate now. This was no longer a

correction – this was a Crash. The dreams, careers and fortunes of all of Wallenstein's thousand traders were crashing down too.

There was no longer any point in following the usual rituals – now they were all alone in a vast market that was careering out of control. The desk managers, tough men feared by their staff, prowled among the traders trying to keep control.

The much-vaunted team spirit of Wallenstein Schlong Turd Brothers disappeared like the nauseous humbug it was. In its place, from beneath the greased hair, the Italian suits, the rawest despair and the lowest hunger were taking over. From worrying about whether they would be able to get a reservation in their favourite restaurant, these people were suddenly fighting for the roofs over their heads.

In normal times, the bankers never dreamed of even visiting the Settlements Department. But now, with everyone selling at the same time, the systems had broken down and the traders were stamping their own sales dockets to make them legal before it was too late. Traders rushed over to the stamping desk and then back to their desks again to continue selling their positions until hundreds were fighting to get to the Settlements Department.

'Let's go help stamp the dockets,' said Wallenstein and joined the rush, which had become a rout. Groom followed with his stately step in his appointed position just behind the boss. Before we could reach the desk to help out, someone began shouting, 'The system's going down.' The traders rushed forward to catch the last moments of the system. This was the edge: if the system crashed before the trade had been checked in, the trade did not exist and they still owned the shares. Their voices were hoarse, their ties wrenched down with their shirts torn open and soaked in sweat.

Standing erect in the full path of the marauding traders, Groom, only hours earlier the proud symbol of Wallenstein's success, was knocked aside, his salver and the *cappuccino* sent flying and bouncing absurdly along the floor beneath the Italian hooves of the well-heeled herd. He lay on the floor, his beloved black tails torn and dirty as the traders jumped over him.

'It's down. It's over,' the voice called. The herd stopped and turned back to watch the screens. There was nothing they could do as the meaningless figures continued to fall. New York had further to fall, but London was finished.

The dazed Groom, who was over seventy, stayed on the floor. No one offered to help him up. We just stepped over him. 'We're fucking wrecked. Twenty million long. Wrecked,' traders were saying, while others were exultant to have got all their clients out before it was too late: 'We're flat. Thank God, we're flat.'

Wallenstein was sitting in his glass office, with his spear twirling in his hand. He pressed an intercom: 'Bring me the Crash scenario,' and then he spun his future predictor to FIRE. 'That is the future,' he said.

'Why did you ask me over?' I said.

He laughed: 'Nelson's share price is . . .' he played with his Reuter's screen . . . '100 pence. It is now worth fuck-all. All those crazy loans to pay for Universal Imperial depend on the value of Nelson. Now it ain't worth nuthin'. That's why you're here. And that's why he's on his way. The party's over.'

He got up and stared out through the glass at the financial ballroom. The traders stood in small groups in front of the screens. The floors were covered in useless dockets. Telephones hung in tangled clusters from the dealing desks. Groom was brushing himself down. Everyone had a story to tell.

'They're just fuckin' traders,' Wallenstein went on, 'they don't know a thing. We took 'em on like the Iranians are using thirteen-year-old children to fight the Iraqis. We gave 'em a gun and a grenade and we said "Charge" and we hoped that some of 'em 'd hit somethun'. When there's a minefield to clear, they send for the thirteen-year-old kids, put 'em in a line and make 'em run across it. It's gonna be the same here. Now, we're at the edge of the minefield and besides, we don't need so many soldiers. Two years ago, we had twenty traders in London. Today, I've got about 1,100. Yesterday, that was fine. Now, they've all gotta go.'

'Are you just going to fire them all?'

Wallenstein swivelled his squat prizefighter's torso towards me. His shirt was undone, and tufts of grey hair showed at the top. He was amused by my scruples.

'Have you ever fired a man?'

'No.'

'Have you ever been fired?'

'No.'

'They are just the soldiers. It's nothing. Business is war, and in war it's the soldiers who die. That's their job. They don't understand the tactics or the big picture. They know nothing. When it began to crash yesterday, before the storm, they were the last to sell. They didn't understand the markets. Look, Joe, when I bought Turd Brothers, I fired the whole fucking firm.'

It was almost the end of the day. The traders were packing up. They all stared at Wallenstein, their hero and general, who had marshalled them across the markets of the world. He smiled at them.

'They've made a bomb in the last couple of years. They'll be all right, but they're just soldiers,' he said again. 'They're loose change.'

'Sir John Nelson and Mr Max Bright are here, sir,' a bodyless voice announced from the intercom.

'Send 'em up,' he said. 'I was in Vietnam. Nam was the best training ground for a banker. Blow away the gooks. Christ, Joe, after what we did out there, firing a thousand traders is easy.'

Nelson and Bright were shepherded across the trading floor by McGill Peabody and Neal von Smith.

'This is the bear market, gentlemen, and it began today.'

'I am not interested in the market, Lew, what about Nelson?' Nelson gave nothing away, though I searched his face for despair. There was none.

'Gentlemen, capitalism is a messy business. The market has wiped out your stock, John. Nelson closed at 90 pence. It'll fall further tomorrow. McGill, how does this affect the structure of the financing?'

Peabody's satisfied face was exhausted and deflated. In his

hysteria, I caught him whispering under his breath the meaningless slogans that had meant so much yesterday: 'Team's a winner. Team's a winner ...' He hardly seemed able to speak. I caught his eyes, and in their sadness I suddenly realized that he had all his own money in the market. Still in the market were all his savings, all those bonuses, all the estates he wanted to buy, the cars, the Eton school fees for McGill junior, all gone.

'Well, Nelson's financing was dependent on the company being worth a certain amount. The necessary share price was 250 pence. If it is now 90 pence, the loans are in default. We can try to renegotiate ... but ...' He opened his arms and closed them again impotently.

'John, you're fighting for your life,' said Lew, holding his spear like a royal sceptre. 'That's the truth. A banker's like a doctor. You tell us how y' feel and we'll tell y' what is really wrong with you. I've given it to y' straight.'

'I want a coffee,' Max announced suddenly. The Crash was spoiling all his fun. He pouted sulkily like a child whose favourite train set has inexplicably broken. 'Where's Groom?'

'Groom is a luxury for the bull market, Max. The chairman can't have a butler in a bear market. He won't be here tomorrow. *Cappuccinos* are for bull markets.'

'Let's put him out of his misery, Fergus.'

'I have enough evidence. The unnatural movements in the Nelson share price; purchases by Swiss holding companies. We have it all, Sir Edwin.'

'Do we know who owns these Swiss companies, Fergus?'

'The Ministry will find that out.'

'So let's call Ken Trumply. I know him very well. He regards Nelson as the vanguard of his new order – the financial spearhead of his ideological libertarian revolution. He was right, of course, but he is Secretary of State for Finance and he will let us act in such a way as to keep the scandal to a minimum. After all, once you've been in the wilderness, you never want to go back. Sheila, can you get Sir Kenneth Trumply at Finance on the line, please.'

Fergus Fox, in a heavy pinstripe, sat in front of Sir Edwin Babylon's desk, which was constructed from part of Napoleon's carriage at Waterloo. He knew that Nelson was close to the Right of the party, and the destruction of Nelson would therefore serve a useful purpose. After all, was not Nelson the worst of the developers? There was something else, which Fox did not deny to himself: Rourke worked with Nelson, though he had little idea at that point how closely I was involved.

That morning he had lain in bed with Sally in their terraced Clapham house. The alarm had gone off. Sally was high-powered in the City. She was a fund manager. Fox said to his wife, 'Do I have to go on with this endless rat-race, always trying to succeed? Always chasing Rourke. I am tired of it. Rourke and I are one of a kind. We're kindred spirits on different sides. Does it have to go on?'

Sally Fox thought, where will we be if he loses his ambition? Nowhere. I married his ambition and now his ambition is my ambition. She said, 'No, don't think like that. You must go on.' She added as a little taunt, 'After all, you have a long way to go.'

So this was to be his vengeance.

Jesse had not been implicated in his destruction, Fergus had decided sensibly, since he was now working for Jesse's father. Sir Edwin was on the telephone to the Secretary of State for Finance.

'Kenneth, it's Edwin. Needless to say, you're aware of the Nelson situation.'

'Hello, Edwin. When someone is described as a "situation", you know they are in trouble. Yes, we are watching the situation.'

'In the course of our work on the bid, we unearthed some facts that your Department should know.'

'We also monitored it. The Department of Finance gave it a clean bill of health. That's all.'

'This is an official conversation, Ken.'

'The government does not want a scandal.'

'That is a truism. Naturally, we also wish to avoid scandal.'

'So we are agreed.'

'No. Some action must be taken.'

'Why?'

'Ken. If you wish to make a point of principle out of Nelson's criminal behaviour, it's up to you.'

'Who mentioned a crime?'

'I do not believe that you wish to leave office . . . again.'

'If the damage can be limited . . .'

'Limited?'

'To one person, Edwin . . .'

'Ahh. We understand one another. The City knows something happened and the City will have to be appeased now or later. We must give them one head. At least.'

'OK, one.'

'One head?'

'One head. If we must.'

'One it is, Ken. Goodbye.'

Babylon put the telephone down and stretched like a cat. He had achieved what he wished. He looked up at the portraits of old Babylons who had owned the bank and knew that he was as clever as any of them. He was a man of his time, as they had been of theirs. He was a modern man.

'Lunch?' said Fox.

'The Club.'

'YUP YUP YUP YUP OUT OUT OUT OUT,' chanted the crowd of gloom-laden grim reapers who had gathered outside Wallenstein's to celebrate the supposed end of the era of the City.

Jewels's old skinhead mates were there: the Crash was the fall of the toffee-nosed silk-tied bastards with prissy birds and smart cars. (Every skinhead also believed that these stuck-up birds enjoyed the lifestyle of their yuppie men but yearned only for the sexual prowess of a real man – like a skinhead for example.) The suits of the yuppies were not just uniforms of law and order, they were also signposts that read: I am richer than you are.

The skinheads were the thirteenth tribe of modern England, for they had no stake in the country at all. Words like socialism and fascism had no real meaning for them, since these were ideas created long ago without a thought for their lot in life. They were not really poor, since they received a variety of doles, but they were social brigands. They were the political flotsam that would turn up at any demonstration.

Barry Syssons was leading the demonstration with a loud-hailer. It was ironic that Syssons and his comrades of middle-class conscience would so often find themselves marching beside the skinheads in their boots and swastikas. Syssons always regarded them as another oppressed minority, while they presumed he was a skinhead who needed a haircut.

When I came out of the Wallenstein building, Syssons spotted me at once and began to lecture me.

'We can never be friends,' he said, 'for you are part of the upper middle class who think only of their own prosperity. All your mates are bankers, rich Jews and capitalists. These years were unnatural. We know that now. Why do you think that freak storm happened? Why do you think the storm caused the Crash today? It is the end of your era. The Crash has punished you. It will make this country one again.'

'You are wrong. This country will never be the same again. As for you and your class, you came from a far more privileged home than us. It's a question of character. Class is a weakling's excuse. Besides, why are all you Cambridge radicals now working for accountancy firms?'

A six-foot skinhead pushed Syssons from behind and then held him by the scruff of the neck:

'So you're an accountant, are y'? You little fucking yuppie.'

'Technically, Sir John, you're bankrupt,' said Mr Ded, the accountant. He had had his single lock of hair cut off, but he missed it. His hand nervously scoured his shiny head for just a hint of that lock that was no more.

'Don't tell me about technicalities, Mr Ded. What exactly is the position as far as Universal Imperial is concerned?'

'It is an asset for which you paid $20 billion but which is now only worth $12 billion. Furthermore, the $20 billion you borrowed is now due to be paid back. That is the position.'

Nelson was calm as the terrified Mr Ded gave him the fatal news. The game was up. He would have to begin again. There would be large sums of money left and he would have to found another Nelson plc. The chair spun around so that he could stare out at his beloved London, the city he had opened with a developer's scalpel.

'Is there anything else?' asked Mr Ded.

'Thank you, Mr Ded . . . for everything.'

'It has been, it is a pleasure to serve such a . . . a . . . such a man.' Ded meant it, for he thought that Nelson had a better understanding of accountancy than any other businessman in the country. That was his definition of a man.

'Shall I go?' I asked him.

'No,' said Nelson. 'I'm expecting something. Let us wait together.' He was still staring out at London. It was dark outside now. We could just see the lights of London and that pink glow on the horizon. 'The developments aren't finished. After so much work.'

'Can I do anything?'

'I loved to build. I enjoyed the early days most of all. Then I did my own building, carried the ladders, and drove the van. We were small fry then, you see. I used to do the paint work myself . . . Building is knowing how to handle materials. You have to love your materials, appreciate them. The bricks, the cement, the tools, the scaffolding. I loved it, and the men were marvellous.'

'How did you get started?'

'When I was a boy, all I remember is my village burning. All the buildings were burning. There were people burning in them. When I got to London, all I wanted to do was build. To make homes. The money came later. I loved my buildings like my own family.'

The intercom bleeped and a voice said, 'Two gentlemen on their way from the Ministry of Finance and the Fraud Squad.'

Suddenly the two men were in the doorway. They ignored me and stared at the back of Nelson's chair and beyond it the Thames.

237

'After so much work,' he said again. He sighed. 'Joe, you will do what you have to do.' He spun the chair around and shook my hand. He then turned to the two men, who stood in their raincoats in the doorway.

'What are the charges?'

One of the men began to read: 'Theft of Nelson Plc funds: two counts. Ten counts of theft of shareholders' funds; eight counts of conspiracy to defraud; five counts of insider trading; seven counts of theft of your own funds . . .'

The policeman stopped reading. He did not understand the list of offences. Nelson looked up.

'Shall we go, gentlemen?' he said at last.

'That would be best, Sir John.' He rose and walked out of the door. I followed the two men.

'That was the nicest office we've seen yet,' whispered one to the other.

'Do you think the Botham-Jaggers are short of money, darling?' said Lady Babylon, as she leafed through the latest auction brochure from Christie's.

'Quite the opposite. After all, they were bought out of Universal Imperial at the height of the market.' Sir Edwin was undergoing one of his wife's periodic visitations. These exhausted him far more than a business meeting. She was like an open wound on his skin, and whenever he saw her he felt the pain again.

'You see, they're selling their Velázquez, so they are probably short of a pound or two.'

'It is rather ugly and Methuselah has never liked it.'

'Poor Penelope!' she said, full of pity and delight, having not listened to a word her husband had said. 'Short of cash.'

'I must get to work. Look, Fergus Fox, my assistant, is here for a meeting,' he said, ashamed that he hated his wife when he had adored her once. He wished she had not drunk, had not lived at cocktail parties and slept with everyone. Nowadays, she slept with her lodgers. It was part of the rent they had to pay, he joked grimly to himself, though she was still good-looking in a blowsy sort of way.

'Hello, Mr Fox,' she said as she left, looking him up and

down. What a charming young man, she thought to herself, I bet he's a great fuck.

Fox watched her go, with a mixture of disgust and a distasteful lust. He regarded her as his boss's only flaw.

'Right,' said the boss. 'Nelson.'

'Under arrest,' came the clipped Presbyterian voice.

'So who did buy the shares?'

'The syndicate – Goncourt, Wallenstein, Hinton . . . subsidized by Nelson with his shareholders' money,' said Fox, as if a murder had been committed. 'Criminals – and they were organized by Rourke. He was the link man.'

'They are not exactly criminals, old chap. After all, until last year, we used to do this on every takeover we ever did.'

Fox scowled, then smiled. He was quick to change with the wind. Now he understood: this was a case of *realpolitik*, not morality.

'We cannot arrest those three. Together with Nelson, that would be just about every talented financier in the country. There is to be minimal scandal.'

'But Rourke is at the very centre. He is the linkman of the case. Without him there is nothing.'

'So what do you suggest, Fergus?'

'His head. The City must have his head too.' Babylon watched him and laughed. What a zealot for justice and purity this Scottish chap is, he thought, especially considering he cheated in elections at Cambridge.

'There is only one head they want. And only one head they get, but the case must be secure. Rourke has to tell everything, so that there's little action in court. If he insists on being a hero and protecting his master, then he'll have to go to the guillotine too. But remember, if you start cutting off heads left and right, it won't stop until you lose your own. One head is enough.'

'Yes, Sir Edwin. One. Or two.'

'Never trust a man whose father and grandfather you don't know,' said Drippy. 'That is the moral of the story.'

The news of Nelson's arrest had electrified London. The diehards from Cambridge gathered at Darling's Chelsea pad like delighted vultures. They were full of the intense excitement one feels when one is close to the protagonists in a terrible scandal. Now they sat among the paintings and the John and Jons on the flawless wooden floor.

'He had four Francis Bacons; he had rashers of Bacons and I sold him a John and Jon last week so, whatever grief he may be in now, Nelson had taste . . .'

'We're not interested in his taste,' snapped Kick, her American accent breaking through. 'He wasn't even English. Have you seen the papers? Have you seen the *Materialist* today? It is just like a mini-series. What a story!'

'I bet he had Jewblood,' lisped Drippy. 'How else could he have been so dodgy and crafty. Something in his profile. Has to be Jewblood.'

'But it sounds so English – "Nelson" – what is foreign about that?' asked Camilla Party-Jones.

'It's all in the paper.'

The media were in seventh heaven. A story of corrupt financiers, of the lives of the very rich, grannies and schoolboys losing their money – it was all there. Somehow, the Blue Rinses and their *Daily Materialist*, the voice of little England that had loved Nelson when he was buying castles, discovered that "John Nelson" was not his name at all.

He had been born Jan Strakosch in an unpronounceable province of a forgotten empire. There were photographs of a little peasant hut in a Central European village ('the home of the Strakosch family') beside the pictures of a great mansion in Park Lane, a Berkshire manor house, Bonnie Prince Charlie's castle and an imposing Scottish hall ('John Nelson-Strakosch's $10 million castle, bought from the 10th Earl of Needapenny – a long way from Moldavia'). It was a foreign story that had ended in a very English way.

'I suppose he was always wather a slippewy chawacter,' said Drippy when Party-Jones had read her paper. 'I mean, what kind of a name is "Stwakosch"?'

'Always doubtful in morals and origins,' agreed Punjab.

'Oh, yes,' Camilla said, 'I always thought that.'

'Daddy tells me he represented the worst aspects of the City. Daddy was on one of his boards – you know he sits on so-o-o-o many boards, very boring – anyway, he sat on some board with Nelson, or should I say Goulash . . .' Yarborough chortled '. . . and they had to shake hands and, of course, he had a slippery handshake. Daddy said he was like a second-hand car dealer.'

In truth, the girls were particularly confused by the whole story. One week their mothers were begging them to have Matt Nelson to stay, and now their parents were telling them that Nelson was a disgusting fifth columnist undermining English values. They had marked down Matt as their friend, their A1 friend, their best friend, and in their dreams they saw his face kissing their lips.

They had imagined walking down the aisle with this billionaire. Now there was to be no peerage, no kiss, no Matt, and all their opinions had to be reversed. They did not feel they had been wrong as such. Instead, they conveniently forgot that they had ever been so keen on Matt Nelson in the first place.

'It's such a tragic situation. For Matt. We knew him, of course, but it was always clear there was something murky,' concluded Joanna. 'To think that all that time, he wasn't who he said he was. He was a criminal.'

It was all so confusing. How could he fall just like that? Did he still look the same now he had fallen? What does it mean, she thought, and who decided that he should fall? Had not the Yarboroughs always been rich and wouldn't we always be, until the end of time? The world was divided. Some were the rich for ever and some were the poor. This man had interfered with this chain of being.

So safe in her income and so satisfied by the people she knew, Yarborough felt suddenly relieved that the dangerous and unsettling influence of Nelson was gone for ever.

Darling was fairer: 'Look, Matt wasn't a criminal. There is goin' to be some strife, that is all . . .'

'Stwife! These impostors emerged out of the Judeo-Slavic zoo, became very wich and now they will disappear again, leaving nothing. No one will never know who they were or where they came from. In the process there will be a terrible scandal.'

'I heard he used to hound his enemies out of the country,' said Jo.

'Mafia-money!' (Punjab.)

'Daddy said he was refused entry to Toffs.' (Party-Jones.)

'Jesse once told me that Nelson never tipped more than 1p in a restaurant.' (Yarborough.)

'My mama heard that he burned down his first factory for the insurance money.' (Drippy.)

At last, Darling said, 'What about Rourke?' There was silence.

'After what he did to Babylon! Now this. He's in it up to here!' Drippy raised his hand over his head. 'We cweated him and we cweated a dishonest spiv.' They all nodded gravely.

'One phone call from me and he will never work in London again,' said Darling.

'He created himself. You created nothing,' said Kick, who could still hear the rowlocks spinning and the boats banging against one another.

'Exactly,' said Drippy. 'Nothing out of nothing comes.'

'I shall have Matt to dinner,' announced Darling. The girls were greatly titillated by the thought of this forbidden doomed hero going to dinner anywhere.

'Poor Matt, having a dishonest father,' said Party-Jones, as if Matt and his father were unconnected by blood.

'To dinner? Here?' gasped Jo.

'What should we say?' said Camilla.

'Watch it, Darling,' laughed Drippy. 'He might steal the silver.'

'You're playing with me.'

'I am playing with the utmost seriousness,' answered Fergus.

'You're playing cat and mouse.'

'Joe, Sir Edwin only plays with people for good reason.'

'So what does he want?'

'Not him, Joe. The City wants . . .'

'Me. No way. I won't martyr myself for the City, for anyone . . .'

242

'Joe. Be calm. Not you. No one cares about you. Who are you? Nothing.'

'Nelson. You want Nelson.'

'We have Nelson whatever, but you're the link.'

'What do you want me to do?'

'You loved Nelson.'

'What do you want, Fergus?'

'Tell me what you thought of Nelson.'

'He is a great man. He has changed his own life and the face of this country. He represents the spirit of this age.'

'And?'

'I admired him.'

'Now you must spike him.'

'What guarantee do I have?'

'You will meet the syndicate at Babylon's house with the man from the Fraud Squad. The syndicate will pay back all profits and pay large fines. You will give an affidavit. Nelson will be buried. He will face trial on his own. Justice will be seen to be done.'

'What if I stand by him?'

'Your hero? You stand trial with him.'

'So I have no choice.'

Fox smiled.

'God, there's Jesse,' said Drippy, who was walking back from Darling's with Jo and Camilla. The three of them stopped, and sure enough a familiar figure walked towards them, with a girl beside him.

'This must be the girl,' said Jo.

'The girl who is not, the one who does not . . .' Camilla didn't even have the courage to say it.

'You mean the yob girl, you silly old tart!' laughed Yarborough.

'She must be after his cheque book,' suggested Drippy.

'But how can he fancy her?' Yarborough and Camilla strained to comprehend the uncomprehensible. How could this friend, one of us, well brought up, an heir to so much, how could he touch an outsider such as this? With her accent, what would Sir Edwin think? wondered Camilla, dreaming

243

of how pleased he would be if Jesse were to bring her home instead. This girl simply wouldn't know how to behave at Goldtrough, decided Joanna, who thought that she herself would be perfect. And what was wrong with them?

'What shall we say?' the girls asked.

'Politely say hello to him and ignore her,' ruled Drippy.

Babylon nodded at them as he passed, but he made no effort to stop and talk. He walked carefully on, his pale hair, grown long in hospital, taunting them as it blew luxuriantly in the London breeze. Jewels, almost dancing as she walked along at his side, did not even give them a triumphant smile. At least then they would have known that the battle for the soul of Jesse was on.

They were shocked by her scar. The stories were right. She really was from the gutter, the forest, the wild. And Jesse, whom their mothers had reared them to covet, was ignoring them for THIS!

Jewels gave them an interested glance, as one looks into the window of a junk shop to see if there is anything valuable among the bric-à-brac, and seeing that there was nothing, she passed on, leaving the three spectators alone in the street. They thought Jesse must have gone mad. They couldn't see that this was his hour, for he was no longer giving himself to fools. Babylon had found a fellow gypsy.

'It's lovely not to have to speak to them,' said Babylon.

'They say it's class they care about, but all they care about is cash,' she told him.

'I agree.'

''Ave you gottit?'

'What?'

'Lolly.'

'Yes,' he said. 'I've got lolly.' Why lie, he thought? Sometimes he missed the social Hoovers and the cargirls and the Chelsea Chicas, but he knew he could go back, and that knowledge was enough in itself.

'Y' don't need it.'

'Everyone needs it.'

'We don't.' She smiled at him so broadly that he wanted to kiss her there and then. There was laughter and strength

244

in her and he loved that. She fulfilled his love of knowing about other worlds apart from his own. He felt exultant that he had found her. She did not need jewels. She did not need anything.

'Everyone has a price,' he said.

'I'm priceless.'

'Why did you want me?' he asked.

'You'd 'ave bin what yer are, wherever y'd bin born, in a slum or a palace.' He hoped she was telling the truth. He was pleased. Then he remembered how he had met her and where she came from. He knew that she was not all good. She was dangerous, and there was cruelty and crudity in her to live as she had lived. He marvelled at how she had lived with those vicious beasts and then him. It was an enigma that he would never unravel.

For her part, she could not believe that they were together. It was an impossibility, but she had pulled it off and she felt that she could pull off anything now, anything. She saw him much as I had always seen him: the leader, tall and thin, always stepping ahead with his feet flying, riding a wave of humour and confidence wherever he went. He made his own fun. Life itself was his favourite comedy. He was afraid of nothing.

'All the others were buyable with something,' he said. 'A ride in a smart car. A nice flat. A title. A fortune.'

'It's gotta be true. Girls can be bought. Some with good things and some with bad. That's the difference between a duchess and slut, innit?'

He didn't answer. She is humanity at its best, he thought, for all her viciousness and her roughness, she is where all the elephants lie buried. He ran his finger over her scar, enjoying the contrast between the rougher scar skin and the smoothness of her face on either side of it. Jesse had always loved contrasts.

'Well done, Joseph. You did it beautifully.' Sir Edwin brought his manicured hands together as if he was clapping silently. 'Do you have everything you need?' he said to the man from the Fraud Squad.

245

'Yes, Sir Edwin. Thank you, Mr Rourke.' The man rose to leave, looking around the office as he did so. It was older and more classy than Nelson's, he decided, but it lacked the view of London. He noticed the painting of Charles I's head held out to the crowd at his execution. History, he thought. Babylon's bank is a house of history.

He saw many offices when he came to question or arrest, and he believed that he was something of an expert.

At last the man was gone and everyone relaxed. Goncourt, Wallenstein and Hinton, the infamous syndicate in the take-over of Universal Imperial, sat at the other end of the long table at Babylon's bank.

'Well,' said Goncourt at last, 'we have avoided most of the agony. Nelson is a real man, don't forget that.'

'No, he was a pig. Look at the shit that's flown. He was bad news from the beginning. That's the last favour I ever do in business.' Hinton's face was red with the emphasis.

'Well, it was a very profitable favour,' I answered him.

'I spent all goddam day firing my guys and then I have to come along here to see if I'm gonna be fired myself,' roared Wallenstein. They knew their positions were not per-manent. Everyone in the room except Babylon had risen to their positions by graft. They knew that the higher you rise, the further you can fall, but they were delighted that this time they had escaped so lightly after such a foolish mis-take.

'So it's over. The scandal is only beginning, but for us, it's over. The era is over. The empire of money has gone,' Babylon summed up.

'What will they say about it?'

'They will say it was an illusion. A lesson against the spending of money that does not exist,' said Sir Edwin.

'Who cares if economists write that this was an economic illusion? England will never be the same again. It may have been a popular fantasy but everyone lived it and the life was exhilarating. Economists can say what they wish, but the ordinary people will tell History that this was a time to be alive.' I was talking, but it was Jesse's voice that spoke.

'Who gives a fuck 'bout these geeks and economists? I

agree with Joe,' roared Wallenstein from the end of the table.

'You have had it every way,' I said to Sir Edwin. 'You were born with a bank and you have cut a man out who came from nowhere. You've had your cake and you've eaten it.'

'What are cakes for?' said Sir Edwin.

Matthew Nelson was waiting downstairs.

'Are you waiting for me?'

'Yes.'

'Why? You know what happened inside.'

'I know. You know my father. So I must talk to you.'

'Where are you living?'

'The houses are all for sale. Everything's for sale. I look back and the Glory Days seem an age ago. It doesn't matter. Five years ago, we lived like anyone else; since then, we've had houses, servants, choppers, horses. Now it all disappears again. Sometimes I wonder if I imagined the whole thing.'

Matt was in the dreadful position of having no illusions left. His face was thin. He saw everything with a savage clarity. He was a Julius Caesar stripped of all the vanities of success and fame.

'Can I do anything for you?'

'No, nothing.' He hated me. He hated everyone, as his father had when he had arrived at Liverpool harbour. The cypher, who had never known where his father was, had become strong and handsome. He feared nothing, for he had lost everything. I was afraid of him. 'How will they re-member my father?' he asked.

'Nothing is finer than the man who creates his own life, for then he truly owns it. He will be remembered for his rebuilding of London.'

'They say he is a criminal. He was forced into all this by bankers. He didn't know what he was doing.' Matt had always been the ordinary English boy. Now his father had fallen, his ordinary life had been ruined. He was quite alone.

'Will he ever get his vengeance?'

'No, never,' he said. 'But I will.'

*

247

I took Emma out to meet my parents at last. We drove up through a London that was under surgery, but Nelson was no longer the surgeon. The trial had been coming up for a year, and Nelson's companies were being broken up and sold off by Government liquidators.

Somewhere in the suburbs of London, we stopped at a red light beside a bus stop. A man in a grey raincoat was waiting alone for the bus. The shelter kept him out of the drizzle and he was reading the *Daily Materialist*. He lowered it for a second. I recognized the Roman face, aged with sadness.

For an instant, our eyes met across the traffic. He straightened himself and tried to arrange his distrait hair. The lights changed and we moved off.

My parents' place was not too far from London, though it was a world away. I had not travelled as far as Nelson. I had not seen villages burning and families massacred, but even I had made a small journey.

Epilogue

Ten Years Later

Britain has many establishments, and they were all at Lord Bright's New Year's Eve party that year.

There were the City men from Oxford and Babylon's bank, at home in the dinner jackets which they had worn since childhood, and their desiccated wives; there were the BBC executives in fashionable black with psychedelic ties; the Jewish property tycoons from North London were in white tuxedos with their hair greased back and a glossy former Miss Israel on their arm; the Indians, who took naturally to wealth, plump and shiny, owning factories in the Midlands, newsagent chains in Scotland, hi-tech companies in Surrey; the bankers from Wallenstein, proudly wearing their abrasive cosmopolitanism like an oppressive uniform; civil servants, bland, well fed and all-knowing, shrewdly combining the pragmatism of *realpolitik* with the prejudices and small-mindedness of little England, whence they came; and finally the dons, writers, actors and pop stars who were always to be found at Max Bright's parties to show that Max appreciated creativity as well as prosperity.

The twin towers of the three-storey Elizabethan mansion were lit up with giant Christmas trees that rose in a tangle of multicoloured bulbs over the battlements, with their stolid red-brick colour, and up into the black December sky. The party was already spinning.

There were women in long skirts sitting outside on the steps, beside men with balding heads and hair that was streaked with grey. Their faces were clear and young, as if success in the world had beautified their skin but had taken a comic revenge on their scalps.

The women sat with long slim legs stretched out over the steps on to the gravel, and they wore the dinner jackets of their husbands over brown shoulders in the clear country air. As we got closer, the sound of laughter and the medley of different musics became so electric that Max's very house seemed to be vibrating and about to take off.

From all parts of the park, more guests were arriving. At first we had felt alone. Then the glitter of women's dresses, in gold and silver and shining turquoise, caught my eyes as we strode up the drive. The lights on the towers played on the jewels and the dresses so that it seemed as if the women were wearing armour. Tall warrior socialites, with jewels glowing where their eyes should be, were going to war in ball dresses of solid steel.

The hall was like a refugee camp for the extremely affluent. The butler had collected all the coats. As he took ours, he bowed and threw them over his shoulder on to a mountain of splendid material, where scarlet was tangled with mink, leopardskin with tweed, velvet with silver fox.

The far wall of the hall was an organ at which a woman with black glossy hair and full brown shoulders was playing old tunes like 'Merrie England' on the vast organ pipes that reached the ceiling. In between her and us was a storm of shouting, yelling people, all brightly coloured in skin and clothes. Waiters stood amid the tempest with poker faces and silver trays filled with glasses of champagne. I grabbed glasses for my wife and myself as we plunged through the crowd.

The waiters were very young, about seventeen or eighteen, local boys hired for the evening. I sipped the champagne and that took me back the ten years to Cambridge. Nero, red-faced, fat and bald, but as ever filled with the joys of life, appeared out of the crowd and confided in me: 'Every time I fall in love with a girl, she turns out to be a callgirl.'

Now the people were older, the waists thicker and most of the old crew had long fallen by the wayside. They had retired to the country or toiled in steady accountancy jobs or they had failed to live up to the expectations of Thatcher's era. They would never reach the world of Max Bright.

Deeper in the house a band was playing, with boys in white tuxedos singing nice clean-sounding songs and banging their tambourines. There was a discothèque somewhere. In other hideaways in the labyrinthine house, different bands were playing so that the noises blended into a buzz of energy in a house crawling with guests whom one greeted, slapped on the back and then tried to avoid.

In this funfair no one was really talking. Above the beating music and the swilling of champagne there was nothing to say, except that the New Year was an hour away.

Everyone was pretending to speak. We were moving our mouths and gesturing with our hands but no meaning was coming out.

Midnight came, with the lights flashing out, the discos and bands stopping. Then the lights came on again as everyone filed into the hall. The woman at the organ did not look round. There was a mirror in front of her. I watched her green eyes scanning the room. She had played hard and there was a light sheen of sweat on her back that made her glitter. The hall, filled to the doors, went quiet. The organist waited, her eyes narrowed, her hands tan spiders on the blacks and whites of the keyboard.

Bright, in a baggy wine-stained white suit with a garish red tie and his bouffant hair now completely grey, came out of the crowd like a magician at a children's party. A waiter handed him a glass. Max shook his head as he surveyed the crowd in his house. He looked us all up and down, as if to say he had quite forgotten he was giving such a grand party. How he loved his own act. Could all these guests be his? And the house?

The clock struck the hour. 'The New Year,' he said, and raised his glass. '1998.' We drank. 'Auld Lang Syne' blew out of the pipes; the party began again.

Now, it was a party of rooms. In an old drawing-room, white-haired patricians sat examining books of prints and asking after one another's children.

'So this girl is marrying him,' an elegant cocktail voice was saying, 'and, as you know, I'm not being snooty: the fact is she will be the next Lady Needapenny – and she just isn't.'

Unfortunately I was spotted before I could escape: 'Oh, Joe,' said the owner of the voice, 'how is your lovely Emma?'

An unmistakable voice suddenly ejaculated, 'Fuck, how much d'you reckon he paid for that picture?' It was that blood and guts Patton of the markets – Lew Wallenstein, stocky and out of place in an absurdly new tweed suit, with a wife, Gladys, who was dressed like an Edwardian tent and had a turquoise rinse hairdo. Wallenstein had not slept with her for twenty-five years.

'Must of cost a million. It's a Van der something,' squawked the wife.

'It's a fuckin' Van der Post, you stoopid bitch. Ya know nuttin.' Why had he married this liability, he asked himself? How could he have made such a fuck-up, even as a young man? He remembered her round, plump Jewish face when he had married her – and how her papa had got him that job at Schlong & Co., his first step on the ladder. He realized he had been hard on her. He remembered Penny and her golden body and his mistresses before and after Penny. Suddenly he realized how much he loved his wife. Gladys was a wise best friend, and he put his arms around her and kissed her. She came from where he came from. Whatever craziness happened, she was there for him.

He softened his voice. 'Don't worry, hon – I'll buy a Van der Post. As a present. This week.'

Gladys grinned with delight. The assembled old aristocrats who had witnessed the scene were repulsed and delighted, as we all are, to have witnessed a *faux-pas*. Yet it was they who would probably have to sell their Van Dycks to Mr and Mrs Wallenstein. In the meantime, they enjoyed their short-lived advantage and wondered who had invited that horrid little American?

A rock star turned squire, who now travelled from stately home to stately home instead of from gig to gig, lay with a rising actress on the other side of a partition that divided the drawing-room from a den. The guitarist smoked little wrinkled cigarettes rolled with shaking nicotine-stained fingers, while the pneumatic starlet talked on and on about the beautiful directors she worked with, what lovers, what darlings they were. The pop star did not look up when I blundered in. 'Yeah,' he was saying, 'Gazza wrote the song in a bubble bath in Frankfurt . . .' He sat looking at her with a stare that was both dreamy and hard. She wanted to get on in the theatre. He wanted to sleep with her: the parts each was thinking of were quite different.

The library was a political salon where a dried-up man who looked as if he worked in the local Post Office lectured young men on what it was like being Home Secretary. The young men wore sober suits and plain ties but their lips were moist and their eyes were dazed with images of distinction. The minister had seen many like these before. He had once been like them, too, but the endless talking to loathsome rivals and duplicitous allies had turned his early enthusiasms into words of concrete.

'How do we get into Parliament?' they said, forming a circle around the Home Secretary.

'Ask Joe Rourke,' I heard him say. 'He's here tonight. He's only been in the House a few years.'

One of the boys asked what had happened to Sir Kenneth Trumply? And they all sniggered. One of them said something about 'belly dancers'; another said 'unlucky'. Was there not some scandal in 1987? The minister pretended not to remember him.

'He was Minister of Defence, and later Finance,' said the boy, his voice overflowing with respect for those offices of state.

'Was he?' said the minister of home affairs, enjoying the thought that he had survived and Kenneth had not. He remembered well how he himself had informed the Prime Minister that Trumply was too close to that bent property financier. If Trumply did not resign again, then who could say, might they not point the finger at the Prime Minister herself? So, for party and state, and the morality of the Blue Rinses, Trumply, who had fought his way back from the wilderness, had resigned again.

'He was almost PM; he was deputy PM,' the boy insisted.

'Yes,' said the minister, 'but he isn't now.'

The dining-room had a long table that reminded me of Henry the Eighth's feasts. Around it sat a dozen men and women without their jackets on. Darling Darlington, in a

Chinese silk smoking-jacket and black slippers engraved with his crest, was telling them about the art world.

'I am a trader like you. I sell and buy pictures just like you trade options and shares.'

The bankers wore braces in bright colours and they wielded their jaws like pistols. The women's dresses were as like suits as possible without trousers. They wore shoes with sharp heels and sharp points and their eyes manoeuvred like the sights of a rifle. They talked about cars. They laughed a lot but their eyes bore the exhaustion of nights spent in the office.

'I judge a man by his car,' said one. 'A Porsche without leather seats is a giveaway.'

They all spoke in a bankerese accent suspended somewhere high in the timeless zone between markets, lost on the tele-phone lines from London to Zurich and on to New York and Tokyo. Their names were strange hybrids too – 'François von Kleist', or 'Charlie Sakomoto'.

'When I go abroad, I'll always hire a car,' said Neal von Smith.

'Sure,' said von Kleist, 'A Merc or a Jaguar.'

'When I was in Thailand, I hired a Roller and drove through the villages.'

'What was it like?' I asked him.

'Why? Why?' all his companions laughed, slapping their thighs, pouring out more champagne so fast that it over-flowed the glasses on to the floor.

'They were so poor, I hated 'em.' The bankers were clap-ping their hands, tears in their eyes. 'I loved it, sitting in the Roller with these villagers like skeletons looking at the motor and me inside, thinking these people are so fucking poor . . .'

'And did you throw hundred-dollar bills out of the window at them?' I said sarcastically.

'I didn't think of that,' said von Smith in all seriousness.

'Next time, next time!' yelled the others.

'Oh yes, next time I'll do it,' he said, as they laughed like rugby players.

This was the next generation. It was ten years since the Crash of 1987. They were aged about twenty-three. Only von Smith had lasted into his thirties. They had probably never heard of the Crash. They are Wallenstein's 'loose change', thought veteran von Smith.

'Markets going up?' I asked.

'They'll always go up,' said von Kleist.

'Cheers,' I said, winking at Neal and making a mental note to sell all my shares at once.

At last I found Max himself in his office. There were some very serious men in the room, with intelligent faces and thinking hands. Max introduced me to them as the coming young tycoon, the future PM. They made a note about me on their little pads with fine gold pens.

'These are the men who run England,' Max informed me, as if they were not there. 'The Permanent Secretaries.'

Each man stood, shook my hand and added 'Treasury' or 'Foreign Office'. They were the real chieftains of Whitehall.

'These boys are there, running the place whoever is in power. They are the eternal government. Politicians, like Mr Rourke MP here, come and go, but you go on for ever. You and they and I can all work together. We know the value of things, don't we?' said Max.

The men in well-cut suits nodded slowly. Max turned to me: 'I'm glad you and Emma could come at last,' he said.

'I'm glad to be here.'

'It's time you were. You've come a long way in ten years. We have a deal to discuss, now we're all here. But first, Joe, do you know what makes me unique?'

'No,' I said on cue.

'Access.' He sat down at his desk and dialled a number. 'Gentlemen, I want you to listen to this.' The gentlemen and I listened.

'Prime Minister? It's Max,' said Max, watching us. 'Yes, PM. Quite. Yes, yes ... Yes ... Yes ... Yes ... Oh, yes, Prime Minister . . .' He put down the mouthpiece. 'That is why the PM likes me,' he said. 'I'm the only person who dares say no to him.'

The Permanent Secretaries had seen many such vulgar displays before, but they still made little notes with their gold pens.

Max continued: 'He is the third Prime Minister I have served. Incredible!' The civil servants, in their dapper double-breasted suits, repeated 'incredible' altogether as one very neutral voice.

'At least this one knows his place. At least HE has no opinions, and even more mercifully, he has no policies,' said the man from the Treasury, speaking through his nose.

'At least HE will leave something behind him, not just worship of money,' said the Foreign Office. They filed out.

'Fashion is a tyrant. They all think She is nothing now,' said Max, now my business partner. 'They think She is just a bitter old woman, but they are wrong. I worshipped Her. They will never know the great things She did. But we'll never forget. She was Britain at its best.'

'Prosperity rebuilt London; theatres have never been so full again; television has never been so creative. Before Her, there was just a grey blur of depression, boredom and weakness. Nothing is created by greyness. It has been the same afterwards. What, apart from the 1980s, has post-war Britain left behind it for History?'

'I am one of the things She left behind,' said Max wistfully.

The waiters had rebelled, obviously unaware in their innocence of the power that resided in the house. I wanted more champagne so I wandered through the halls hoping to find the kitchen. The waiters were drinking it themselves out of bottles. When I asked if I could have some, they were quite nonplussed.

'Fuck off, y' rich bastard,' one said, and slammed the door.

Outside the kitchen, I bumped into Mr Party-Jones, the father of Camilla, the stockbroker.

'I've followed your career.' He and I stood face to face in the empty corridor. 'You've done extraordinarily well.' He looked me up and down, as if recalling the bemused boy he had met all those years ago. 'Extraordinarily well,' he said again, rather rudely.

He was thinking to himself: Rourke is one of those chaps who has worked damned hard and done extremely well for himself. I don't begrudge him it one bit, though he was rather mixed up with that Strakosch-Nelson character . . .

There was the essence of my success. I was always second best: since Cambridge, how many more talented Babylons and Nelsons had I seen dashed to smithereens by their own brilliance. How I had envied and worshipped their superiority and how sorry I had been to see them fall. Each time it was I, the one who couldn't speak, the one who was just a pawn, it was I who was there after it was over. Somehow, I didn't cause the usual offence of new money, for I understood in my bones the English way: the tortoise will always beat the hare.

'I don't like the atmosphere here. This is advertising money. You're a Cambridge man. Were you at Augustus?'

'Yes.'

'In my day, no one went to Augustus. I was at Hytler.'

'Well, now no one goes to Hytler . . .'

'But Camilla, my daughter, was at Hytler . . .'

'Quite, Mr Party-Jones.'

We opened one door where we found five teenagers snorting coke out of a hundred-pound note. One of them saw us. 'Excuse me,' he said to us, 'whose house is this?'

'Lord Bright's.'

'Where is it?' said the boy.

'Norfolk.'

'Good,' the boy said to his friends. 'We are on earth.' They nodded and took another line.

'You could have fooled me,' grunted Mr Party-Jones.

Emma was lounging in the hall with her usual retinue of adoring males in attendance. She pulled me over to her and nodded her head towards the far corner of the vast room, over near the organ.

'See that woman, sweetai,' she said.

'You mean the organist?'

'You know who she is?'

I still did not know.

'She is Max's mistress and once Sir Edwin's . . .'

'Really?'

'Look over there.' I followed her glance, and there standing near the organist was Kick Seamark. I compared the two women.

'Max's mistress isn't her mother?'

'You got it, sweetai,' said my wife. 'The mother's called Josephine.'

Kick Seamark raised her cheeks one by one to be kissed. I kissed them obediently.

'Are you still in love with me?' said the voice from New England.

'Of course.' I was being gallant.

'I cannot get away from boys in love with me.'

'Really? Like who?'

'The royals, for some reason, just adore me . . .'

'Which ones?'

'. . . And if not royalty itself, then men who are more or less royal.'

'What do you mean?'

'Brand names are the sexiest thing. You're driving along and there on a pint of beer, or on a pub or on a supermarket, you see the surname of the boy who is in love with you and you just think that you're there with him and you're making love. What you're making love to isn't a man of bone and skin, it's an empire that's inside you.' I saw there and then that there was no stopping her.

Kick was a modern horizontale. She was a pair of brown legs straddling the jet-set world from Mustique to Monaco that everyone who was anyone had to pass through, like an exclusive airport lounge. Her sex smelt of money, and her money smelt of sex, and it was a long time since she had been able to tell the difference. I saw by the way she kissed me and the way she squeezed my hands that she was now only capable of providing pleasure. Her eyes had been given a silver shine by the 'Ecstasy' and tablets she had been fed, and her Barbadian tan was so deeply brown as to be almost vulgar.

'You'll breed daughters like Kick Seamark,' I remembered Babylon saying to me at Cambridge. 'And when you see what you have created, you'll wonder why you worked so hard, why you destroyed men to produce creatures so empty and so base.'

Her mother came up to us. She looked fortyish but somehow younger than her daughter. She was taller and less brown and her features had gained the regularity that is the mark of looks that last. She was dark like her daughter, but the bones of her back and her face were works of delicious delicacy. They were collector's pieces.

'You are an old friend of Kick's from Cambridge and you have done so well since. You're married to Kick's friend Emma. Max has told me all about you.' She spoke precisely and slowly, taking the words as they came, enjoying the lilt of her Boston accent, which was stronger than Kick's.

'And he's still in love with me, mama,' said the husky-voiced daughter.

'Are you?' said Josephine, watching me, with a cruel curve to her lips.

'Oh yes.' I was playing to the mother.

'Not everyone can always be in love with you, my darling,' the mother smiled viciously at Kick.

'My mother is kept here by Uncle Max . . .' began Kick to me.

'I don't blame him at all,' I said into mother Josephine's smooth-skinned face. She was enjoying the destruction of her daughter and rival. I was happy to watch the bout and be the prize. Not that the winner was in any doubt.

Kick was still ranting. '. . . And mother always has men so in love with her, if you want to use the word "love" liberally, that they will give her houses, cars, anything, even money. Yes, she takes cash too . . .' The mid-Atlantic gravel I had once so admired was now desperate. I asked Josephine to dance.

'What an invitation. Goodnight, Katherine.'

'Go to bed, Kick,' I said to the international plaything.

Josephine danced so that once again there was that gleam on her long brown shoulders. We danced close.

'I hate this modern dancing, it's so cold,' she whispered in my ear below the thuds of the disco. 'I like to be held.'

259

I held her close. Then I almost kissed her. She moved her face away.

'I am Max's,' she said.

'I am married,' I said.

'You're different,' she whispered.

'You're no one's.' I risked a kiss in the darkness.

The room was so dark that the other dancers were only what the shafts of light from the door threw on to the floor. Beside us in the beating blackness was a dancer whose face I couldn't see.

I couldn't tell if it was a man or a woman. The figure danced with the wildest enthusiasm, throwing its arms up over its head, squatting on the floor in a dozen positions before leaping up like a Cossack towards the ceiling, a hand outstretched. It was a boy. There was something boyish in the smallness of the hips and the way he kicked his legs out. Then, in the changing light, I saw in the fullness of the face in the shadows, in the hips, in the chest, it must be a girl.

When I stared again, they were once more reversed but what a scene, I thought, how they enjoy life, whoever they are! And how they moved. There was a fitness and an energy about the figures that seemed familiar.

When the door opened again, I saw that thin face I had known well, but it was so sunken I had to look twice to check. There was no doubt, though. The dancer was Babylon.

I closed my eyes as we danced, dreaming of her knowledge, imagining the tricks and games this woman of a thousand gifts must know. I had forgotten her silly daughter. When I opened my eyes, loving the lingering odour that an older woman carries, the stench of the knowledge of evil and evil, the couple were gone.

We left the discothèque. Max and Emma were outside, watching the door. Josephine went over to Max, but she turned as she went: 'I'll come back to you tonight. I'll find you,' she whispered in my ear. She did not look back at me, but she walked in steps that sent the muscles in her back astir, and that showed the line of her hips and the straightness of her legs.

Max put his arm round me. 'I don't care,' he said, the middle-aged smoothness a trifle strained. There was desperation in his affluence. 'I can spare her. I have too many women anyway. I've got too many ties, too many shoes, too many houses. I've got too many friends. I can spare her. I've got too much of everything.' He stole away into the mob of his friends, with Josephine on his arm.

Emma was half disgusted and half amused. 'How could you? In Max's own house. His mistress in his house.' She spoke with a kind of delight. 'You are out of hand. In his own house! You're the Devil.'

'Did you see Babylon?'

'Yes, he's here. With Jewels. He looks awful. He must be ill.'

'Where is he, darling?'

'Outside,' she said. 'It's morning, the first day of a new year. Find Jesse, sweetai. Go.'

The dawn was spreading in the sky so quickly that I felt God must be in a hurry to begin the day. Without me really noticing, it was suddenly light. That morning light is the finest. It was freezing, so I pulled my jacket around me and tightened the bow tie. The dew was still on the trees so that they glittered as the first rays of a new year's sun caught the leaves and the blades of the thick grass.

Jesse still lived with Jewels and was still asked everywhere, for he could hold a dinner party in rapture for a whole evening, talking his usual blend of high brow and low life. He had had a book or two published. But on the terms of our old friendship, he had failed. He was too complicated to succeed. He had once wanted so many things that, unable to make up his mind, he had settled for one – Jewels.

We had met at Scrubber's wedding to the Marquis of Treasurehunt. There was a touch of the gypsy about Babylon. There always had been. He had swum against the tide and I had swum with it.

They were waiting for me. She had worn well, as I had known she would, and she still could not be bothered to spend cash on clothes. A leather mini-skirt was the closest she came to evening wear.

'So another new year,' I said.

She went very quiet then. Her Cockney voice was like a sharpened scythe: 'It's a time of nothing. What is there but money and unemployment? What is there to hope for? It's a dark age. It's your age.'

She walked off towards the house. In the light it looked like an old mental hospital. In a way, it was a new one. She was the girl I could never find, the unbuyable girl. She walked angrily but there was charm in her bitterness.

There was charm all about her.

There were tears in Jewels's eyes as she walked away, little tears like droplets of dew on the trees. When he turned back to me, there was something very wrong in his face. It was all planes and shadows. I was shocked to look at him closely. He had no flesh on him. When the morning wind began to blow he was so frail it blew him back a step. His hair was thinner too and his skin had a yellow tinge. Only his eyes shone. The way he stood, I felt he wanted me to examine his face.

'Seen any Cambridge people?' he said, fingering the scarf on his neck.

'Some.'

'Still going strong?'

'They're all alive.'

'I see.'

'All doing their own thing. No one's died of AIDS yet. All this fuss is just panic, isn't it?'

'No.'

'Do you know someone who's died of it?'

'No.'

'Do you know anyone who's got it?'

'Yes.'

'From Cambridge?'

'Yes.'

'Our year or . . .?'

'Our year.'

'Do you know him?'

'Oh, yes.'

262

'Do I?'

'You too.'

'Do you know him well?'

'Very well.' My stomach turned cold.

He was silent for a second, watching me. Suddenly the rising sun threw its light over the house and on to us. It lit up the grass around so that it bore the dew as if it were a shower of diamonds.

'I know him better than I know anyone.'

I understood, and when I looked at him, he smiled at my shock.

'I hope you don't mind me telling you like this,' he said. 'It's difficult to tell.'

'Is this person actually . . .? Is he going to . . .?' I could not say the words. Why did he not weep? He had done with weeping.

'I am dying.' I could not imagine it. Could he return to the earth? Where would all that energy go? There was no dust good enough for Jesse Babylon.

'You must fight it,' I said, clenching my fists. He listened impassively.

'Nothing lasts, Joe. That's the beauty of it.'

'How can you just leave everything?'

'You leave the things you won't feel any more. You make a list of the feelings you have loved, and one by one you cross them out. When there are no more, you are ready.'

'But how did you catch it?' Suddenly, I thought of myself. Where had he caught it? I had to know. What if . . . Scrubber or . . .?

'Jewels is a carrier.' He took off the scarf. His neck was a mass of red sores. 'The mark of the leper,' he said. 'There's no fun in it. If there were, I'd find it. When I first found out, I wanted to take everyone with me. Go on a binge. Pass it around.'

'Like Hitler in his Bunker.'

'I can't complain. To everything, there is a season. But I thought you had to be good to die young, and I am not good.' He enjoyed saying that. He liked not being good.

'Those whom the Gods love . . .'

263

'AIDS is a bad death. It's strange to die of having lived. That's the consolation. Most people die without having lived at all.'

'It must be hard for Jewels.'

'It's not hard now.' He peered out across the lawns to where she was watching us. 'I'll go quietly.'

She was outlined in the wide doorway of the French window. Jewels had matured but kept her big generous cheeks and her legs and the thick red-brown hair. I looked at her, trying to understand how she could give life – and bring death.

The party was over now. The halls of the mansion were empty. The stained glasses, the bottles and the odd shreds of gold lamé that lay across the floors were like finding the dusty toys of a lost child. It was only the rebellious waiters who were still partying. They were drinking Max's Bollinger. Every now and then, a pair would rush through a room, chasing some waitress, knocking a Picasso or a Chagall off the wall, smashing it in their excitement at being let loose in an abandoned castle.

'She made me happier than I had ever been. She taught me the worth of everything. I owe her a great deal.'

'And this.' I meant AIDS, but I could not bring myself to say it.

He turned to the sun, giving me the silhouette of his profile against the towers of the house and the dawn.

'Life carries within it the seeds of death.' He struck the pose with a smile that enjoyed the theatre of a good cliché. If he was going to die, he might as well live death to its full.

'Why did we sleep with all those girls?' I don't know why I used that expression. I didn't mean 'sleep' at all.

'They were like reading books,' he laughed. 'The more you read, the more you knew.' I tried to join in the joke but I was afraid lest I cried when I wanted to laugh.

'There's no such thing as a good woman, but she's the nearest to it,' he gestured towards the house. Even now, I envied him.

'What will she do?'

'You must keep an eye on her.'

264

'Does she have money?'
'I've made a will.'
'Leaving it all to her?'
'I wanted to.'
'So, she'll be fine.'
'She didn't want it. None of it.'
'Why?'
'She didn't want to be owned.' She was never bought.
'Your family?'
'They don't need it.'
'It's not really my business.'
'Oh, but it is.'
'How come?'
'I've left it all to you.'

He moved away from me as if I were the one with the Plague. She came out of the house to meet him and neither of them looked back. Only the money was good enough for me.

An arrow of flying geese crossed the sky. We heard them honking and looked up. The haunting creak, as their wings beat the air, stayed with us as the arrow disappeared into the sky.

'Where are they going?' asked Jesse Babylon, but he didn't expect us to answer.

It was daylight. The sun was up.

'Well,' I said loudly, shaking myself. 'I must get back to London. I've got meetings. Tomorrow's a busy day.'

FOR THE BEST IN PAPERBACKS, LOOK FOR THE 🐧

In every corner of the world, on every subject under the sun, Penguin represents quality and variety – the very best in publishing today.

For complete information about books available from Penguin – including Puffins, Penguin Classics and Arkana – and how to order them, write to us at the appropriate address below. Please note that for copyright reasons the selection of books varies from country to country.

In the United Kingdom: Please write to *Dept E.P., Penguin Books Ltd, Harmondsworth, Middlesex, UB7 0DA.*

If you have any difficulty in obtaining a title, please send your order with the correct money, plus ten per cent for postage and packaging, to *PO Box No 11, West Drayton, Middlesex*

In the United States: Please write to *Dept BA, Penguin, 299 Murray Hill Parkway, East Rutherford, New Jersey 07073*

In Canada: Please write to *Penguin Books Canada Ltd, 2801 John Street, Markham, Ontario L3R 1B4*

In Australia: Please write to the *Marketing Department, Penguin Books Australia Ltd, P.O. Box 257, Ringwood, Victoria 3134*

In New Zealand: Please write to the *Marketing Department, Penguin Books (NZ) Ltd, Private Bag, Takapuna, Auckland 9*

In India: Please write to *Penguin Overseas Ltd, 706 Eros Apartments, 56 Nehru Place, New Delhi, 110019*

In the Netherlands: Please write to *Penguin Books Netherlands B.V., Postbus 3507, 1001 AH, Amsterdam*

In West Germany: Please write to *Penguin Books Ltd, Friedrichstrasse 10–12, D–6000 Frankfurt/Main 1*

In Spain: Please write to *Alhambra Longman S.A., Fernandez de la Hoz 9, E–28010 Madrid*

In Italy: Please write to *Penguin Italia s.r.l., Via Como 4, I-20096 Pioltello (Milano)*

In France: Please write to *Penguin Books Ltd, 39 Rue de Montmorency, F-75003 Paris*

In Japan: Please write to *Longman Penguin Japan Co Ltd, Yamaguchi Building, 2-12-9 Kanda Jimbocho, Chiyoda-Ku, Tokyo 101*

A CHOICE OF PENGUIN FICTION

Humboldt's Gift   Saul Bellow

Bellow's classic story of the writer's life in America is an exuberant tale of success and failure. 'Sharp, erudite, beautifully measured ... One of the most gifted chroniclers of the Western world alive today' – *The Times*

Incline Our Hearts   A. N. Wilson

'An account of an eccentric childhood so moving, so private and personal, and so intensely funny that it bears inescapable comparison with that greatest of childhood novels, *David Copperfield*' – *Daily Telegraph*

The Lyre of Orpheus   Robertson Davies

'The lyre of Orpheus opens the door of the underworld', wrote E. T. A. Hoffmann; and his spirit, languishing in limbo, watches over, and comments on, the efforts of the Cornish Foundation as its Trustees decide to produce an opera. 'A marvellous finale' (*Sunday Times*) to Robertson Davies's Cornish Trilogy.

The New Confessions   William Boyd

The outrageous, hilarious autobiography of John James Todd, a Scotsman born in 1899 and one of the great self-appointed (and failed) geniuses of the twentieth century. 'Brilliant ... a Citizen Kane of a novel' – *Daily Telegraph*

The Blue Gate of Babylon   Paul Pickering

'Like Ian Fleming gone berserk, the writing is of supreme quality, the humour a taste instantly acquired' – *Mail on Sunday*. 'Brilliantly exploits the fluently headlong manner of Evelyn Waugh's early black farces' – *Sunday Times*